THE TRIBULATION CULT: A POWERFUL NEW SERIES FROM BEST-SELLING AUTHOR MICHAEL PHILLIPS

The Invisible War: Book 1, A Novel
9781956454321 / 9781956454338 eBook

Birth of a Remnant:
Book 2, A Novel
9781956454499 /
9781956454505 eBook

"SHOCKING!!! The first book in this series was riveting—great characters—I felt emotionally connected to them! Sitting on the edge of my seat, I couldn't stop reading!!! I felt empowered learning the enemy's historical tactics and knowing the enemy's weakness. We *can* be a threat for *good* and overcome the darkness that makes the Left's anti-America agenda seem stronger than it is."

— Sandra Guerra, Anaheim, California

"The first book in Michael Phillips's new series is all I hoped it would be: gripping, prophetic, hard-hitting. It's a winner."

— Nick Harrison, Eugene, Oregon

"*The Invisible War* by Michael Phillips, the first book in the Tribulation Cult series, is a powerful fictional interpretation of the transformation of America since the Vietnam era. It clearly and precisely portrays the methods used to attack the conservative, religious, and family structures in our country. When marching in the streets to protest the Vietnam War did not have the desired result, the teaching of Saul Alinsky

opened the eyes of his followers to play the 'long game' to infiltrate and destroy religion, family, and our country as we know it.

"Having grown up during this era, reading this book has the 'hair on my arms standing up.' It is a powerful, well-written, fictional work that is a reminder to understand what has transpired, the need to be strong, and to put on The Full Armor of God."

— George Laman, BA political science and American history, firefighter/paramedic (Ret.)

5-STAR REVIEWS FROM AMAZON FOR BOOK 1: *THE INVISIBLE WAR*

Joseph Dindinger
Couldn't put it down!

"I've read Michael Phillips before, and this has a lot of the same heart, and depth of characters, but a whole new, and very relevant setting—our world today. Can't wait to see where the next volume, and the next, and the next, go!"

Cheryl Bussler
Michael Phillips books

"I love reading most everything from my all-time favorite writer/author Michael Phillips!"

Linda C. Livingston
Good read

"My favorite author, always a great story!"

Deanna Mosier
Great insight!

"The book starts in 1973 and goes to 2033, and follows four friends, two follow their faith and two go a different way. The author goes into society's changes through the years and has great insight into these years in America. I really enjoyed the depth of insight, the characters' growth, and listening to the excellent narrator. Looking forward to the next book!"

HIDDEN JIHAD

MICHAEL PHILLIPS

HIDDEN JIHAD

TRIBULATION CULT BOOK 3:
A NOVEL

Fidelis Publishing ®
Winchester, VA • Nashville, TN
www.fidelispublishing.com

ISBN: 9781956454956
ISBN: (eBook) 9781956454963
Hidden Jihad
Tribulation Cult Book 3: A Novel

Order at www.faithfultext.com for a significant discount. Email info@fidelispublishing.com to inquire about bulk purchase discounts.

Author photos by Melanie Bogner, DuoParadigms Public Relations & Design
Cover design by Diana Lawrence
Interior layout design and typesetting by Lisa Parnell
Copyediting by Amanda Varian

Manufactured in the United States of America

10 9 8 7 6 5 4 3 2 1

Contents

Contents

Contents

"The political horizon affords as fine a prospect . . . with returning harmony . . . with the irresistible propagation of the Rights of Man, the eradication of hierarchy, oppression, superstition and tyranny over the world, by means of that soul-improving . . . palladium of all our national joys . . . whose value . . . cannot be sufficiently appreciated by those who would disdain to better the image of God."

— Dr. Nathaniel Ames,
after the presidential election of 1800

These fine enlightened sentiments could be taken as a manifesto of the Secular-Democratic Consciousness. The new age had just experienced a miraculous revival.

— Page Smith
on Ames's diary entry, December 31, 1800*

* Page Smith, *The Shaping of America,* Vol. 3 (McGraw Hill, 1980), 309.

> *"For there shall be a sowing of peace; the vine shall yield its fruit, and the ground shall give its increase, and the heavens shall give their dew; and I will cause the remnant of this people to possess all these things."*
>
> **— Zechariah 8:12**

PART 1

NEW ADMINISTRATION BRIGHT WITH PROMISE

SPRING–SUMMER 2050

1

The Western Presidential Manor

May 2050

SILKY SOUNDS emanated from a seven-piece jazz ensemble to one side of an expansive lawn, bordered by trim hedges and colorful azaleas and rhododendrons.

Three smoothly seductive lead saxophones interweaving their interpretive harmonies created an atmosphere more evocative of New Orleans than what had been dubbed the Western Presidential Manor on Bainbridge Island. Opposite the musicians a lavish portable bar dispensed a full range of offerings. Wine, brandy, champagne, and assorted liqueurs, among the most expensive money could buy, flowed freely. Two or three hundred high-ranking and formally attired guests mingled casually, drinks in hand, amid an intoxicating aura of power.

The president had made no appearance yet. He was not expected to effect his grand entrance until every name had been checked off, and the elite from around the globe was on hand to witness his triumphant emergence.

The tidewaters of Puget Sound lapped gently on a four-hundred-yard length of private shoreline as carefully maintained as the manicured grass sloping down to it. Bainbridge had long represented one of Washington State's most exclusive districts, isolated as it was from the Olympic Peninsula to the west and the mainland to the east. Though serviced by a two-lane bridge at its northern extremity, the island was most easily accessible from Seattle by ferry, or, if you liked, helicopter. That the island boasted as many private landing pads as swimming pools gave some indication of the tax bracket of its residents. Google-Microsoft, Amazon-Starbucks, Apple-Boeing, Social Media Enterprises LTD, Alaska-Delta, Global AI, and other notable Washington-based conglomerates maintained hideaway compounds here for the use of their executives.

This particular expanse of gravelly seafront and private harbor was now the most restricted piece of waterfront real estate in the country, guarded twenty-four-seven at both extremities by Secret Service agents with automatic weapons. A high electric fence surrounded the rest of the fifteen-acre compound. Well behind the main house sat a spacious helipad and hangars for two aircraft in addition to Marine One. The newly installed runway half a mile away could handle a modest-sized Bombardier or smaller private jet, but nothing so large as a commercial airliner. Air Force One was therefore hangared at Paine Field.

Neither rifles, fence, nor round-the-clock military guard, however, could prevent a steady flow of sea craft of all sizes and shapes, from tiny motorboats to luxury yachts and ferries, streaming by. Their owners and captains knew enough to keep their distance. Every vessel that ventured within a quarter mile was scrutinized and its identity quickly checked. This did not stop the passengers on those boats, large and small, from intently scanning the shoreline, binoculars keenly focused, to see whom they might be lucky enough to catch a glimpse.

The day was sunny, breezy, and warm—in the mid-sixties. On the shores of Puget Sound, it was as warm as anyone had the right to expect in May. Expansive gardens spread out from the lawn in all directions. The profusion of color from beds of tulips, daffodils, and roses bordering the larger flowering species, accented by infinite shades of fresh green tips bursting from trees and hedges and shrubs, evidenced spring in the full glory of its recreative miracle. Surely the northern hemisphere's month of May brought a smile to the Creator's heart, annually reminiscent of the eternal proclamation: God saw all that he had made, and it was very good.

All segments, not merely of US society but of the global family, had been included on the president's selective cast of characters for this momentous day. The multi-varied dress and skin color told the tale. Burqas, niqabs, sarongs, sherwanis, even a few colorful African tribal costumes, were plentifully represented. With them walked black tuxedos and twenty-thousand-dollar dresses from the most exclusive Parisian designers. The guest list gave no doubt that Jefferson Fitzsimmons Rhodes was indeed the world's president. This gathering to celebrate the half-century mark over which history had chosen him to preside in every way confirmed him as the planet's most powerful and popular man.

Most of those who had been invited occupied the top rung of their respective ladders. Leaders from business and education, banking and commerce and law, and every other segment of society were on hand. This was the crème de la crème. Not just the movers and shakers, but those of a select elite who told the movers and shakers what to move and shake. Every major capital claimed representation on this day—Beijing, Buenos Aires, Edinburgh, Rome, Hong Kong, Mexico City, London, Tokyo, Moscow, Singapore, Shanghai, Baghdad, Berlin, Rio de Janeiro, Tehran, Kiev, Cairo, Paris, Ottawa, Sydney, Istanbul, New Delhi, Jerusalem, and all the rest.

Politicians, of course, dominated. Besides leaders from both houses of Congress and most of the justices of the Supreme Court, at least two dozen presidents and prime ministers, along with numerous foreign dignitaries, had flown in to this northwestern outpost on the opposite coast from the nation's capital. A surprising number of so-called holy men rubbed shoulders with them. They included ayatollahs, rabbis, cardinals, priests, ministers, and the especially revered new Dalai Lama. One small contingent from California, however, was noticeably out of place. The president had his own reasons for including them.

Bainbridge Island, on this day, was truly the center of the human universe. This was the president's shindig. He made sure he was surrounded by fawning admirers. Nor could anyone deny him such an obvious perk of his position. Who wouldn't relish in the luxury of being surrounded by so many in the political world, and from every nation on the planet, who thought he walked on water. In this era of unanimity and accord, what in former times would have been called "the opposition" was almost a distant memory. This president, more than any other, had done what most would have considered impossible a generation earlier—united the human species. Its infinitely diverse coalitions seemed to be dwelling, as the saying went, with peace on earth and goodwill toward men.

At least so the president and his powerful and recently renamed Progressive Party led the US public and world to believe. Not even all his fellow former "Democrats," however, endorsed the change which President Rhodes had unilaterally imposed. What about the party's illustrious history that was intrinsically linked to the Democrat name?

More serious undercurrents than the name of his party existed within the Rhodes vision of utopia. Thought all but dead a decade ago, Christianity was showing surprising resiliency against the uniform onslaught against it from nearly every segment of society. It was unclear what role the churches and clergy of organized Catholicism, Orthodoxy, Protestantism, and Evangelicalism played in the sudden resurgence of interest in traditional spirituality. Whatever was happening seemed to have originated outside the world of official Christendom. Those who were paying close attention noted its genesis as coinciding with the publication of Dr. Charles Reyburn's book *Roots: America Reclaims Its Heritage* two years earlier, just months prior to Rhodes's landslide victory.

On his part, the president had given little thought either to Reyburn or Christianity since the death of his former friend and roommate Ward Hutchins on the night of the election.

Until planning this mid-century bash, that is. Suddenly the uptick of Christian activity appeared on his radar. In making out the guest list, he recalled a news briefing from several weeks earlier about a Christian event in Texas that, for unexplained reasons, struck him as worrisome.

Even with Ward gone, he couldn't become complacent. Few things concerned him more than a rebirth of Christian fanaticism. He needed to know what was going on. He didn't want news briefings. He needed someone on the inside. After some thought, the guest list had been revised accordingly.

A thorough contingent of the media had also been invited to Bainbridge Island—WNN, no secret the president's chosen mouthpiece, most prominent among the rest. All the other US networks and most of their reputable international counterparts were on hand as well, though with strict orders that they would film only the president's address later in the afternoon. No interviews with guests were allowed.

In the meantime the journalists and their cameramen waited inside several large rooms of the expansive Rhodes estate, cooling their heels with the same expensive potations being imbibed outside. They passed the time speculating on the nature of the president's upcoming address. It was billed as setting forth more significant policy initiatives than the bland predictabilities outlined in his State of the Union a few months earlier. The Presidential Manor had released a statement a week before, heightening rather than lowering expectations.

Anson Roswell, the president's press secretary, tagged it his State of the World speech.

2

INVITATION

THE ORNATE envelope arrived at the Circle F Ranch in the California foothills northeast of Sacramento in mid-April of that same year by special courier.

It was a Saturday. Only Ginger Forster—finishing two papers and looking ahead to finals as her third year at Jessup University drew to a close—and her mother, Grace, were home. Mark and Craig were in Grass Valley with Mark's parents and neighbor David Gordon, helping with the final load of Bob's and Laura's move back to the Forster ranch. It had taken a year after Mark's resignation from the pastorate of Foothills Gospel Ministries to sell his parents' condo in Grass Valley, get the family who had been leasing the ranch re-situated, and then complete the move to the ranch themselves. No one was happier with the new living arrangement than Robert Forster himself.

"I've got it all drawn up, Dad," said Mark when he laid out his plan on his parents' kitchen table, rolling out a sheet of drawings. "You and I will add a bathroom and outside entrance on the east side and remodel the three bedrooms of that wing into a master suite and new living room for Grace and me. We'll convert the third bedroom to a kitchen with windows looking east toward the mountains. Grace and I will have our own apartment. You and Mom can take up residence in the main house like before."

"What about Ginger and Craig?" asked Mark's mother.

"We'll find rooms for them. It's a huge house. Even when Janet and Gayle and I were growing up, there were spare bedrooms. We'll knock out a wall somewhere and add a room or two if need be. With Ginger and Craig in college, they may not be with us much longer anyway. We could also add bathrooms and convert the bedrooms into small student apartments."

"I'm overwhelmed, Mark, my boy," said Robert softly. "I hardly know what to say. Of course, your mother and I are appreciative. You know how much I've missed the ranch. But . . ."

He paused and glanced at his wife, then back at Mark.

"I told you a few years ago when we talked about the ranch," he went on, "that we understood that you had your own plans—that you had your own life to live. No regrets on our side. We loved the ranch but it was time to move on."

"I know, Dad," nodded Mark. "But things have changed for us."

"I understand. But I don't want you making this offer for us, if you know what I mean. We appreciate it, of course. But you have to do what is best for you. We don't want to tie you down to the ranch. Other opportunities may present themselves for you that would be—"

"Dad," interrupted Mark, "Grace and I have been praying about this for months. The church ministry—I should say the pulpit ministry—is over for me. That is a certainty. The other certainty is that we are staying here in the Sacramento area. We have prayed about many options. The only thing that has presented itself, and that has grown stronger, is to return to the ranch. I think I would like to raise horses and maybe take in problem animals. I've spoken with the Wests and Heather Marshall about possibilities, and about Heather working for us and helping set it up. Yes, a career change at my age can be a risky business. But with the ranch debt-free and that I grew up knowing the business, and if you would join me—heck—we could get the thing up and running in no time! I'm eager to get back into the ranching life. Grace and I are planning to move to the ranch regardless, even if you two decide to remain in Grass Valley. With your okay, of course. The ranch is obviously still yours and you have tenants there."

Mark's parents again looked at one another.

"We'd love to join you at the ranch!" said Laura.

Mark's father said nothing, only glanced away and brushed the back of his hand across his eyes.

Now a year later, with the remodeling at the ranch reaching its final stages, the last of Bob's and Laura's furniture and boxes and possessions was making its way to the Circle F where they had spent most of their married lives. Much had remained at the ranch or in storage. With a pickup and David's flatbed, the move was not difficult.

Tomorrow night, Sunday, they would sleep again in their former bedroom. Mark and Grace and their family planned to make the move to the ranch in the summer. Their home in Roseville was currently on the market.

Mark's cell phone sounded about three o'clock on Saturday just as he and Craig drove up to his parents' condo in Grass Valley for another load. David and Bob were a few minutes behind in the flatbed.

Mark got out of the pickup and returned Grace's call.

"Hey, Gracie! Just pulled into the condo. You called?"

"You'd better go in and sit down," said Grace.

"Why . . . bad news?" said Mark.

"No. But I think you may want to be sitting down anyway."

"I don't think there is anything left to sit on!" laughed Mark. "Most of the chairs and two couches went in the last load. Okay," he went on as he walked, "I've found a place outside."

"Is Craig with you?"

"Right here."

"Put your phone on speaker."

"You're being very mysterious!" laughed Mark again. "Okay, we're ready."

"Hold onto your hats," said Grace. "We just received a packet by special courier, with official seals on the envelope. The return address was just two lines, The Office of the President of the United States, the Presidential Manor, Washington, DC."

"Whoa!" exclaimed Craig.

"Inside were three invitations to a special presidential reception next month in Seattle."

"Amazing!" said Mark. "I thought Jeff had forgotten his childhood pal."

"Apparently not."

"Why three? Did they leave one of us out?"

"Just the opposite. I guess they figured with two college students in the family maybe there would be a boyfriend or girlfriend in the picture. One invitation reads Mark and Grace Forster are cordially invited, etc. Another reads Ginger Forster plus one, and the third Craig Forster plus one."

3

Tremors of Approaching War

ON BAINBRIDGE Island, an hour passed.

Waitresses and waiters attired in subdued gray skirts and white blouses, gray slacks and white shirts, lending a professional tone without calling undo attention to their owners, wove their way inconspicuously among the rich, powerful, and famous. Their skilled hands bore silver trays laden with unusual delicacies and concoctions—colorful, exotic, and definitely not to be found in your neighborhood delicatessen. These ranged from caviar and sushi to cakes and truffles and petits fours and chocolate-covered strawberries along with a multitude of colored things whose identity could only be guessed at.

The bright smiles and laughter and the atmosphere of culture and command belied silent but ominous undercurrents the perceptive observer might have detected beneath the serenity of the afternoon. The distant cadence measured by the approaching kettledrums of history was too faint. They accented dissonant chords intruding into the superficial symphony of peace and goodwill. It took keen hearing to discern those strains. Few were aware of them.

How could these who had come together on this day know the façade of ebullience for what it was? They were part of the charade. They were incapable of recognizing its hollow ring. The offices of power they occupied and the praise of the masses lavished upon them were poor training grounds for the development of true eyesight and hearing. As

One said so long ago of the masses surrounding him, they saw but did not perceive and heard but did not understand.

A cataclysm of world events lay on the horizon. But who would behold its approach? The storm had been invisibly gathering for decades, if not centuries. No one was more keenly aware of that fact than Harvard Professor of Religion Hamad Bahram. His tall, commanding, swarthy demeanor ensured that he was noticed wherever he went. He was a man of few words. He kept his own counsel and let his penetrating black eyes speak for him. His pedigree, stretching back into the indistinct shadows of Iran's intellectual elite, was unknown to anyone in the West. For now, he was watching and waiting, making sure he was seen by the right people. The years of patience had paid off. He had risen steadily in academic circles and now stood poised at the threshold of world power.

His association with Mike Bardolf through the Palladium organization had garnered him an invitation to the prestigious event. He intended to make the most of it. After he met the president personally for the first time on this day, he would make sure Rhodes never forgot him.

When the upheaval came, these men and women, and many like them, would be at the eye of the hurricane. Helping usher in that era of crisis and change, they were themselves the least capable of detecting the portents of its advance. Professor Bahram, however, saw them clearly. It had gradually been borne in upon him that his family's moment of destiny might arrive sooner than his visionary grandfather Nasim or father Sonrab had foreseen.

As the afternoon wore on, smiling faces, gay laughter, tinkling champagne glasses, and myriad happy sights and sounds each wove its own subtle melody through the ensemble's rendition of peppy favorites from the nation's historic jazz repertoire. It was obvious that the crowd was enjoying basking in the self-satisfied glow of its own importance. Many of its number felt the flush all the more after two or three glasses of expensive wine from California's Napa Valley.

Standing almost at attention among them were a surprising number whose faces betrayed no hint of emotion, who partook of no alcohol, engaged in no conversation, and lapsed into no smiles. Intently scanning and surveying, their eyes remained vigilant, narrowly focused, as if expecting danger.

The Secret Service was well known, of course, as the most no-nonsense agency in the government. That the size of one particular ultra-private branch of the Service had recently been expanded, however, was not widely known. That fact was buried beneath so many layers of bureaucracy as to completely avoid scrutiny from prying eyes on Capitol Hill.

Some might have called the precedent alarming, too reminiscent of a secret police force than what was necessitated by mere protection. As none but the president's close advisor Mike Bardolf, now Deputy Director to FBI Chief Erin Parva, knew of the memorandum creating the unit, it was likely to remain hidden from view. The congressional oversight committees whose duty it was to regulate national security knew nothing of it. In truth, Bardolf already considered it his own private security detail.

Several small yachts eased up to the private landing where more celebrated guests disembarked. Two or three helicopters landed on the helipad. Once their cargo was safely delivered, they lifted noisily off again and returned to SeaTac.

The German prime minister, Russian president, and UN Secretary General arrived together on the last of these. All three were greeted with fanfare and aplomb as they stepped out of the lavish electric shuttle from the small air field into the midst of the crowd. Quickly they found themselves swallowed into the throng of well-wishers who had been awaiting their arrival. Chinese Premier Jiang had come early as the president's most special guest of all. The foreign dignitaries completely overshadowed Vice President Elizabeth Wickes Hardy who, if his staff had not seen to it, the president would probably have forgotten to invite at all.

No more guests were due. The list was complete. All that remained now was for the man at the center of the world stage to grace the gathering with his presence.

4

Day of Grief

NOVEMBER 5, 2048

LINDA HUTCHINS Trent, youngest justice of the Supreme Court, just months shy of her fiftieth birthday, nearly tossed the presidential invitation into the trash moments after opening it. Yet something prevented quite such a rash response.

She replaced it in the ornate packet and set it on the sideboard with the day's other mail, though she had no intention of attending.

Although—it would be a good excuse to go home again, to personally visit with Deidra more than she had been able to during her trip out for Ward's funeral. Also to see her older brother . . .

But no. It was out of the question.

The thought of Sawyer sent her into another tailspin back to that dreadful day following the election.

Her *brother*. Now she had only one.

She had watched the election results seventeen months earlier with many conflicting emotions. Jeff's victory was never in doubt. But his post-election speech and the spectacle of the Space Needle celebration had revolted her, saddened her, and now in retrospect also infuriated her. Deep inside she could not prevent the gnawing sense that the honorable President-Elect Jefferson Fitzsimmons Rhodes was responsible for Ward's death. She had not learned of the shooting until the next day, along with the rest of the country. She would not have gone so far as to claim that Jeff had actually ordered the mob-style hit—he was too careful and clever for that. But immediate suspicions swept through her.

She had grown up hearing those of former generations talk about where they were the moment they heard JFK had been assassinated. It was the defining moment of a generation. One of her grandfathers talked about being on a golf course, how seemingly everyone on the course heard almost at the same moment, and how from every direction on all eighteen holes, play suddenly stopped, and gradually a mass silent exodus toward the clubhouse had begun—hundreds of balls left where they lay—in a mournful procession of shock, not a word spoken as the clubhouse filled with disbelieving men and women crowded in to watch Walter Cronkite on a small black and white television set.

For her parents, that defining moment of seared memory had been watching the Twin Towers of New York's World Trade Center collapse.

The only world event that history would remember from November 4, 2048, was the day-after victory celebrations of the new incoming president.

But it would be the day after that which would forever be the watershed of Linda's own life.

Her Kennedy moment—*Where were you when you heard . . .?*—came midway through the morning. It was Thursday, November 5. The Court's morning arguments were in full swing about yet one more case involving sexual and gender nonsense that had dominated the national and legal cultural battleground since the right to abortion up to six months following birth had been codified into US law, and upheld by numerous Supreme Court decisions in the years since. The new case was brought by a trans "man" who had kept her uterus in working order, had given IVF birth, and was suing FNN and its correspondent Denver Stone for hate speech, having referred to her on national news as *her*, hoping thus to establish the legal precedent that "men" could also give birth. Transphobia was now one of the regular hate-accusations against conservatives. Twenty years before it might have been hailed as a landmark case for "women's rights." But the terminology was tricky these days. Was this a landmark case for *women*, for *men* . . .

For whom exactly? What gender was actually involved?

Even the justices occasionally stumbled over themselves not wanting to inadvertently use a pronoun that would offend somebody.

It was not for the case that Linda would remember the day. But rather for the shocking news she received from Seattle in the midst of oral arguments.

Interruptions when the Court was in session were rare. They always signaled one of two things—a personal emergency or a governmental crisis. The justices were never interrupted for *good* news.

When the clerk came through the door behind the eleven robed, seated justices, the sound of its opening stopped Justice Heyworth in mid-sentence. Eyes turned to see their chief clerk, whose responsibility it was to weigh the urgent communications that came during open session. His appearance alone signaled something important.

He walked behind the justices to Linda and handed her a single folded sheet of paper. She opened it.

Phone call waiting in your chambers, she read. *Come immediately. Family emergency.*

Her face went white. She drew in a breath, then stood.

"I'm sorry," she said to her colleagues. "Excuse me. I seem to have an emergency call."

She walked out through the back door and to her office, while the clerk privately relayed the situation to the other justices.

Linda sat down at her desk, picked up the telephone, and opened her private line.

"This is Linda Trent," she said, her voice soft and shaky.

"Linda . . . it's Mom," she heard.

The relief at hearing her mother's voice was but momentary. She could hear the tears in her mother's trembling voice.

"Mom . . . what is it? Is it Dad?"

"No, honey . . . it's—"

Eloise Hutchins broke down sobbing.

"Oh, Mom!" said Linda. She could do nothing but wait.

It took some time before Mrs. Hutchins could regain enough composure to haltingly convey the terrible news.

"It's . . . it's Ward, honey . . . he's been shot."

"Oh, God! Is he . . ."

Again Mrs. Hutchins burst into tears.

"Linda, honey . . . he's dead."

A torrent of sobs sounded over the phone as Linda sat numb. Her eyes filled and she wept freely.

A full minute went by. Neither mother nor daughter could speak.

"Dad . . . Sawyer . . . Deidra . . .?" said Linda at length.

"Ward was alone," replied Eloise. "Deidra found him in his office half an hour ago. She called the police first of course. Then she called me."

"What happened?"

"I don't know. He'd been shot during the night."

"How is Deidra?"

"In shock, of course. Her mother is with her, while the police . . . you know . . . while they investigate everything. I called you first. I'll call your father and Sawyer when we get off the phone."

"I'll get a flight this afternoon, Mom," said Linda. "Or tonight, as soon as I can. I'll be there by tomorrow morning."

"Can you get away?"

"Yes. I'll read the transcripts later. It's a disgusting case. I'd rather not hear the details. There are so many disturbed people in the world, Mom. I sometimes wonder if they all think of the Supreme Court as their personal ally to legalize their depravity. Half the time we go along. What does that make us? Nevertheless, I will be glad to get away. We're not scheduled to vote on anything for several weeks."

"What should we do about a funeral?"

"We'll talk with Dad and Sawyer when I get there, Mom."

"Ward was a famous man."

"You're right. We'll have to think of the public reaction. It will be all over the news."

"What do you think . . . you know . . . Mr. Rhodes is in Seattle . . . do you think he—"

"Harrison?"

"No, I mean, you know . . . your friend."

"Jeff—of course! He's in town for his big celebration."

"Would he want to attend . . . maybe say a few words?"

"Probably. And make a show of what good friends he and Ward were. The thought of it turns my stomach. I do not want him at the funeral. Though by the time we get something planned, he'll likely be back here, the conquering hero returns to the capital."

"I never liked him much either. But we couldn't keep him from attending. He will be the next president."

"So it would seem," said Linda sardonically. "But leave Jeff to me. I'll find out his schedule and we'll make sure the funeral is at a time when it will be impossible for him to attend."

☆ ☆ ☆

Sawyer and Truman Hutchins had only just both spoken on the phone with Mrs. Hutchins and Linda separately when word of Ward Hutchins's assassination the previous night exploded over the national news. Linda barely had time to inform her colleagues—who recessed the proceedings for the remainder of the morning—when her private cell phone sounded.

She suspected who might be calling. She was right.

"Linda, it's Jeff. I just heard—I am so sorry."

"Thank you," she replied placidly without emotion.

"Are your folks okay?"

"Of course not. They just lost a son."

"I know . . . I mean—"

"Forget it. I'm sorry. I'm raw too. I only found out from my mother an hour ago."

"Well, please convey my condolences to the rest of your family. If there is anything I can do?"

"Thank you," said Linda, trying to keep calm. She wanted to shout, *Haven't you already done enough, you two-faced hypocrite!*

The call ended leaving Linda with turbulent emotions oscillating between grief and wrath.

Predictably, the president-elect issued a press briefing later in the day, which was played and replayed on every newscast that evening, extolling his dear friend Ward Hutchins as one of the most principled and finest men he had been privileged to know, a man of virtue and character and courage to stand firm for his convictions, and who would be sorely missed by the nation and by him personally.

Her phone kept ringing for the rest of the day. Linda did not watch the news reports nor respond to a dozen requests for comment regarding her brother's mysterious murder.

By nine o'clock that evening she was on a red eye from Obama International to SeaTac.

5

Suspicions

2048

THE SEATTLE police held their own press briefing after that of the president-elect—watched in the nation's capital with great interest by one Court Masters—the gist of which amounted to a précis of the facts:

That Ward Hutchins had been found dead early that morning in his study, slumped over his desk, his Bible open to the book of Revelation. A single shot had been fired from a long-distance sniper rifle, killing him instantly. Time of death was estimated between eleven and one o'clock the previous night. The location of the shooter had been determined to be the top floor open-air parking garage atop a thirteen-story condominium building two blocks away. A single shell casing had been found. There were no fingerprints anywhere, nor did they have any suspects at this time.

Though the cases were entirely different—poison and a high-tech sniper's bullet—Masters immediately thought of the still unsolved murder of President Adriana Carmella Hunt fifteen years earlier. That he had been on the former president's police detail that day in Baltimore caused him naturally to take the assassination personally, as probably did every policeman and agent charged that day with protecting the president. It wasn't guilt, exactly. Just the sense that he hadn't done his job. The later clandestine assignment—given him by Secret Service head Erin Parva, now Director of the FBI—to investigate the case, and his inability to uncover any actionable intelligence in the years since, only added to that sense of failure. Parva's yanking him off the case, then showing obvious displeasure two years later when he began asking questions about Domokos's biographer and now presidential aide Michael Bardolf, left him with lingering doubts about both Parva and Bardolf. But he'd unearthed nothing more about the Hunt assassination, even with his wife Stella's help with the weird yet fascinating world of artificial intelligence.

Now this—another high-profile murder. His investigative instincts exploded again to life.

The thought flashed into his brain immediately when he heard about events in Seattle that the two political assassinations—which he had no doubt also characterized that of Hutchins—were linked. How, he had no idea. But years on the DC metro police force had taught him to trust his gut. The moment he heard the news, he smelled a rat.

Hutchins was former roommate to Rhodes. Bardolf was now closer to Rhodes than anyone. Parva had something on Bardolf or he had something on her. And their affiliation went straight back to Patterson Park!

The detective was awake once more.

Yet now more than ever, with Bardolf in the Presidential Manor and Parva heading the FBI, there was probably nothing he could do.

6

A Global Family

MAY 2050

ON BAINBRIDGE Island, another forty minutes went by.

Gradually a low buzz began to circulate that the moment was approaching. News teams were given word to file outside where their cameras were mounted in readiness behind where the chairs were set. The jazz ensemble quieted. Its musicians melted unobtrusively into the house. Adjustments to the microphones at the podium in front of the seating area signaled that the afternoon's high point was at hand. The chairs filled. A hush descended.

All stood in perfect readiness. At last the president strode out from his private precincts in the house. Into the sunlight of a Puget Sound spring afternoon he came, as if heaven itself were shining its spotlight upon him. Rousing applause met his upstretched arms and smiles and gestures of greeting to those especially honored world leaders seated in the first few rows.

"Good afternoon . . . hello and greetings to all of you!" the president said loudly, though his voice was drowned out by cheers and applause. "Hello . . . thank you . . . it is good to see you all . . . welcome to the great state of Washington!"

It took some time for the approbation to die down. Its pace, crescendo, and gradual decline, as nearly all aspects of this president's public persona, was carefully orchestrated. The loud greeting of the crowd was assisted by the volume control for the speakers surrounding them that helped those in attendance to know how long to keep clapping. Those few seated near them heard the piped acclaim for the president. But though it was a standard feature included in all his public appearances, the news cameras never knew it. Those watching around the world only saw and heard frenetic acclaim that seemed to go on forever, confirming the desired image of this president's wild popularity wherever he went.

Gradually the sound controls were dialed back. The crowd followed suit. And after many *Thank yous* and further words of welcome, the president began his momentous speech.

A litany of bland introductory pronouncements followed, eventually giving way to a series of priority initiatives whose widespread consequences were but scarcely hinted at, and then in the most veiled of terms.

"My hope and commitment to you," the president was saying, "is to continue devoting my presidency not merely to the affairs and future of the United States itself, but to the larger community of the entire planet. America has always been a leader in the family of nations. It is now time for America to step forward and lead again, in new ways for new times—lead by stepping out of the limelight, lead by becoming one in that great family without insisting that we remain the head of that family.

"With that vision of a global family of equality, it is my commitment to act more than merely as *America's* president. I hope those of you who lead the diverse races and tongues of humanity will think of me as equally your president, ready to fight for the freedom and equality of all peoples everywhere, *all* nations, *all* minorities. It is my earnest prayer that the future will look back on this era as one when every vestige of racism and inequality were at last ended among us, when freedom became a reality everywhere, not just for the few but for all.

"Toward that end, I will be establishing presidential commissions to monitor and oversee progress toward liberty, equality, and unity in several key areas of vital importance culturally, socially, and governmentally. As we move toward the future, I envision these commissions drawing upon the voluntary assets from many of your nations, not just our own. Education, world poverty, hunger, religion, climate control, finance, complete global elimination of fossil fuels in the developing nations as we have accomplished in the US—these and other areas of concern present challenges to unity and equality that I believe we can overcome in our lifetime. Their mandates will be to tear down walls of bias, inequality, and segregated opportunity. Eventually I would hope that these Freedom Commissions would be invested with more than a mere advisory role, helping to shape and implement a global vision of freedom for all peoples everywhere."

7

Journalistic Hiatus

TODD STEWART sat with a glass of Perrier at the back of the expansive lawn of the presidential home on Bainbridge Island where the crowd was seated listening to the speech. He could not prevent his mind drifting, and his gaze wandering out over the waters of Puget Sound.

It was hard to imagine that four days ago he had been a quarter of a world away, staring out over a very different ocean, the surprisingly temperate waters of the Moray Firth of the North Sea in northern Scotland, trying to decide whether or not to accept the president's invitation. Part of him wanted to remain where he was, in the idyllic small former fishing village where he had gone, planning to stay for two weeks of R and R.

And yet—four days later—now he was staring across the water at the Space Needle and Seattle's skyline.

Most in his position, needing to take a break from work and able to afford it, would doubtless have chosen Baja, the south of France, or Hawaii. But the proverbial "friend of a friend," or in his case the friend of a friend of a nephew, told him of an isolated stretch of Scotland's coastline unlike anyplace in the world. A little chillier than Hawaii or the Mediterranean perhaps. But the water was crystalline, the air fresh and clean, the coastal walks spectacular. Best of all—no crowds. His friend might also arrange a place for him to stay.

Todd had jumped at it. It did not take long for him to have so fallen in love with the little village of Portlossie that he had remained fourteen months rather than two weeks and was well begun on the novel he had always wanted to write. The president's invitation barely reached him in time, once he decided to attend, for him to make travel arrangements out of Aberdeen's airport sixty miles away.

Thus, here he was, still a little jet-lagged, feeling like a fish out of water in the very environment that had once been so intoxicating to him.

His heart wasn't exactly still in the highlands, as the famous Scottish ballad put it. But some part of him had been left behind on the coast of the North Sea.

All around him sat three or four hundred other lucky ones who had been invited to the Western Presidential Manor. He should feel honored.

Probably in a way he was. But he knew the president had invited him because of his journalistic connections, hoping to entice him back into the game, and secure one of the country's most popular young media stars in his corner. Todd knew Rhodes liked him. But could he guarantee the president favorable treatment in the future? His outlook on many things was changing. That fact could not help alter his journalistic perspective.

He was uncertain what his future held. He had taken a leave of absence from NBC and gone away to find out. But over a year later, no answers had come.

He tried to return his attention to the president's speech. He had heard these kinds of speeches so many times, they now did little more than put him to sleep. But having decided to accept the invitation, the least he could do was try to listen.

"I propose further," Rhodes was saying, "that revised legal standards be established to which all nations can ascribe. These standards will complement the work of my Freedom Commissions in order to implement and enforce their recommendations, rooting out bigotry, inequity, and financial and other forms of disparity that exist. In all these ways, together we will move in unity and accord toward a common vision of bringing the good life and equitable living conditions to all. Toward this end I propose that a world Judicial Council be established to recommend and ultimately enforce these standards of freedom and equality. I hope that all the governments of those of you represented here will join the United States in supporting and contributing to the functionality of this council by investing it with authority to carry out its vision.

"We will also seek to expand access to global financial markets for those traditionally excluded from the economic benefits of those markets. Our new Midwest Stock Alliance Trade Center, under construction in St. Louis and scheduled to open two years from now, will handle all manner of investments, but will focus on bringing our expanding immigrant and minority communities into the world of finance and investments. To this end, I will propose to Congress a 2 percent surtax of taxable income on all native-born American individuals of European or Asian descent to be distributed to first-time investors of Latin and African decent, both citizens and non-citizens, in the form of subsidies on purchases of stocks, bonds, mutual funds, and other financial products through the new Midwest Stock Alliance.

"As another example, I exhort the world's religious bodies, organizations, and faiths to come together in harmony in greater ways than has been possible before now. I believe that the era of religious wars is past, that Muslim and Jew and Christian, like the fabled lion and lamb, can at last come together to dwell in peace, harmony, and mutual respect. It is not my intent that their differences be ignored, but rather that the religions of the world move toward the ultimate goal of functioning as a world family of faith. Toward that end, I am announcing today that the first of the Freedom Commissions, the Commission on Religious Unity, will be inaugurated this week. Hopefully, it will lead the way with a vision that can be embraced by all fields of human endeavor where men have been too long divided."

The president paused and drew in a breath as he surveyed the crowd. He had his listeners exactly where he wanted them, softened and receptive for what would doubtless be received by his critics as the most far-reaching of his new policy initiatives.

"Our US Constitution has served us well, as have those of your nations," the president continued after a moment. "I now propose that we venture boldly into the future with a World Constitution. Toward this end I will be contacting other world leaders in the coming months with the goal of establishing a Presidential Alliance made up of world leaders and scholars to recommend a framework upon which to build. The aim will not be to replace any of the historic documents that have provided a useful foundation for the governments of the past, but rather to move into the future as a global family that must find increasing ways to pool and link our talents, resources, and our governmental mechanisms in order to make binding decisions for the good of all. As city-states gave way to larger states and as states and regions gradually coalesced into nations, the time has now come for nations to follow that same progression toward higher forms of global unity."

The president continued for another thirty minutes, offering little in the way of specifics but much in the way of grandiosity of vision. Among the gathered politicians of the nations, for whom platitudes were the name of the game, his smooth words and polished presentation slipped fluidly into the world mind like so many innocuous idea-seeds. There they would invisibly send down roots into the collective consciousness of a planet that seemed eager to embrace this man to lead it forward into a new Promised Land—an imagined Nirvana of universal brotherhood and goodwill that could become reality simply by dreaming it.

8

Disquiet

THE IDYLLIC garden setting masked undercurrents of disquiet in the heart of one discerning man who, for reasons he still did not understand, had been included with those gathered on this celebratory day.

As Mark Forster sat listening with wife, daughter, and friend, he felt far different stirrings in his breast than optimism concerning the future. He sensed tremors that originated from far beyond the horizon of earthly sight. David Gordon's years of influence had deepened within him insight into the human spirit and the cultural war which had been underway for decades.

Thus he *saw*—he *felt*—he *heard*—he *understood* much to which the men and women around him were oblivious.

That he knew the man at the center of the day's event as well, or in some ways perhaps even better than anyone present, though in other ways not at all—at least he had known him *longer*—only added to his inner qualms. But Jeff had changed since the early days of their friendship. He wondered if he really knew him now at all.

Perhaps today he would find out. Flattered on the one hand by the singular honor of the invitation, Mark knew Jeff well enough to be suspiciously curious why he would choose now to rekindle their former friendship. Was it possible, he wondered, that the strain of the presidency had become burdensome? Perhaps Jeff simply wanted to talk to an old friend in the tradition of Billy Graham's many visits to the White

House. That would be wonderful, Mark thought. But it was impossible to hold out much hope that such was the reason.

He had not spoken to Jeff for eighteen years—not since prior to his first election to the House when Jeff tried to enlist his support. Why now, he wondered, staring intently into the face of the man who had once been his best friend, and now was the most powerful man on earth.

The speech was gradually winding down.

"As the boundaries from old paradigms and structures gradually collapse," the president was saying, "to be replaced by new global paradigms, we must take courage to lead bravely and boldly. Some segments of our varied constituencies will not grasp this lofty vision. The small-minded will object. They will fight to preserve perspectives of the past that have fed the bigotry and inequality from which we must emancipate them. They may not understand. Even though we are trying to liberate them from archaic prejudices, they will struggle to retain them. I stand before you today saying that we must persevere. For their own good and the benefit of humanity, we must liberate the pockets of backward thinking that remain. Only so will their children and grandchildren be able to grow up in a world free from the bigoted belief systems of the past.

"The texts of the past must also be rewritten to prevent their errors being perpetuated. Valuing our history, we must move beyond it. History is fluid, not static. It requires new interpretations in every generation, some of them dramatic. Honoring those who have come before, we must now climb on their shoulders and point to a new vision that was impossible for them to see.

"Join with me today, my friends. Join me in this vision. The path to peace leads out of the old and into the new. You and I must lead the way with courage and forcefulness."

The president's conclusion, and the rousing response that followed, did nothing to mitigate the disquiet the speech had stirred within him. Mark still had no idea why he had been invited. He obviously did not move in these circles. He was an insignificant nobody. He didn't even own a tuxedo. He hoped his plain black suit, the same he had worn for years to officiate at weddings and funerals, did not call too much attention to itself. And as he looked around, he doubted any of the others had been invited to bring family along.

The speech over, the four rose, drifted across the lawn, their guest moving off on her own. Mark and wife and daughter milled about aimlessly, quietly discussing the speech they had just heard.

9

Away from the Throng and Tumult

As THE applause gradually died away, Todd Stewart rose from his chair toward the rear of the assembly and glanced unconsciously in the opposite direction. Quickly the music from the ensemble started up again. Dozens of invited dignitaries swarmed forward to congratulate the president on his moment of triumph.

Todd had no interest in being part of it. His gaze drifted along the coastline to the west. Maybe he would again acclimate himself to the lofty world of politics. On this day, however, it seemed hollow and artificial alongside the resplendent silence of the Scottish coast he had so recently left.

He was no more given to the superficial political conversation now than when he'd left the country shortly after the election. As he wandered away from the crowd, he assumed himself the only unsociable person in attendance. A hundred yards away, however, he saw another solitary soul walking away from the crowd.

She stopped and seated herself on a large stone near the water's edge, then sat looking out over the water. He could tell nothing about her age from this distance. She appeared to be a teenage girl, which may have explained why she was uninterested in the president's speech. She was turned away, gazing toward the mountains of the Olympic peninsula in the distance.

Who was she, he wondered. What was a young girl doing all alone in such an august gathering? She almost seemed lonely. Maybe he could cheer her up and get away from the hubbub at the same time. He continued along the shoreline toward her.

As he drew closer, she heard the crunch of his feet on the gravel and turned.

Todd stopped in his tracks as she glanced toward him. She was no girl at all!

If anything, she was near his own age. Nor did she appear lonely! She wore the most contented expression he had ever seen. Her peaceful countenance, so unexpected, shot through him.

He stood speechless.

She stared up expectantly, then broke the awkwardness.

"Hi," she said with a smile.

"Uh, hello," he said somewhat clumsily. "I saw you sitting here alone and thought, I don't know . . . that you might be . . . sorry, I didn't mean to intrude."

She laughed.

"But I see you are just enjoying the day and probably don't need my company," Todd added.

"I *am* enjoying the day," she replied. "But if you were concerned about me, thank you. That was very thoughtful."

"I don't know how thoughtful it was. I'm not feeling particularly sociable either. I just returned from overseas and am still feeling the effects of jet lag. I suppose I felt like getting away from the crowd."

"Where were you?"

"Scotland," replied Todd, easing himself down onto the gravel slope of the beach.

"Oh, I'd love to visit Scotland some day. One of my favorite authors was Scottish. What were you doing there?"

"R and R, I guess you'd say—professional burnout. I needed a break."

"What do you do?"

"Right now, not much of anything—sort of unemployed. Long-term leave of absence. What about you?"

"I'm a nurse in a care home. I also work with horses."

"Like a vet?"

"Not exactly. I help troubled horses after the vets are through with them. I help them get back to normal."

"Interesting. An unusual combination—care home and horses."

"It is—but I love both. I think of them the same—helping people *and* horses either recover from or learn to live with whatever ails them. What were you taking a leave of absence from?"

"I'd rather not say. I hope you don't mind. I was involved in the political world."

"Which would explain why you're here."

"I suppose. It finally got to me. I realized I'd had enough. At least for a while."

"But you're here."

"Yeah. I'm not quite sure why I decided to come."

"You must be somebody important to have been invited."

"I don't know about that. I used to be known by a few movers and shakers."

"I thought so!"

"I could say the same—*you* must be someone important."

She laughed. "I am here as a guest—a plus-one, I think is the technical term."

"With your boyfriend?"

She laughed again. "That is as funny as that I'm someone important. No, some friends asked if I'd like to come on their invitation. Believe me, I am as complete a nobody as you will ever meet. I'm still not convinced about you. There's something you're not telling. You *are* someone important—I know it."

Now it was Todd's turn to laugh.

"Maybe once, but no more. The only reason I'm here is that I think the president has always had a soft spot for me."

"You know the president!"

"I knew him *before* he was president. I haven't spoken a word to him since."

"I'm not sure I believe you. But I'll let it go for now."

She glanced back toward the house and grounds.

"I probably ought to rejoin my friends. They will be worried about me off by myself. Like you were. People tend to worry about me, not realizing how content I usually am."

Todd rose.

"Here, help me stand," she said reaching up her hand. "One of my legs is shorter than the other. I can manage, but it's easier with help."

Todd reached down, took her hand, and pulled her to her feet.

"Oh, my goodness—you're tall!" she said, laughing lightly.

"And you're short!" rejoined Todd, laughing with her. Just as quickly he caught himself. "Oh, I'm sorry," he said. "I meant nothing—"

"It's fine. I *am* short. I've always been short. I'm not embarrassed by it. My name's Heather, by the way."

"I'm Todd."

As they began to walk back toward the festivities, Todd now noticed her limp.

"An accident?" he said.

"Rattlesnake bite. I was nine."

"Gosh!"

"It was pretty bad. I almost died. It stunted one leg. But it was the best thing that ever happened to me."

Obviously astonished by her statement, before Todd was able to ask what she meant, they found themselves again swept into the swirl of humanity.

10

Memorable Meeting

As THEY approached the crowd, Heather's host family was standing toward the back of the activity, wondering, like her, what they were doing in this world so far removed from the reality of their lives. Seeing the two walking toward them, Grace's eyes widened.

"Oh, my goodness!" she exclaimed softly. "Look, Mark—look who Heather's with!"

"I see! But I don't believe it!"

Ginger was listening to their confidential tones.

"Who is it, Mom?"

"Todd Stewart," replied Grace, keeping her voice low.

"*The* Todd Stewart—the television journalist!"

"I'm pretty sure that's him," replied Grace.

Heather and Todd now joined them.

"And you thought you wouldn't find anyone to talk to!" said Mark as they approached.

"Todd, this is Mark Forster," said Heather, "—and his wife, Grace, and Ginger, their daughter. I'm Ginger's plus-one, like I told you."

"Pleased to meet you, sir," said Todd as he and Mark shook hands. "And you, Mrs. Forster. I'm Todd Stewart."

Ginger pulled Heather aside as Todd and her parents chatted informally.

"How did you meet him!" whispered Ginger excitedly.

"He just came over and started talking."

"You *do* know who he is?"

"Yes, I just introduced you—his name's Todd."

"But you know *who* he is?"

"What do you mean?" said Heather. "He just returned from Scotland. I know nothing more than that. Though actually he did say he knew the president."

"I guess so, Heather! He's a famous reporter. Even I've seen him on TV!"

"I hardly ever watch the news. He didn't tell me anything about himself."

They turned back to the other three. Mark had just noticed Ward's sister across the lawn.

"Oh, Grace—there's Linda," he said. "I'd like to see her. Do you know Linda Trent, Todd?"

"*Justice* Trent?"

Mark nodded.

"I've never met her."

"Would you like to?"

"I would, yes. But—"

He paused and lowered his voice, then leaned toward Mark.

"I was actually going to see if I could introduce Heather to the president," he whispered.

"Then you go ahead," laughed Mark. "That will make her day. I'll be sure you meet Linda before the day's over."

Todd turned toward where Heather and Ginger stood listening, Ginger still agog.

"What do you think, Heather?" he said. "Would you like to meet the president?"

"What—really! You're kidding!"

"Come on. We'll see if we can get close enough in the midst of his admirers."

They walked off together, Ginger following with eyes wide in amazement. By now Mark and Grace were moving away in the opposite direction.

"This may take a while," said Todd as he and Heather squeezed through the crowd toward where the president was surrounded by dozens waiting to shake his hand.

As they went, many approached Todd and greeted him with friendly handshakes.

"Haven't seen you around lately, Stewart."

". . . heard you were out of the country . . ."

". . . good to have you back, Todd."

"Everybody seems to know you!" said Heather. "They're looking at you like you're a movie star. Ginger was right."

"What did she say?"

"That you were famous."

Todd laughed loudly. More heads turned. Before long a sizeable crowd was clustered about them.

"She said I should have known who you were," said Heather. "To be honest—I didn't. I never watch the news on television. I didn't recognize you at all."

"Just as well," rejoined Todd. "Most of it's not worth watching. You wouldn't have seen me for over a year anyway."

"Strange thing for a journalist to say—that the news isn't worth watching."

"That's one of the reasons I took time off—trying to figure out that exact thing, and if I want to keep being part of it."

"Sounds serious."

"I suppose for me it is. Long story, as they say."

"Did you get any answers while you were away?" asked Heather.

"Not really," answered Todd. "But I think I'm beginning to ask some of the right questions."

"That's always the most important first step." She glanced about unconsciously, noticing all the eyes turned toward them. She inched closer to Todd and lowered her voice.

"What are they all looking at!" she said.

Todd laughed. "Us!" he said. "Don't worry about it."

Before Heather could reply, a man approached through the cluster of bodies.

"Hey, Todd!" he said. "I was hoping you'd make it. You were hard to track down."

"Hello, Anson," said Todd as they shook hands. "—Heather, meet Anson Roswell, an old friend from my university days and now the president's press secretary."

Heather smiled. Roswell glanced down at her, forcing a somewhat awkward smile though not extending his hand. To him she appeared a little girl. He wondered if she was Todd's younger sister. He turned back to Todd.

"I was hoping to introduce Heather to Mr. Rhodes," said Todd.

"He wanted to see you too. We weren't sure if you were going to make it. I only located you in time to get the invitation sent off."

"Well, it found me, and here I am!"

"Let's see if we can get you through this crowd," said Anson, leading the way. "It's a madhouse."

"You sure landed on your feet," said Todd. "The presidential press secretary."

"A rough job, but somebody's got to do it, right!" laughed Anson. "Mike Bardolf's tight with Rhodes. He put in a good word for me."

The name sent Todd into brief morose reflection. Mike Bardolf was one person he hoped he did *not* see today.

"Wait here," said Anson. "I'll tell the president you're here—though I'm sure he's spotted your tall crop of blond hair above the crowd. You're hard to miss."

He hurried off, leaving the two alone again.

"You do know all the important people!" laughed Heather. "I had no idea what I was getting into when you sat down beside me over there!"

They waited another five or ten minutes, chatting easily, interrupted by frequent handshakes and greetings to Todd all along the same lines—hadn't seen him around . . . missed his newscasts . . . heard he'd been away . . . nice to see him back.

Anson Roswell reappeared, again told them to follow, and led them through the throng. A minute later Heather found herself face-to-face with the president of the United States.

He and Todd exchanged a few words in much the same vein as if they were best friends. Jefferson Rhodes was the kind of man who made *everyone* feel like his best friend.

"Mr. President," said Todd, "I would like you to meet Heather—oh, gosh!" he said, turning quickly to Heather. "I don't even know your last name! We just met, Mr. President," he added back to Rhodes.

"Marshall," said Heather with a smile. "It's Heather Marshall."

"Well I'm glad that's settled!" said the president, offering his hand. "Hello, Miss Marshall. I am glad to meet you. But . . . *Marshall*—I know that name from somewhere? Where are you from?"

"California."

"A friend of mine used to talk about an author from California he knew. I think the name was Marshall. A religious author."

"He was my grandfather."

"Well, well—that is remarkable."

"Unless you mean Catherine Marshall—she is the other well-known Christian author with the same name."

"No, it was a man. A British-sounding name."

"My grandfather was Stirling Marshall."

"That's him! So how do you come to be here? I don't remember your name on the guest list. You're not a gate-crasher, are you, Miss Marshall?" added the president with his winning smile.

"I came with the Forsters—Mark and Grace Forster. I think technically I'm known as Ginger Forster's plus-one."

"Ah, so that explains it—small world! Mark Forster's the man I was telling you about who used to read your grandfather's books. He's an old friend."

He turned to Todd.

"I will see you later, Todd," he said. "I hope to find you again with all your cohorts at the Manor keeping me honest."

"We'll see, Mr. President," said Todd. "Thank you for taking the time for us."

They turned away through dozens of others still clamoring for their own opportunity to grab a few seconds in the presidential glow. Heather felt the stares as they squeezed through, silently looking down on her—both literally and figuratively—wondering who *she* was to merit the president's attention.

"What did he mean by keeping him honest?" she asked as the crowd gradually thinned.

"Just a private little thing he says to me," answered Todd. "He considers me an ally in the press corps."

"Are you?"

"I used to be."

"And now?"

"I don't know. I suppose that's the question I've been asking myself for a year."

11

The President's Son

SOME IDEA of the intrinsic difference between the two young men attending the presidential fete on Bainbridge Island may have been surmised by what each held in his hand and by which young ladies drew their attention. Todd Stewart had just set down a glass of mineral water accented with a slice of lemon when, a short time earlier, he walked toward the young woman whose face he could not see. When she did turn toward him, he found himself drawn to her countenance rather than her features, which, though highlighted by a radiant smile, according to the standards of most young men would have been considered plain.

The other young man might have been given some degree of latitude in the shallowness of his perceptions as being more than a decade younger. Yet the tumbler of Scotch in his hand—which he held for show—in fact he hated the stuff—and eyes roving the grounds of the estate for unattached pretty faces nevertheless spoke of character flaws he had not yet, in his twenty-three years, seen need to recognize.

He had taken note of a particularly good-looking young lady he had never seen before—twenty or twenty-one by his estimation. He had been eyeing her for a while. The great majority of those in attendance were older and knew him, which was not always to his advantage. A fresh face who might *not* know him presented a double allure. Trying out his charms on an innocent unsuspecting girl, sizing up the right moment to drop the bomb and watch her wilt—it was a game he enjoyed.

But the young woman across the lawn had been surrounded all day by a man and woman he took to be her parents, hovering much too close to give him the freedom he needed to exercise his considerable charms. The three had been joined a minute or two earlier by a tall man and tiny young woman who stood at least a foot shorter.

He continued to assess the situation out of the corner of his eyes while making small talk with dignitaries who felt duty bound to make conversation with him.

His opportunity finally arrived. The tall man and short woman left the other three. At the same time the older man and his wife walked away in the opposite direction, leaving the girl momentarily isolated. He was on the move instantly.

Experience made him an expert in the wily art of the casual saunter, creating the illusion of an accidental encounter. It worked to perfection.

"Oh . . . hello," he said, as if noticing her at the last minute as he strolled slowly by. "Great day, isn't it?"

"Beautiful," the girl replied. "I don't remember a more gorgeous day in Seattle in all the time we lived here."

"You're from Seattle?"

"Used to be. We moved to California six years ago when I was sixteen. I haven't been back since. It really gets hot where we live. That's why I expected to be chilly today. But it's so pleasant with the smell of the water. That's one thing I really miss—the water."

"You don't live on the coast, I take it. No surfing and all that?"

She laughed. "No, we live in a hilly region east of the central valley. Rivers and hundred-degree days, but no ocean."

"Why did you move?"

"My dad's a minister. He was minister of Puget Sound Vine Ministries. But he felt it was time for a change."

"Really," he said, suddenly aware of the glass of Scotch in his hand. He hadn't been prepared to find this knockout of a girl the daughter of a minister. "I may have heard of him. What's his name?"

"He's Mark Forster. That's my mom and dad there talking to Mrs. Trent, the Supreme Court justice. I haven't met her, but she and my dad are friends from college. I'm Ginger, by the way—Ginger Forster."

"I'm happy to meet you, Ginger Forster. So you're the daughter of a well-known man?"

"Probably that might have once been true—here in Seattle at least. But not so much anymore. He resigned from his California church two years ago and we moved to the ranch where he grew up. Now we raise and train horses."

"That's a big change—from being a minister to a horse trainer!"

"He loves it! We all love the ranch, though my brother and I are in college, so we don't have a lot to do with the work at the ranch. Our friend Heather—that's her over there with Mr. Stewart—works at the ranch. She has a gift with horses. What about you? Do you live here in Seattle?"

"We used to, like you. But my family moved when I was young. I barely remember Seattle. I was only six when we moved."

"Where do you live now?"

"Washington, DC."

"Oh, probably like half the people here," said Ginger. "Like the lady my folks are talking to. What about you? Are you still in school?"

"No. I put in three years."

"You quit with only a year before graduating? That's a shame."

"I just couldn't take it anymore."

"And since?"

"There's not much to tell. I bounce around from thing to thing, trying to keep out of trouble. Actually, you might have heard of my dad too," he added as if it were an afterthought, flashing the trademark family smile that usually caused the opposite sex to go weak in the knees. "That's him over there talking to the chairman of the Joint Chiefs," he added, gesturing toward the front where the crowd was still clustered around the president.

"You don't mean—" began Ginger.

"Yeah, that's him. I'm Bradon Rhodes. The guy there, the president—that's my old man."

"Now it's my turn to say wow!" laughed Ginger. "You certainly outdid me in the famous father department."

"Yeah well, what can I say?" rejoined Bradon, again flashing the Rhodes smile, though inwardly surprised that she was showing no sign of being mesmerized. "Can I, uh . . . get you something to drink?" he added. "Scotch, a martini?"

"No, thank you. I don't drink."

"Not even a beer."

"No, nothing."

"Oh, right. I probably shouldn't have asked. A minister's daughter and liquor don't go together. Sorry. I'll just get rid of this," he said, handing his still-full glass to a passing waiter. "But how do you survive in college without at least letting down occasionally?"

"I go to a Christian college. Not that there aren't those who go a little too far sometimes. But I'm not interested. Virtue and character are more important to me than having a good time. Besides, I *wouldn't* call drinking having a good time. I can't think of anything worse."

"An unusual thing for a college student to say."

"I'm sure you're right. So is it true what they say about you, young Mr. Rhodes?" she asked.

"What do they say?" laughed Bradon.

"That you *do* like having a good time enjoying the party life and as a result have dropped out of three colleges so far."

"You seem unusually well informed on the president's ne'er-do-well son!"

"I keep up on the political scene. I'm minoring in Political Science."

"Well, then, I suppose what you've heard is true. Let's just say I haven't found my niche yet."

"Do you live in the White House?"

"I do. But don't you mean the Presidential Manor?"

"We still call it the White House."

"Why?"

"Because we don't want to concede to all the ridiculous changes progressivism has forced on the country."

"Whoa! You'd better not let my father hear you!" laughed Bradon.

"I don't care if he hears me. I would say the same to his face. The new liberalism of the last half century has nearly ruined the country. I know our fathers used to be friends, but they've followed much different paths since."

"Well I leave the controversies to my dad!" laughed Bradon.

"While you enjoy having a good time?"

"Something like that! Not every twenty-three-year-old has the chance to be voted the capital's most eligible, though somewhat disreputable, bachelor. Hey, why not enjoy the notoriety while I can!"

"You like being considered disreputable?"

"Why not? I have to beat away the girls with a stick."

"And you're proud of that?"

"Like I say, you're only young once."

"You don't want to get an education, a job, be respected like your father?"

"Maybe some day. But I enjoy the single life too much to settle down. You know what they say—why limit yourself to one fish when you can swim in the whole ocean."

Ginger did not smile. She found the remark offensive and juvenile. It brought to mind what she had heard about the president's son through the years—that he was a playboy and proud of it. That he was devilishly handsome could not be denied—tan hair in a perfect Robert Redford cut.

Her expression did not escape him. "You object?" he said.

"Who am I to object if that's the way you want to live your life," replied Ginger, "but it's not a very noble sentiment. Nor, I must say, a very mature one. It sounds more like the statement of a teenager than a grown man."

Bradon laughed, hiding the fact that the words stung. "You are blunt, I will say that!" he said. "The only trouble with your argument is that I never claimed to be noble or mature."

"Don't you *want* to be?"

"I don't know. Maybe later. Why worry about that kind of thing when you're young? Youth is the time for having fun. Or would you disagree with that too?"

"Youth seems to me to be the time to form the character you will have through the rest of your life. Do you honestly think you can *not* be noble through your youth and then one day suddenly decide to become noble all at once? It doesn't work that way. You become what you have always been. Or I should say you become what you have been making of yourself all along."

"My, my—a philosopher as well as a beauty! Well, as I say, I don't worry about all that. Maybe I will be noble and mature one day, maybe I won't. Who cares? What difference does it make?"

"It makes all the difference in the world."

"To whom?"

"To yourself. For me, to myself. Being a person of character matters to oneself."

"But as I said, who cares?"

"Don't *you* care what kind of person you are—deep down? Don't you care what kind of person you are *becoming*? I care what kind of person I am becoming. What else could matter so much as who you are inside?"

"Maybe you're right. You sound like my sister Melissa, she's around here someplace. She's the studious type, nose to the grindstone—thinks I'm frittering my life away when I should be getting a degree. But I come back to what I said before, I don't care. I'm young and I figure life is to enjoy."

By now Bradon Rhodes was a little nettled. He did not like being put in his place, especially by a girl, and a beautiful one at that. He expected it of his sister, but not a stranger. He was accustomed to weaving his charms and flashing his smile and having girls fawn over him. He was well aware that he was one of the paparazzi's favorite targets, that his picture was everywhere, and that any girl he looked at twice could become famous overnight if the moment were caught on camera.

He turned absently and wandered a few steps away, whether to impress her or just as a diversion, he didn't try to analyze.

"Hello, Madam Vice President," he said, approaching Ms. Hardy where she stood talking to a tall man Bradon did not know.

"Mr. Rhodes," nodded Hardy.

"Please," laughed Bradon. "That sounds like you're talking to my father! I'm sure you know my reputation well enough not to confuse the son with the father!"

"No comment," smiled the vice president. "I am politician enough not to step into that one. Do you know Dr. Bahram?" she asked, indicating the man beside her.

"Sorry, no."

"Let me introduce you. Dr. Bahram, this is Bradon Rhodes, the president's son. Bradon, Dr. Hamad Bahram of Harvard."

The two shook hands. "Harvard—that's a little out of my league," said Bradon. "What's your field?"

"I am chair of the Religion Department," answered Bahram in a resonant, almost musically deep voice. "My specialty is Muslim studies, though I also teach the history of Christianity and all the major faiths."

"Fascinating. Never had much use for all that myself. Maybe I should sit in on one of your lectures. Who knows, you might convert me."

"But to what, Mr. Rhodes? That would be an important consideration."

"Good point!" laughed Bradon. "I suppose not all religions are created equal."

"Well, you would be welcome any time."

After another minute or two of desultory conversation, Bradon drifted away, his brief annoyance dissipated, and returned to where Ginger still stood.

From the moment he had eyed her during his father's speech, not so much as a doubt had entered his mind that she would wilt at the sight of him. He was not used to being bested in a philosophical discussion by a girl. He had a good mind to turn the tables on her. He would enjoy watching her squirm in embarrassment.

"So tell me," he went on, "—as a minister's daughter . . . what about you? Are you a virgin?"

Ginger's eyes shot open in astonishment.

"Does my question shock you?" said Bradon.

"It totally shocks me," replied Ginger.

"People talk openly these days about their sex lives."

"Noble people don't."

"Do you claim to be more noble than me?"

"I claim nothing. But I think your question is disgusting and insulting."

"Will you answer it?"

"I will not. No gentleman would talk so crudely to a lady."

"I lay no claim to being a gentleman."

"Then you would seem to be succeeding. Please, excuse me, Mister Rhodes—this conversation has gone quite far enough and I have no interest in pursuing it further."

She turned and walked down the sloping lawn toward the water. It was obvious she did not wish to be followed.

12

Palladium's Legacy in a New Era

SEVENTY-FOUR-YEAR-OLD LORING Bardolf watched the president's speech with a multitude of complex feelings. On the one hand, he should rejoice. The new president, though not a member of Palladium like his two predecessors, was nevertheless articulating to perfection the public face of its agenda—of necessity in somewhat bland terms, though the code words were easy to discern.

Too much so. Though couched in jargon the public would swallow by the gradual inoculation method they had been using for decades, he recognized all too clearly the undercurrents that could have come from only one source. Some of the words and phrases were almost word for word. It could not be coincidental. Whoever had written this speech must have had the Domokos Final Declaration—supposedly top secret—in front of him.

The mystery of the break-in to the Mira Monte safe, if Storm Roswell's suspicions were correct, resurfaced in his mind. The speech he had just heard certainly gave credibility to the theory.

Jefferson Rhodes was a shrewd politician. He reminded Loring of the old pre-disgrace days of William Jefferson Clinton and not just because of the intersection of their names. Both Jeffersons were masters of the game. He had no doubt Rhodes mostly believed what he said. But the man was no intellectual giant. In that regard he couldn't hold a candle to Clinton. Neither was he a visionary like Marx or Alinsky or

Domokos or his own father. He would not go so far as to call Rhodes a lightweight. But there was no way he could have formulated the ideas contained in his speech on his own. Its points coincided too precisely with the outline of Domokos's final secretive document.

Bardolf's eyes strayed from the president on the television screen in front of him. Cameras continued following him after his address, panning the crowd as pundits pointed out myriad US and world leaders milling about the grounds of the Bainbridge estate. He caught frequent glimpses of his son standing so close behind the president that his face was occasionally visible during the speech. He had to hand it to him—Mike had managed to worm his way to the summit of world power without Palladium's help *or* his own. And he had brought young Roswell up with him. A deviously clever move. Two of Palladium's future League of Seven were now in the Oval Office with the president of the United States.

He wondered if it had been wise to keep Mike out of the organization's highest echelons of power. Even Anson Roswell had been made a member of the seventy-two last year and would be promoted to the League of Seven if old Storm, whose health at sixty-seven wasn't the best, passed on to his final reward. He knew Mike was furious to be passed over in favor of Anson, nine years his junior. He would be even more furious if he knew that his own father had cast the deciding—though forever confidential—vote in Anson's favor. By that time Rhodes had already named Anson his press secretary. He wondered how their working relationship as two of the president's closest confidants had been affected by the change.

He thought he had been doing the right thing to advance Mike slowly in Palladium's leadership. Now he wondered if he should have brought him in sooner.

Truth be told, he was a little afraid of his son. Mike had a ruthless streak. In his secret heart he harbored dark suspicions about what his son might be capable of. He could not prevent visions of Mike supplanting him, even—if events somehow made it possible—taking the unprecedented step of voting him off the League.

Mike was a cagey one. He had managed to circumvent Palladium altogether and was now in a position of power greater than any of the hundred-and-forty-four or the seventy-two. Greater even than his own father's.

Officially Mike was only in charge of the president's Secret Service detail. But he knew that his true position, invisible by design, was far greater. He not only had Rhodes's ear, Mike was in a position to call as many shots as he dared while remaining out of the public eye. He probably could have been named chief of staff instead of the bureaucrat Trent Randall. But invisibility was the key to Palladium's power. Such had been Palladium's strategy since the 1970s. Mike had co-opted it to his own advantage. He had done an end-run around his own father.

Loring smiled with begrudging pride in his son's stratagems.

Yet the underlying dilemma remained. The theft of the Domokos Declaration from the safe at Palladium headquarters was unsolved. He'd half suspected Mike at the time, though had said nothing to Storm. The president's speech all but confirmed it. Unless Rhodes was more clever than he gave him credit for being and knew all about Palladium and had someone *else* on the inside. There remained his troubling mention of *Four-Six*. But he doubted Rhodes knew anything. If Mike hadn't written this speech directly from the Declaration, thought Loring, he was very much mistaken.

He wasn't *certain* what role Mike had played in the old man's affairs during his final days. Mike never divulged the details of his work with Viktor. Maybe he *hadn't* possessed a copy. That would explain the break-in. Perhaps Viktor had faded mentally after writing his Final Declaration and giving it to Palladium following his final speech at Mira Monte in December of 2032. It could be that the writings Mike was part of later were incomplete or that he wanted to compare them with the Declaration.

Yet if Mike *had* helped Domokos write the thing, why had he broken into the safe? He might never know, thought Loring. In any event, he was all but certain that Mike was now in possession of the copy that had gone missing from Mira Monte.

Two pressing questions remained:

Had he shown the document to Rhodes? Or had he fed Rhodes the content for the speech? Or had he written the speech himself?

And secondly, if Mike had taken it upon himself to break into the compound—there was no record of his being anywhere near Mira Monte during the entire time in question—how had he done so? Was he to be trusted sufficiently to be elevated to Palladium's highest leadership?

Had his own son, the grandson of Palladium's founder, gone off the reservation? If he was taking matters into his own hands, would he have to eventually be cut loose? Such a thing would be unprecedented, especially for a Bardolf. No one from Palladium was ever cut loose. Once on the inside, they knew too much.

Elimination in the old-fashioned sense of the word was the only option. It had only been resorted to twice that he was aware of—both times during his father's tenure as Grand Master. It would be unthinkable in Mike's case.

Perhaps it didn't matter. So long as the agenda went forward, what was the difference whether it came through a pawn like Rhodes, aided by a little cunning manipulation on the part of his son?

The entire ethos of Palladium was founded on duplicity, manipulation, and secrecy. Maybe he was being too hard on Mike. He was using Alinsky's Rules and what he had learned from his association with Domokos to maximum advantage, both to himself and for the cause. He should be proud of the young blackguard—a chip off the familial block!

But did he have an obligation to the League and Palladium that superseded ties of blood? Others of the League were sure to notice the similarity between the Rhodes speech and the Final Declaration. Would their suspicions also fall on Mike? Or perhaps Anson? Perhaps he ought to take steps to ensure it was the latter.

Probably the best policy at this point was to bring Mike into the fold. Keep your enemies closer. Bring him back onto the reservation. Getting him confirmed as one of the seventy-two would be easy. Placing him onto the League would be more difficult. Never had *two* Bardolfs or Roswells served simultaneously.

Proposing it would be a daring gambit. But nothing would heal whatever breach might exist between himself and his son like bringing him all the way to the top of Palladium beside him. There were sure to be objections. He would have to weigh matters carefully. Give Mike *too* much power and he could find his own position precarious.

Keep your enemies closer, but still don't trust them—that might be the more appropriate motto. Meanwhile, he would keep his suspicions about the theft of the Declaration to himself. If Mike could be reined in by making him part of the organization's inner circle, it wouldn't matter anyway.

13

Reunion of Roommates

AFTER HER uncomfortable interview with Bradon Rhodes, Ginger rejoined her parents as they were walking away from their visit with Linda Trent.

"Who was that you were talking to?" asked Grace.

"Bradon Rhodes," said replied Ginger rolling her eyes.

"The president's son!"

"Yes, but he's nothing to rave about. I think he was trying to impress me with how worldly he was. It was kind of disgusting. Do you know him, Dad?"

"Only by reputation."

"Well what you've heard is true!"

The three ambled down the slope toward the water. Gradually the crowd thinned.

"I don't know about the two of you," said Mark, "but as much as I appreciate the invitation, I'm ready to think about taking the ferry back to the mainland. I've seen Linda and don't know anyone else."

"You know Mr. Rhodes, Dad."

"I wasn't counting him!" laughed Mark.

"I've had enough," said Grace. "I wonder where Heather's got to and if we can pry her away from the dashing Mr. Stewart!"

"She might not be ready to leave!" added Mark.

As they were talking, they hadn't noticed a number of individuals and small groups moving in their direction. The crowd seemed to be following them toward the water's edge. Grace was the first to notice.

"Uh . . . Mark," she said.

By now Ginger had also seen the reason for the general movement toward them. She stood staring with wide eyes.

"Don't look now, Mark," Grace added, "but . . ." She nodded her head slightly.

Mark turned just in time to see the man of the hour walking briskly toward him, his entourage and surrounding crowd in his wake.

"Mark, my old friend!" said the familiar voice. "I'm so glad you could come."

There was the president approaching, hand outstretched. The owners of a hundred pairs of eyes around the lawn were wondering who was this unknown man dressed in a bargain-rack suit that the president had singled out from among so many world leaders.

"Mr. President," said Mark, taking the president's hand and shaking it warmly, "it is good to see you again."

"And you, my friend. It has been far too long. Hello, Grace," added Jeff, turning to her at Mark's side. He took her offered hand and kissed it lightly.

"And this is our daughter, Ginger," said Grace.

"Ginger!" said Jeff enthusiastically. "I have known both your parents a long time. It is a pleasure at last to meet you."

Ginger smiled and shook his hand but was too speechless to reply. She had heard her father and mother talk about "Jeff" for years. Suddenly she was shaking hands, not with Jeff but with President Jefferson Fitzsimmons Rhodes!

"And all of you," said Jeff, turning to the woman at his side, "meet my wife, Marcia."

The three Forsters shook hands with the First Lady.

"I have been hearing about you, Mr. Forster," she said, "since before Jeff and I were married."

"I won't ask what you heard!" laughed Mark. "But please, call me Mark."

"He speaks of you fondly, I assure you," said Mrs. Rhodes.

The president now sidled close to Mark.

"Have you seen Linda?" he asked. "She's around here someplace."

"Yes, we had a chance to catch up a few minutes ago," replied Mark. "Brief, but it was good to see her. She seems to be doing okay—after Ward, you know."

"Yes, terrible thing. It's too bad he wasn't able to complete the reunion."

Gradually Jeff led Mark a pace or two from their wives.

"I would like to talk to you away from all this," he said when they managed to distance themselves somewhat from the press of the crowd that was abuzz with the question who was the man the president was talking to. As they moved away, Grace and the First Lady continued to chat freely, attracting equal curiosity from the onlookers.

"You are one of my oldest and most trusted friends, Mark," said Jeff. "I believe history will look back on this day as a turning point. I wanted you to be part of it. What did you think of the speech?"

"I, uh . . . it was sweeping in its vision, Mr. President," replied Mark, caught off guard by the abrupt question. He could not help being aware that hundreds of eyes were staring straight at him.

"A noncommittally vague response," laughed the president. "But I should have known better than to ask. You were always one who kept your own counsel until you were sure you had something to say. In my game it's called keeping one's powder dry. While others were happy to spout off at the drop of a hat, you remained silently in the background. You were the quiet one back in those days during our heated political discussions."

Mark smiled, but, true to the other's words, offered no reply.

"So let me rephrase my question. When you have a more in-depth response to my speech, I would like to hear it."

"I willingly accede to your request, Mr. President," nodded Mark. "That I can and will give when the time is appropriate."

"Where are you staying?"

"At the Coastal Budget motel in Tacoma," replied Mark. "We drove up from Sacramento."

"The Coastal Budget!" exclaimed Jeff. "We can't have that. I will make arrangements for you to stay here with me for as long as you like."

"Surely you have more important people to—"

"None more important than you," Jeff interrupted. "We have much catching up to do."

"That is very kind of you, Mr. President. But honestly, we are fine at the motel. Please, have no worries about us."

"Nonsense. Marcia and I would love to have you here. There's another young lady here with you, I believe—a friend of Ginger's—her too of course. I'll have one of my people talk to you and arrange everything. Then you and I will talk at more length, tomorrow morning perhaps. I have plans for you, Mark."

"You have plans for *me*!" laughed Mark.

"I do indeed. We shall talk about it at more leisure later. But—" added the president, glancing about, "there are many other people I need to greet."

14

Presidential Guests

MARK, GRACE, Ginger, and Heather did not return to their motel. Preparing to leave the event where they knew almost no one, the unexpected attentions of the president made them a center of interest and conversation for the next two hours. Suddenly they were surrounded by dozens of men and women wanting to shake their hands and introduce themselves, all with variations of the same question: "How do you know the president?"

By the time the afternoon began to wind down, with exhaustion setting in from relentless visiting with strangers, one of the president's "people" approached Mark. He was informed that their belongings had been picked up and transported to one of the guest cottages on the estate, their bill at the motel paid, and arrangements made for their car. One of the president's staff would show them the way to the cottage. Not altogether comfortable with strangers packing up their things, they were assured that the president had people whose job it was to take care of just such details.

They found everything in order when the young lady who had been assigned to attend to their every need took them to their new quarters—far more luxurious than their budget motel—complete with three bedrooms, each with its own bathroom, fully stocked kitchen, sitting room with wide-screen TV and home movie system, and outfitted office desk and equipment occupying one corner, outdoor jacuzzi, and private garden. She left them with a menu from which their meals and anything else they might want would be brought to them—any time, day or night.

"This is unexpected to say the least!" said Mark as Ginger and Heather disappeared to explore their rooms and the jacuzzi in back. "Even for a former roommate, it's not like Jeff to roll out the red carpet like this."

"He is the president," said Grace.

"I know, but given our dramatically different political outlooks—we haven't exactly been close. Our last meeting years ago was strained. I expected to pay our respects and be on the way home tomorrow morning."

A knock on the door interrupted their conversation. Mark went to the door.

There stood the president's son.

"Hello, Mr. Forster," he said, offering his hand. "I am Bradon Rhodes."

"You seem to know me already," said Mark as the two shook hands. "I am pleased to meet you. Please, come in—this is my wife, Grace."

"Hello, Mrs. Forster," said Bradon, shaking her hand in turn. "I met your daughter earlier. Is she . . . uh, is she here?"

Ginger and Heather were just returning through the sliding glass doors from outside. Ginger saw their guest too late to avoid him.

"Hello again, Miss Forster," he said. His reserved and respectful demeanor was entirely altered from before. "I came by to make sure you were comfortable and to see if you need anything," he said to Mark.

"We're very comfortable, thank you," replied Mark. "And have you met our friend Heather Marshall?"

"I haven't had the pleasure—Bradon Rhodes," he added, reaching his hand in Heather's direction. She shook it as she nodded with a smile.

Bradon turned again toward Ginger. "I, uh, wanted to apologize for being offensive before," he said. "I did not represent my father as well as I should have. I am very sorry."

"Thank you," nodded Ginger, though without expression.

"I wanted to ask you to join me for dinner, as my way of making up for my rudeness. I thought we could take the ferry into the city."

"Thank you," replied Ginger, still without expression, "but I already have plans."

"Oh, okay," said Bradon in obvious surprise. "Well, then," he added, turning toward the door, "maybe another time then."

He turned and smiled at Grace. "It was nice to meet you, Mrs. Forster, and you too, Miss Marshall—and you, sir," he added, again shaking Mark's hand. "Let me know if you need anything."

The moment the door closed behind him, Grace glanced around at the others. "He seems nice," she said.

"No comment," said Ginger.

"What plans do you have?"

"To have dinner and spend the evening with you and Daddy. I've already been looking over the menu. Unless the two of you want to be alone!" she added with a grin.

"Never from you, my dear!" laughed Mark. "I can't think of anything better than an evening with our two girls."

"You will have to spend it just with me, Daddy. Heather *is* going over to the city."

All eyes turned in Heather's direction. Her face reddened.

"It's nothing, it's just—" she began.

"The capital's most famous and handsome television reporter is taking you to dinner," said Ginger playfully, "and it's *nothing*!"

"He's just, you know, being nice. He said he felt sorry for me when he saw me sitting alone after the president's speech."

"Yes, and then spent the whole afternoon with you and ended the day asking you out on a date."

"It's not a date! He's just being nice, I tell you," laughed Heather in embarrassment. "He'll forget about me when this is all over. I'll probably never see him again after—"

Heather stopped abruptly.

"Okay . . .?" said Ginger, drawing the word out quizzically. "After *what*?"

Heather smiled almost mischievously and glanced away briefly.

"It's nothing really. But he sort of invited me to go sailing tomorrow."

"I told you!" laughed Ginger. "It's not nothing!"

"Lucky you," said Grace. "That sounds like fun!"

"I told him I wasn't sure if I would be here long enough. I didn't know when we were leaving."

"We would not want you to miss that!" said Mark. "We will be here long enough for your sail. Besides, Jeff wants to see me tomorrow. We will be here at least until the afternoon. When you see Mr. Stewart this evening you can accept his invitation. We will not leave Bainbridge without you!"

Another knock came to the door not two minutes after the departure of the president's son. Ginger immediately disappeared into one of the bedrooms. Wondering if it might be Todd, Heather remained. Grace opened the door.

There stood a uniformed officer.

"Mrs. Forster?"

Grace nodded.

"A message for your husband from the president," he said, handing her an envelope. He turned crisply on his heels and walked away.

Grace closed the door and handed Mark the envelope.

"Apparently I am to meet privately with Jeff tomorrow morning," he said after reading the enclosed sheet. "It does not sound like an informal chat. I will be *sent for*."

"Very mysterious!" said Grace.

"Maybe we will finally find out why we were invited," said Mark.

"Depending on what is involved," said Grace, turning to Heather, "it sounds like you will definitely have time for your sail with Mr. Stewart."

"I still have no idea why he would want to go sailing with me! Look at all the famous people who are here. If what you say about how well known he is, he could have asked anybody. I'm a nobody!"

"Nobody is a nobody, my dear," said Mark. "Besides, you're Stirling Marshall's granddaughter. Not Todd Stewart, not even the president of the United States, can match that!"

15

Old Friends

AFTER AN exquisite dinner from the presidential kitchen, Mark and Grace went out for a walk along the water's edge, leaving Ginger in the jacuzzi and Heather across the Sound in the city. Turning away from the water, they followed one of the many paths on the estate into a light grove of pine and fir, gradually circling back toward the guest cottages which sat behind the main house of the Rhodes compound. The lowering sun behind them over the hills to the west shown upon a solitary woman walking slowly toward them.

As they drew closer, recognition dawned. It was Linda Hutchins Trent.

They continued forward. This time, away from the eyes of the multitude and unconcerned about her reputation in the eyes of the nation's political elite, one at a time Mark and Grace embraced her affectionately.

As they stepped back, tears flooded Linda's eyes. She too felt emotions flowing more freely than she had allowed earlier.

"I wasn't sure you would recognize me before we met earlier," she said in a husky voice, "or even if you would want to see me. I had hoped to talk to you again."

"Oh, Linda," said Mark, "why would we not have wanted to see you? We were delighted to see you!"

"Thank you, Mark. You were always so kind—one of the most gracious men I ever met. But I wasn't very kind to you back in the day, once

I fell under Jeff's spell. I'm afraid I said some unkind things to you and Ward."

"Water under the bridge. We were all young back then. One of life's important lessons is that relationships are infinitely more important than politics. You will always be a friend."

"Thank you. Thank you both," said Linda, glancing back and forth at the two with a smile.

"Is Cameron here?" asked Mark.

"No, he couldn't make it—though even if he hadn't had a scheduling conflict, he might have declined. Not Jeff's biggest fan."

Mark did not reply.

"We are so sorry about Ward," said Grace, as they continued toward the cottages, Linda walking between them. "It is a dreadful tragedy."

"Thank you," replied Linda, drawing in a steadying breath. "His loss is nearly as great for you. You were closer to him for years, Mark, than I was. We did have a wonderful visit before his death. We were able to put much of the past behind us. It was very healing. Had we not had that time, I think I would die from the guilt. I still have many regrets. It's a pain I will have to live with. I turned away from him for so many years. But knowing we were able to express our love for one another at the end makes a big difference."

"Have there been any developments in the case?" asked Mark.

"Nothing. We'll probably never know who was responsible or why. But Ward was a controversial, even divisive, figure. And more outspoken about politics than I wish he had been."

"You said earlier that your husband wasn't able to come," said Grace. "What does he do? I'm sorry, I should know. I'm sure Mark's told me."

"He's an attorney. He's in the middle of a big case. He doesn't like Jeff much anyway. Not just because of the former boyfriend thing—he doesn't trust him. He was glad for a reason not to come. But I felt I should."

"Before we saw you earlier, I didn't think we would know a soul," laughed Grace. "This is an amazing atmosphere for us! Talking to the president, meeting the First Lady, senators and congressmen and foreign heads of state everywhere, then walking along and running into a Supreme Court justice."

"Correction," smiled Linda, "—running into a friend."

She grew thoughtful. A curiously self-conscious expression came over her face. Mark sensed the change. He saw that she was struggling with emotion.

"Actually," she began again, "the main reason I accepted the invitation, besides the chance to see my folks again—they're back together, by the way. I don't know if you knew that."

"Ward kept us up to date on your family," said Mark. "That's wonderful about your parents."

"What I was going to say is that the main reason I decided to come was in hopes of talking to you."

"Us!" exclaimed Mark and Grace together.

"Even Supreme Court justices have their informants! I got wind that Jeff had invited you."

"We still have no idea why," said Mark.

"Nor do I," rejoined Linda.

"We will find out tomorrow," said Grace. "Jeff's asked Mark to meet him in the morning."

"Hmm," Linda nodded. "Interesting. I would say the same thing to you that I did to Ward shortly before his death—be careful, Mark. I'm sure he's got something up his sleeve."

"You're probably right. If I know Jeff, he's always got something up his sleeve. But why did you want to see us?"

"I'd rather wait until we can sit down and talk uninterrupted."

"Would you like to come over to our cottage for dessert?" asked Grace. "Where are you staying—are you here on the island?"

"No, I'm staying with my folks in the city. I need to be getting one of the presidential ferries back over."

She paused and thought a moment.

"Would you . . . I mean, I don't know how long you're staying and I realize presidents tend to trump everyone else. But I would love for my dad to meet you. Do you think you could come over and have supper with us tomorrow evening? My mother would be thrilled to see you again, Mark."

She paused. A smile came over her face.

"She had her eye on you for me, you know. She was so fond of you. Sorry, Grace!" she added with a sheepish smile.

"Who wouldn't love Mark!" laughed Grace. "But I was the lucky one who snagged him!"

"If Jeff has no plans for us, we'd love to," said Mark. "Don't you need to ask your mother?"

"Believe me—she will be excited to have you."

"Shall we call you tomorrow, then?" asked Mark.

"I'll give you my number."

"What about the girls?" asked Grace.

"Girls?" said Linda.

"Our daughter Ginger and another young lady who came with us, Heather Marshall. Apparently, the president's son has taken an interest in our Ginger."

"I'd keep her away from him," said Linda. "There are stories that would make any parent uncomfortable. But by all means both girls are more than welcome."

"One of us will call you as soon tomorrow as we know if we will be free for the evening."

16

Madcap Abduction

MIKE BARDOLF made certain that he was the one to personally escort Mark Forster to the president's West Coast version of the Oval Office at 9:45 the following morning. The two had never met and circumstances did not afford opportunity for introductions or personal exchanges. He presented himself stoically at the door to the guest cottage punctually at 9:40, then led the way crisply to the main house, divulging no more than had he been a low-level flunky on the presidential food chain.

Both men, however, were students of people and experts at reading the signs of motive and character. Without a word being spoken, when they parted, both knew more about the other than the other suspected. In that subtle unspoken game, in this case Mike Bardolf had the decided advantage. Not only was he a master at sizing people up, he had possessed a complete dossier on Hutchins's friend and fellow pastor for years. If a stranger and evangelical Christian was going to be close to the president, he wanted to know everything about him—down to what he said when leaving his wife and daughter for the auspicious meeting. The details told him more than anyone suspected. It was why he knew the president far better than the president would ever know him. It was a matter of feeling the other's vibes, as his 1960s-raised grandfather might have said.

When he left the president's former friend to be fussed over by staffers offering him coffee and a plate of fruit and Danish, Bardolf was confident that he had learned what he needed to—that the man was no firebrand like Ward Hutchins. Gracious, soft-spoken, gentle, courteous—he was one who could easily be "handled."

"Hey, Pine, my old friend!" exclaimed Jeff walking in at 10:03.

Mark rose and the two shook hands.

"Mr. President," said Mark with a respectful nod.

"Mark, Mark!" said Jeff effusively. "None of that here. It's *me*! We're behind closed doors, no tape recordings or eavesdroppers. It's Jeff—or Pike. Otherwise I will promptly kick you out."

"Okay, *Jeff*—you win," laughed Mark.

"Did they get you what you need—coffee, anything else?"

"I'm good."

"And your accommodations?"

"Wonderful—very comfortable. I can't thank you enough. The three women are still in disbelief to be the president's guest."

"It's the least I can do. But . . . the *three* women?"

"We brought a young woman with us—Heather Marshall."

"Oh, right—I met her yesterday. She was with young Stewart—daughter of that author friend of yours."

"Granddaughter. Her parents are dear friends. And your son, it seems, has been paying his respects to our daughter."

"The rascal! And your, uh— Ginger?"

"She's a little wary."

"Smart girl!" laughed Bradon's father.

As Mark and the president visited casually, Grace opened the door of their guest cottage. She was shocked to see the First Lady standing in front of her, apparently alone, without escort or Secret Service detail.

"Mrs. Rhodes!" she exclaimed.

"Hello, Mrs. Forster," said Jeff's wife. "I'm sorry to call unannounced . . ."

"We are your guests. I am at your service."

"I wondered if you would like to go for a walk. It would give us a chance to visit while our husbands are talking."

"I'd love to. Just let me get my sweater. The morning is a little chillier than I am used to in California."

A few minutes later the two women were making their way through the trees that were numerous throughout the estate, chatting comfortably.

"What *are* our husbands talking about?" asked Grace, laughing lightly. "In fact, what are Mark and I doing here at all!"

Marcia Rhodes laughed. "All Jefferson told me was that he and your husband are old college friends. Beyond that, I know nothing. You knew Jefferson back then too, didn't you?"

"Only as being Mark's girlfriend."

The path they had been following emerged out of the trees. The huge open expanse of the small private airport known as Rhodes Field opened before them. Its 7,000-foot runway stretched away through a clearing in the trees all the way to the Sound where the water curved around from the front of the estate into a wide inlet, which provided a perfect approach to the runway. Though the estate's main small harbor was located in front of the large house, a smaller collection of docks extended out into the water at the end of the runway to accommodate the sea planes that made regular runs to the mainland.

As they came into the clearing, Grace saw two helicopters sitting at the helipad and several private jets, as well as a half dozen four- and six-seaters.

"Oh, just look at that cute little Cessna 375!" exclaimed Grace. "I've read about it but never seen one."

The First Lady glanced over at her in surprise. "Do you know airplanes?"

"Yes, I love planes. I'm a pilot."

"No!"

"I've been flying since I was seventeen."

"Will you take me up for a ride?"

Grace stared back, assuming Jeff's wife was joking.

"I'm serious," said Mrs. Rhodes.

Grace continued looking at her, incredulous. "You're not *really* serious?" she laughed.

"I am—absolutely. I can clear it."

"Wouldn't I get arrested or something?"

"Not if you're with me. They'll do whatever I say. I'll tell them I made you do it."

Grace laughed, still not sure how seriously to take her.

By now Mrs. Rhodes was excitedly leading her forward toward the hangars.

"This is our hangar here," she said as they walked inside the largest of the three. "I assume you don't want to try out the Gulfstream. But here are three Cessnas. I don't know who that one you saw outside belongs to, but you can take your pick of any of these. I'll go clear it with Martin."

She turned to go, then paused.

"Come to think of it, he'll just say no or call Mike Bardolf and he will definitely put the kibosh on it. We'll just go and ask forgiveness instead of permission. Let them eat cake. What are they going to do, shoot us down or arrest me?" she added with a laugh.

"Are you—I mean, I don't want to get you in trouble," said Grace. "I don't want to get *me* in trouble!"

"Mrs. Forster, this is a presidential wife's order—go pick out one of those planes and make ready for takeoff."

Trying to sound stern, there was yet a twinkle in Marcia Rhodes's eye. Still reluctant, yet unable to avoid a flutter of excitement, Grace turned toward the planes.

"I know all three models. I can fly any of them. I guess I had better check the fuel levels and maintenance logs."

"Be quick about it before Martin spots us."

17

An Offer

BACK IN the president's office, at last Jeff got down to the purpose for which he had brought Mark to Bainbridge Island.

"I don't believe in beating around the bush, Mark," he said. "So I'll get right to the point. My sources tell me that you've left the pulpit of your church and retired from the active ministry."

"I have," nodded Mark. "I felt it was time for a change."

"Is the change permanent?"

"Probably. I can't say for certain. When you're walking with God, nothing can be permanent. One has to keep his options open to whatever God might have you do."

Ignoring the spiritual implications, Jeff seized on Mark's words, though in a different vein than Mark had intended.

"Good, I am glad to hear it," he said. "Was your stepping away prompted by a change in your religious convictions?"

"Not at all. They are stronger than ever. It is because of my deepening convictions about many things that I resigned my pastorate."

"Ah . . . good, that's fine—I am delighted to hear it."

The whine of a Cessna engine came gradually into their hearing, passed overhead, and faded in the distance. Neither man took notice.

"I must say, Jeff, that surprises me."

"Why?"

"It is no secret that we do not see eye to eye on the cultural and political direction the country has been moving since Obama's time."

"Exactly. What I have to propose lies in your world—religion and spirituality, not politics. Perhaps it is *because* we do not see through the same political lens that I have asked you here. Because we are different, we balance each other. We were always a team, not necessarily because we were alike. Pike and Pine—different but a team! We were good together. You have your finger on the pulse of the religious world and the religious climate of the country in a way I am incapable of. That is your world, not mine. Which is why—"

Jeff paused for effect.

"—which is why I asked you here to invite you to join my administration. I want you to be part of my team, Mark."

Mark stared dumbfounded at his former friend.

"I have no idea what to say," he replied slowly, "—how even to process your words. It is so out of the blue, so bizarre. I am probably the most *unpolitical* man you know. Where did this come from, Jeff? Why me?"

"Don't you see—because you're the *perfect* man—as an old friend, as an honorable man for whom I have the greatest respect. Were I to choose someone with political baggage, he or she would never be able to represent and be accepted by the entire religious spectrum. *Only*, as you say, an unpolitical man could garner that kind of respect."

"But to do what? I'm a political babe in the woods. I have nothing to offer."

"That's where you're wrong. I want you to head up the new Commission on Religious Unity that I mentioned in my speech. I want to bring spirituality and religion back into the national discussion. You and Ward always insisted that the country was losing touch with its religious foundations. I now see that you were right. The book published by Dr. Reyburn two years ago touched a chord of latent spirituality in the country. We need to listen to that. You are a respected leader and spokesman. I doubt if you have an enemy in the world. If I might say it, I believe that Ward's mantle as evangelicalism's foremost spokesman has passed to you. Our connection together and with Ward—God bless him—will immediately place you in the spotlight, and bring attention to the new commitment of the Rhodes administration to the spiritual values of our nation, exactly as Dr. Reyburn wrote about."

"You misjudge my standing," said Mark. "I am no longer a spokesman for anything. I am a simple rancher now. If Ward had a mantle, it hasn't passed to me."

"Let me be the judge of that. You are the man I want."

Jeff said no more, allowing Mark to absorb his persuasive monologue. Still shell-shocked, Mark began gathering his wits sufficiently to form a few questions.

"I guess the first thing I need to ask is what it would entail," he said.

"Ninety percent of the world's wars," replied Jeff, as if reading the talking points of his sales pitch from a script, "have religion at their foundation. For the world to truly come together, religious hatred must be eliminated for all time. There will always be different religions and sects within those systems of faith. But hatred must cease. Acceptance of those of differing faiths and harmony between them, must light the way toward the objectives I spoke of in my speech—unity and freedom for all people on the planet. The Commission on Religious Unity will bring together leaders from every major religion to plan a strategy that can be implemented worldwide to bring about a new era of harmony. My vision for the commission is like nothing ever attempted before.

"What I see," he went on, "is leaders coming together with joint proposals, spearheaded by you, to take back to their individual constituencies, there to be implemented at the grass roots level of their churches and synagogues and mosques—strategies that will be practical, that will have teeth, that will bring people together not separate them, strategies, too, that will have the full support and backing of the administration."

"What you describe sounds wonderful, of course," said Mark, though with a note of caution. "Though also somewhat utopian. Do you really believe that religious divisions can be eliminated through political commissions?"

"Not eliminated, obviously. But significantly overcome."

"It has never succeeded before."

"You're right. So why should we not be the first to make it succeed? The world is evolving, Mark. Towns and cities were once autonomous. Then they became city-states. Those city-states became larger states, then countries. Progress tends toward a great coming together, a coalescing of separate interests into a gradual unifying of their objectives. Unity is the great goal of progress. It is inevitable that this same progressive evolution will ultimately sweep religious differences into it, just as cities and states and nations have come together. Why should we not stand at the vanguard of this new view of religion from a global not a sectarian foundation? Why should you and I not lead the way?"

"A sweeping vision," nodded Mark.

"Call the position I am offering a Religion Czar, if you like."

Inwardly the words grated on Mark's sensibilities like fingernails on an old-fashioned chalkboard. If Jeff was trying to sell him on the idea, he could not have used a more inappropriate expression. But he let it go.

"I want you, Mark, to take your place along with the other leaders of our nation," Jeff went on, "to be this administration's religion guru and spokesman to the spiritual community—to all faiths of the world."

Again, Mark squirmed inwardly. "And you would envision Grace and me moving to Washington?" he said.

"Of course. We would work together every day. The good we could do to bring the people of the country together would be unparalleled. It goes without saying that your compensation would be sizeable. Your parents are aging, I believe. You would be in a position to see to their every need."

Mark drew in a long breath, then exhaled slowly. It was silent for twenty or thirty seconds.

"Well?" said Jeff at length.

"All I can say at this point," replied Mark slowly, "is that I am overwhelmed. I am appreciative that you would have such a level of confidence in me. Of course, I will have to talk with Grace and Ginger and Craig. The four of us will pray earnestly about what is God's will in the matter."

"But you will do it? You will accept the position?"

"As I say, we will pray to see if we believe it to be God's will."

"What is there to pray about, Mark? I am offering you the opportunity of a lifetime."

"I realize that. I am grateful, Jeff. Believe me, I will weigh everything you say seriously. But I cannot accept until or unless God makes clear it is what *he* wants me to do."

"What about what *you* want, what *I* want?"

"They matter nothing. Only what he wants."

"Ah, right, I see," nodded Jeff. "Well then, get to praying. I'm anxious to move on this."

"You can be assured I will, as you say, get to praying immediately. I began as you were speaking. One more question—is this confidential? May I discuss it with some of my close friends and counselors?"

"Of course. Not confidential at all."

Suddenly the door opened and Mike Bardolf strode in.

"I apologize for the intrusion, Mr. President," he said. "There has been a major breach of security."

"What is it, Mike—anything serious?"

"That is uncertain, sir. One of the small Cessnas has taken off from the landing field, and the First Lady is missing."

"What! Has she been . . . what is it, Mike—has she been abducted!"

"It does not appear so, Mr. President. Martin was able to raise her on the radio. She was laughing."

"Where were your men, Mike! The Secret Service is supposed to prevent things like this. There'll be hell to pay. Who in blazes is flying the plane without clearance?"

"It has not been confirmed, sir."

Bardolf glanced toward where Mark sat listening.

"It appears that Mrs. Forster may be with her."

"What!"

Jeff turned toward Mark.

"Do you know anything about this?"

"Not a thing. Grace is a licensed pilot, but I cannot imagine—"

Jeff did not wait for him to finish.

"Get to the bottom of it, Mike!" he barked. "Find out where they're going and get the choppers in the air. We've got to get them back on the ground before this turns into a major incident. That's all we'd need is for some lunatic to get wind of it and turn an automatic rifle on them. Get on it, Mike!"

The discussion of the presidential commission was obviously over. Mark left the "Oval Office," leaving Jeff inwardly fuming both at his hesitancy in accepting the offer and at what he was convinced was Grace's complicity in the escapade involving the First Lady.

By days end he had already decided, if Mark turned down his offer, that he might bring charges against Grace for stealing a presidential plane and taking the First Lady hostage.

18

An Evening at the Hutchinses

THE SUPPER that evening with Eloise and Truman Hutchins was the happiest social gathering Linda's parents had enjoyed since their son Ward's murder eighteen months earlier. For one evening at least they were able to put the memory behind them and enjoy the presence of one of Ward's best friends. Mark's grief, if not equal to their own, was enough for them to know that he deeply shared their pain. For Linda, too, the evening was cathartic.

Not surprisingly, Grace was the center of attention for her madcap adventure with the First Lady. Their unauthorized Cessna flight made instant news, including recriminations from the FAA. By the time two helicopters were in the air after them, enough curious onlookers around Seattle heard and saw them and, with the president in residence, were curious what might be going on. Film footage of the two military choppers in pursuit of the tiny Cessna were all over the internet and evening newscasts.

Press Secretary Anson Roswell issued a statement with the presidential runway in the background, accompanied by film clips of the Cessna coming in for a landing escorted by the two helicopters. Cameras, by then on hand filming the landing, zoomed in on the two women exiting the plane in high spirits. Across the country the pressing question was: Who was the woman with the First Lady flying the plane!

“You’re famous, Mom!” said Ginger when Truman Hutchins turned off the television.

“How did it all happen, Grace?” asked Eloise.

“It was completely spur of the moment,” laughed Grace. “Mrs. Rhodes came by for a visit during Mark’s meeting with Jeff. We went out for a walk, came to the airstrip, and I mentioned that I had a pilot’s license. Before I knew it, we were strapping ourselves in and taking off. I didn’t know what to think. But she wouldn’t take no for an answer. I probably should have refused, but she was so insistent. And I have to say, it was fun. Though after all the hoopla it caused, I hope I don’t get in trouble. They could take my license away.”

“I’m sure Jeff won’t let it go that far,” said Mark.

“Where did you go?” asked Ginger.

“Just over the city then inland and around Mt. Rainier. It was an amazing sight. By then we had two helicopters, one on either side of us, ordering us by radio and loudspeaker to turn around. Marcia—I mean, Mrs. Rhodes—was loving it. ‘Just ignore them,” she said. ‘What are they going to do, shoot down the First Lady?’ She grabbed the mic and told them she was fine and to leave us alone. They didn’t, of course, and we’d had our fun. So we followed them back. By then the whole compound had emptied and was waiting at the field when we landed.”

“I don’t think Jeff was pleased,” laughed Mark. “That was quite a sight when you touched down! I’d love to be a fly on the wall of the presidential bedroom tonight!”

“From what I’ve seen, Marcia can hold her own,” said Grace. “Though before all that happened, when we were walking together, she was surprisingly frank. She doesn’t seem to be enjoying the First Lady role. I don’t think she likes the spotlight.”

Unconsciously Mark and Grace glanced toward Linda.

“I never really knew Marcia,” she said. “I knew his first wife from law school. There was no love lost between her and me. Marcia and I only ran into one another a time or two at social functions in Seattle. She always hung back—never pushed herself into the limelight.”

“Ward once described her as a trophy wife.”

"That wouldn't be my characterization. His first wife, yes. Marcia is a very handsome woman, there's no doubt about that. But my sense is that there is more to Marcia Rhodes than the public sees. There have been rumors too, that the marriage isn't altogether idyllic, that she didn't want him running for president."

"Well, she seems to be handling it fine," said Grace. "I liked her. Obviously, it is a day I will never forget! My mom was on the phone ten minutes after we landed," Grace laughed. "It didn't take long for it to be all over the news about the mystery pilot who abducted the First Lady!"

Sensing that Linda and her two friends needed to talk, the two Hutchinses excused themselves after dessert. Ginger remained with her parents.

The moment the four were alone, the three women, to whom Mark had as yet said nothing about the morning, all turned to him bursting with questions about his meeting with the president.

Mark smiled at their exuberant curiosity.

"Don't keep us in suspense!" said Grace.

"My hesitation," Mark replied slowly, "is only because I'm not yet quite sure what to think of it myself."

"Then just tell us."

"Okay. Hold onto your hats. Jeff asked me to join his administration."

Grace and Linda stared back as if they hadn't heard him.

"What does that mean, Daddy?" said Ginger.

"You're *serious*?" said Linda.

"I am. As for what it means," he added, "I'm still not really sure."

"For what position?" said Linda. "I mean—I think the world of you, Mark, but let's face it, you're . . ."

She broke off, not sure how to put it delicately.

"Hardly qualified for a high-level government post," laughed Mark.

"That wasn't exactly what I meant—more not the type. You're no political animal."

"For any existing position in the government, I *wouldn't* be qualified. But he wants to create a new position, something like a Religion Czar to oversee his new Commission on Religious Unity. He wants me to head it."

Mark went on to recount the conversation in detail. When he was through, the room was silent.

"Seriously, Mark," said Grace at length, "you're not actually . . . us—moving to the East Coast! Just after we have the ranch up and running again."

Mark exhaled slowly.

"I don't know," he said. "On the surface of it—of course not. How could I possibly consider such a thing? For the rest of the day, whenever I thought about it, I could hardly keep from laughing. The idea is ridiculous. I found myself wondering if it was nothing but a scheme by Jeff—the invitation to the reception and speech—to exact his sweet revenge on me for not endorsing him all those years ago when he first ran for Congress. Was this his chance to show me he didn't need me, dangling the brass ring in front of me to show how high he had risen while I was still a nobody."

"I wouldn't put it past him," said Linda sardonically.

"Yet he seemed absolutely sincere, as if we were still the greatest of pals. I know Jeff can be a chameleon. I suppose I have a naïve and trusting streak, but I did not detect insincerity or duplicity. I know I haven't been around him in years. Maybe I'm too naïve for my own good. He seemed almost annoyed when I did not give him an answer immediately. But it seemed for real. I think he really *wants* me to accept."

After another thoughtful silence, again Linda spoke.

"I've said this before, Mark," she said. "I would be very careful. He may be sincere in his own way. Politicians can be entirely sincere and yet completely duplicitous at the same time. Opposite as duplicity and sincerity seem, politicians become so self-deluded they have no inkling how two-faced even sincerity becomes. I've been living in that bubble all my professional life. From Jeff's perspective, I'm sure he is convinced that everything he is trying to accomplish is for the world's good. That's the delusion of the Left. They're not aware how unscrupulous their methods have become. Even in the Supreme Court, there have been times when my colleagues and I have gone so far as to justify lying and murder in cases where the final objective somehow fits into the noble purpose of the liberal agenda."

She paused momentarily.

"All this to say that I would be reluctant to trust Jeff too far," she added. "I have never been able to completely eliminate the thought that he may have had something to do with Ward's death."

"Are you serious!"

"I have nothing to base that on, only a suspicion. There are rumors in Washington. Nothing about Ward, but linking Jeff to people you don't want anything to do with—dirty tricks on opponents that make Nixon's seem like child's play."

Linda paused again and looked at Mark with a serious expression.

"I mean no disrespect, Mark," she said. "In fact, I mean it with the *greatest* respect, but in some ways you are an innocent. The people in that world—Jeff's world—would chew you up and spit you out."

Mark nodded. "I know you're right. My inclination is to see Jeff as soon as we get back to the island tonight and tell him no. But I have to be true to my word and pray about it. What if the Lord might actually want me to accept?"

"Mark, you can't be serious!" said Grace again.

"I don't know. Don't we have to be *willing*? I can't think of anything I want to do less than move to DC. The idea of being at the center of power and influence doesn't move the needle a hair's breadth for me. But I have to ask God, *Is this something you want me to do?*"

"Just be careful, Mark," repeated Linda. "As you pray, be careful."

"I will heed your cautions, I promise."

The silence this time signaled the end of the discussion. The others knew the matter would be decided in Mark's prayer closet. Even Linda, though she had not considered herself an active Christian for years, knew Mark well enough to know that.

19

Friendship Restored and Renewed

"THERE IS something else I want to talk to the two of you about," said Linda at length. "I hope you don't mind, Ginger," she added. "I need to talk to your parents alone."

"Of course not," replied Ginger.

"Should we go out for a walk?" asked Linda, glancing back and forth between Mark and Grace. "It will be light for another hour or so."

They left the house. Linda led the way in silence.

"It's completely unrelated to everything we've been talking about," she began after a minute or two. Personal, I guess you would say."

She paused and drew in a deep breath.

"This is hard," she went on, smiling almost nervously. "Here I sit on the Supreme Court. I'm at the pinnacle of my profession. Yet deep down inside I'm just . . . *me*. Obviously there's a lot of water under the bridge—we've all changed since those carefree days at Humboldt, what was it, over thirty years ago now? Hard to believe! Yet as I reflect on those years, part of me is still the same. That's probably hard for you to believe. I know I became more liberal than you and Ward might have liked. I slipped into progressivism without any good reason, except that I followed Jeff's lead all those years ago. Then you're surrounded by people who make it all sound so plausible. The bubble of like-mindedness takes over and dictates how you perceive everything. Before you know it, years go by and you've never subjected your beliefs to the kind of critical thinking we're supposed to do on the Court.

"But I've been, I don't know, reevaluating some of those perspectives. I'm sure Ward's death has a lot to do with it. But I was wondering about things even before that. You're probably shocked by that, though I suppose I am still a liberal at heart. But the book by Dr. Reyburn forced me to think about much I hadn't thought about carefully."

"You read the Reyburn book?" said Mark.

"You're surprised?"

"I suppose I am."

"Maybe I'm surprised too. I don't know what prompted me to buy it. Shortly afterward I had a wonderful visit with Ward. It turned out to be the last time I saw him. I knew I needed to apologize for misjudging him for his strong views. We were able to affirm our love for each other. In light of what happened, I am so thankful for that time."

Again she paused and looked away.

"I need to do the same with the two of you," she said. "I want to apologize for being so critical of your beliefs and your faith, for cruel things I said, to you especially, Mark, all those years ago when we argued about Trump. Mostly for being critical of your desire to live your faith in a practical way I never did and that I couldn't understand back then. I see now what honorable young men you and Ward were and what honorable men you both became. And you too, Grace," she added, glancing toward Grace with a smile. "You probably don't know this, but I admire you. You exemplify your name."

"Oh, Linda!" said Grace, reaching our and taking Linda's hand.

Linda looked away, tears flooding her eyes.

"I'm sorry," she said softly, "—sorry I wasn't able to see who you were sooner."

Mark stopped and turned toward her. Linda faced him, and they embraced.

"I hope this means we can be friends again," he said as they drew back, "like we were when we first met."

"I would like that," smiled Linda, glancing back and forth between him and Grace. "I know we live three thousand miles apart. But I want to, I don't know, maybe get in touch with God again. I was so immature back then, so easily swayed by Jeff. I wonder if I ever knew God at all. My mom took us to church, of course—she was the religious one of the family. But did I ever *really* know what it meant to be a Christian like she did, like you both and Ward did? Now I'm not so sure. For the first time, I really want to. Maybe Ward's death has caused me to think about life in a new way, and how quickly it passes. Maybe it's turning fifty, maybe it's Jeff's election and seeing who he's become—maybe it's the Reyburn book. For whatever reason, I know I need to make some changes—inside, where I have to live with myself. There's no one else I have to turn to but the two of you."

She looked away and began weeping softly.

They continued to walk and talk for another hour. By the time the three Forsters left the Hutchins home, they only just made the eleven o'clock presidential ferry back to Bainbridge Island.

20

Momentous Times

A MORE UNLIKELY locale for one small segment of the worldwide rebirth of the first-century church could scarcely be imagined than the foothills of northeast California. What possible link could exist between ancient Galilee, Samaria, Jerusalem, and Bethany and this region of lakes, rivers, forests, and valleys a third of a globe away?

It was in the homes of individuals that Christ's church was born, not in synagogues or temples. There were no buildings in which to house that ancient Church. It was housed in hearts, living stones of men and women fitted and joined together by the mortar of unity as a dwelling place for the Spirit of God.

It was in such homes that the faithful remnant of that primitive Church was now coming alive at the two adjacent ranches of the foothills and in other homes scattered about the environs of California's state capital.

Nor was it the only such place where remnant cells were springing up. What was taking place in California was but a "type" of a worldwide move of that same Spirit, preparing his people for tribulations to come. Yet it was also one of the most significant by virtue of its links to author Stirling Marshall, whose writings were giving those quiet birthings a foundational vision for a new era in Christianity's long history, and a new era in the ongoing raising up of the living Temple which is his eternal Church.

History unfolds with curious twists and turns. The notoriety of those eras, places, and people whose names become known to later generations are capricious, elusive, unpredictable. They invariably seem more ordinary to their own times than they are viewed by posterity.

The settings where change originates are usually of little consequence in themselves, until they are impregnated with significance by the people who inhabit them. A stable in Bethlehem . . . a church door in Wittenberg . . . a large hall in Philadelphia . . . the homes of faithful men and women in Dorado Wood, California, Hillsgrove, Kentucky . . . Austin and Houston and Indianapolis and Nashville and Elgin and Eureka and Cullen and Atlanta . . . none can tell where the *next* such seemingly unremarkable place will emerge as the site of some unseen human earthquake that will set future histories rumbling.

Similarly, the individuals who move history's compass are rarely taken note of during the formative years of their preparation for that destiny. The seeds of those personalities first send down invisible roots that nurture and nourish the trees upon which the fruit of greatness grows. Likewise, the precursors of the events that sweep such individuals into their train germinate years, decades, even centuries before. Their impact remains unobserved, miniscule, seemingly commonplace, until the moment of truth is suddenly at hand.

None can tell when, or where, or through whom the tide of human affairs may dramatically shift at an unlikely place, or because of one man or woman, or its waters gush in a new direction from a single decision or otherwise unremarkable event.

History is, after all, the story of individuals more than places or events. It is men and women who spawn the events that make up history's progressive unfolding. Most of those personal dramas are never known. Some of their stories rise from amid the rest to exercise an impact upon future generations far greater than those men and women would have thought possible.

Mark Forster had no more idea as he saddled his favorite mare—a gorgeous Lusitano of eight years, light dun in color, keen of hearing, and equable of temperament—in returning to his roots and stepping down from his pastorate, that he and Grace and their family had embarked on a destiny of eternal import. Everything had changed since their deepening involvement with the mentor of Mark's youth and the family of Timothy and Jaylene Marshall. They were now intrinsically connected by inseparable bonds with those others who, more by accident than intent, viewed themselves as an informal coalescing of brothers and sisters of a commonly-shared life. With David Gordon and Timothy Marshall, Mark Forster was now acknowledged as one of the spiritual leaders of what they unofficially referred to as a Fellowship of Common Life.

All he was thinking about at this moment was putting the recent trip to Seattle behind him in the most pleasurable way possible—on the back of a horse.

Many things lay heavy on his mind. The trip north had taken a major unexpected turn. He now had to figure out what it meant. And how to respond to Jeff's request.

He, Grace, Ginger, and Heather had driven south from Salem the day before, arriving home about sunset. The drive had been full of animated conversation—mostly among the three women—which largely centered around Grace's madcap flight with Marcia Rhodes, Ginger's attempts to avoid the persistent visits of Bradon Rhodes, and Heather's detailed account of her dinner and sail on Puget Sound with Todd Stewart. For one who had never been on a date in her life, the evening and afternoon with Todd had been as unique for Heather as it was exciting. She was old enough and wise enough, however, not to be schoolgirl giddy over it or to read too much into it.

"I don't know how he managed the boat," she said, "—I suppose from the president somehow—there were quite a few tied to the docks—or how he knew so much about sailing, especially being from New Mexico. Maybe he learned to sail on a lake there. But he knew everything. We went in and out of little inlets when I could see nothing of the city, around some small islands, and then suddenly there was the Space Needle again. I know you all used to live here and have sailed before, but I've never done anything like that in my life!"

"And with someone so famous," said Grace.

"And good-looking!" added Ginger.

"I don't know about that!" laughed Heather. "He was just Todd. Nice, considerate, soft-spoken. I'm glad I didn't know who he was when he came over and sat down beside me after the president's speech. I would have been scared to talk to him. But we just started talking. I've never talked like that, you know, to a guy. I wasn't even nervous."

"He didn't tell you anything other than that he had taken a leave of absence from his job?" asked Mark.

"He didn't even tell me what his job was. I had no idea until you told me."

"I'd wondered why he dropped off the radar. He was on the news every night. Then suddenly he disappeared."

"Are you going to see him again?" asked Ginger with a mischievous grin.

"I doubt it. How would I? He lives in the east, or I think so. Actually, I don't know where he lives. For all I know he'll go back to Scotland or New Mexico where his family is. I can't imagine how I would see him? But it will be a wonderful memory."

"You gave him your address?" said Ginger.

"No, he didn't ask for it."

"But you'll write him?"

"How? I have no idea where he lives."

21

Mentor and Protégé

By THE time they were unpacked and had enjoyed a light supper, night had fallen over the Circle F. Heather spent the night, as she often did, in the room that was effectively hers in the large ranch house where Mark had himself been raised, now also shared with Mark's parents.

Mark was up and outside the next morning at first light, saddling the Lusitano and heading out, relishing in the crisp spring air at 2,500 feet above the valley floor thirty miles east. Giving him a goodbye as she still lay in bed, Grace knew where Mark was bound. She and he had talked and prayed the thing out at length. Now he needed to talk to his mentor.

Mark's future, though yet beyond his ken, would carry more weight in annals still to be written than the lifetime of achievements and accolades being heaped on the friend of his youth who now stood at the pinnacle of worldly power. To all appearances, the one had achieved so much, the other so little. The world, however, is rarely capable of accurately judging life's significances. Indeed, its perspectives often reflect the precise inverse of reality, as the reflection of a mountain on the glassy surface of a lake—beautiful, every detail perfectly in place, yet pointing in the wrong direction. The world is too swayed by the cult of personality, by the heady aphrodisiac of fame, and by the fleeting allure of the moment, to recognize Truth where it quietly dwells in life's hidden places. It is the men and women of noble character who write the eternal histories that will remain long after the approbations heaped upon their ambitious contemporaries have faded in the blinding light of eternity's dawn.

The sprawling ranch known as the Circle F once boasted more than twenty thousand acres of prime valley and foothill grazing land. Those were the glory years of the late nineteenth century when Macgregor Forster was one of the west's leading land barons and on intimate terms with California tycoons Leland Stanford, Henry Huntington, and Eureka lumberman William Carson.

That his acreage extended deep into the rugged Sierra eastward had occasionally filled Mark's boyhood thoughts with dreams of fantastic mineral deposits waiting to be unearthed. That there was probably still gold in abundance throughout the Sierra, perhaps even beneath the land of the Circle F brand, there could be little doubt. The very roads and towns, peaks and valleys and lakes everywhere through the region spoke legendary reminders of the gold rush—Sonora, Angels Camp, El Dorado, Hangtown, Calaveras, Jackson. Some so-called mining experts claimed that 90 percent of California's gold deposits still lay buried in the earth.

By Macgregor's time, however, most of the easy gold had been found and the mines picked dry. After a few halfhearted attempts to resurrect two or three of the abandoned shafts in the rugged mountains of his estate, he gave up the effort. His mysterious disappearance in his seventy-seventh year gave rise to speculation that he had fallen victim to that lethal disease known as gold fever. It is true that he was last seen heading east into the mountains, alone, on his favorite mount, with a second horse following behind laden with equipment and supplies.

He was never seen again, nor his body found. Thus, the mystery remained. Stories also abounded that he had found the fabled "lost vein of Calaveras" and had been murdered for it. But no gold was ever seen, no claims filed, no untoward activity noted on his land. Wherever he had been bound, whatever had been his destination, and wherever was his final resting place, Macgregor Forster's secrets died with him.

Macgregor's four sons, perhaps predictably, squabbled over the enormous inheritance, a dispute rendered all the more contentious by the fact that there was no will.

Generations passed. Marriages within Macgregor's lineage were curiously few and the children produced fewer, a peculiar anomaly that resulted in the large original tract of land remaining substantially intact, though of necessity divided into smaller and smaller segments as each generation gave way to the next. For the following century, the former lands of the Circle F remained substantially in the hands of the Forster family and their offshoots, the ranch itself passing from Macgregor to son Fergus to son James to son Jonathan, and thence to Mark's father Robert.

The economic challenges of the late twentieth century began at last to alter that trend, along with cultural shifts and the inevitable havoc to family estates caused by divorce, remarriage, and the fragmentation of family values.

Even with such changes in the wind, by the time Jonathan Forster passed down his portion of the family legacy, his only son, Robert, was still in a position to inherit some three thousand prime acres, including the original ranch house built by Macgregor Forster with the help—and donations of incalculably valuable old growth redwood from his mills on the state's north coast—of his friend William Carson. It was the only sizeable share left of the original and still boasted a rusted iron sign above the entry gate that read Circle F. The remainder of the original acreage had by then passed to second, third, and fourth cousins, much had been sold off, and most of the rest had been divided, fought over, redivided, and parceled out to one claimant or another in the courts.

Fifty-year-old Mark Forster was not thinking of his family's heritage or of the mystery surrounding his great-great-great-grandfather's death, as he rode away from the ranch house on the well-worn trail that led to the Bar JG neighboring ranch of his father's friend David Gordon. He was in a thoughtful mood and needed to be alone. The event on Bainbridge Island and the extra days he and the three women spent at the presidential compound, left him full of a veritable hurricane of thoughts and emotions.

He was ill at ease. But not for the reasons he would have expected—neither from the melancholy of seeing his childhood friend again and realizing how far they had drifted apart, nor from Linda's cautions, nor even from the inevitable reminders of his friend Ward's tragic death. Something else lay at the root of it.

He was not as experienced as he might have wished at discerning the leading of God's voice. He was learning. But sometimes he rued what a slow learner he had been. He had been eager to be God's man during the youthful enthusiasm of his college days. He thought God had led him into the pastorate. But after seventeen years and growing stale in the pulpit, he wondered if the leading had been God's at all.

Perhaps it had been. Perhaps all had worked out for his ultimate growth. He recalled one of Kempis's prayers, *You know what is expedient for my spiritual progress, do with me according to your will and good pleasure.*

Maybe his years in the pastorate had indeed been expedient in their own way for his spiritual progress. But now, six years after moving from Seattle to Roseville, and two years after stepping down, and a year after taking over the family ranch in partnership with his father, he sometimes felt that he was still a novice in the high things of God. Hearing God's Voice seemed more difficult now than when he was twenty-five.

Was that because at last he was seeking to hear *deep* things—eternal things?

Suddenly the stakes were much higher than a week ago.

Telling David about the invitation before their trip to Seattle, his old friend had come out with one of the frequent pearls of wisdom that so often emerged from his mouth.

"He who does what God puts before him to do," David had said, "leaving his cares, his plans, his ambitions, and the result of that doing in the hands of the Master, can never tell what mighty oaks may grow from the acorn of that small obedience. Go and meet with your old friend, Mark, my boy. God will show you what you are to do next."

He rode the rest of the way replaying the conversation with Jeff in his mind, and later his discussion with Grace and Linda, until at last the familiar sign of the Bar JG came into view ahead of him.

"Mark, my boy!" exclaimed David, walking out onto his front porch as Mark rode up. "I've been expecting you. It would appear that you survived your visit with your friend unscathed. Though I'm not so sure about your wife's reputation!"

Mark laughed as he dismounted and tied the mare to the rail. "We all survived some rather unexpected developments. I guess you already know about Grace's adventure. For my own part, I find myself coming to you again seeking wisdom and counsel."

"Come in and tell me everything!"

"I see you've got a few new horses in your new paddock there," said Mark, glancing toward David's barn and the new fenced corral between it and the house.

"Actually, those three are from the Wests. They ran short of space. I said I'd take care of them."

They walked into the house. Soon Mark was giving David a full account of the trip.

"A momentous few days," said David. His voice was soft and thoughtful. "We definitely need to pray."

"Obviously I will turn down the position," said Mark. "What else can I do? It's out of the question. But I have the sense that Jeff will not be pleased. I have no idea why he wants me. But when I hesitated and said I would need to talk to Grace and pray, he seemed miffed."

"What *does* Grace think?" asked David.

"She's horrified at the prospect of moving to Washington."

"Would a move be required?"

"That's what Jeff said."

David nodded. They sat for some time in silence.

"A couple of things come to me," said David at length. "I'd rather say nothing for the moment. I need to pray about my response as well. But first I would ask—is this something you *want* to do, that you would like to do?"

"Oh, gosh—no!" answered Mark quickly.

"It doesn't excite you in any way?"

"Not at all."

"I see. Well, the only other thing I would say is that we probably also need to talk to Timothy and Jaylene—that is, if you feel it would be appropriate. A multitude of counselors, you know."

"I was thinking the same thing."

22

Where Two or Three

TEACHING IN a Christian university, even in the radically progressive environment of the mid-twenty-first century, Timothy Marshall had not faced the same pressures as a Christian in the world of academia that his father had encountered in the previous century. He had continued as head of Jessup University's history department well into his sixties before scaling back his schedule. As honorary professor emeritus he had, now at seventy, been semi-retired for several years, mostly delivering lectures on special occasions.

During the previous ten years, at the urging of the Common Life group and the many individuals with whom he, Jaylene, and Heather maintained a correspondence, he had devoted more of his time to writing. At first his efforts were focused on republishing his father's writings, augmenting them with compilations, overviews, compendiums, and collections of his shorter articles. Gradually he began publishing his own work, surprised at the reaction of readers from their continually expanding mailing list, most of whom said that his writing sounded just like his father's. Everyone clamored for more, not because he was Stirling Marshall's son, but because they were eager to be fed by his *own* insights, which even, some said, went beyond his father's in certain areas of scriptural inquiry. He added a parallel volume to his father's commandments book, which he titled *Unspoken*

Commandments of the Old Testament, then followed it with two more—*The Father of Jesus Revealed in the Old Testament* and *Christian Truth in an Era of Untruth.*

Two books, however, though unwritten, steadily rose to the top of his "must do" bucket list. The first was a major biography of his parents which he tentatively envisioned as *Stirling Marshall and His Wife.* It was a book he knew he had to write. The second was a proposed overview or summary of his father's *Benedict Brief.* He would write it in his own voice, adding and explaining as necessary, simplifying perhaps, in order to distill the message and make it more easily assimilated by a broad cross-section of Christians.

Not knowing when, or *if*, the *Brief* would ever be made fully public, and conscious of being faithful to his father's final instructions, he hoped to convey most of its important points without compromising the imperative of its being shared only with those able to receive its truths. Without watering it down, he hoped perhaps to till the soil of readiness with his own ideas gleaned from his father. He hoped this would ensure that whatever controversy or criticism resulted was directed at him and would not detract from his father's writings or the eventual reception of the *Brief* at some future time. He had no clear vision for what structure his compendium or synthesis of the *Brief* would take, or how exactly he would intermingle his father's ideas with his own. He had nothing more at this point than a prospective title: *An Underground Survival Guide for Christians in a Hostile World.* Meanwhile, he was praying for further insight and direction.

Timothy's wife, Jaylene, was still teaching full-time at Jessup University as head of the Science department. Her writings over the years had been more scientific and apologetic than her husband's. She had developed the initial course that had led to her removal from the California university system years before into a book titled *Discovering Einstein in Genesis.* It was followed by *Science Rediscovers Its Creator: Scientific Proofs of God's Existence*, whose inspiration had been the writings of mathematician and physicist Wolfgang Smith, and her most recent title, *Pascal, Darwin, Einstein, Smith, MacDonald, and Paul: A Conversation in Heaven.*

Mark had called on Thursday asking to talk to them. Both Marshalls were awaiting their arrival when Mark, Grace, and David arrived two days later.

"We are eager to hear all about the reception in Seattle," said Timothy. "Mixing with the movers and shakers! Heather filled us in somewhat, but didn't give us many details."

"We watched the president's speech on television," said Jaylene. "We tried to catch a glimpse of you."

"We kept to the back!" laughed Grace.

"I thought I saw Heather briefly when they did a distance view of the estate after the speech ended, walking away from the crowd along the water. But I couldn't be sure. Now we know!"

"No doubt your daughter has told you all about her new acquaintance."

"Not that much," answered Jaylene. "Just that she went sailing with someone she met. She didn't even tell us his name. It was all we could do to pry it out of her that it was a young man."

"Not just *someone*," rejoined Grace. "She was probably embarrassed. I think we made too much of it on the drive home. But the young man who took her to dinner in the city the night of the speech, and sailing on Puget Sound the next day was Todd Stewart."

"The reporter!" said Timothy and Jaylene almost in unison.

"The very same."

"Goodness! Maybe we shouldn't be surprised," said Jaylene. "You were mixing with an elite crowd up there. Heather did say she met the president and First Lady. After that, why should anything surprise us!"

"She also told us about the stir you created, Grace," said Timothy.

Grace laughed. "I was afraid I might be arrested for kidnapping. So far the FBI hasn't appeared at our door."

"Ginger was admittedly giggly about Heather's weekend," said Mark. "Heather downplayed it. But I think her time with Mr. Stewart was more special than she let on."

"She probably is embarrassed, like you said, Grace," nodded Jaylene. "No boy, or man, I should say, has ever looked twice at her, the poor dear. She has a heart of gold, but knows she isn't the first face young men notice. At this point in her life, she doesn't expect that to change."

"I think she was so surprised by Mr. Stewart's kindness," said Grace seriously, "and the fact that they could talk so easily, that she had no idea what to make of it."

"She'll need time to absorb it. Even if she never sees him again, we're happy for her to have had those two days. Thank you for taking her."

"She's one of our family," said Grace. "An extraordinary young woman. She is a role model of godliness for our daughter. Ginger loves her."

"And is your Craig kicking himself for not going along—meeting the president and everything else."

"He's got no interest in politics," replied Mark. "The only thing he said was wishing he could have been on the plane with Grace and Marcia Rhodes."

"*Marcia*—my, my! First names!" laughed Jaylene.

"If I'm going to call the president Jeff, it hardly seems necessary to be formal about his wife."

"So tell us about Seattle," said Timothy. "What was it like seeing your old childhood friend? Did you call him *Mr. President* to his face?"

"Only the first time or two. Once we were alone he insisted on *Jeff*. Altogether a surreal experience."

"You met with him *alone*?"

Mark nodded. "A private meeting the day after the speech, capped off by an unexpected twist."

Mark went on to detail his meeting with the president.

"Remarkable!" said Timothy. "I had the sense something of import took place. But Heather said nothing. She takes seriously the principle of not passing along information that is not hers to pass on. So what did you say to Mr. Rhodes?"

"That I would talk to Grace and that we would pray earnestly. It seems obvious that I cannot accept. That's why Grace and I want to ask for your prayers. After all that has happened recently, and with the fellowship we share with you and Heather and David, not to mention the FCL group, we realize more than ever that our lives are bound up with many others—even people we don't know. What God has begun among us has implications—widening concentric circles...eternal implications. As you said when you shared the *Brief* with us, a great responsibility rests on us all now to be faithful stewards of what God has entrusted to us, and of what he is doing among us. We are part of a legacy bigger than any of us."

Mark paused and drew in a thoughtful breath.

"I cannot think this opportunity, Jeff's offer, whatever I might call it—I cannot think it accidental. We have committed our future to God. In some way I do not yet understand, his hand must be in it. I feel it imperative to evaluate this unexpected turn in light of our fellowship, the *Brief*, the many believers God seems to be raising up in other areas. Grace and I are not an island unto ourselves. In a sense, I feel this offer has come to *all* of us—to those of us bound together here in our small part of God's remnant Church. How to balance and intermingle the spiritual and political worlds is difficult."

Mark smiled feebly. "Actually, I'm very perplexed," he said. "I still feel that there is no way I can accept. Yet every time we talk about it, Grace says that I am protesting too much, though she hates the thought of it as much as I do. Maybe we are *both* protesting too much!" he laughed. "Is this a case where God wants us to be willing to do the thing our flesh *doesn't* want to do? I have no idea what God is up to. Whatever this means, it involves us all. It is a decision we must make together."

The room fell silent.

As if by common consent, the two Marshall and Forster couples waited for their elder statesman who had not yet spoken. As was his custom, David was not anxious to fill the silence with his own voice. When at last he spoke, his tone was soft and thoughtful.

"You know," he began, "what a firm believer I am in the old truth of *waiting on the Lord*. Too often we are in a rush to hear from him, more *eager* for his leading than our spirits are quietly and patiently *receptive* to his leading. At the same time, when we are experienced from much practice in the process of listening, heeding, and obeying, it is also true that the Spirit occasionally speaks quickly. The sense has come upon me as I sat here to suggest something that I would not suggest to our entire group. But I think it appropriate for the five of us. It may not give direction. Yet if the Spirit has prompted me to suggest it, I have to believe there is a reason for it."

He paused, as if waiting for final confirmation to go ahead.

"What has come to me is this," he said after a prolonged silence, "—for us all to pray silently, and listen for the *first* sense that comes. Sometimes we can overthink, over-discuss, and overanalyze. In this case, I am sensing that perhaps the answer has already been given, and that we need to listen to the first impulse that comes in answer to our *What wouldest thou . . .?* We may not all sense the same thing. Yet this is what has come to me."

He glanced around the room at the four others.

"I trust what you say," said Mark after a few seconds.

The others nodded.

David rose and walked outside. Grace and Timothy rose also. Grace left the house. Timothy went to his office. Jaylene and Mark remained in the living room. Not a word was spoken for fifteen minutes. When David reentered, the other four were seated quietly. Again they waited for him to take the lead.

"An interestingly different prayer experience," he began with a smile. "I was not altogether surprised. The moment you told me of your conversation with the president a few days ago, Mark, I immediately sensed a nudge which I wondered if was from the Lord. I said nothing to give him time to confirm or point me in a different direction. I suggested we pray in this manner, to give the Spirit opportunity to counterbalance my own thoughts if I was hearing incorrectly. Before I say anything further, I would like to ask you, Mark—did any nudge come to you when you first said, *What wouldest thou . . .?*"

Mark smiled, then slowly nodded.

"Yes—yes it did," he said. "It was the same nudge I felt faintly even as I was leaving the meeting with Jeff to find out what was going on with the two women who had been flying around Mt. Rainier in a Cessna. It was neither what I expected nor wanted to hear."

23

A Journalist in Wyoming

EARLY JULY 2050

TODD STEWART did not return to Scotland after the event on Bainbridge Island. Instead he returned to his Washington, DC, apartment.

Though on an indefinite leave of absence from his job, his thoughts had not been idle. He loved what he did. He had lived every young newsperson's dream. But knowing he was not his own man eventually ruined it. Even if he somehow managed to scrape together the two hundred fifty grand to repay Mike Bardolf or whoever else was responsible for footing the bills for his last two years at UCLA, he knew that unless he did Bardolf's bidding, his career as a top-level journalist was probably over. It wasn't about the money. Bardolf wanted to control him. He had the feeling the network execs were in on it too.

He had cited the vague catch-all "personal reasons" as the excuse for his Scotland trip, adding, when pressed, burnout from the long presidential campaign. The only decision he had reached while overseas was that he definitely could not resume his job as before. There had to be a change. Other than that, the future was murky.

Only one idea had been with him since the election—to interview ex-senator and presidential candidate Harvey Jansen.

Todd had smelled a rat before the election. He knew the accusations against the GOP candidate were false. In good conscience he knew he had to do what he could to set the record straight. He had participated in the attempted disgrace of two men—Ward Hutchins and Harvey Jansen.

His thoughts were also consumed with his conversations with Heather Marshall. What if Ward Hutchins was actually more like Heather Marshall than he, or anyone in the press, ever knew? She was nothing like what progressives thought of Christians. Maybe Ward Hutchins wasn't either.

He could do nothing about Ward Hutchins. But he could do what lay in his power to right the wrong done to the Jansens in the closing days of the campaign.

He had to keep his plans secret. Otherwise Bardolf, or even the president, would find some way to kill his idea. There was only one person in the news business he trusted implicitly, his college friend Deke Barnes. Last he knew he was working for a local station in Phoenix, though they hadn't spoken in two years. Deke would keep the thing under wraps until he could take the completed and edited footage to Cheyenne's NBC affiliate KGWN with promise of an exclusive that not even network headquarters in New York would know about.

When Harriett Jansen opened the door of their Laramie ranch house to see Todd Stewart standing in front of her, she nearly slammed the door in his face.

"Hello, Mrs. Jansen," he began, "I'm Todd Stewart. I wonder if I might—"

"I know who you are," she interrupted. "How dare you show your face here after what you did to my husband."

"You're right. It was unconscionable," said Todd. "All I can say is how sorry I am. I mean that sincerely. I have come in hopes of doing what I can to make it right."

"It's a little late for that!"

"Again, you are right. What happened cannot be undone. I hope you and your husband will allow me to publicly apologize to you both on camera and give you the opportunity to tell your side of the story. I'm not here on behalf of the network."

"Who sent you then?"

"No one. After the election, partially because of what happened to your husband, I took a leave of absence. I have not been on camera since. I'm here on my own, for no reason other than for how bad I feel that I was part of what was done. I want to give you and your husband the chance to address the nation. I want the country to see what an honest and honorable man and woman you are."

By now Todd's sincere tone had mitigated Harriett Jansen's initial anger.

"Well . . ." she said slowly, "Harvey will have to decide. If he thinks it's okay, I won't object. He's out taking hay to the horses. He won't be long. But how do we know you won't use something we say to make Harvey look foolish just like you all did before?"

"I can only give you my word," replied Todd. "I am not the same man I was then. I promise that you will see the completed interview and that we will redo anything you are uncomfortable with before it airs. I mean *anything.* If there is so much as one word you do not like, one expression on either of your faces, one of my questions—anything at all—we will re-shoot and re-edit. It will be *your* interview, not mine. I hope you will be able to trust me."

24

Decision . . . with Terms

MID-JULY 2050

"THIS IS the Presidential Manor," answered a receptionist.

"Hello, my name is Mark Forster," said Mark. "I am a friend of the president. I imagine you will have to check on that. But if the message could be given him that I called, he can reach me—"

"Please hold the line a moment, Mr. Forster," she interrupted. "We've been given instructions to put you through immediately."

A little shocked, Mark waited. Three minutes later, he heard the familiar voice on the line.

"Mark," said the president enthusiastically, "I am delighted you called. I only have a minute. I have Speaker of the House Biden here. But you and I can talk more later. Tell me you have good news for me."

"Actually," replied Mark, "I am quite surprised myself—but yes, I suppose I do. I have decided to accept your offer, as long as—"

"That's wonderful. Fantastic. We'll go over the details later. I'll call you."

Suddenly the call was over.

Mark hung up the phone with a deep sigh. Well, it was done, he thought. Though it wasn't quite a done deal yet. Whether Jeff would agree to his terms remained the big question.

Two days later Mark received a call from the Presidential Manor setting up a telephone call with the president for the following day. Mark was by the phone, Grace at his side, fifteen minutes before the appointed time.

Finally, his phone rang.

"Hey, Mark, it's Jeff," he heard after being connected to the Oval Office. "I've got a couple minutes. So tell me, how soon can you get here?"

"I need to talk to you about that, Jeff," replied Mark. "I didn't get the chance when we spoke the other day. My willingness to help with your commission isn't exactly open-ended."

"What do you mean?"

"There are conditions to my feeling comfortable about it. My *terms*, I guess you'd say."

"What do you mean conditions? What kind of conditions?"

"Well, first of all, there is no way I can move my family to DC. Ginger and Craig are both in college, though Ginger's about done. Both our parents are aging and are in California. Our home is here."

"I thought I made it clear I would need you here."

"You did. But I didn't get the chance to say what I was trying to add two days ago—that I would accept your offer as long as I could do so and remain in California."

The line was silent a second or two. Mark could tell Jeff was annoyed.

"That would make it very difficult," he said after a moment.

"I understand. If you feel that would make it impossible, I perfectly understand that you may want someone else."

"I will think about that. Is there anything *else*?" Jeff added stiffly.

"That would depend on what you have in mind, how often I would need to be in the capital, who else would be involved, and exactly what I would be doing. If, for example, I can fly to DC for a week every two months, or even Monday through Friday once a month, I would need a place where Grace and I could be comfortable and feel at home—a small apartment perhaps. I couldn't do it if we were living out of suitcases."

"Grace would accompany you?"

"Occasionally."

"I see. Well, accommodations could certainly be arranged."

"I assume you will need to think about all this further and decide if you'd rather have someone else. If so, I will completely understand and will always be grateful for the opportunity, and for our friendship."

"Yes, of course. I will consider everything you've said and get back to you."

The call ended without further pleasantries.

Mark turned toward Grace with a smile and shrug.

"Jeff wasn't pleased that I didn't just jump. He's used to having things his way."

"He assumes he can manipulate you."

"You're probably right. He always took the lead, even when we were boys."

"You won't let him?"

"That's why I have you—to keep me on my toes! He may pull the plug on this whole thing anyway."

25

High Summer in the Foothills

LATE JULY 2050

THE HOT sun of late July had turned the Sacramento valley into a dry sweltering cauldron. A week of 100-plus days, capped by the previous afternoon's record smashing 114° had Californians longing for the slightest breath of wind.

With Ginger and Craig now in college and both working summers, the "Forster Family Saturdays" were less frequent than when they were younger. Throughout the summer, however, they managed to coordinate their schedules every two to three weeks, sometimes on a Saturday, sometimes Sunday. With triple-digit heat as their next outing approached, Craig wanted water! He had done his homework before springing his plan on the family.

"I want to go rafting on the river this Sunday," he said at supper on Tuesday when the three generations of Forsters were seated around the table.

The others looked at him with questioning expressions.

"You mean the Sacramento—" began Mark.

"No, the American. I've got it all figured out," said Craig excitedly. "We'll rent a big rubber raft. There are places on the river where you rent them. You put in at Sunrise, then float down to River Bend Park. We can either take two cars or there are shuttles to drive you back to Sunrise when you're done."

"That sounds awesome!" said Ginger.

"It does sound fun," laughed Grace.

"Then we'll have a picnic at the park," said Craig.

"You've got it all figured out!" now laughed Mark. "Let's do it."

"What about you, Grandma and Grandpa?" asked Ginger.

"Are we invited!" asked Mark's mother.

"Of course!" chimed in Mark and Grace together.

"Can we invite Heather?" said Ginger.

"And Uncle David," added Craig.

"This is turning into quite the party!" said Mark.

Hearing that Bob and Laura were digging out their swimming suits, "Uncle David" Gordon was not about to be left out.

In the foothills surrounding Grass Valley, the elevation managed to keep the thermometer between 90° and 95° for the rest of the week—hot enough, but on the edge of tolerable. Everyone was looking forward to the weekend's adventure on the river.

While Heather still worked three days a week at the care home, helping Mark and Robert Forster over the past year reestablish the Circle F as a horse rather than a cattle ranch gave her a new sense of purpose. Though she was only able to devote four days a week to the ranch, Mark called her his foreman.

It wasn't true, of course, as Heather was quick to point out. Old Bob Forster—happier than he had been in years to be sharing the ranch with his son's family—knew more about horses and ranching than she ever would. But they all recognized her gift with animals. It probably was true that they would not have been able to do what they did—raising, boarding, and rehabilitating horses—without her.

In a little over a year, strictly by word of mouth, they were receiving so many requests, both for boarding or for Heather to consult with horse owners throughout the state, that David at the Bar JG boarded their occasional surplus. Craig and Ginger shared Heather's love for horses. But next month Ginger would be a senior at Jessup, Craig a junior at Sac State. Craig spent most Friday and Saturday nights at the Bar JG working side by side with David all day Saturday and half of most Sundays. During the summer months Craig was his right-hand man, though David, now at seventy-nine, was inconspicuously keeping his eyes open for a full-time live-in foreman when Craig returned to school.

As she did on most Thursdays, Heather Marshall spent the night at the Circle F, anticipating a full day on Friday.

Shortly after 10:00 a.m. a car drove through the gate and along the long gravel drive to the Circle F ranch house. No one was outside to notice. Craig was at the Gordon ranch, Ginger was visiting a friend in Roseville. Robert and Laura were seated at the kitchen table with Grace when the door knocker sounded. Grace rose to answer it.

The sight that met her eyes was so unexpected, all she could do was stand and stare with her mouth half open.

"Oh, my goodness!" she exclaimed under her breath. "I mean, I'm sorry—Mr. Stewart! I just didn't—"

"Hello again, Mrs. Forster," said Todd Stewart with a smile. "I am sorry to show up at your door unannounced. I see I have come at a bad time—"

"Oh, no—not at all! I was just shocked to see you. It is I who should apologize! Please, won't you come in."

Todd followed her inside to the kitchen. Seeing a stranger he did not recognize, Robert rose from the table.

"This is my father-in-law Robert Forster and his wife, Laura," said Grace. "Bob, Laura—meet Todd Stewart. We met when we were in Seattle."

"Stewart," said Robert, gripping Todd's offered hand with a strength Todd did not often encounter in Washington, DC.

"Hello, sir," said Todd, "—Mrs. Forster," he added, offering his hand to Laura.

"Won't you join us for coffee," said Grace, offering him a chair. "I'm sorry, but Mark is across the valley with a neighboring rancher. He will probably not be home for a couple hours."

"Thank you," replied Todd, smiling as if embarrassed. "Actually—it's nice to see you again, but to be honest I'm not here to see your husband. I'm looking for Miss Marshall. I knew she came to Bainbridge Island with you folks, but I've been unable to track her down. I was hoping you might be able to give me her address."

"I can do better than that," said Grace. "Heather works for us several days a week. We keep a room for her at the house. She's here now, working out in the barn."

"Really!" exclaimed Todd, his face brightening. "That's perfect!"

"Let me show you," said Grace. "I'll take you to her."

She turned and led the way outside and down the porch steps.

"She's there, in the biggest of the two barns," said Grace as they made their way across the grass, "—straight ahead."

"If you don't mind—could I go alone?" asked Todd. "I'd like to surprise her."

"Believe me," laughed Grace, "you will definitely succeed in that!"

Todd continued. Grace watched as he made his way alongside the corral and to the large open end of the barn.

"I don't believe it!" she whispered as he disappeared inside.

26

The Interview

MID-JULY 2050

TODD STEWART'S friend Deke Barnes's ambition was to be a Hollywood cameraman, even a director one day. He hadn't caught his big break yet. But he'd outdone himself with Todd's Jansen interview. Even sitting in the car while Todd went to the door hoping it wouldn't get slammed in his face, Deke's brain was spinning with possibilities as he gazed across the Wyoming countryside.

Once he learned that Harvey Jansen was no mere gun-toting school-teacher, but also an expert horseman, his ranch sitting in the shadow of the Tetons, the music for the piece—what else but one of the exquisite evocative melodies by Jay Ungar and Molly Mason—was already playing in Deke's head. Images continued. He would rebrand Harvey Jansen as a rugged man of the West, not only with courage to diffuse a potentially explosive situation at his school but with the yet deeper courage of character to suffer the indignity of being ridiculed in a presidential election for the sake of his Christian convictions and his belief in traditional American values.

He would turn Harvey Jansen into a heroic figure—bold, strong, courageous, the very antithesis of how he had been portrayed in the media two years before.

He succeeded beyond even his own hopes.

His piece opened with a panorama of the mountain range to the accompaniment of Ungar and Mason's majestic "Blue River Waltz" and "The Mountain House." It might have been the opening of a Ken Burns documentary if not a John Wayne film, panning the countryside until a rider came into view in the distance, galloping closer and closer, the very image of the fabled Marlboro man, until Harvey Jansen came into focus. He dismounted and walked toward the waiting familiar figure of Todd Stewart, outfitted for the occasion in boots and cowboy hat, compliments of Laramie's premier ranch store.

It was a stirring opening. Deke then cut to a film of Jansen's daring exploits at his school confronting Brad Childress with the cool calm of James Stewart, then a few film clips from election speeches. They portrayed Jansen confident, measured, and mature as he articulated his conviction that America had taken a wrong road and must regain its roots or eventually die an ignoble death.

By the time the interview itself began, alternating between the two Jansens in their living room along with scenes of the former candidate and Todd walking about the ranch, the image was not of a humiliated politician but an all-American man's man. After only five minutes it was more than obvious that the portrayal by the news media, and by now-president Jefferson Rhodes, had been almost entirely false.

"I believe this is the first interview you've done since the election, Senator," began Todd as the sit-down dialog got underway.

"*Former* senator," corrected Jansen. "I was never comfortable in the role. I accepted the brief appointment reluctantly. If you don't mind, I would prefer you simply call me Mr. Jansen or even more preferably *Harvey*, though protocol may prohibit you feeling comfortable being quite so informal."

"It would indeed!" laughed Todd. "You were, after all, only four percentage points away at one point from possibly becoming president of the United States."

"For a very brief moment!" laughed Jansen. "But yes, you're right—this is my first televised interview since then."

"Well I am most appreciative of the opportunity to sit down with you and your wife. And thank you also, Mrs. Jansen," said Todd, turning to where Harriett Jansen sat beside her husband as Deke swung toward her. "You weren't so happy to see me when I turned up unannounced at your door!"

"You took me quite by surprise," she replied, reddening as the camera pointed at her.

"Again, as I expressed before, I do apologize for just showing up. I was afraid you might not agree to the interview otherwise. I *had* to see you—for myself as much as for you. It was something I knew I had to do even before the day of the election. I want to take this opportunity, in public," Todd went on as Deke now zoomed close in on his face, "to apologize both to you and to the country for my part in reporting what turned out to be completely false allegations against you."

"I'm sure you were simply reporting what was given you," nodded Harvey graciously.

"Be that as it may," rejoined Todd, "a journalist has an obligation to truth. I was not careful enough to make the effort to discern truth at the time. Like too many in my profession, I was a puppet of the Progressive Party's talking points. I hope I have finally come awake from the deception of that media hypocrisy. In any event, I am deeply sorry, and I hope I have learned from the experience."

"Thank you. All is forgiven," smiled Jansen. "And honestly, Todd," he added, laughing lightly, "I didn't want to be president anyway!"

"I knew you were a long shot, but is that really true?"

"I only accepted the nomination because, after prayer with Governor Fox and Harriett, I felt God wanted me to run—for the good of the Republican Party, and perhaps in order to shine a tiny beam of God's light into the national dialog where it had been so desperately missing for so long. I don't suppose I succeeded very well but such was my motive."

"But had you won, you would have served?"

"Of course. But I only accepted the nomination out of obedience to God, not because of any desire to be president."

"That is an incredible statement. Most politicians would give anything to occupy the Oval Office."

"I am not one of them. Besides, I'm no politician."

"You served as a United States senator."

"As a favor to Governor Fox. I am still no politician."

"How would you describe yourself then?"

"A husband first, a school teacher second, a Westerner, a rancher, a man who loves the outdoors, who loves this country, an American who values America's past, its history, its roots, its exceptionalism. I am not blind to the flaws of that history, just as I am not blind to the flaws in my own character. But I hope I am a growing man. Likewise, I believe America has been a growing country, not perfect but pointed toward goodness. It is that foundation of goodness that progressives have become blind to. Most of all, I am a Christian whose primary business is to do what the Lord commands his followers to do."

"You have no doubt read Professor Charles Reyburn's book?"

"I have."

"What is your opinion of it?"

"I consider it an inspired, if not prophetic warning to America. I consider Dr. Reyburn one of the truly courageous, even heroic figures of our time."

"And if Dr. Reyburn's challenge to the nation to reclaim its roots were to result in a groundswell of new religious, even conservative sentiment in the country, would you consider another run for the White House?"

"Don't you mean the Presidential Manor?"

"Oh, yes—of course. Would you consider another run for the presidency?"

"I would not."

"Under no circumstances."

"None that I can foresee. I am no standard-bearer for change. I am merely one man trying to live my life as God's child as best I can where he has planted me. Obviously, if I felt God leading me otherwise, I would be attentive to that. But that ship has sailed. I think it unlikely to sail again. Better Dr. Reyburn than me as a standard-bearer for a return to America's core values. He has articulated that imperative far better than I ever could."

"Do you know something about his plans?" asked Todd, his voice perking up at the scent of a breaking story.

"No. I should have said nothing. Forgive me. I only meant that I admire the vision and perspective he has laid out."

"Do you know Dr. Reyburn?"

"We have never met. I wrote congratulating him on his book and telling him exactly what I told you. I received a very warm and gracious reply. He is an honorable man."

"What is your opinion of our current president, your former opponent?"

"He is our president. He has my best wishes. Harriett and I pray for him."

"What do you pray when you pray for him?"

"That his eyes will be opened to truth."

"Do you bear him any ill-will for the events of the final days of the election?"

"Of course not. I am a Christian. We are not allowed to bear grudges. I am commanded both to forgive and to pray for him. I have done the former and I continue to do the latter."

"There are some who have suggested that he may have had a hand in the allegations that were brought against you."

"I have no information to indicate that, nor would I speculate."

"But if it were true—"

"Please, Mr. Stewart. I'm simply not going to go there. He is our president."

"Fair enough. May I ask, then, if you endorse his policies, his agenda?"

"I support Jefferson Rhodes as a man created in the image of God, as my brother in the family of humanity. I pray that he will know God as his Father in increasingly personal ways, which is exactly the same thing I pray for myself. I honor the position of the presidency which he now occupies. That entails a certain degree of honor toward the man as well.

"But that is a difficult honor to know how to practice when a man believes in and pursues perspectives and practices that *dishonor*, even blaspheme the God I serve. I admit that I struggle mightily knowing how to love and honor those individuals whose lives and practices and beliefs dishonor our heavenly Father. As a Christian who bases my worldview, my beliefs, and my cultural perspectives on the truths of the New Testament, and believing that much of the agenda of progressivism and the Progressive Party directly opposes those truths, how can I do otherwise than oppose that agenda?"

"Would you care to elaborate on specifics?"

"No."

"What about you, Mrs. Jansen?" said Todd, turning to the former senator's wife. "Would you care to tell viewers more about your personal perspectives?"

"No."

"Tell me this, then, Mr. Jansen," Todd went on. "You are still one of the most popular public figures in Wyoming. Would you consider another run for the Senate?"

"I would not."

After a break, Todd and Deke moved the remainder of the interview outside, capturing both Jansens on horseback, then walking casually on an informal tour of their ranch, during which the discussion ranged from issues confronting farms and ranchers in the West to changes in wildlife habitat, to the global warming and cooling cycles that had disrupted weather patterns during the previous quarter of the century, eventually circling back around to a firsthand account by Harvey and Harriett Jansen of the events at Laramie Christian School six years before that had vaulted Harvey Jansen into national prominence. More film footage would be included. There was no lack of different angles from a hundred handheld phones that had captured the event and were now easily obtained.

Having arranged for the use of their facilities with WGWY, Deke and Todd returned to Cheyenne that afternoon, spent the next day editing the film and dubbing in music and footage of the school incident. An interview was arranged with Brad Childress, then in his first year teaching second grade in the state capital. He nearly broke down in tears on camera as he said, "Mr. Jansen saved my life. I owe him everything." It was the most moving moment of the interview.

Returning again to Laramie with the completed interview on his computer for the Jansen's final approval, though prepared to re-edit if they were uncomfortable with anything, Todd and Deke waited in silence as Harvey and Harriett watched the interview from start to finish.

Before it was over, Harriett was in tears. "I can't thank you enough, Todd," she said. "You have exonerated my husband for all the world to see."

Todd turned to her husband with an expression of question.

"Don't change a thing, Todd," he said.

When Todd Stewart left Laramie the day after the initial filming of the interview, he knew he had two new lifelong friends.

27

Fresh Breeze of Reality

RATHER THAN flying, Todd had driven across the country from DC to Wyoming. Much in his outlook was changing. He wanted to be alone. There was no better environment for *thinking* than behind the wheel enjoying scenery speeding by. An extended road trip could not have come at a better time.

The interview concluded, he considered driving Deke back south and visiting his mother in Tucson. But his solitary road trip had not yet accomplished all it needed to. He'd made no plans after dropping Deke off at the small Laramie airport. Even while concentrating on the interview, however, he had begun to suspect in which direction he would leave Wyoming.

As he watched Deke's plane lift into the air, he walked back to his car, left the airport, reached Interstate 80, then turned onto the westbound on-ramp leading to Salt Lake City, across the salt flats and the desolate high plateau of Nevada which he had never seen, to Reno, up over the Sierras, and finally down into the Sacramento valley.

There was someone else he wanted to see.

He hoped the information he had managed to dig up on the president's special guests at Bainbridge would be sufficient once he reached California. It would be a long way to drive on a wild goose chase.

A recurring theme on his mind during his hiatus in Scotland, besides Mike Bardolf and how to get free of his clutches, was the superficiality of life in the political world. People were shallow. What should be important issues were not analyzed rationally. Responses were mere political talking points. No one thought for themselves, especially in the media. Everyone regurgitated the company line. Where was the reality, the honesty, the courage to *think*. The political world was filled with robots programmed with the progressive agenda.

The worst of it was that he had been a robot himself! That was the most bitter reality—he was as superficial as the rest!

He'd accepted the president's invitation to Bainbridge Island not even knowing why. He was not anxious to jump back into that world. Maybe he hoped it might have changed under the new administration. Or that *he* had changed.

Then had come the incredible moment.

Suddenly the noise and ambition and talking points and agendas and politics and the superficiality of personalities faded into a quietude broken only by the gently lapping waters of Puget Sound against the gravelly shoreline. And a face of peace, contentment, and serenity turned toward him and looked up into his eyes.

Before that moment, the sight of her walking away from the crowd was a visual image that hit him with undefined force. While the rest of the throng was bustling and talking and laughing, caught up in the pomp and show of political power, there was one walking in the opposite direction, turning her back on that world, immune to its fleeting allure, refusing to be drawn in, choosing her own life path.

Perhaps he was reading too much into it. Yet somehow the imagery spoke powerfully, even if subconsciously. The sight of her with her back to that world resonated with the same disquiet that had led him to the distant shores of Scotland.

Without thinking of the symbolism of it, he found himself following her. The girl's solitude in the midst of the crowd drew him. On that day he did not ask why.

Then she turned toward him. In that moment life had changed.

He had never seen such an expression. He could not have said whether the girl he had taken for much younger was twenty-five or forty, whether she was pretty or plain, whether she was tall or short. He could hardly remember the color of her hair or what she was wearing.

The radiance of her countenance dominated all.

The light in her eyes pulled him into its depths. It was the light of tranquil self-knowing. He had encountered a contented soul, at peace with the world, and at peace with herself.

As they began to talk, he recognized a difference greater merely than her expression. She was not of the world of the crowd behind them. They were in the middle of it—special guests of the president of the United States.

But she was not *of* it.

As they talked, he felt as if the breeze off the water was blowing something new and clean into his soul. It was the fresh wind of reality. Here was an authentic human being playing no games of personality, with no one to impress, no agenda, ruled by no talking points. She was nothing more than simply herself. He doubted she was even capable of playing games or trying to impress anyone. She was of another world entirely than everything surrounding them.

After another day, however, enchanted as he was, enjoying her company as no one's he had ever met, he had still not discovered the origin, the source, the reason for the light in her eyes. He could say no more than that during those brief hours, he too had felt at peace, whole, complete, more authentically *himself* than he could remember feeling for a long time. Her peace had spilled over, and gotten inside him.

He had to see her again.

28

The Visit

HEATHER MARSHALL'S first thought when she heard soft footsteps enter the darkened barn was that Bob Forster had come to see how she was getting on.

She glanced toward the sound. The sun's rays from the open end of the building revealed only a silhouette in the dim light.

A tall silhouette!

She shielded her eyes. A *very* tall silhouette. One with no sign of the ancient, stained, creased cowboy hat which Bob never left the house without. It *couldn't* be Mark or his father!

An involuntary gasp escaped her lips.

She was glad for the darkness. A hot flush rose from her neck into her face.

"Hello, Heather," came the voice she would know anywhere.

"Todd!" she exclaimed, her eyes at last adjusting enough to see his crop of blond hair. "What are you . . . I mean . . ." she stammered, fumbling for words. "How did . . . I can't believe . . . what are you doing here!"

Todd laughed, as delighted to hear her voice as he was to see her.

"I came to see you, what else?" he said. "We hadn't finished the talk we began out on Puget Sound."

Heather set aside the pitchfork in her hand, hardly thinking of the manure splatters all over her jeans and caked on her boots from the two cattle stalls, a far messier operation than when cleaning up after the horses. Slowly she came forward with her characteristic limp.

"How in the world did you find me?" said Heather as she came. "This isn't even where I live—I mean I work here and stay here part of the time, but how would you know that? I mean . . . how could you possibly . . . oh, gosh, I'm babbling like an idiot!"

Again Todd laughed. Slowly Heather led the way out of the barn into the sunlight.

"It's my fault," he said. "I should have let you know. But I wanted to surprise you. I was halfway here. So I decided to keep driving."

"Halfway—from where?"

"From Washington. I was doing an interview in Wyoming."

"Oh, of course. We all watched it last night. One of the Sacramento stations broadcasted it. Todd, it was a wonderful thing you did for poor Mr. and Mrs. Jansen. I felt so bad for them after the election. They seem like really nice people."

"A wonderful couple. Just think what our country could have had."

"I had no idea you were such a star until we were on our way home from Seattle and the Forsters told me about you. Why didn't you tell me!"

"It didn't seem important. It's all in the past. I was just enjoying talking to you. I saw no reason to bring it up."

As their eyes adjusted to the sunlight, suddenly Heather became aware of her clothes and hair and gloves and boots—wet and brown.

"Oh, gosh—what a sight I must be!" she said. "I was cleaning out . . . I guess I don't need to tell you. I'm sure you can smell what I was doing! This is so embarrassing!"

Todd laughed. It was the first hint of self-consciousness he had seen in Heather. It was refreshing to hear her talk so. Everything about her was *real*.

"Don't worry—really," he said. "It's a ranch. If you can find me a pair of jeans and boots that fit, I'll help you. We'll make quick work of those stalls."

"Are you kidding! I wouldn't think of it. You didn't come all this way to clean manure out of cow stalls. Especially now that I know you're famous."

"Stop with the famous stuff!" laughed Todd. "If you treat me one iota different, I'll turn around and leave."

"Okay, I wouldn't want that!" laughed Heather. "Let's go into the house—just let me get cleaned up. I'm a total mess!"

Heather hurried as fast as she could toward the house, Todd walking beside her taking one step to every two of hers.

"Did you see the others?" she asked.

"Mrs. Forster met me at the door."

"Oh, of course. That's how you knew where I was."

"She introduced me to the older couple."

"Yes—Mark's parents. This is their ranch. Mark was raised here."

Grace had just gotten off the phone with Mark, telling him that he might want to get home as quickly as he could. Still too amazed by this turn of events to keep from watching, she was standing at the window as Heather and her visitor emerged from the barn and headed toward the house. She stepped back quickly. The front door opened a minute later.

"Grace," Heather called through the open door. "Oh, there you are—this is Todd . . . but you've already seen him! What am I thinking. I'm going to go change my clothes. Just look at me! Can you entertain Todd for a few minutes? I'll go around back so I can dump these clothes in the laundry room. I don't want to smell up the house!"

She turned and hurried off the porch and around the side of the house.

"Unless I miss my guess," said Grace, leading their guest inside, "you have caught our young ranch foreman quite by surprise. Heather is about the most even-keeled person I know. I don't think I've ever seen her quite so . . . *flustered*."

Todd laughed. "I would be too if she suddenly showed up at my door in DC! But like I said, I wanted to surprise her. It may have been stupid of me. What if I hadn't been able to find you all? I didn't get her address in Seattle. What if she'd been away? Or for all I know she has a boyfriend and I might not exactly have been welcome. She laughed when I mentioned that in Seattle, but you never know. I suppose I didn't really think it through. I just came."

"Well if you wanted to surprise her, I think we can assume you succeeded!" laughed Grace. "Come and sit down. Maybe you'd like that cup of coffee now."

"That sounds good, thank you," replied Todd, again greeting Mark's parents and joining them at the table. "Is Heather really your foreman?"

"That's what we call her. Not politically correct, I suppose, but Heather wouldn't hear of being called foreperson, or forewoman. She hates all that."

"All what?"

"Political correctness—the ridiculous jargon progressivism has forced on the culture. She is no feminist, that's for sure. None of us are. I realize you are part of that world, but we're pretty traditional around here. We women recognize our men as the leaders of our marriages and as our spiritual heads."

"That's not something you hear much these days. Actually," laughed Todd, I don't think I've *ever* heard it. A revolutionary perspective of marriage."

"A *traditional* perspective," now said Laura Forster. "And a biblical one. A marriage of equals where there is no head or even where the woman usurps the man's role—*that's* the revolutionary perspective. And an unscriptural one."

"That will take some time for me to get my head around," said Todd.

"By the way," said Grace, "we saw your interview with the Jansens."

"Heather told me. I had no idea if anyone outside Wyoming would see it."

"I think it's being played all over the country—at least on conservative outlets. I doubt your network will air it. But people are seeing it. Many news sites have mentioned it. It was extremely well done."

"Thank you."

"It was obvious that you've changed in your perspective since the election."

"Absolutely," said Todd. "I feel terrible about my part in all that. Even by the time of the election I determined that I would interview them to let the country see who they really were."

"A very kind and responsible thing to have done," said Grace. "But to return to your question—Heather works here four days a week. Mark and Bob might technically be considered the bosses. It is your ranch, right, Bob?"

"Used to be," replied Mark's father. "I like to think of it as yours and Mark's now. But we couldn't do half of what we do without Heather. She is a hard worker and a genius with horses."

"Seeing her in her own environment, now I know why she felt like a fish out of water in Seattle. Though the instant I say that, I realize there was more to it—she simply wasn't part of that world."

"None of us were," said Grace. "We all felt, as you say, like fish out of water."

"I think I'm beginning to understand that feeling myself."

"Even though you're part of it."

"I was for a long time," rejoined Todd. "Things are looking different to me now."

"Is that where you've come from—Seattle?" asked Grace.

"I live in DC. I drove out for the Jansen interview, then kept going."

"Do you have other business or interviews out here?"

"Nothing. I came to see Heather. I know we only had a short time together. But to be honest, Mrs. Forster, I hadn't had my fill. I've never talked to anyone so easily and comfortably. It was like we'd known each other for years."

"Speak of the angel!" said Grace as Heather came through the hall into the kitchen. "That was fast."

"At least I managed to wash off and get into clean clothes," said Heather. She glanced toward Todd, smiled, and took a seat at the table.

By the time Mark walked in forty minutes later, Grace and Laura were busy setting out a sandwich buffet for lunch.

Hearing the door open, Todd turned and rose.

"Hello, Mr. Forster," he said, standing and offering his hand. "It is good to see you again."

"And you, Mr. Stewart. Welcome to California's gold country."

"Thank you. The rest of your family has been giving me a very warm welcome. And congratulations to you. I hear you'll be working in Washington before long."

"All still tentative," rejoined Mark. "How do you know about that?"

"There are no secrets in Washington. I still have my sources. All I had to do was mention your name when I was trying to figure out how to make contact with you and Heather," he added, glancing toward her, "and I learned all about the president's offer."

"Interesting. But nothing's been finalized yet."

"I invited Timothy and Jaylene for supper tonight, Mark," said Grace. "Heather is eager for them to meet our famous guest."

"Hardly that!" laughed Todd. "I told you," he said, turning to Heather, "if you persist in playing the *famous* card, I will get in my car and leave!"

"I know, I'm sorry," replied Heather. "But compared with all of us, you are."

"Maybe once that might have been a little true. But no more. I'm not sure the network will even want me back. I had my five minutes in the spotlight and that may be the end of it. People will forget all about me in a year or two."

"Why did you step away, if you don't mind my asking?" said Mark.

Todd drew in a thoughtful breath. The room quieted. Though Mark had only just arrived, the conversation around the table between the others had been so free-flowing that no barriers to honesty remained. It was an atmosphere that encouraged openness. These were nothing like the exchanges Todd was used to in the world of Washington. He found himself speaking with a freedom he would never dream of at a cocktail party or among his colleagues at work. Something here was different.

At length he smiled. "You know," he said slowly, "I'm still not exactly sure myself—at least that I can put into words. Most people would say I was committing professional suicide by stepping away. That may be true. I realize I was living a dream. There was talk that I would be tapped as the president's press secretary. If not, there I was years shy of forty in front of the camera most nights. People were talking about me as NBC's future anchorman. I feel funny saying it, but the fact is I suppose I was one of the network's stars."

He glanced at Heather with a sheepish smile. "So there—I guess I admitted it, right?" he said.

She returned his smile with a kind expression.

"Who would walk away from all that?" he added.

He paused again, almost sadly.

"The moment I learned of Rev. Hutchins's death, something snapped inside me. I knew I had to step back and reassess my life or maybe reassess the whole world of politics to which I had given my life. In that instant I knew something was wrong. Though there have been no specific allegations and though the case may remain unsolved, something in my gut told me that his murder had political overtones. The world and culture I was immersed in was somehow responsible for his death, though I can point to nothing specific."

Again he paused thoughtfully.

"I had been feeling misgivings for some time," he resumed, speaking slowly and quietly. "It was not only the sense that something was wrong in that world—what back in Trump's day they called *the swamp* of Washington. It was also the sense that I was being used, even manipulated by forces outside myself to further narratives that weren't true. I was often merely handed a script to read. At first I thought little of it. I was too caught up in the excitement and heady life of being a national journalist. Gradually I started listening to myself. I didn't like what I heard. My reporting, first about Rev. Hutchins, and later about Senator Jansen was patently false. I was part of it. That's why I had to try to make things right with the Jansens.

"That night outside the Hillsgrove graduation ceremony when I basically told the world that Rev. Hutchins was a cheat and liar and the same when I was in Los Angeles reporting on Senator Jansen's arrest, in both cases, as they say in Scotland, I knew it was all a load of rubbish. I had been handed the scripts and I dutifully went along. My soul searching began that night on the plane ride back to DC from Hillsgrove, though it didn't get deep enough into me soon enough to prevent me smearing Senator Jansen.

"Once you start thinking seriously about things, more thoughts tumble into your brain. It was a slow process. I wish it had come sooner and progressed more rapidly. Looking back, I see that deep inside I had begun to question the whole ethical fabric, not only of the political world but also of the media.

"Where was the quest for truth? I found myself hard-pressed to answer that. It was all about the accepted narrative, the almighty and sacred *Agenda* of the progressive culture, what those in control of that narrative *wanted* the public to think and believe, what I was *told* to say. I couldn't help thinking of *1984*. I wondered if I had become a pawn in a real-life Orwellian drama."

Todd paused and turned to Mark.

"I know you were Rev. Hutchins's friend," he said turning toward Mark. "I feel compelled to apologize to you for my false reporting. You were swept up into the falsehoods. Terrible things were implied about you—and I must apologize for that to you also, Mrs. Forster," he added, turning to Grace. "I know it must have been an awful time for your family. I am so very sorry. If I hadn't been in DC at the time for Senator Rhodes's announcement of his candidacy, I would probably have been sent out here to cover Rev. Hutchins's appearance at your church. I might have publicly said untrue things about you as well. The people I was working for had been doing their best to dig up dirt on you. That whole gay story—everyone knew there was nothing to it. I am sorrier than I can say—to both of you."

Mark smiled and nodded. "Thank you," he said. "But no lasting harm done. We will face worse in the times to come. *The days are evil*, as the Bible says."

Todd took in his words thoughtfully. It was quiet a moment.

"The plot to implicate poor Senator Jansen was the last straw," he went on. "The cruelty of it—trying to ruin a man's reputation with lies for the sake of an election. And then Rev. Hutchins's murder. I knew I had to walk away—for how long I had no idea. I just knew I couldn't face the camera again. I went to Scotland, where I was until just days before the event on Bainbridge Island. At first I wasn't going to accept the invitation. I had no interest in the president's speech or in seeing any of those people again. But for some reason I decided to attend. And I'm glad I did."

He glanced around the table, smiling, pausing for a brief instant as he caught Heather's eyes.

"All the time I was in Scotland I vowed that I would not resume my job—if I still had a job—until I had sought to make what amends were possible. I would interview the Jansens on camera, hope to apologize to you, Mr. Forster, for my part in things that were said about you even if indirectly, and also hope to see Mrs. Hutchins and set the record straight about her husband if she would allow me to interview her. I also determined to try to visit Dr. Reyburn, not because of anything false I reported on him, but just because I feel I need to meet him. In any event, I have recently discharged the first two of those four debts—though I guess wanting to meet Dr. Reyburn doesn't exactly fall into that category. Nevertheless, I am hoping you might be able to pave the way for Rev. Hutchins's widow to see me. She would have every right not to."

"I *know* she will see you," rejoined Mark. "I will be happy to talk to her on your behalf."

"Thank you."

"But why did you come *here*?" now asked Heather. "Her tone was sincerity itself, with no suggestion that *she* might be the cause.

"I told you—to see you," replied Todd.

"I know you said that in the barn, and that's very nice of you to say," rejoined Heather with a hint of red again rising in her cheeks. Quickly she added, "but surely there must be more to it."

"Fair enough," nodded Todd. "I suppose you're right. I mentioned Dr. Reyburn's book. It was like no book I had ever read—not only because of its religious content, which was completely new to me, but also for his summary of America's history from a traditional, shall I even say a conservative viewpoint You have no idea how utterly foreign such a perspective is in the environment of liberalism in which the media is immersed. In my world, you *never* hear the kinds of things Reyburn said. As I read, something awoke inside me in answer to the questions that had been harassing me about what I was doing parroting back lies in front of the camera. Suddenly the contrast between the lack of ethics and truth in the world of politics and the media, and what I sensed was the nobility and virtue in Dr. Reyburn, was stark and plain. That's when I knew I had to talk to him personally. I had to find out if the man himself was as real as he came across in his book.

"All that was in my mind during my time in Scotland. But I had no plan. I didn't know what I was supposed to do next. Then came the invitation to the event in Seattle. Though my first reaction was to pass, I finally decided to attend just to see what presented itself. As if in direct answer to my contempt for the political scene, seeing so many people I knew from before but with no interest in talking to them, I saw in the distance what I took to be a teenage girl walking away from the crowd and sitting down on a rock next to the water—"

He glanced toward Heather.

"Sorry," he said, "but from a distance I couldn't tell . . ."

Heather laughed. "Don't worry. I get that a lot. I know I'm small."

"So I wandered toward this *girl*," Todd went on, glancing around the table at the others, "wondering why she wasn't part of all the hoopla. I soon discovered that I had just met a young *woman* who was not like anyone I had ever met. She talked freely about God and the Bible and doing what God said. I'd never heard anyone talk like that. I had zero exposure to religion growing up. It was a completely new language. Yet it was the same language Dr. Reyburn spoke in the latter portions of his book. And when I asked about something—I can't even remember what it was—and you said—"

He turned toward Heather.

"—you said, 'I am a Christian,' without a moment's hesitation, without an ounce of embarrassment, not trying to hide it, I was almost stunned. *Nobody* would say such a thing in my world for fear of being ridiculed. I'm sure there are Christians in politics and the media. But they would never talk openly of it. But you said it as if you were *proud* of it."

"Of course I am proud to be a Christian," said Heather matter-of-factly.

"That's exactly what I mean. In my world—politics and the media—for someone to unabashedly say, *I am a Christian, I pray, I talk to God, I order my life by the Bible*, would be as unthinkable as, 'I just returned from Jupiter.' And to say, 'I am *proud* to be a Christian,' would be more scandalous yet. Honestly, Heather, I have never heard someone say what you just said."

He shook his head, obviously still trying to process it all.

"On the heels of my misgivings, even guilt, for saying what I did about Rev. Hutchins and after what we of the media did to Senator Jansen, and the impact of the Reyburn book, when I walked up to you and saw such a contented look of peace on your face, and when we talked—it was so real, so unaffected. No hidden agendas and motives. After so many years in Washington where no one is completely real, I had to find out what made Heather Marshall tick."

He smiled almost in embarrassment.

"I'm sorry—I don't mean to put you on the spot like that or to make you into some kind of saint. I'm just telling you everything that was going through my brain."

He turned to Mark.

"You asked me why I took a leave of absence from my job—you just got the whole nine yards!" he added laughing.

"An amazing story!" said Grace. "Thank you for sharing so openly with us."

"And you found me in a barn covered with manure!" laughed Heather.

"What could be more real than that!" rejoined Todd, then grew serious again. "Maybe in a way, that's exactly why I came, what I was looking for. I was searching for *reality*. So here I am."

29

Journalist in Gold Country

"WHERE ARE you staying, Todd?" asked Mark.

"I spent last night at the Best Western in Grass Valley."

"What are your plans? How long will you be in California?"

"Honestly, I have no plans, other than hopefully, as long as I'm on the West Coast, to see Mrs. Hutchins after I leave."

"You do know how far it is to Seattle?"

"I am beginning to realize that distances here are greater than in the east," laughed Todd. "But I have no job to get back to. Right now these things I've been talking about are more important. I don't know what my future holds, or even what I want to do."

"You would be welcome to stay here at the ranch for as long as you like. We have plenty of room. It has always been a working ranch. There was a time when a half dozen hands lived here permanently, right, Dad?"

"Maybe more," nodded Bob. "Though that was in my father's and grandfather's time. My grandfather had bunkhouses up in the hills when he kept cattle in the high country for nine months of the year. Small cabins, in disrepair now and probably too far from the ranch to be practical. Both ranches used them—now that I think about it, ours and the Bar JG, I'm not sure who actually owns them," he added laughing. "But the point is—absolutely, we've got room. We'd love to have you stay on."

"Our son and daughter share an apartment in Roseville to make their school commutes easier," said Mark. "They come up on weekends. Heather is here three or four nights a week depending on her other commitments. We have guest rooms, plus the old bunkhouse in the barn."

"Oh, Mark, no one's stayed there for years!" said Laura. "There's plenty of room here in the house."

"Thank you very much," said Todd. "That is very gracious of you all. I feel overwhelmed by your kindness."

The Circle F "foreman" took the rest of the day showing Todd about the ranch, teaching him the basics of getting on and off a horse, and riding around the precincts of the barn. They managed to find a pair of boots and a hat to fit, though jeans for his tall, lanky frame were more difficult. A pair of Robert's were the closest, though came down only halfway over the boots.

Todd was not satisfied unless Heather allowed him to help with some of her work. He did not want to be treated like a guest, though no one was particularly concerned about the ranch work. There were no time clocks. Reluctantly Heather agreed but refused to subject him to cleaning out stalls. They spent much of the afternoon working with two horses that had been entrusted to them—a mare and her newborn colt whose perilous delivery had threatened the lives of both, and whom they were nursing back to health.

Timothy and Jaylene arrived about five o'clock that Friday afternoon. They had of course heard about Todd after Heather's return from Seattle. She had so downplayed their meeting, however, implying that he was just one of the crowd, all but ignoring their half-day sail together, that they had no idea how things stood. For that matter, neither did Heather. She was as shocked to hear Todd's voice in the barn as were her parents when Grace called to tell them that one of the most famous television journalists in the country had driven a third of the way across the country for the express purpose of visiting their daughter.

Seeing Todd Stewart up close and personal, at six-three, handsome and a national figure, towering over their five-foot-one and admittedly plain-featured daughter, they could not help wondering about the purpose of his visit. They loved Heather to death, but no young man had ever paid the slightest attention to her.

The evening was enjoyable for everyone. Todd held the others spellbound with spirited discussion and stories and inside glimpses into the world of high politics, accompanied by much laughter and many questions. Having been together all afternoon, on her home turf, so to speak, Heather was completely relaxed. She and Todd carried themselves as the best of friends, without a hint of awkwardness.

Everyone was completely taken with their guest. He was so at ease that he no longer seemed a guest at all. His gentlemanly respectfulness toward the older Forsters and Marshalls was plain, as was his youthful energetic humor with Ginger and Craig, who were not about to miss the evening. Though nothing was *said*, it was impossible not to be aware of the relational undercurrents, nor could Ginger keep from an occasional wide-eyed glance toward Todd and Heather sitting together on the couch.

As the discussion drifted toward plans for the weekend, Craig wasn't about to let *his* plans be forgotten.

"What about the river?" he said.

The others looked around at each other.

"Sorry, Craig," said Mark, "I'd forgotten all about it. We might have to reschedule it."

"The raft's rented and I've paid a deposit, Dad."

"Hey, don't change your plans on my account," said Todd. "I can go see some of the sights in Sacramento."

"I wouldn't think of leaving you on your own," said Heather, then looked around at the others. "You all go ahead and enjoy the river without me."

"No way," said Craig. "You and Todd have to come too."

Todd glanced around with a questioning expression. "What is this you're getting me into, Craig!"

It didn't take much persuasion on Craig's part before Todd was as excited about the trip down the river as he was.

Heather was scheduled to work at the care home on the following day, a Saturday. After returning to his motel Friday night, Todd returned to the ranch for Saturday lunch and accepted the Forsters offer of a room for the remainder of his stay. Mark and Timothy took the opportunity to get to know him a little better. The three, along with Mark's father, drove over to David's after dinner.

The hours with the older men was unlike anything Todd had experienced in his life. His own father had died when he was seven. He'd spent the next six years, until his mother remarried, without a man in his life. This was his first exposure to such men of deep conviction and rugged manliness, integrity, and good humor—men of strong character and virtue anchored in spiritual conviction. Why were men like David Gordon, Timothy Marshall, and Mark Forster not running the country instead of the superficial shells that made up the elite world of progressive politics, thought Todd as they drove back to the Circle F in the darkness. By day's end his desire to return to the empty life of Washington, DC, was even less than before.

The import of it did not strike him until later, when suddenly Todd realized, in all his time with Heather and her family and close circle of friends, that he had not heard a single word of profanity, not so much as a hint of the many commonplace mild versions that were unthinkingly sprinkled throughout every conversation in Washington. He had heard not a single reference to *God* as an exclamatory punctuation to conversation.

Though Bob said little, in his own way he too was absorbing more than the others realized. In the twilight of his life, his son's and best friend's common sense Christian faith was slowly finding its way into new places within him.

30

Reflections in the Oval Office

July 2050

MIKE BARDOLF walked into the silent Oval Office, strode with confident step across the legendary oval carpet, and sat behind the presidential desk.

He was familiar enough with the august surroundings. He had been here dozens of times for meetings with the president and others. He also came in whenever the president was out of town. Sitting here alone, in the quiet, was a heady experience even for him. There was nothing quite like the intoxication of knowing he had reached the top, that the president of the United States was out in the world doing and saying exactly what he wanted him to.

There had been a few arched eyebrows, but no one tried to stop him the first time he'd entered the private inner sanctum without the president. No one had questioned it since. He was head of the president's Secret Service detail. The entire staff of Presidential Manor guards worked for him. The only person above him was FBI Director Erin Parva, and she was rarely here.

Moreover, in the Palladium hierarchy, it might have been an interesting question who worked for whom between himself and Parva.

He set a sealed envelope containing a single page document on the desk. *Presidential Eyes Only* was stamped in red. It contained a list of names with a brief précis of proposed objectives for each. He hoped the president was ready for the bold initiatives he had taken the somewhat dangerous step of committing to writing. He had been working behind the scenes long enough, laying the groundwork. It was time. He hoped he had not misjudged either the president or the timing.

He would get the president alone as soon after his return from Saudi Arabia to make sure he read his memorandum, then retrieve it. He'd made no copies. No one else could ever see it. No copy could be left with Rhodes. But he wanted him to see it and read it in *writing*. Only so would it have the necessary impact.

As he sat at the Obama desk—a gift from the icon of Progressivism after the election of President ACH—his thoughts drifted back to the meeting here shortly after the Rhodes inauguration eighteen months earlier.

The pivotal meeting between President Jefferson Rhodes, Mike Bardolf, Press Secretary Anson Roswell, and the president's Chief of Staff Trent Randall—who wondered why the head of the presidential Secret Service detail was there at all—had taken place in the Oval Office two months into the new administration. Enough time had passed for the country to become accustomed to its new president—a bit of a culture shock as the first white heterosexual male to occupy the office in almost two decades—and for things to settle into a comfortable routine.

Rhodes and Randall had known one another for twenty years. Randall had been his right-hand man behind the scenes in Congress, though few in the country had heard of him until he was named the incoming president's chief of staff. Rhodes trusted Randall implicitly. He knew that his primary benefit was administrative Mike Bardolf, in the president's view, and true enough, was a strategist—a big vision man with links, useful in their own way, to icon Viktor Domokos. He was a man who didn't think twice about getting his hands dirty.

Now that Rhodes had reached the pinnacle, he would need both men—each with his own talents—to consolidate his power and secure his reputation as an even more transformative president than Obama. He knew that Bardolf and Rhodes didn't like each other. He was confident in being able to use that fact to his advantage. A little competition for the president's approval would keep both men on their toes.

Rhodes, however, had little idea to what an extent he was himself being manipulated by Mike Bardolf and the forces for radical change he represented. Once Bardolf began writing his speeches on the campaign trail, it became easier and easier to subtly inject elements of the Domokos master strategy into the president's words. Before long, Jefferson Rhodes fully believed the ideas his own. The first time Mike privately handed the candidate a draft he had prepared for an upcoming event, Mike insisted that no one ever know who wrote his speeches. Rhodes was so taken with the speech that he completely ignored the one given him by his normal speechwriters.

His listeners were surprised at his seemingly impromptu remarks. But even his speechwriters had to admit that the speech was good. Better than good—it had garnered standing ovations. Mike was careful after that not to write *every* speech or make suggested changes every time the candidate came to him to evaluate what had been given him by his team of speechwriters. He intruded just often enough to stay invisible and for Rhodes's staff and the public to think Jefferson Rhodes more gifted with the golden tongue of oratory than he really was.

As hints of Domokos's vision came drifting through in the president's words, the transition was so imperceptible it was scarcely noticed, even by Jefferson Rhodes. His inauguration speech, cleverly annotated by Bardolf from the official version, contained in germinal form—shrewdly worded so as not to be recognized—nearly every aspect of the Domokos-inspired sweeping agenda, which Mike would amplify in coming months.

As the morning's highly confidential Oval Office meeting got underway that March of 2049, even Mike Bardolf had not anticipated how quickly the planted seeds of his stratagems, sown not only in speeches but also in private conversations as they traveled to numerous public appearances, would take root.

"What we embark on today is historic and will be built on utter dedication to our cause," the president began. "What we discuss today must never leave this room. We four are confidants with each other and no other. I know you, Trent, were surprised at some of my cabinet selections. They seem a bit more traditional than you expected. All part of the master plan, I assure you."

He paused. The others waited. On Bardolf's part he was not surprised in the least. He had suggested that very thing, though so unobtrusively he doubted Rhodes even remembered the conversation.

"In the year leading up to the election," the president went on, "there was an uncomfortable resurgence of conservative religious sentiment in the country. It was not only because of my one-time friend Ward Hutchins, whose unfortunate demise I admit is a relief but also from the Reyburn fanatic. Had the unthinkable happened and that bumpkin Jansen been elected, imagine the catastrophic setbacks that could have resulted. This country could have been plunged back into the dark ages of the 2020s.

"It is my goal in this first term to set in place a strategy to keep that from ever happening. You will be my trusted lieutenants to lay the groundwork for that strategy.

"The Reyburn book remains at the top of the *New York Times* list," Rhodes went on. "The fallout from the Hutchins murder continues to stir up the evangelical faction. I purposely chose individuals with moderate views, tending more right than those involved in recent administrations, to calm those stirrings down—to prove that Jefferson Rhodes is not the antichrist as many in the Bible Belt are convinced Ward was about to announce. I must win them over, lull the religious world back into the slumber that has kept the progressive agenda rolling steadily forward since the Trump aberration. I do not consider this Reyburn flurry serious. Yet we must be prudent. As a result of my cabinet selections, I am already showing 55 percent approval among evangelicals, when it was at 35 in the days following Ward's death."

"But won't those traditionalists hinder our objectives?" asked Randall.

"Not at all. When has any cabinet member been influential in directing major policy? They are figureheads. They will give their speeches and present a calm public face to their agencies. Behind the scenes, the new Presidential Commissions will do the heavy lifting. The Commission heads will, in a sense, be my shadow cabinet, out of sight except when it suits our purpose to give some aspect of the agenda a public face. I am thinking of commissions for media, literacy, and so on. We already control medicine, finance, business, and education, and of course the more political agencies."

"A very shrewd strategy, Mr. President," assented Bardolf. "I salute your cunning foresight."

It had obviously been lost to the president's ken, if he had even realized it at the time, that Bardolf planted in his mind the seeds of this precise strategy.

"Thank you," said Rhodes. "Eventually I will want you to bring me potential names and to submit your ideas for the proposed immediate and long-term agendas in their respective spheres. I want to let things settle for a year or so, keep our ratings high as the Christian menace gradually goes back to sleep. We'll begin moving, as I say, behind the scenes, next year when the time seems right."

Inwardly Mike could hardly keep from smiling. He had already earmarked half of the more radical Commission appointees, every one, as would be the rest, from the highest echelons of Palladium's leadership. By the time Jefferson Rhodes's second term began, every agency of the US government would be under Palladium's control. The League of Seven would effectively be running the country. And one way or another, by then he would be running the League.

"One idea I am mulling over, specifically to counteract the religious threat to our plans, is to bring some visible evangelical into my administration."

"An evangelical!" exclaimed Randall. "My God, why on earth—you might as well bring in a two-year-old."

The president smiled.

"Trent, haven't you been listening? I want to lull the religious right back into the cocoon of its contented coma. How better to do that than by bringing one of its own onboard to quietly sing the lullaby, *It's all right . . . there's nothing to worry about . . . President Rhodes is watching out for us too . . . he's a good Christian man . . . go back to sleep, all is well . . . the country is safe . . . sleep . . . sleep Christian, sleep.*"

Bardolf smiled again. The president was indeed cunning. Almost as cunning as he was himself.

"In what role would you place such an individual?" asked Randall.

"I am considering that very question," replied the president. "It has crossed my mind to establish a Religion Commission among the others. Rather than trying to eliminate religion from the public square, as Christians have been saying the Progressive Party wants to do, we will assuage those worries by highlighting that, far from being anti-religion, the Rhodes administration is bringing religion back in America."

"The Left might mock you for pandering to the religious faction."

"Let them. Once they see the end result five or six years from now, with Christianity more soundly asleep than ever, churches closing, Reyburn and Ward Hutchins distant memories and no new prophets on the horizon, they will call me a genius. Give me ten years. By 2060, Christianity will be dead in America."

"*Ten* years, Mr. President?" queried Bardolf, with a tone that spoke volumes.

"I misspoke. *Eight* years. In the meantime, I want names for my commission czars."

Bardolf's thoughts returned to the present. It hadn't taken him long to come up with his recommendations. He had been refining his list, mostly from among Palladium's seventy-two, since before the election, waiting for Rhodes to think of the very thing he was making sure he eventually thought.

The list was nearly complete. He had just been waiting for the right time to give it to the president. He knew Randall was talking to Rhodes behind his back. He would have to walk with care. He couldn't overtly undercut Randall. Like everything he did, he had to make his moves subtly, so that Rhodes never suspected his true motives.

The speech on Bainbridge Island had been well-received. The president might as well have read straight from the Domokos Declaration.

What was contained in the memo now sitting on the president's desk signaled the opening of the final offensive against the remaining enemies of his progressive vision. He would continue to refine it so that his multi-pronged strategy was fully in place before the next election.

He harbored not the slightest doubt that within the next six years his invisible tactics would sweep away the final roadblocks to the implementation of the Marx, Alinsky, Domokos—and now the *Bardolf* vision for the future of the world.

Central to everything was controlling the narrative he wanted fed to the public. He had been grooming Todd Stewart for exactly that purpose for over a decade. He had lined it up so that he should have been network anchor by the time he was forty—his own personal mouthpiece delivering the news nightly to the public. He intended to make Todd Stewart the reincarnation of Walter Cronkite, the mid-century's "most trusted man in America." His had been the first name when he had begun his czar's list—*Media Czar: Todd Stewart.* His was the only name he had included who was *not* a member of Palladium, though as soon as he was on the League of Seven, Stewart would be proposed for membership.

Then the young fool had disappeared off the face of the media map.

He had tried to get a line on him for months before learning that he was in Scotland. His first thought was to hop on a plane and go after him. But what would he have done—brought him back by force?

Suddenly he turned up at Bainbridge acting strange and standoffish. He knew Todd was purposefully evading him. To top it off, the Jansen interview last week! He'd watched the thing in mounting fury.

D—— the young imbecile! What was he thinking! After all the money he'd invested in his education! He would make him pay, one way or another!

He had no choice but to scratch his name from his list that same night. The paper in the envelope in front of him now had a blank after "Media Czar." He'd been so confident in being able to control Todd to do his bidding that he had no backup.

If Todd wasn't going to play ball, he would see to it that his days as a media star were over. There were plenty of others he could get who would do *anything* to land a network gig. He hated the thought of starting over after investing so many years in Stewart. He still hoped he could rein him back in. Ambition and power were compelling allures. He probably needed to rebait the hook with something more enticing. Probably money wouldn't do it. He'd already thrown millions at him.

Maybe a woman.

He'd expected Todd back in Washington by now. But no one had seen him for over two weeks. He hadn't been at his apartment. He wasn't answering his phone. To all appearances he'd disappeared again!

Todd, Bardolf thought angrily, *where the h—— are you!*

31

Day on the River

When Sunday came, Heather's parents were also included in the outing on the American River. The diverse group loaded into two cars. Mark and Timothy dropped everyone off at the Sunrise Recreation Area to make arrangements for the raft, then drove the two cars downriver to leave one of the vehicles at journey's end, complete with picnic and barbeque supplies packed in coolers, then returned to join the others.

Half an hour later, outfitted with life jackets, sunscreen, hats, and water bottles, the eleven adventurers set off in their large yellow raft down the gentle flow of the river. Their float to River Bend Park would last three to four hours.

Craig, as official group leader was beside himself. At every deep pool, he was overboard into the river, though sometimes had to swim hard to catch back up to the steadily moving raft before being hauled back onboard by Timothy and his father. College man that he was, he was the youngest present and not above a little exuberant showing off in front of their esteemed guest and his new idol.

"Todd," he called out from the river, "it's not too cold. Come and join me!"

"This sun is pretty hot," said Todd. "Okay, look out, here I come!"

Getting his body and long legs over the side, without kicking or splashing anyone else in the crowded raft, took some doing. But after an initial exclamation from the sudden cold, Todd was soon swimming rapidly in Craig's direction.

"You too, Uncle David," yelled Craig.

David laughed. "I would never be able to get back in! I'm fine here with your grandfather."

"Both of you can come in. Grandpa, you can do it."

"Craig, my boy," laughed Robert Forster, "I don't think you have any idea how old I am."

"Look out—I'm coming in!" said Ginger, at last getting up her courage to jump overboard and join her brother.

"Wait for me!" exclaimed Heather.

Though she was closer to Grace's age than Ginger's, the little girl in Heather Marshall was never far from the surface. In spite of her leg, she could swim almost as well as she could ride. She was in the water in seconds swimming toward the others.

The parents and grandparents and honorary uncle laughed and shouted encouragement as the four young people cavorted and swam about the raft. Though it hadn't been apparent all weekend, compared with David and the three married couples, Todd, too, was in some ways still a fun-loving boy. The three generations that had come to the river together were suddenly separated by those remaining in the raft and those four laughing and splashing each other and racing and yelling like children in the river. Mark and Grace were used to it. They had been watching Ginger and Craig's antics all their lives. For Timothy and Jaylene, however, it was a new experience, watching their daughter playing and laughing like a girl, with a young man splashing her in the face and dunking her and challenging her to a race to the other side of the river, Heather obviously loving every minute of it. Jaylene was quiet as she watched. Not all the water around her eyes was from being splashed by the energetic swimmers.

"Uh-oh!" said Timothy. "I feel the current picking up. I think there's white water ahead. You four better climb back in before you're stranded on the rocks!"

Three hours later, their raft returned to the rental company, the swimmers showered in the park's outdoor facilities, the older adventurers glad to be back on dry land, Craig was exuberant at the success of his outing. Food and drinks from the coolers were spread on a picnic table, and eleven hungry rafters began digging into sandwiches, chips, potato salad, and an assortment of still decently cold drinks.

"A wonderful idea, Craig," said Laura Forster. "I haven't been to the river in ages."

"As long as we have lived here," said Jaylene, "I have never done this. Thank you so much for inviting us, Craig.—Have you, Timothy?"

"No," Timothy replied. "I was nearly grown before I came to the area."

"Some call the river float a rite of passage if you live around here," said Mark.

"All the girls at church have done it," said Ginger.

"I'm surprised the youth group doesn't come to the river regularly," said Mark.

"They used to," said Timothy. "Several years ago some of the parents thought it wasn't safe, so it was discontinued."

"Do you go river rafting in the east, Todd?" asked Craig.

"I've never done this or had so much fun in my life," answered Todd. "There's rafting in New Mexico but I've never done it. Thanks for including me, Craig."

It gradually quieted as they ate.

"How did you and Laura meet, Bob?" Timothy had just asked.

"We met in high school," answered Mark's father.

"And . . .?" said Timothy, when nothing further was said. "There must be more to the story."

The elder Forster did not answer immediately.

"Come on, Dad," laughed Mark, "tell him. It's a great story—young love leads to a fifty-year marriage. They were high school sweethearts."

"Now I *am* intrigued!" said Timothy. "I want to hear it."

"Me too, Grandpa," exhorted Ginger. "I don't know about this romance!"

"Ginger, dear," said Laura. "Your grandfather was quite the charmer."

By now all eyes were on Robert. A smile was playing on his lips, but still he said nothing.

"Dad was a football star," said Mark. "He and David were big stuff in Grass Valley in the late '80s. Mom was a cheerleader and had a crush on him."

Hearing his father's comment, Craig wandered closer.

"Is this true, Bob?" asked Timothy.

"I suppose—yeah, Laura was a cheerleader."

"I mean about the football star."

"It *is* true," now added David. "He was Grass Valley's starting quarterback as a sophomore. We won the league championship all three years. He took the team to state his senior year."

"We might have won too," said Robert, finally chiming in, "if you'd had the good sense not to graduate a year ahead of me!"

"What's this, David?" said Timothy, turning to David.

"I happened to be on the team too," replied David with a smile. "But Bob was the star."

"Come on, David—tell them the truth. He wasn't just on the team. David was all-league wide-out three years running. He was my go-to receiver. My junior year, when David was a senior, we connected for a league record twenty-three touchdowns."

"In one season—that's amazing!"

"Tell them about the homecoming game, Dad," said Mark.

"They don't want to hear—"

"I absolutely want to hear about it!" laughed Timothy.

"It's no big deal," said Robert. "It was my junior year. We were playing Folsom—they were always a powerhouse. Huge football program—went to state every year. They led us 20–0 at halftime. It was a blowout.

"So at halftime, David and I huddled in a corner of the locker room and decided to take matters into our own hands. We had grown up playing together. We had all kinds of patterns and plays we used to run, just the two of us. We had been throwing the football around at our two ranches from the time we were ten. Once David's speed began to develop and we discovered that I could throw a decent ball, we devised all kinds of crazy plays—the R-shove, the down-out-go, the T-2, the reverse-waggle, button-and-go, pitch-and-run, the sideline fake—I can't even remember them all. In those few minutes in the locker room we decided to scrap the coach's playbook and use our own."

"What happened?"

"They got the ball when the second half started, but we managed to stop them. So when we huddled after their punt, I called the play the coach sent in. But when we broke, I whispered to David, *Button-and-go.* He split out wide, the rest of the team did what the coach had called, but I ignored it and dropped back deep so I'd have time. David sprinted out twenty years, turned and stopped dead in his tracks. I pumped hard. Their safety bit. Before the safety knew what hit him, David had spun back around and was sprinting for the post right past him, and I launched a bomb. David was fast in those days, I mean *fast.* I thought I had overthrown him by at least twenty yards. I mean I unleashed it with everything I had. Somebody later said it went fifty-five yards in the air. But David sprinted right under it and hauled it in."

By then David was laughing at the memory. "It worked exactly like we drew it up with a stick in the dirt!"

"Just like that," Robert went on, "it was 20–7. We stopped them again. Next time it took us three plays. What were they, David?"

"I think you hit me with a T-2 for only fifteen or twenty yards, then the R-shove—"

"Right, now I remember. I got sacked pretty good on first down after that. Then we did a down and out, then the reverse-waggle—"

"What was that, Grandpa?" asked Craig excitedly.

Robert laughed. "Nothing fancy. I would just tuck the ball in tight and sprint for the left sideline like I was going to run wide. David lined up on the opposite side and broke left with the rest of the team. Once we had their whole team moving with us to our left, I stopped just before reaching the stripe, spun around and threw back across the field. By then David had faked a center-crossing left and was sprinting back the other way across the grain. It didn't matter where I put the ball, he could find it."

"Not exactly true, Bob," said David. "You could put the ball on the head of a pin at a dead run. Your leads were so perfect I never broke stride."

"Well, whatever," laughed Robert, "we were a pretty good duo."

"I take it you connected on that one too?"

"We did, though on that one David had to use a little fancy footwork and his speed to get past their safety. Six minutes into the third quarter, we'd cut it to 21–14."

"What was the final score?" asked Timothy.

"We won 35–28. It was Folsom's only loss the whole season. David scored four of our five touchdowns."

"They were furious!" laughed David.

"And the fifth."

Robert hesitated.

"Tell him, Bob," said David.

"I'd called the reverse-waggle again," said Robert. "By then they were getting wise to David and were triple-teaming him. When I dashed toward the sideline, I realized that their linebackers and safeties were sticking on him like glue, and that I had a pretty clear shot myself. So instead of stopping to pass, I kept the ball and swept around the left and down the sideline and managed to get in."

"*Managed*?" laughed David. "He tip-toed down the sideline, straight-arming three of their guys before he got clear, and ran forty-eight yards for the touchdown."

"Tell Timothy about the homecoming king and queen," said Mark.

"Let me guess, Bob," said Timothy. "You and Laura, the cheerleader and quarterback."

"You're half right," said Robert. "The king and queen were *David* and Laura."

"I was a senior," said David. "Bob was the star, but it was my final year—the sentimental choice, you know."

"You should see the pictures!" said Mark. "These two guys were real hunks in their day. No wonder my mom had a crush on you, Dad!"

"Pictures?" said Timothy.

"Mom and Dad were homecoming king and queen the next year."

"Amazing—your mom was homecoming queen two years in a row, with both these two guys!"

"She was a stunner in high school," said Mark. "I'll show you the pictures."

"I'll agree, she was gorgeous," laughed Robert. "I was lucky to land her. And lucky David had no designs on her."

"She only had eyes for you, Bob," laughed David. "She was looking around for you the whole night of the dance when she and I were king and queen."

"Well I am very impressed," laughed Todd. "I am sensing another interview in the making."

"You can count me out, son!" said Robert. "I will deny everything you just heard!"

Engrossing as the story had been, Craig had had enough inactivity. He jumped up and sprinted away with his soccer ball. Heather, Todd, and Ginger leapt and went after him on the expansive grass laughing, trying to get the ball from Craig—though not very successfully. He had played soccer in high school. Two girls, one with a limp, were hardly worthy adversaries. But then Todd chased after him and Craig dashed away, kicking the ball in front of him, shrieking in terror.

An hour later, the river party had separated into three groups. The four older men wandered away from the table across the park and were chatting casually. The four young people were playing two-on-two soccer, brother and sister against Todd and Heather.

Grace, Jaylene, and Laura Forster were still seated at the picnic table.

"It must have been a remarkable thing" began Grace, "being part of the Marshall family—Timothy's parents being so well-known and, I don't know, spiritual giants I guess you might say."

Jaylene laughed. "They weren't at all like that. Just normal people. Yet I suppose I do consider them amazing. Yes, I was very fortunate to know them. Being a *Marshall* is an honor. But, oh my—what a culture shock it was for me when I first met them."

"How so?"

"I was an atheist in college when I met Timothy."

"No way!"

"It's true," laughed Jaylene. "My father was pretty well known in his field too. I sort of went from one well-known family to another. He was a geologist. I grew up in a thoroughly secular environment and went away to college as a card-carrying atheist."

"What happened?" asked Laura.

"What else—I met Timothy."

"I want to hear the story!" said Grace.

"Timothy often says he was slow to see his father's vision. I think he carries some regrets that he wasn't as fully aware of his father's greatness sooner. That's one of the reasons he admires David so much," Jaylene added, glancing at the four men walking together in the distance. "But David was older. I tell Timothy that it's natural for David to have been further along that road. But when I met Timothy, *he* seemed like a spiritual giant. When I read my first Stirling Marshall book, which Timothy gave me when I was still an atheist, it sounded just like Timothy."

"How *did* you meet—an atheist and Stirling Marshall's son?"

"I was, I suppose you might say, an unusual kind of secularist. Most of the students and faculty I knew in college were self-satisfied. Even in a university environment, they weren't looking to expand their perspectives beyond what they had been taught to believe."

"But not you?"

"I was a *hungry* atheist," Jaylene went on. "I wasn't satisfied with the pat answers the scientific world gave about beginnings. I should rephrase that—I wasn't satisfied with the complete *lack* of answers. I was fascinated by absolute beginnings but science had no theory to put forward. I wanted to understand *both* sides of the creation and evolution debate. So I checked a Bible out of the university library and was reading in the first chapter of *Genesis* seeing if I could make sense of it. I was sitting by myself on a bench on campus, hoping no one I knew saw me reading a Bible. A young man happened along, saw me reading a Bible, and stopped."

"Timothy?"

"That was him. I knew absolutely nothing about God or Christianity or Jesus. Truly—*nothing.* Three months later I was in the Marshall home for Christmas, Stirling and Larke welcoming me like family, though I was still somewhat bewildered at the tidal wave of changes that were sweeping over me. And the rest, as they say, is history."

32

Moving into the Depths

"YESTERDAY WAS really fun," said Todd when Heather arrived at the ranch the following morning.

"And you have the sunburn to show for it," laughed Heather.

"A lasting souvenir from the American River! But I think I should probably be leaving tomorrow."

"Are you still planning to drive up to Seattle before going east?"

"I am. Mark talked to Mrs. Hutchins last night. She said she will be happy to see me. Then I can return to the East knowing that I've seen three of the four people I vowed I needed to see. That will leave only Dr. Reyburn."

"Have you heard of Zacchaeus?" asked Heather.

"The name's familiar. Somebody in the Bible, isn't he?"

Heather nodded.

"Why?"

"Nothing, only what you said reminded me of him."

It was shortly before noon on Monday. Todd had been at the Circle F through the weekend, and Heather had determined to take him on a long but easy ride. She did not want him leaving California until he was not only comfortable in the saddle but able to enjoy it. After short tutorial rides on Friday and again on Sunday after returning from the river, he was willing to put his fate in her hands and head off on horseback into the hills.

"I had hoped to have the chance to have you over to my house," said Heather as they saddled the two horses. "My grandparents' house, really—though technically mine now—mine and my parents. I'd like you to see it, just because it reminds me of my grandparents. I'd like you to know a little more about them."

"I would enjoy that."

"Would you like to come over this evening and I'll make us dinner? After our ride."

"I would like that a lot," replied Todd.

The differences in their height were not so apparent as they set off on horseback, though Todd's legs dangled low on his mount's sides. Heather's stirrups, on the other hand, were set so high on Cinnamon's flanks that her boots did not even reach the bottom of her mount's belly. Cinnamon was the daughter of Nutmeg, her first horse, now over twenty-five. Todd was mounted on nine-year-old Dusky Lady, the gentlest horse in the Forster stables who had never been known to bolt, buck, or throw a rider.

"I've been meaning to say something for a couple days," said Todd as they moved slowly along the trail through the pasture north of the barn that led into the forest and gradually up into the hills. It was the route most rides started with, the trail branching off repeatedly in different directions—toward the Bar JG, another up to Rustler's Butte, and others throughout the foothills among numerous streams, waterfalls, even small lakes that fed the North Fork of the American River. "I haven't seemed to find the right time. But I wanted to say that I hoped I didn't embarrass you Friday with all I said when we were with the Forsters."

"You did, a little," laughed Heather. "All that about wanting to see me again and that talking to me was different—who wouldn't be embarrassed?"

"I am sorry. But it was true."

"I know. So I don't mind. That's part of your story. The time in Seattle was special for me too—though in different ways. I felt the same freedom to be myself. Not that I would have dared show up unannounced at your door!"

Todd laughed. "Okay, I suppose I went a little overboard!"

"I'm glad you did. It's been really fun. Everyone loves you. Craig adores you!"

"He's a great kid."

"So have you found out what you came for?" asked Heather.

"What makes Heather Marshall tick, you mean?"

"I'd forgotten about that. Another one of your embarrassing statements! Surely there was more to it."

Todd thought a minute.

"You were different than anyone I'd ever talked to," he said. "I wanted to find out why. But when I was with the Jansens, I felt the same thing. I felt *goodness* and humility in them. I think I came away from the interview more changed than anyone. Like you, they talked freely and openly about their faith. Everyone I've met here exudes that same spirit. It's fresh and clean, wholesome somehow. That afternoon and evening with your father and Mark and Mr. Gordon—that was one of the most extraordinary times I've spent in my life. They are three remarkable men. Their love and respect for one another—I've never seen such a level of honor and humility between men."

He paused. They rode along for several minutes enjoying the quiet rhythmic sound of the horses' hooves on the hard-packed path.

"I read Dr. Reyburn's book," said Todd at length. "But he talked about spiritual things mostly in the context of the country and America's foundations and the country's uniqueness. I don't suppose I internalized his spiritual references. But when talking to you, and hearing you speak so openly about being a Christian, then the Jansens, then everyone here—I am suddenly being bombarded with people all speaking a common language. I suppose I was a victim of the standard progressive assumption that no one *really* believes all that anymore and that churches are just religious social clubs. But being with you all, I've not heard the word *church* once. Mark used to be a pastor, yet none of you even went to church yesterday. We went rafting on the river, for heaven's sake! For you people, Christianity is *real*. It doesn't seem to have anything to do with church. Nobody's giving me tracts. Instead of taking me to church I was invited to go river rafting. It's completely upside-down from my expectations about Christians."

Heather could not help laughing.

"So you're right—it *is* about more than just you. *Everything's* new to me. I'm curious about what makes *all* of you tick. What is this strange new form of Christianity that fills you with such energy and makes those four men such examples of manly virtue, that fills them with such love for each other? A lot of people call themselves Christians. But those I've met in my circles are no different from everyone else. But you, your parents, the Forsters, the Jansens—you are different."

"I don't know that it's any more complicated," rejoined Heather, "than that we take what we believe seriously. Our worldview, our outlook, our perspectives are based on learning to look at life and the world through God's eyes. How that translates into daily life and who we are is in trying to live by what Jesus said, living the way he says we are supposed to live. Like I said, it's not really very complicated."

"But who can do that?"

"No one."

"But you just said—"

"I said we *try*. I should make it more personal. I try. No one can live by what Jesus said perfectly. The question is whether or not that is your life's objective—to grow more capable of doing so. That *is* my life's objective. That's what Heather Marshall is all about—the desire to grow more able throughout my life to do what Jesus said."

"That is a remarkable statement. I've never heard anyone say that about their life. *How* do you grow capable of it?"

"By doing what you *do* know to do and *can* do. We simply call it obedience. Obeying what Jesus said to do, thinking as he told his people to think, behaving as he told his people to behave, conducting relationships as he told his people to treat others. People often think Christianity is nothing but rules and do's and don'ts. I don't see it that way. It's so much more practical than rules—be kind, do good to others, forgive those who wrong you, speak graciously, don't swear, don't talk too much, treat others unselfishly. Who wouldn't want to do those things? Doing what Jesus says really just boils down to *Be nice, be kind, be good, be unselfish.*"

She paused a moment.

"And do you want to know something, Todd," she went on, "you may not think of yourself as a Christian and you say you know nothing about it—but you do half those things yourself. You're kind, you're nice, you went to the Jansen's and asked forgiveness, you speak graciously, I've never heard you swear."

Todd nodded thoughtfully. "That's nice of you to say. But before I began reevaluating, I was so immersed in the liberal mindset that I did hurt people—like Ward Hutchins and Mr. Forster."

"And now you are taking account for it and trying to change. That's what I mean by *trying*. You, too, are trying to live by many of Jesus's commands without even knowing it."

"That's a remarkable thought."

"It's true."

"You make Christianity sound so simple."

"In a way, I think it is. Not *easy*, but simple. Simple to understand, I should say. Christianity isn't hard to understand. But it's hard to do if you're serious about being a Christian. It's *hard* to be good and kind and unselfish. It's just that not many people try. Even most who call themselves Christians don't try—that's not their life's goal. But it is mine. I want to grow to become like Jesus."

"But why?"

"Because I believe—we all believe—that Jesus is the Son of God. That he came to reveal God, to show us the kind of people we're supposed to be and how we're supposed to live and think. If that is true, how can a person of truth not embrace it? That's what life is all about—living as Jesus told us to live, getting to know God the Father as he knew him, living by the truth that God is *good*, and—well, I said it before—becoming like him."

"An amazing thing to say."

"If you want to know what makes me tick—that's it."

"You say it's simple, not complicated. But there are many things about Christianity that *are* hard to understand. That's why there is so much confusion about religion in the world."

"Sure. That's a good point. Much of the confusion, however, is not because it's hard to understand but because people want their own way."

"How do you mean?"

"They don't want anyone telling them what to do—not God, not Jesus, not anybody. They want what *they* want, which is the complete opposite of Christianity. Because Christianity is also about right and wrong. It's not only about being good. Jesus also says, *Don't do wrong, don't sin, embrace truth not falsehood.* That's when it starts to get difficult for people who want to go their own way, people who *want* to sin, who *don't* love truth. Christianity is about embracing another's will rather than your own."

"God's, you mean."

"Yes. That's why what Jesus says is so important—he tells specifically *how* to embrace and live by God's will not our own. That's what you're trying to do—embrace truth in your life."

"And you would say all this is not only what makes you tick, it's why being with those men was so different, why *they* were different? It's also what makes them tick?"

"That is exactly the difference. Imagine living for twenty or forty or, in David's case I think, over fifty years trying to model your life after that of Jesus, learning for fifty years to see through God's eyes. What powerful depth of godliness has been infused into those men, including my father. What I said before is true—none of us live the life perfectly, not my dad or Mark or David either. But the Christlikeness that is evident in them is clear. It is the fruit of a lifetime trying to do what Jesus said. What can I do but want to follow their example?"

Still trying to absorb this new way of looking at life. Todd remained quiet for several minutes as they wound through the trees and the trail began to climb more steeply.

"How are you doing?" asked Heather.

"Fine, actually. This is fun. I feel like John Wayne."

Heather laughed. "If you get tired or saddle sore, we can stop and take a break. I'd like to take you up to Rustler's Butte. We can have lunch there. It's another half an hour. From the summit you can see down to the Forster ranch and David's in the distance."

"I'm game. Lead on!"

33

Rustler's Butte

FORTY MINUTES later they were seated on a well-worn dirty blanket used expressly for laying on the dry dusty ground, as all the ground for a hundred miles was at this time of year. The simple picnic lunch from their saddle bags was spread between them. The horses were tied to two trees munching on the oats Heather had brought.

"It's quite a sight from up here," said Todd, "seeing the two ranches spread out so far below. "Your man David Gordon—a bit of a mystic is how he struck me."

"In a way I suppose."

"Has he never married?"

"No, a confirmed bachelor," answered Heather. "He grew up on the Bar JG and has been there all his life. He's a man who has spent most of his life growing into the image of Christlikeness. He was a protégé of my grandfather's. Much of who he is he credits to my grandfather's influence."

"You continue to say the most unusual things. The *image of Christlikeness*—another phrase I've never heard before. Your grandfather and Mr. Gordon must have been, and must *be*, extraordinary men to think in such terms."

"They were and are," nodded Heather. "After my grandfather's death, I suppose you might say David filled his shoes or that my grandfather's mantle passed to him. He became a mentor to my parents and to Mark and Grace too, in the same way that my grandfather had been to him."

"Does Mr. Forster believe these same things you're talking about—obedience and the image of Christlikensss and doing what Jesus said and everything else?"

"I would say yes, that Mark and Grace are similarly minded."

"And your parents?"

"Yes."

"And you?"

"I told you—those things are what my life is all about."

Todd began chuckling lightly.

"What?" said Heather.

"I was just thinking that if Mr. Forster starts talking like that when he gets to Washington, they will laugh him out of town."

"That may happen. I wasn't involved too much in Mark's decision, though I knew it was being discussed. He prayed with my parents and David before accepting the president's offer. He had to seriously weigh that very thing and try to discern what God wanted him to do. It was a hard decision."

Neither spoke further. The stillness of the high altitude—broken only by a gentle breeze, the temperature down a few degrees from the valley and from the previous day's 103° on the river—was peaceful, quiet, almost solemn.

Todd rose and walked to the overlook. He stood gazing down over the two ranches for several minutes, then walked about the plateau in both directions, taking in the views toward the high Sierras, then turning again westward toward California's great central valley in the distance beyond the rolling landscape of the foothills.

When he returned, his face wore a deeply thoughtful expression.

"I'm sorry to be asking so many questions," he said with a sheepish smile. "I feel like a kindergartner. You call me famous," he added with a smile, "yet I feel like a dunce. I'm so ignorant about spiritual things. You are light-years ahead of me. I appreciate your being patient with my questions."

"Oh, Todd—of course," replied Heather with a gentle smile. "Questions are how we learn and grow. In a way, this is new for me too."

"How so?"

"I've never been in the position of being asking what I believe and what Christianity means. I help my parents answer the mail. And sometimes there are questions I try to answer. But it's different one-on-one."

"The mail?"

"Readers writing about my grandfather's and my dad's and mom's books. Talking to you is different than that."

"I *am* interested," rejoined Todd. "I don't know what to think. All I know is that the world I left behind in Washington is superficial. There are no deep answers to anything in politics. I don't know what I was expecting, or what I was looking for in Scotland. I suppose maybe for the first time in my life I want to know what truth really is. An odd thing for a journalist to say. But when I realized that the media was *not* about truth, I suppose that's when my search for truth began."

He paused a moment.

"It's not that I've never known religious people," he said. "You hear people in Washington say, 'I'm a Catholic,' or 'I'm Methodist,' or 'I'm Episcopal.' But you said, 'I am a *Christian*.' You've never once mentioned church. I always thought Christianity *was* the church. That's something that puzzles me. What's the difference between being a Catholic, say, and being a Christian or an Episcopal or anything else. What are *you*—are you any of those things?"

"No."

"Just a Christian?"

"I hope so."

"What's the difference?"

"Those other names are names of church denominations. People join churches like they join any organization. That makes them members of a church. Being the member of a church doesn't make you a Christian. To answer your question—a *Christian* is a follower or a disciple of Christ. In other words, a person who is dedicated to following Jesus and doing what he said, living like he told his followers to live."

"Obeying, like you told me before."

"Yes."

"So are Catholics and Baptists and Episcopalians and Presbyterians and all the rest Christians?"

"Some are, some aren't. Being any of those things is no different than being a Republican or a Progressive or a Rotarian. There are Christian Republicans and Republicans who aren't Christians, or Rotarians or whatever. Being a Christian has nothing to do with membership in anything, including any church."

"You continue to throw new things at me!" laughed Todd. "Are you saying that there are Catholics who are Christians and Catholics who go to mass and do all the Catholic things, but who *aren't* Christians?"

"Yes."

"And the same with Baptists and Presbyterians and Episcopalian—some are Christians and some aren't?

"Yes. And with Republicans and Progressives—some are Christians and some aren't. Though I seriously wonder sometimes how any dedicated follower of Jesus *can* be a Progressive with all the horrifying things the Progressive Party believes. But it's not my place to say."

"You must realize how shocking what you say is—that many church people actually *aren't* Christians."

"It may be shocking. But it's true. Christianity has nothing to do with church. It has everything to do with modeling our lives after that of Jesus. Some churches help people do that. But most don't. Churches have become institutions that teach all kinds of other things but mostly ignore the commands Jesus told his followers to live by."

"Isn't that what the church is for—to teach that way of life?"

"It should be but usually isn't. Christianity and the church *ought* to mean the same thing. Jesus intended them to mean the same thing. I think it breaks his heart that they don't mean the same thing. The two diverged more than two thousand years ago. The church and true Christianity have been growing further apart ever since."

"Do you go to church?"

"Sometimes."

An hour later Heather was leading the way back toward the Circle F by a different route than they had taken up to Rustler's Butte. Their conversation on the descent was lighter, both sharing more about their lives up to the point that had brought them together on a sunny day on the shores of Puget Sound.

"Is there still gold in these hills and rivers?" Todd asked.

"They say a lot," Heather replied. "Some claim that only a fraction of the total was ever found."

"That's amazing. To think that so much might be down there—right under where we're riding for all we know! Maybe that's how I'll frame the story of my trip here—that is *if* I ever write about it—*A Journalist Finds Gold in Gold Country.*"

"A catchy title!" laughed Heather. "You wouldn't be the first journalist to write about the gold country."

"There've been hundreds, I'm sure."

"One of the first, probably the first woman was named Corrie Belle Hollister. She lived not far from here in a little town called Miracle Springs in the 1850s and 1860s. Then later she reported on the Civil War."

"I've never heard of her."

"Not many have. But the books she wrote about her experiences are wonderful. I read them when I was young and have read them all again since. Besides the gold rush and Civil War, she writes about many of the same things we've been talking about—how as she grew older she learned what being a Christian meant and how to live practically as a Christian. I've got a set of her writings at the house. I'll show them to you tonight."

34

The House in Dorado Wood

NONE THE worse for their long ride earlier in the day, showered and clean, though with some soreness in his hindquarters, Todd arrived at the house in Dorado Wood about six that evening. Heather had driven straight home after the ride and had supper nearly ready when Todd arrived.

She took him around the house with its numerous family photographs, showed him the books of her grandfather's library, telling about his life in brief, explaining about the ongoing work related to her family's writings, including those of her own parents, and about the group meetings she and her parents hosted.

"In other words," said Todd, "your grandfather's legacy lives on through his writings."

"I couldn't have said it better."

"And you and your parents are carrying on that work by keeping his books in circulation and keeping readers aware of his life. And adding to his legacy as well. Your parents have both written books, and you are the third in the generation of Marshalls. Will you carry on that tradition?"

"Write books, you mean?"

Todd nodded.

"I doubt it!" laughed Heather. "They sometimes jokingly call books the family business. But I could never do what my parents and grandparents have done."

"You might be able to explain things in a different way—just like you have done with me."

"I've never thought about writing a book. You're the journalist, not me!"

They sat down at the table, continuing to chat freely.

"I'm sorry again for asking you a million questions," said Todd as they enjoyed the meal.

"I told you before, I love it."

"Okay, then, here's another one. Do you believe that Christianity is still relevant in the world? I mean, I think I understand what you are saying about trying to live by what Jesus said—as much as a neophyte can understand! But is it still for everyone? In today's modern world, so few people care about spiritual things."

"It's more relevant now than ever."

"Why do you say that?"

"Because when you embrace what Jesus taught, everything in life comes into it. Christianity is about right and wrong, about truth and virtue and integrity and righteousness. The world's morals and values and standards of right and wrong are crumbling before our eyes."

"Do you really think it's that serious?"

"I do. The moral depravity of our country is awful. Surely you can see it. It's disgusting and depraved, there's nothing else to call it. Sin and evil and immorality are so commonplace that everyone thinks it's normal. That's what the Progressive Party has brought to our country—the disintegration of right and wrong and truth. Modernity has so lost sight of right and wrong that it no longer believes something like sin even exists."

"That reminds me of something Dr. Reyburn said in his book," nodded Todd. "He said that politics was incapable of dealing with the world's problems at their root."

"Politics makes it all the worse by normalizing and legalizing sin," said Heather. "How can politics help the human situation when one of the root beliefs of progressivism is that right and wrong no longer exist?"

"Do you think Mr. Forster would agree that politics is incapable of helping?"

"You'd have to ask him. Probably."

"Why would he accept the president's offer then?"

"He felt God was leading him to. I don't think he wanted to accept."

"Really! But he did because God wanted him to?"

"As I understand it."

Todd thought a moment.

"Back to what you said a minute ago about the Progressive Party . . . I hope you won't think worse of me, but I'm a Progressive. At least I always thought so. It's the norm in my world. But there are Progressives who consider themselves Christians—maybe not many, but some. Yet they probably hold views you would call disgusting and sinful. Are such people not Christians then?"

"That's a hard question. We struggle with it every day. What I would say is that it is a question I don't believe we're supposed to ask. Everyone has to ask *themselves* if they are living by Jesus's commands. I can't ask that about anyone but myself."

"And that's what makes a man or woman a Christian—living by Jesus's commands."

"*Trying* to—making it their life's objective."

"But you won't say that people who aren't making that their life's objective are *not* Christians."

"That is correct—I won't say that about anyone. That is between them and God in their hearts. What if they are trying in ways I cannot see? What if they have *begun* that process but are so early on the learning curve that no one can see it yet but they are on a road that will pass me spiritually one day? What if they *haven't* begun yet, but God is preparing them to turn around and begin trying to live as a Christian, maybe tomorrow or the next day? What to all appearances may look like unconcern for the deeper realities of obedience may be about to change? There are many reasons why I cannot judge whether or not anyone else is an obedient and trying and sincere Christian. My only business is to be a true Christian myself."

"By trying to do what Jesus said?"

"Yes."

"What about all the other things that Christians have so many views on? Does none of that matter?"

"Much of it doesn't matter. Some doctrines matter a lot. Some matter nothing. The foundation remains doing what Jesus said. Everything else is secondary. None of those other things, even the important beliefs, make you a Christian."

"And that's why you say church doesn't matter so much, because it emphasizes the unimportant things?"

"In my opinion—yes. Many Christians would disagree. I'm just one young woman telling you what I think. But it is true that when most people hear the word *Christianity*, they think of church and doctrines and theological beliefs and a thousand things that Christians disagree about. Being a follower of Jesus is completely different from all that. I'll spend the rest of my life trying to obey even the simplest of his commands."

"Such as?"

"Oh, I don't know . . . how about do good to those who treat you badly. That's hard! Who can do that perfectly? I was treated so mean and made fun of when I was young because of my limp. I didn't obey that command very well, I can tell you!"

"I don't remember ever hearing about doing good to those who treat you badly."

"Well, I put it in my own words. What Jesus said was to love your enemies and pray for those who spitefully use you. To me that translates as: Do good to those who treat you badly."

"That exactly describes the Jansens!"

"That's what I mean. They have been a living example of true Christianity to the whole country. If you're serious about living by the commands, you have to personalize them. That's why going to church and singing hymns and studying doctrines and debating a point of theology isn't the same thing. If that's all someone wants to do, it's easy.

Obeying what Jesus told his followers to do, thinking his thoughts, treating people as he did, listening to God's voice, modeling your life after his—that takes a lifetime. I've got my hands full just trying to obey a simple command like forgive those who do me wrong, or do good to those who mistreat me, or don't worry about tomorrow."

"I see what you mean."

"That's why I don't give much thought to all the peripheral things—heaven and hell, the crusades, miracles, were Adam and Eve historical people, is the devil real, not to mention all the trappings of the church like robes and incense and sermons that people sleep through and rote prayers that mean nothing to anyone, and all the hypocrisy the world loves to throw at Christians and the terrible things that have been done in the name of Christianity. Those are all pointless debates that just prove my point—none of those things comprise *true* Christianity. Harvey Jansen didn't talk about theology or wear his spiritual convictions on his sleeve when he ran for president. He just *lived* as a godly man, and let his life speak for itself."

They continued to talk and share.

"I think you would like my mom's book about Einstein and Genesis," said Heather as the discussion drifted toward historical evidences for the Bible. "She explains Christianity from a logical scientific standpoint. I think it is as significant as my grandfather's book on the unspoken commandments."

"Maybe I should read them both," nodded Todd.

"I think you'd like them."

Gradually the evening grew late.

"I am so appreciative of the time I've had with you," said Todd. "Thank you for sharing with me. And for trusting me with your thoughts and ideas."

"I would say the same," rejoined Heather. "You have been very open. It has been a special few days. We'll both be mentally exhausted for a week!"

"I'm sure my brain will be working to process it all the way back to the East Coast. But since I'm leaving, one more request if you don't mind."

"Of course not."

Todd thought a few seconds.

"How would you put it all together. Tell me in twenty-five words or less—I'll give you a hundred! I'll give you as many words as you need. Tell me boiled down what you think true Christianity is. What is its essence, what it means to *you*. When you said, *I am a Christian*, tell me the *essence* of what that means. The simplified version, the elevator speech. I know—the commands, doing what Jesus said. But give me the larger scope of it, the overview of the whole thing—the essence of *true* Christianity from your perspective."

"That's an enormous question, a huge thing to ask. I don't know that I want to answer on the spur of the moment without giving it more thought."

"Take as long as you like. Maybe I had better give you five hundred words!"

Heather laughed, then it grew quiet.

"I would rather try to write it down," she said after a few seconds. "Can I write it to you in a letter?"

"Sure, whatever you are comfortable with. I can wait."

When Todd walked out to his rental car a short while later, he was carrying copies of Stirling Marshall's *Does Truth Matter?*, along with Timothy's *Christian Truth in an Era of Untruth*, and Jaylene's *Discovering Einstein in Genesis*. He would spend his last night in California with Mark and Grace at the Circle F and be on his way to Seattle by six o'clock the following morning. Heather would not see him again.

He turned to her in the light of the streetlamp outside the house. Their eyes met.

Neither said a word. Todd smiled, held her eyes a moment, then opened the car door.

"I'll expect a letter waiting for me when I get back to Washington in a week or ten days," he said.

Heather nodded and smiled again. She did not dare speak.

A minute later the car disappeared down the street. Heather walked inside and sat for a long time in what suddenly seemed a silent and lonely house. Not even the surrounding memory of her grandparents could console the strange new empty feeling that swept through her.

Sleep was out of the question.

She was glad she would be working at the care home for the next two days. She was not ready to face the flurry of questions that would surely bombard her from Ginger or Mark and Grace and her own parents.

When she returned to the Circle F on Thursday, she kept mostly to herself. The others saw her alone, walking about or sitting quietly.

They all knew the reason.

35

The Commands Continue to Take Root

Early August

THE LETTER that arrived in a packet of mail in early August of 2050 was the first from that country which Timothy had received. He therefore read the letter with particular interest.

Dear Mr. Marshall,

Let me introduce myself. I am Leon Morales. My wife and I live in Machala, a city of a quarter million on the southern Ecuadorian coast. We both had the good fortune to be from affluent families and to have been educated in the US. While at the University of Florida, which was during your Pérez presidency, we became Christians through an underground campus organization—all the Christian groups were forced underground during those years when US colleges and universities became so deeply what was called Woke back then. Being from Latin America and knowing what a gift of freedom people in the US had, we saw the futility of American progressivism. We became involved in a secret Christian group. One of the books that was spread around our group—though once word of it got out, the campus Gestapo (that's what we called the leaders of the Woke movement and social justice warriors as they thought of themselves) put it on the list of banned books which were forbidden on campus. Anyone finding a copy was ordered to destroy it. The book was called The Commands.

We returned to teach mathematics and English at the Technical University of Machala and raise our family in the city we love. Once back in Ecuador, we started a similar Christian group for the students at our university. It has thrived in the years since. Thankfully our country is not infected with the loss of religious freedom as in the US, so we are able to be open about our Christian faith. Though most of the students know some English, they are not proficient enough to understand deep spiritual truths. We have made great use of a Spanish translation of the Commands book. We hoped to find more books by the same author in Spanish. We wrote to his son and learned of one additional title, Hazme Como Jesús, which we have ordered. He also told us about your father's writings and was kind enough to send us a copy of Unspoken Commandments. He suggested we contact you to see if any of your father's books have been translated into Spanish. He also gave us your address.

I hope this will reach you. My wife and I are enjoying your father's book on the commandments very much.

Sincerely,
Leon Morales

Timothy began writing a reply immediately.

Dear Leon,

How wonderful to hear from you. I am familiar with the Commands book you mention. The author and my father corresponded for many years, though both are now gone. In fact, we are in touch with the lady who translated the Commands book into Spanish—your fellow Ecuadorian—and she is at work on a Spanish edition of my father's Unspoken Commandments as well.

Unfortunately, there are no more books from either author that I am aware of in Spanish. I hope that will change in the future.

In the meantime, I am enclosing a list of my father's books which we have available—in English only, I'm afraid. If we can send you anything, we would be privileged to do so. Please do not hesitate to ask.

We would love to hear more about your ministry to students in Ecuador!

Thank you for writing, and God's best to both you and your wife.

In Christ,
Timothy Marshall

36

Taking Stock of Life

TURNING SIXTY in itself hadn't been especially traumatic for Court Masters.

That the milestone came a week before the president's much-heralded speech in Seattle the previous May made it impossible to say which event contributed more significantly to his decision. But within ten days of the "Big Six-O," which he and his wife celebrated at home with three couples from church, he knew a turning point had come.

Taken together, the combination of the two events hit him squarely between the eyes: *I may not have that many active working years left—why am I spending those years as a cop in a city in which everything is controlled by a government that is corrupt and is ruining the country?*

He let it settle for a week before talking to Stella, making sure he wasn't simply reacting emotionally to his birthday and the Rhodes speech. When he mentioned it, she wasn't surprised.

"I'm thinking of turning in my papers," he said one morning over coffee. "I've got thirty-five years in. I'll make almost as much retired as working. It's time for a change. Our government's going down the toilet. I don't know why I've stayed part of it so long."

"What will you do?" his wife asked.

"I've got some ideas. I want to know what you think—nothing's set in stone. But you don't seem surprised."

Stella smiled. "You forget how well I know you," she said. "I saw it on your face after the president's speech a week ago. You're not thinking of investigating the Hutchins assassination like you did the former president's?"

Court smiled. "I can't say I'm not intrigued," he said. "I'm convinced the two murders are linked. But if they are being covered up, I'm not willing to jeopardize my life and our future by turning over those rocks. I don't want to become a third casualty. It's obvious that whoever's behind these events plays for keeps."

"You don't know what a relief it is to hear you say that!"

"You thought I might start nosing around again?"

"I saw the gleam in your eye."

Court laughed. "No, my thoughts of retirement are sincere. So what do you think?"

"Like you say, it's probably time. You haven't been really happy with your job for a long time, even more so after we went to California."

"I suppose you're right. That changed everything. I didn't put it in so many words at the time, but that's when the center of gravity in our lives began to shift. I think the handwriting's been on the wall ever since, though it's taken till now to realize what it's saying."

"Which is?"

"Get out of that world," replied Court. "I've just been going through the motions. That's not my life anymore."

"What *are* your ideas? You're not the sit-around type."

Court drew in a long breath and thought a minute.

"It's a little vague," he began, "but I'm wondering if there aren't ways I can make myself of service to people—you know, those who are just learning about these new ways of thinking and how they fit into their lives . . . people who are struggling with what coming out of the world means, trying to figure out where church fits now that they are seeing things differently . . . people who are asking the same questions we've been asking since coming back from California. I'm still asking them! Do I quit my job? Do we leave church or stay? Do we start a home group? It's hard to know how to apply the principle of separation from the world when we live in the world. I'm trying to figure it out myself."

"Are you thinking of starting a Bible study or that we should start a group like the Marshall's?"

"That's not the kind of thing I meant. I'm not the type to lead a group. Just helping people."

"In what way?"

"Whatever they need. I don't know what I'm thinking—just trying to be there for people who are new to this different way of looking at what the body of Christ means. We've got no children. We've both made good money. We've got more set aside than we'll ever need. Maybe God will bring into our lives people we can help financially. Maybe I can help people with projects around their houses, lend a hand to David Gordon at his ranch—he's getting too old for some things. Who can tell, if times continue to get dangerous for Christians, I may be in a position to make the same offer to others I did to Dr. Reyburn. That's my background, my area of expertise—security and protection. God uses our gifts and experiences. I'm not a writer or Bible teacher like Timothy and Mark. Maybe God can use me in different ways."

It fell silent. Both realized something new in their lives was at hand.

"Do you think I should quit *my* job at the temp agency?" asked Stella at length.

"I don't know," Court answered slowly. "Even doing temp work as you are, you're still in the tech world. It's going downhill just like the politics. That's a decision only you can make."

"Like you said, I could use my experience to help Christians rather than contributing to the spiritually bankrupt world of high tech. You're right, we don't need the money. We should use the years we have left investing in people's lives."

Court filed his thirty-day retirement papers the next day. Stella followed a few weeks later.

Even before his final day on the job, after some back and forth with Timothy and Mark in several telephone calls, Court had composed a letter and sent it out to the regulars of the FCL group, most of whom lived in California or the adjoining states, along with three dozen names and addresses Timothy supplied from around the country. In the letter Court told of his recent retirement and offered his services to anyone whom he might be able to help—whether house maintenance, remodeling, even financial assistance. He did not know cars or plumbing, he said, but could usually figure out most other things.

When the second letter went out a month later—which included a dozen such notices they had received from others volunteering their services and listing the areas *they* might be helpful in—Stella volunteered her computer skills to accompany her husband's.

The response was overwhelming. More men and women continued to write back *offering* their own services on a volunteer basis than there were *requests* for help.

By midsummer Stella had designed a full-fledged monthly newsletter prepared to go out to more than a hundred addresses around the country, with a list of three dozen names and their particular areas of interest. They called it *A Helps Newsletter—an interactive message board for gifts, skills, and needs for Christians seeking to practicalize the commands of Jesus, disengage from the world, and live in the unity of daily discipleship.*

In early July, Court helped a former pastor in North Dakota—who, like Mark Forster, had stepped away from the ministry and was struggling to make ends meet—re-roof his house. Over the next month and a half, an assortment of jobs in the DC area kept him busy. He helped a young man near Baltimore whose wife had left him, move into an apartment, loaning him the money for his security deposit at no interest and no repayment schedule.

"Pay me only if and when you can," he said, "and only as much as you can afford."

He added an extra pair of hands to two remodeling projects within two hours of DC. And he and Stella helped a recently widowed woman in their church downsize, sell some of her things, and move into an assisted living facility.

Meanwhile, the requests for Stella's help with various computer and software problems were even more numerous. As they did not involve travel, she was able to handle them from her office at home. She was soon writing regular articles in response to a wide range of computer questions.

In August they flew out to California for a few days, renewing what were now among their closest spiritual friendships. Court helped David with a project at the Bar JG, the nature of which neither he nor David would divulge. Stella spent an afternoon with Jaylene and Heather addressing envelopes, even answering a letter or two.

37

News from Russia

TIMOTHY MARSHALL missed teaching, missed the energetic engagement with enthusiastic young people. However, his own energy was not what it once was. He had always considered his father a dynamo. It had been almost a shock to see him gradually decline in energy through his seventies and eighties. Now Timothy understood it! He'd just turned seventy himself. The years were creeping up on him just as they had on his father.

He had to admit that he enjoyed life's slower pace which gave him more time to write. His father had hoped to write about his generational ancestry but had not progressed far before death overtook him. Now Timothy hoped to bring the Marshall and Stevens heritage into the telling of his parents' lives. Whether anyone would read it, Timothy had no idea. But he and his father were historians. It was what they did—record the past and try to understand it. As C. S. Lewis once said, source-hunting was in their blood. He hoped he would be able to put his father's and mother's lives not only into the perspective of the era in which they lived, but also into a prophetic perspective of the future, and the perilous times in which he, as their son, now lived.

Timothy was also grateful for more time to devote to correspondence. His father would never have anticipated the ongoing impact of his writings. Nor could Timothy have foreseen that of his and Jaylene's as well. It hardly mattered *why* people contacted them or what book they had read. The common thread was a new outlook on living their Christian faith in an increasingly Godless world. Now Heather was an intrinsic part of that correspondence. They were at the center of something expanding within the body of Christ—a coming out of the world and its worldly churches, a coming out that was dedicated, not to organizations but to Christlikeness, obedience, and unity with others of like mind. It was a coming out that was invisibly being knit into a worldwide fellowship. A remnant of shared life was being birthed and was sending down roots in many places simultaneously.

The letters that came were infinitely varied. When he sat down at his desk early one Sunday morning, those emotions went especially deep. He had been waiting to answer two letters until he knew he would not be interrupted, both from far distant friends he had never met. Both contained familiar return addresses. He smiled as he opened the first. The correspondence had gone back and forth with some regularity ever since their Ecuadorian friends had first contacted them.

He read the letter, then opened a new file on his computer.

Dear Leon and Alita,

How good to hear from you again. The recent family photo you included is a treasure. Your little Jaime and his sister, Evita, are growing fast. Even in a year I can see a difference.

The news you share of the Bible study with your students is wonderful. I'm glad the chapter-by-chapter translation of my father's book you are developing is striking a chord. Imagine—young university students in this age of worldliness committing themselves to living by the Sermon on the Mount.

What an extraordinary thing! You two are indeed ambassadors for the Lord!

We are still working on a Spanish translation of my father's New Testament books. It is a daunting undertaking, but we trust eventually it will have an impact in the Spanish-speaking world.

Meanwhile Jaylene and Heather are both doing well . . .

Ten minutes later, Timothy's fingers stilled. He printed the letter, signed it, and set it aside.

The next envelope was from an even more distant part of the world. It was clear that persecution was coming. It would surely fall most heavily on those determined to stand against the world's lies. The churches of man would be spared because they were no threat to the headlong rush of progressivism into the abyss. Its fury would instead fall on those of the remnant who dared proclaim by their lives, "I stand with Jesus. I stand for truth. I stand against sin. I rebuke the Lie."

That tribulation was coming. That it would probably come upon them all was starkly confirmed by the letter he now read from their dear Russian friend.

Dear Timothy and Jaylene.

As I told you, after first corresponding with you, we began meeting with a few friends to share the ideas we have discussed together. We hoped perhaps to study your father's book, which I was translating one command at a time into Russian. We were astonished how widespread was the spiritual hunger in Moscow. Within a year, others were meeting in their homes. So many came to us, hearing about our group and wanting to live true discipleship, that we began meeting in many homes throughout the city.

I have been careful in sharing the principles you and your father write about, especially about the true Church versus the church of man, and separation from the world and obedience to the commands. Most who hear these things are filled with excitement. They have never heard such things from the priest in our Orthodox church or even in the smaller Catholic or Protestant churches. They recognize the truth immediately. There are also Mormon, Jehovah's Witness, Baptist, and Pentecostal churches in Moscow, but their numbers are small. None of them teach or preach what you and your father do.

Yet remarkably, life is springing up in our many home groups. We don't even know what to call it. It has no name—it is a fellowship of shared life! What more needs be said than that? You know me—I am a plain and humble man. I am scarcely educated, though God be praised I know English so I can speak freely with you and read your books. That such a move of God could be happening through Anya and me is unbelievable. Yet perhaps I am no more unworthy than a fisherman! I envy your education and your wisdom, though I know you will rebuke me for thinking it. You will say, "We are brothers. We share a common life. There is no hierarchy in brotherhood—no more educated or less educated, or more skilled or less skilled. In brotherhood we are equals and God uses all our gifts, different as they may be, to accomplish his purposes."

You would be right, and I stand rebuked for my envy. I am so filled with humble gratitude for that brotherhood.

I am writing of many thoughts because this may be my last letter to you for some time. Two Orthodox priests in Moscow heard about our group, or groups as it now is. No one thought meeting with other Christians should be kept secret. Why would priests not rejoice that Christians were coming together. However, talk began to circulate in a few of the churches that said we were subverting the church. These two priests went to the police with reports of a strange new cult of believers in strange practices that was teaching people to leave the church. They said we were teaching that the Russian government is corrupt and must be replaced by a new kingdom.

These rumors reached the Kremlin and reprisals began immediately. Several of our groups were raided during their meetings, police with guns storming in, some of the people beaten and arrested. Most have thankfully been released, but they have been forbidden to meet. There was no meeting at our home during the raids, so we and our small fellowship are safe. The others were interrogated and demanded that they tell who was the leader of the seditious movement. No one betrayed us, but it is only a matter of time before we are discovered.

There have never been secrets. Even the children know our names, so we will easily be found out. Some of our number have learned that the PPF, the People's Police Force, have orders to arrest the cult's leader, as they call it, which I suppose is me, and make an example of him, and kill him if he resists. Some of our people have come to us in secret, begging us to leave Moscow, even to get out of Russia entirely. Others have already left for different parts of the country, determined to take the life we have found elsewhere where it can be planted and flourish. We are determined as Aleksandr Solzhenitsyn said in his final message to the Russian people before his emigration to the west, to live not by lies.

Therefore, at the urging of our brothers and sisters, we are leaving Moscow tomorrow before daybreak. A friend will mail this letter for us. We only leave behind our parents and three brothers and sisters. We pray no harm will come to them. Russia has not yet degenerated back to the days of the USSR, though it may come to that again. If we can reach Poland or Germany safely, we hope they will be able to join us. I have a cousin in Poland, and we have been in close contact with Monika and Fynn in Germany after you put us in contact with them.

Pray for us, as we do daily for you. The world is crumbling, but God is at work and his people are being drawn together as the coming out continues.

It would be best that you not write in case the letter should fall into the wrong hands. We will be away tomorrow anyway. I know your hearts and know that you will want to help. You would probably offer to send money. But we are well provided for. God has blessed our fellowship. We have no material needs. Russia needs the light of truth. We are willing to stay, even die if it comes to that. But all in our group unanimously exhorted us by the Lord's leading to go and to seek a place where our fellowship can live and thrive and bring light to a lost world.

So we are leaving tomorrow morning. Pray that God will blind the eyes of those searching for us even now, if it is indeed by his will that we survive this sudden outbreak of persecution. Do not write. Only pray. We will contact you when we are safe.

Yours in the unity of the fellowship of discipleship and in the shared life of Christlikeness to which we are called.

Grigor Popov

Then Zerub'babel the son of She-al'ti-el, and Joshua the son of Jehoz'adak, the high priest, with all the remnant of the people, obeyed the voice of the LORD their God, and the words of Haggai the prophet, as the LORD their God had sent him; and the people feared before the LORD.

—**Haggai 1:12**

PART 2

A REMNANT GROWS

FALL 2050–WINTER 2051

38

Machinations in the Heart of Islam

August 2050

HAMAD BAHRAM returned from the event on Bainbridge Island the previous May thinking long thoughts—deep into the past . . . far into the future. The invitation secured by Mike Bardolf had been fortuitous. Meeting the president for the first time, even more so.

It was but a brief moment. Yet a pivotal one. It would lead to more.

As he and the president shook hands, he felt an imperceptible psychic tingle, certainly unnoticed by one like Rhodes, as if power was coursing through the president's hand into his.

The significance of the encounter remained with him. He took it as a sign. Something had been transferred in that moment, as if the ancient dream of his people was suddenly stirring to life and flowing into him for a new era of destiny.

He had been thinking of his father and grandfather and great-grandfather ever since. They had carried Islam's dormant dream for a century. Now their vision rested on him.

The deep-hidden objective of the small Iranian leadership cartel spawned by his great-grandfather Husain a century earlier had been to place one of their own in the Oval Office—a devout Muslim committed to planting Sharia law into the heart of the Western world. From that foothold they would expand the faith throughout the West.

Husain Bahram had immigrated to the US after the Second World War and became a citizen in the days when Iran and the US were allies of convenience. His son Nasim, a natural-born American, grew up listening to his aging father's dream of an Islamic state. It was Nasim who turned the dream he had imbibed from his father into a bold and controversial strategy.

When Nasim Bahram envisioned the potential of moles in the Palladium organization, he could have no way of knowing how long it would take, or that his own grandson would be given the opportunity to step into that destiny and fulfill the millennia-long hopes of Islam.

Ever since their stealth ally had occupied the then–White House between 2009 and 2017 and had removed restrictions on their nuclear program, their countrymen back home had been working on a new generation of fissionable materials, some not using uranium or plutonium at all. Hamad's cousin Ada was head of the new program experimenting with highly complex synthetic elements. He managed to keep in contact with Ada and abreast of developments through invisible extensively circuitous familial back channels.

Back in the Khomeini and bin Laden days, his predecessors had wrongly assumed that a frontal assault would succeed against the Great Satan. To be sure, terrorism could inflict damage, kill people, and instill fear. But none of these would ever defeat America. Its people, its national identity, was too resilient, its economy too strong, its resources too vast, its will too fiercely proud of its inveterate Americanism. That spirit could only be defeated by slowly cutting off its life-source, poisoning the well from which America gained its strength. Only then could the ultimate objective of an Islamic Caliphate be achieved.

To make that possible, the *soul* of the United States had to die.

But the death of the colossal *idea* of America could only be brought about invisibly. The poison must infiltrate the national *consciousness*, the national *will*, and the national *morality* one invisible step at a time. Undetected, unseen, until that character, that undefinable ethos that the very word "America" represented in the history of the world, was dead.

It was Hamad's grandfather Nasim who beheld how that death could be effected. It would happen of its own accord, organically, from the lethal poison flowing through the bloodstream of America. Their opportunity lay in taking advantage of it when, at some future propitious moment, the soul of America was ripe to be extinguished and its nationhood stolen.

Nasim Bahram had been educated at Stanford and was in his youthful thirties teaching in the California University system during the counterculture explosion of the sixties. He had shrewdly observed the events of these years through the lens of his father's vision.

He saw that the liberal progressivism taking shape around him would in time take over America. It was that progressive tidal wave that would give Islam its opportunity.

When all Iran was chanting *Death to America* during the heady days of Ayatollah Khomeini's humiliation of Jimmy Carter, exulting in Iran's so-called victory, an epiphany came to Nasim. The realization was startling for a loyal Iranian.

What he saw was shocking: The Ayatollah and the mobs chanting and burning American flags in Tehran's streets were nothing but short-sighted fools.

In a blinding flash, suddenly his father's vision crystalized.

America would *never* be defeated by such means. Armed conflict and suicide bombs could not possibly defeat the *idea*. It could only be defeated from *within*. In that moment of clarity, he saw the ingredients of the lethal poison that would defeat the Great Satan of the West.

It was all around him!

The pot mixing that poison and spreading it into America's bloodstream had been bubbling and brewing throughout the sixties and seventies. It had been in front of him all along!

John Lennon and Jane Fonda and Malcolm X and Saul Alinsky and Angela Davis and Timothy Leary—*they* were fermenting the poison. They didn't know it, but they were paving the way for Islam's final triumph! The student revolt and sexual revolution of the sixties and seventies was the greenhouse of the future Caliphate!

The feminism, free sex, homosexuality, anti-authority, globalism, counterculture of rebellion, and anti-capitalism of the new leftist movement provided the lethal mix that, if given long enough, would kill the *idea* of America. Progressivism *itself* was the poison that would bring about America's death.

As all this came to him, Nasim Bahram also saw how to exploit it. It was the most shocking realization of all. He was shocked himself when he beheld the strategy in all its counterintuitive brilliance:

He would *join* the radical leftists. He would *participate* in spreading the poison into America's cultural bloodstream.

There was, however, one danger. One preventative to the death of America, a single antidote to the poison—Christianity.

Only Christianity could save America. For Islam to triumph, it must render Christianity powerless. To achieve that objective, Christianity must be infiltrated with the *same* liberal poison. Then Christianity would die along with the idea of America.

If they could normalize homosexuality into the bloodstream of America's thought, Christianity would collapse from within. The strength of family would die. The ideals of Western civilization would all die.

Ultimately, with one of their own inside the Oval Office, Canada, Mexico, then the rest of Central and South America would follow.

As odious as it would be, Nasim's shocking strategy would require him to ingratiate himself as a mole into the very progressive movement every true Muslim despised. A new kind of mole. Not a terrorist mole but a progressive one. He would launch a new kind of jihad—using the West's own decadence and apathy against them.

First lull *Christians* to sleep.

Then lull *Americans* who once loved their country to sleep.

Then lull *conservatives* to sleep.

Then, as the preliminary to the final thrust, once they assumed their agenda secure, lull *progressives and liberals* to sleep.

Then they would strike.

Checkmate.

Nasim's far-reaching plan to infiltrate the progressive movement was unthinkable to every Imam with whom he shared it. They called it betrayal. He called it a strategy that would ensure Islam's triumph.

He also knew, however, that those who carried the plan into the future would have to pretend to be progressives. Theirs would be a sacrifice greater than strapping suicide bombs to their chests. Yet their odious sacrifice of *pretending* to embrace the very thing they hated would gain the ultimate prize.

Nasim was a pragmatist. Theirs had always been a war of centuries. The temporary deception would yield final victory.

Sleeper cells, of course, were nothing new. His use of the idea, however, was revolutionary—a sleeper cell in plain sight! Wide awake while America slept, while the *idea* that had made it the greatest nation in history slowly drifted into a coma from which it would never awake.

In one of his classes at UCSB, Nasim made the acquaintance of a young man by the name of Slayton Bardolf. He recognized him immediately as one to watch. Through Bardolf, he had become a member of Palladium or the Alliance of Progress as it was called in those early days. His son Sonrab followed after him and eventually his grandson Hamad.

Nasim Bahram's bold, daring, controversial strategy was discussed in certain select and very private circles in Iran during visits back to the Middle East. As a result, he was ostracized as an infidel. Yet half a century later, the infidel Nasim Bahram had proved the prophet.

On its surface, his vision was contrary to everything Islam stood for, except the one thing that mattered more than anything—defeat of the West.

From their earliest days, the daring strategy had been instilled into Nasim's son and grandson Hamad. With a gradually widening Palladium network at their disposal, they had successfully planted stealth moles deep inside the substructure of American business and academia, the scientific community and the arts, entertainment and the media. Every one, to all appearance, was a faithful progressive. Through the years the invisible army expanded and moved into higher positions of influence and power within their respective fields.

They would all be in place when the time came.

39

Secret Commissions Take Shape

THE FACT that Mike Bardolf maintained two offices greatly annoyed his FBI boss Erin Parva. In spite of their Palladium connections, Parva was protective of her position. Ever since bringing him into his second senatorial campaign eight years earlier, she realized that the president had a special connection with Mike Bardolf. She had no idea what the fascination was. Half of what Mike did had nothing to do with the FBI or Secret Service. For whatever reasons, Rhodes didn't want him listed among his official presidential staff.

Parva suspected more to it than met the eye. Otherwise, why did Mike maintain an office in the Presidential Manor only two doors from the Oval Office—with no name on the door and no official title? All she knew was that Mike often helped the president with his speeches. Other than that, even as head of the FBI, she had been able to discover little more than that the president made clear, in spite of the FBI organizational chart, that Mike Bardolf was answerable only to him.

She rarely saw Bardolf now. He used his FBI office only when the president was out of town on the rare occasions when Mike did not accompany him. But she knew that to raise questions could put her in the president's doghouse. So she raised none.

Mike Bardolf sat at his desk in his *other* "official" office at FBI headquarters on Pennsylvania Avenue. Today's business he wanted to think through away from curious glances at the Presidential Manor.

He smiled to himself as he thought of Parva's consternation. He had always been adept at keeping people off balance in their perceptions of him. It was exactly how he wanted it. Even Rhodes had no idea who he was dealing with.

He thought another moment, then pulled several files from one of the desk drawers.

Most of the official Secret Service cohort were in Florida with the president where he was campaigning for Progressive candidates in the upcoming midterms. They would be walking about, guns in shoulder holsters, eyes scanning the crowd, whispering into hidden microphones, pressing a close circle around the president, keeping the crowd at bay, watching the perimeter—the usual Secret Service functions. All routine. Though Rhodes liked to have him at his side, Mike knew he wasn't needed in Florida. Neither was the president for that matter. There was no danger of a midterm slump in the elections. They had Congress sewn up for life. But Rhodes felt it necessary to go through the motions, delivering a few religion-friendly speeches in the Sunshine State to gauge reaction preparatory to the rollout of his new Religion Commission.

Mike opened the top file in his hand. He had been working on his proposal since before his meeting with the president and Trent Randall a year earlier. The Bainbridge speech and inauguration of the Religion Commission finally set the wheels in motion to move toward Phase Two of the agenda, as he saw it. The president read over his July memo with interest but thus far he'd kept his more sweeping proposals to himself. Rhodes had to be brought along carefully.

Mike glanced over the first page.

Twelve Freedom Commissions for Progress to be established to carry out the details of the Global Progressive Mandate, each of twelve members, to set cultural and social direction to be incorporated into policy directives, Commissions headed by Directors making up a Presidential Alliance with decision-making authority, subject to the president's approval, to forcefully execute and implement the president's agenda through executive order. The overarching objectives of the FCP Presidential Alliance will include, but not be limited to the following priorities: reproductive services equity, bias eradication, lifestyle freedom, diversity, religion, wealth and opportunity equity, gender neutrality and confirmation surgery, humanism, inequality remediation, justice, minority equity, hate eradication, global brotherhood.

One chairman to preside over the Twelve, he thought, smiling to himself at the clever use of the familiar quote that came to his mind—one chairman to rule them, one chairman to find them, one chairman to bring them into the light and bind them all to the cause. And with the same power to control events as the fabled ring of legend.

If all went according to plan, Palladium would be in control of the country in less than five years.

He would select men and women he could mold in his own image, thought Mike. A few might be older than his own fifty years, but without his connections and range of knowledge. He knew many in the organization still dismissed him as the third most important Bardolf, though his place at the president's side put much of that to rest. His father may have kept him down, but his time would come. Most of Palladium's members realized that he would be ruling the roost eventually. Many were already subtly currying his favor. Mike Bardolf was a man to be reckoned with. Everyone in Palladium knew it.

His list of commissions and potential directors remained a work in progress. But his vision was taking shape as he continued to refine his ideas for the transformation of America.

His first proposed agency would in many ways be the most important of all, setting in place the underlying priorities and directions of the whole. The progressivism of his predecessor generations had been infused almost invisibly into the culture since his grandfather's time, more openly after Obama's tenure, through the US public education apparatus. That network of indoctrination would continue to mold future generations in the new realities of social, racial, and financial equity, woven into the new progressive perspectives of history, race, religion, sexuality, marriage, and global brotherhood.

He read over his previous draft, then added more notes, and continued through his visionary prospectus.

EDUCATIONAL COMMISSION. *Mandate:* Establish protocols, programs, curriculum, teacher training, and testing, based in an enlightened secularist worldview, to inculcate tolerance, hate eradication, gender and marital-lifestyle choice, multiculturalism, to instill a personal awareness in white students of the destructiveness of systemic white racism, and to eradicate the last vestiges of Christian or supernatural myths from the educational sphere. Public funding of education at all levels to be offset by taxation increases of private educational institutions, ensuring that the educational greenhouse of progressive ideas continues to flourish. All curriculum in all subjects to be infused with the perspectives of the FCP Presidential Alliance agenda, eliminating all links to Christianity. Mandated high school and collegiate courses expanded to include multicultural and social justice ethics ahead of math, science, and bilingual Spanish and English requirements. These mandates to include strict supervision of non-public institutions, home schools, and private schools at all levels, including colleges and universities. Those institutions not adhering to the mandates of the Commission and curriculum and course mandates to be fined, then, if still uncompliant, shut down. Education Enforcement Agency to be established to enforce mandates of the Commission. All public school teachers required to be members of Progressive Party or certification shall be withdrawn. All teacher contracts shall include a legally binding "belief clause," disavowing belief in God, Christianity, or supernaturalism.

Proposed Director: Imala Petruso

INTERNATIONAL ADVOCACY COMMISSION. *Mandate:* To use America's leadership to bring the family of nations together—promoting world unity and goodwill, global brotherhood, poverty elimination, crime reduction, drug trade eradication, animal rights; wealth distribution from developed to poorer countries; enhanced food production, sustainability, and distribution; finding remedies to ecological concerns such as the current global cooling trend and the global water supply. Immigration standards and levels to be established internationally rather than by individual nations, ensuring access of developing peoples to the full rights of citizenship in the world community.

Proposed Director: Anahid Tate

Banking, Finance, and Tax Commission. *Mandate:* To work directly with the World Bank in establishing internationally uniform banking regulations, investment protocols, wealth redistribution, and equity guidelines, and, within the US, to continue implementing fair-share taxation standards, salary limits, and universal basic income standards that expand qualifications and raise levels beyond those of the 2032 Universal Income Act. Universal income established for immigrants in conjunction with World Bank and world immigration standards. Reparations for African Americans and other minorities extended beyond the ten-year window provided by the Reparations Initiative of 2034 and made permanent on a need-based scale.

Proposed Director: Conrad Rian

Technology, Media, and Communications Commission. *Mandate:* To bring together advances in technology, artificial intelligence, robot capability, transhumanism, and computer implant technology with media and communications networks to advance the well-being of humanity throughout the world. To use ongoing technological advances, working with media institutions, to infuse the overarching principles of the FCP Presidential Alliance agenda into the minds and hearts of the populace. Development of AI infiltration digital robotic technologies for thorough internet, phone, and in-home surveillance, and reporting of subversive religious elements. Media guidelines established to regulate all media outlets and organizations to ensure compliance of right-wing institutions with the FCP Presidential Alliance agenda.

Proposed Director: Sidney Torrance

RELIGIOUS UNITY COMMISSION. *Mandate:* Under the banner of seeking unity and brotherhood between diverse world faiths through bias eradication, tolerance, and inclusion, to gradually eliminate the influence of religion nationally and globally, with the ultimate objective of eliminating Judaism and Christianity from the public square. With the recognition of Christianity's role as the leading purveyor among the world's religions of intolerance, racism, bigotry, and hatred, an emphasis on reframing Christian teaching will be essential. A new lexicon of definitions will be established and introduced in schools to rebrand former Christian terms with secular meanings. Mandated texts will be established to be taught in churches, including standardized statements of faith presenting Christianity as one faith-option among many. If alternate opinions to Christianity are not presented—

Mike's concentration was jarred with the importune sound of his phone.

40

Unexpected Call

"MR. BARDOLF," he heard when he answered, "this is Todd Stewart."

Bardolf drew in a sharp breath of surprise. It was quickly followed by a volley of silent imprecations as his anger at his media protégé rushed into his mind.

"Todd," Mike replied, managing to keep his voice calm, "you are still alive after all. Not hearing from you in so long, I was beginning to wonder."

"I am sorry about that. I've received your messages. I thought it was time I finally contacted you."

"I'm glad you did. After your leave of absence, then seeing you on Bainbridge, I wanted to know when you'd be back at the network. There's a lot going on. I need you on my team."

"I understand, but—about that—I'm going to need a little more time."

"Time for what?" rejoined Bardolf testily.

"Personal things."

"What kind of things?"

"I suppose you'd say I got burned out. That's why I needed the time off. I still haven't got it all worked out, which is why I need to—"

"Got what worked out?" barked Bardolf. "Come on, Todd, you're talking in riddles. What's going on?"

"What it boils down to is that I'm not sure how comfortable I am in front of the news cameras."

"That's what you do. It was your dream. That's why I paid for your education. I've got a lot invested in you."

"I am aware of that. I am very appreciative. I know I owe you my career. I'm just trying to be realistic about whether I can go back to business as usual at the network."

"Why not? What's preventing you?"

"I've been at NBC for ten years. I've enjoyed it, and again, I'm appreciative for all you've done for me. But I'm not the same man I was fresh out of UCLA. People grow and change and—"

"Look, Todd," interrupted Bardolf. "Go ahead and grow and change all you want. But don't forget who bankrolled your career. You *are* on my team. Nothing can change that. You're right, you owe me and I want you back in the game. So get your growing and changing over with and get your head back on straight. Where are you, anyway? Let's get together. Maybe I can help you with your indecision—sweeten the pot, shall we say."

"Actually, I'm in Seattle again."

"*Seattle!* Doing what?"

"Personal business I needed to take care of. I'll be on my way to DC soon."

"Then get it taken care of, whatever it is, and get in touch with me when you get back. This hiatus of yours has gone on long enough. I'm in the middle of something, so I need to end this. Get in touch with me when you're back."

41

Stratagems Continue

BARDOLF HUNG up the phone and finally gave vent to his annoyance, swearing loudly.

After a moment he picked up the religion file he had been perusing.

Todd sounded strange, he thought to himself. He just hoped he hadn't gone off to some ashram or monastery and got religion.

It took several minutes before he could refocus his thoughts on the Religion Commission and his directorship recommendation. He began reading again:

> If alternate opinions to Christianity are not presented, pastoral licenses will be revoked, and, if necessary, churches shut down. Churches and clergy required to sign and conform to legally binding contractual agreements, renewed annually or be shut down and licenses revoked. Influential Jewish and Christian leaders, churches, and organizations to be scrutinized and regularly monitored. Church Compliance Agency will be established to oversee and enforce implementation of mandates for all Jewish congregations and Christian churches, with authority to levy fines and close institutions not complying with mandated FCP Presidential Alliance standards.
>
> Proposed Director: Hamad Bahram

Calming after the irritating phone call, he continued through his file.

LITERACY AND PUBLISHING COMMISSION. *Mandate:* To establish FCP Presidential Alliance standards and guidelines for publishing, along with a Publishing Compliance Agency to monitor and enforce them. Magazines, books, newspapers, and other publications, including online content, to be reviewed prior to publication. Those not in compliance will be blocked from publication. Underground publishing to be rooted out, subjected to fines and publication blocked. Jewish and Christian publishers and authors heavily scrutinized. All religious content required to include FCP Presidential Alliance content.

Proposed Director: Trista Casale

MEDICINE AND VACCINATION, HEALTH AND WELLNESS COMMISSION. *Mandate:* To promote health and wellness nationally and globally in ways that engender physical, mental, psychological, and sexual health, working toward a holistic approach to personhood by eliminating masculine and feminine paradigms in medical care. Underlying the elimination of outdated paradigms and continuing the principles of the Harris-Cortez Freedom Affirmation Bill of 2031, all birth certificates will list a "Temporarily Assigned Gender" specified by the attending physician or midwife, but with "Chosen Gender" options available to mother, with or without father's consent, and also available to the child after age ten, these chosen gender options to be legally binding and superseding temporarily assigned genders. Birth certificates to be considered living and changeable documents. Additional key priorities to include international equity of health services; abortion, contraception, and reproductive service equality and availability; gender confirmation surgery availability for all ages at public expense, children presented with gender options from second grade and annually thereafter; tracking and monitoring health and potential disease of all citizens with chip technology; establishment of birth defect survivability quotas; expansion of the Dignified Freedom of Death Act of 2035 by establishing governmental panel with decision-making authority concerning life-sustainability feasibility parameters for individuals over the age of ninety and younger when disease or conditions are incurable. Vaccination systems and technologies expanded according to the top-secret Mosquito Protocol outlined in the addendum to the Global Progressive Mandate.

Proposed Director: Hester Vali

Legal and Judicial Commission. *Mandate:* To enforce with the full weight of the legal and judicial system the mandates and guidelines of the twelve Commissions. Working with the president, the Commission will develop and assist in the drafting of new legislative initiatives to propose to Congress with FCP Presidential Alliance objectives to enhance minority equity, expand prison reform, and reduce racism by criminalizing white and specifically Christian hate crimes. Commission to work with Education and Religion Commissions to establish strategies for employing the judicial system to root out right-wing religious churches and groups potentially resistant to the FCP Presidential Alliance mandates and take appropriate legal action.

Proposed Director: Judge Felix Harriman

Standards, Guidelines, and Mandates Commission. *Mandate:* To establish and monitor guidelines and standards regulating scientific exploration, industry, mining, ecological and pollution issues, climate issues, and the exploitation of global natural resources. Guidelines to be established enforcing each item of the overarching FCP Presidential Alliance agenda in conjunction with all Commissions in their fields and areas of control. Cultural, medical, religious, and ecological goals established, also subject to those of other Commissions, to provide framework for mandates of enforcement in all areas.

Proposed Director: Kanika Marland

Statehood Expansion and Unification Commission. *Mandate:* To explore methods, timetables, and strategies to gain public acceptance of unification with Mexico and the Central American countries, and develop a plan for establishing the borders of new states to be added to the US.

Proposed Director: Sally Foma

World Constitution Commission. *Mandate:* To work with United Nations and representatives of other countries to assess proposals, then to draft a world constitution, to which all nations will subordinate their individual governing institutions. This will entail a long process of negotiation and multiple drafts, changes, discussion, and compromise. The Commission will spearhead these efforts to keep momentum focused toward final acceptance, passage, and implementation.

Proposed Director: Rufus Biggs

And most secretive of all, thought Mike, leaning back in his chair and exhaling slowly—the enforcement arm, a private Palladium-directed police force and security apparatus, probably set up initially as a division of the FBI whose official mandate would be shielded from public view.

Intelligence, Police, and Enforcement Commission. *Mandate:* To work with the various compliance agencies to investigate infractions and enforce the mandates, directives, standards, and guidelines established by all twelve commissions. Full investigative, arrest, detainment, and incarceration authority shall reside in the Commission, subject to and in concert with the guidelines and recommendations of its twin enforcement arm, the Legal and Judicial Commission.

Proposed Director: Chief Lamar Royce

Mike set the papers aside.

What *wasn't* in his directive he would keep to himself, the fact that the Commissions would effectively represent a governmental arm of Palladium. By calling it the *Presidential Alliance*, or PDA, few would recognize Pd as the symbol for Palladium, atomic number 46 on the periodic table. Only its members would know that PDA secretly referred to the *PallaDium Alliance*—the fusing of the organization's originating names.

He was, of course, the obvious one to lead the twelve Commissions.

Thus far he had been satisfied to work toward his objectives behind the scenes. One day his name would stand beside that of Karl Marx and Barack Obama as the third millennium's architect of the new progressive world order. It might soon be time for him to step out of the shadows and into the limelight. That day would come when the president named *him* Chairman of the PDA.

Who could tell what the next few years might bring? His father was aging. He would be on the League before long. Maybe he would run for president in 2056, Mike thought with a smile.

He continued working late into the night. When he finally printed the latest draft of his work, he knew it was not the final document. It would remain a work in progress. But he had taken the vision of his mentor several major strides forward. This document would provide the foundation of what was to come.

He would soon succeed in bringing Viktor Domokos's Final Declaration into the Oval Office—not something even Viktor could have accomplished. Rhodes himself would never know that the ideas he considered his own had originated at the bedside of the dying Romanian financier. Nor, Mike thought, would anyone ever know his own role in Viktor's final days.

As architect of an agenda of vastly more sweeping globalist progressivism, they would know his name one day. Whether or not he decided to follow Jefferson Rhodes into the Oval Office, a Nobel Prize with his name on it was not out of the question. Thus far Palladium had not been successful in gaining a clear majority on the Nobel committee. They owned Congress, the Motion Picture Academy, and the media. But the Nobel committee had eluded them. By the time he was president or in his second or third term, they should easily have that too under their control.

Mike Bardolf wasn't given to self-analysis. He was so confident in his ability to get anything done, he didn't need it. He knew he could get people to do things, even *think* things, never realizing that he was manipulating them to his bidding. He had wormed his way into the inner sanctum of Viktor Domokos's mind, just as he had that of Jefferson Rhodes. Eventually neither man could do without him. He not only made himself indispensable according to that basic principle of Business 101, he had invaded their most private psyches by stealth.

The one man he had never been able to manipulate was his father. But the dynamic of the father-son relationship was complex. The long shadow cast by his grandfather was not easy for either Loring or Michael Bardolf to escape.

42

Expanding the Brotherhood

Early September 2050

IT HAD been two weeks since Grigor Popov's letter arrived at the Marshall home. They'd heard nothing further and were obviously concerned.

The expansion of the Popov fellowship of friends was far from unique. Wherever the principles of Stirling Marshall's *Benedict Brief* were discussed and lived, the enthusiasm was electric. For all Timothy and Jaylene knew, there might be dozens of groups around the country by now, perhaps hundreds, many of which they knew nothing about. Groups began, splintered off into others, which in turn spawned more.

When Timothy and Jaylene next visited David and the plight of the Popovs came up, he merely nodded and let out a thoughtful sigh.

"It begins," he said. "I fear this is but a hint of things to come. A sinister tribulation has been fomenting for years and is about to boil over. It may not be with guns here in America, though arrests may well come. One thing is certain—freedoms will be taken away—freedom of belief, freedom of thought. The remnant may eventually be forced underground."

"Do you seriously think it will come to that?" asked Jaylene.

"I do. And in my lifetime," replied David. "It is coming—sooner than many realize. The halcyon days of meeting together openly apart from the church of man will not last. The world and the Ally will see to that. Man's church does not like its flaws exposed any more than progressivism wants its hypocrisies revealed in the sunlight of truth."

"I wish there was something we could do to help Grigor and Anya," said Jaylene.

"Has there been word from the Sievers?" asked David.

Timothy shook his head. "They received much the same message we did."

When Timothy arrived back from Jessup a week later after a special lecture on the Reformation, on a day when Jaylene had no classes and had remained home, the enthusiasm was visible all over her face.

"You look like you've had a good day away from school!" laughed Timothy.

"You know how we invite people who write us to visit if they're ever in California—and how many of the foreign letters say they wish they could meet us?"

Timothy nodded. "I sent a letter to Monika and Fynn in Germany two weeks ago," he said, "and said that very thing, especially now that their fellowship has grown through nearby farming communities."

"That's what I've been trying to tell you!" said Jaylene. "You won't believe it. They wrote back—they want to come!"

"Monika and Fynn!"

"They're talking about mid-spring, maybe March or April. They're already investigating plane fares."

"That's fantastic!" exclaimed Timothy.

"They're not the only ones. We heard from six couples today, all expressing the same thing—the desire to come and meet us. It can't be a coincidence. It's a sign, Timothy. I think God is saying the time for waiting has done its work. The seeds have been planted. It's time to think more publicly about what we're doing—to open it up. God is preparing to expand the vision, I'm sure of it."

"What are you thinking—that it's time to make my father's *Brief* public?"

"Probably not that. God will have to lead more specifically before we take that step. But I sense something stirring. There was another letter from the Campbells in Scotland. Their group is still growing.

Two of their people have started groups of their own—one in Glencoe, another in Spean Bridge. So many of the people we've written to have started their own groups. It may be time to get them together."

"An amazing idea. What a thing that would be. The Constables in London wrote last week too. Maybe God is indeed saying that a new season is dawning."

"But look— this is the best news of all," said Jaylene, handing a letter to Timothy. He recognized the handwriting immediately.

"Grigor!" he exclaimed, then quickly scanned the letter. "They're safely in Poland!"

He finished the single page and glanced up at Jaylene. "I don't know why but somehow this confirms exactly what you were saying—that we need to get together with these people and these groups that are springing up. What a joy it would be to meet Grigor and Anya!"

"We could raise enough money in our own group to bring them here."

"Everyone would consider it a privilege! Imagine our people being intimately connected to a remnant fellowship in Russia. We've known that God's drawing out, the spiritual rapture out of man's church, has been taking place quietly and invisibly for years. This is such a personal and present example of the persecution that will increasingly accompany it."

"You're right," said Jaylene excitedly. "Our people will *want* to help!"

"If we announced it in the *Master's Helps Newsletter*, the response would be enormous."

"Why don't we extend an invitation in the spring?" Jaylene went on, "An open invitation to people who have written us, like the Popovs and those who wrote today, to meet and mix with others who share the same vision—in the States—anyone who's written us!"

Timothy laughed. "What if five hundred decided to come?" he said.

"Can you imagine that!" laughed Jaylene. "It would be wonderful. How many people do you suppose have written to your folks and us through the years?"

"Easily thousands. We'll use both ranches this time—David's *and* the Circle F. We'll put up tents!"

"But you know what your father said, and I've heard you say it too, Tim—the message of the true Church, the message of the remnant, the message of discipleship-obedience is for the few not the many. There *wouldn't* be five hundred who came. It wouldn't be a new version of Woodstock. Coming together to celebrate self-sacrifice, obedience, separation from the world, and living by the commands—that's not a message that will attract multitudes. That vision might only attract ten."

"You're probably right," nodded Timothy. "But we know of eight or ten other groups similar to ours in the States. That number is growing—not just in Scotland and Germany and Russia."

"The numbers don't matter anyway. Even if it's only ten or fifteen—or five hundred if that's what God has in mind!—what an opportunity for however many it is to taste and experience bonds of unity outside a traditional church setting and to be an intimate part of what God is doing around the world."

"That's my father's vision of the church—*people* meeting fellow disciples. Obviously, those from our group would help us host it."

"What about the church—Foothills? There are still rumors going around."

"Maybe that can't be helped much longer. A new season is dawning."

"And your father's *Brief*?"

"I don't know. We'll have to see how God leads. It may be that some, even if only one or two or three, *may* be intended to read it. I'm sensing no answer to that question yet. It *may* even be in God's plan for my father's vision to flourish first in another country, in which case it may be time for the seeds of the *Brief* to be planted elsewhere—Scotland, Russia, Germany—perhaps even Israel. There is Rabbi Hoderov who has been writing regularly. Hana and Gidon are so eager to bring Jesus's commands to the land where he walked and first spoke to hungry and receptive hearts."

"You truly think the *Brief* may be intended to take root elsewhere?"

"I don't know. Yet I question whether it is even possible here. America's spiritual demise may not provide the best soil for the next era in the growth of the Church—the remnant Church, the Tribulation Church.

One thing I am certain of, that there are probably other documents similar to my father's *Brief* being written around the world even now. Rabbi Hoderov mentioned that he was writing something in Hebrew."

Timothy paused thoughtfully, then slowly nodded. "I think it's time—let's pray specifically about a gathering of some kind."

"It will be difficult to keep it secret. People in the church and the community will find out."

"It's probably time we don't worry about that."

After lengthy talks with Mark, Grace, David, and Heather, Timothy and Jaylene set plans in motion for a gathering of readers and the FCL group for early spring at David Gordon's ranch. If too many people expressed an interest, they would assess the logistics of also using the Forster ranch. For now they merely set a date in early April, then began praying specifically that God would bring those who needed to be there.

Though they decided against quite so public an announcement as the *Master's Helps Newsletter*, the gathering was announced in personal letters sent out over the next two months to give people time to make plans.

43

Letters Crossing the Country

SUMMER 2050

THE CORRESPONDENCE between Heather Marshall and Todd Stewart was sporadically regular during the five weeks since his leaving California. That Todd had been circuitously *en route* back to the East Coast for three of those weeks meant that most of the letters—four in all—came addressed to Heather from Todd, while he, on the road, was unable to receive any of hers that were piling up in his mailbox in DC.

July 29, 2050

Dear Heather,

This evening I met with Rev. Hutchins's wife and mother, Deidra and Eloise.

I took two days driving up to Seattle after leaving you, taking the long way through Oregon so I could see Crater Lake—a spectacular sight. I spent the night in a motel in a small town in the middle of Oregon, drove the rest of the way up yesterday, then today made arrangements to meet with the Hutchinses. It's late now—I just returned from Eloise Hutchins's house. I'm too keyed up to sleep for a while.

Obviously, it was an emotional visit—more tears than laughter. But Rev. Hutchins's wife and mother were wonderfully gracious to me—accepting, kind, understanding. It was as if my apologies opened wellsprings of love within them. When I explained the remorse I felt for contributing to the negative press about their son and husband and how it had begun a process of reevaluation and change within me, from that moment on I might as well have been one of Rev. Hutchins's best friends like Mr. Forster.

Though it was a visit of only two hours, I know that what happened this evening will never leave me. I drove away from Sacramento having experienced—as I fumblingly tried to explain—what I can only call the reality of the Christians I was meeting. But tonight, after being with Deidra and Eloise, I realized I'd experienced something equally different that was just as new.

That was forgiveness. They had every reason to resent me, even hate me. But they forgave me for what I had done. It was the same with the Jansens. They, too, opened their hearts to me. Somehow the force of simple forgiveness had lain dormant since my time in Wyoming. Suddenly tonight it exploded within me like a tidal wave. What an unbelievable power is contained in forgiveness.

It was extraordinary. It was like being washed all over with fresh cleansing water of healing. For the first time in several years, I felt free of the guilt I had been carrying about my role in spreading so many falsehoods.

I don't know what more to say. I'm close to tears. I think I will just say good night.

Todd

August 1–5, 2050

Dear Heather,

I left Seattle and am staying with an old friend in Denver. I've written bits of this and have been adding to it over several days.

I've been in no hurry, especially not knowing what I will do when I get back to Washington. So I am taking my time, deciding my route day by day, stopping often, taking side trips as the mood strikes me.

I've also been reading the three books you gave me—reading them slowly, trying to absorb many new things. I thought I was beginning to understand Christianity after talking so much with you. Now I realize how little I really still understand.

Funny, the one Marshall I want to know more than the others is . . . well, obviously I mean you! But I am reading books by your grandfather, your father, and your mother, and getting to know them instead. They are all amazing writers and able to articulate such remarkable truths and insights. These are like no books I've ever read. My goodness—your mother's unbelievable take on the beginnings of the universe! Who would ever put Einstein and Genesis together like she has done! To use an old-fashioned expression—these books are blowing my mind! The principles of Christianity explained like I've never heard. I wish you had written a book too!

I drove from Seattle over the Cascades, through Idaho and Montana and down into Yellowstone, where I spent two days. Then Jackson Hole and Laramie where I visited with the Jansens again. They invited me to stay the night. Of course I told them all about my visit with you and your people there. They knew about your grandfather and have his book on the commandments. We had a very interesting conversation lasting till after midnight. I'll have to tell you more about it.

Then on to Denver where I am now. The friend I am staying with is a confirmed atheist. Imagine our conversations! Now it's me trying to explain this new kind of Christianity to him, when I'm just trying to figure it out myself!

I'm not sure how I will go from here—probably across the plains, through the Ozarks, and to Kentucky. I'm feeling strangely random and spontaneous. My year in Scotland must have done that to me. I am hoping the drive will help put what we talked about into perspective.

I hope you are working on my request for a 100-word—or 500!—version of Heather Marshall's "What comprises the essence of Christianity?" I am eager for it, yet will be patient.

I know important things like that take time to sift and sort and settle in the brain. Even if it does not come together for you in a way that you can set down on paper for a year, I will wait. Though I hope it will not be that long! I so value your thoughts and perspectives!

Todd

August 11, 2050

Heather,

After arriving in Kentucky, I contacted Dr. Reyburn. I am scheduled to meet him at Hillsgrove tomorrow.

I will tell you later about my travels from Seattle, my conversations with the Jansens, and then my atheist friend in Denver, who now thinks I'm nuts . . .

Todd

August 14, 2050

Heather,

I had the most extraordinary visit with Charles and Regina Reyburn. They knew who I was and I sensed their reservations at first, especially from Mrs. Reyburn. But like the others, they soon realized I was sincere and warmed up. It was a different kind of visit. I didn't have anything specifically to apologize for. But I wanted Dr. Reyburn to know how important his book had been in this journey of reevaluation I'm on, if that's what it should be called. Everything has worked together—my gradual qualms about my reporting, his book, my time in Scotland, meeting the Jansens, then you and your family and the Forsters, then the impact of the three books you gave me. In a sense meeting the Reyburns was like bringing the whole process full circle.

I don't think it ever came up when I was in California but I was surprised to learn that the Reyburns knew your father. One more unexpected connection in this strange but wonderful circle of people I am meeting. And to think it all began when I saw a young woman walking away from the crowd along Puget Sound! Meeting the people, I mean. My reevaluations began in 2046 when I was covering the Hillsgrove graduation. That's why meeting the Reyburns is like coming full circle. Flying home to DC from here is when I first began to ask what kind of person I was and wanted to be. When I told Dr. Reyburn that, a strange look came over his face.

"I remember that night well," he said. "I watched your broadcast. Even though it angered me, I saw something in you that told me what I was witnessing and what you were saying did not represent the real you. I was prompted to pray for you that night, which I did, and which I have continued to do ever since. I had the sense that God's hand was on you. I knew we would meet some day. Then yesterday you called, said you were in town, and asked if we could meet. I could only smile to myself. I was not surprised."

What an extraordinary thing for someone to say, that God's hand was on me. I don't even know what that means. It's one more thing—among many!—that I have to process. I'm at last on the final leg of my trip and should arrive back in DC in several days.

Actually, I'm not anxious to get back to the city. What will I do then? That's the big question.

Thinking of you more than ever.

Todd

Todd's first stop after driving into DC was to pick up his mail. Walking into his apartment fifteen minutes later, he hardly glanced around, only set down his two bags, turned on a light, then flopped down in his favorite chair with the seven letters from Heather that were waiting for him. He glanced over the postmark dates, then opened and read them in order.

July 27–31, 2050

Dear Todd,

I know you just left yesterday and won't read this for a week or two or three or however long it takes you to get home. But I had to write, if for no other reason than to tell you how much I enjoyed your visit and how honored I still feel that you would want to visit. I will never forget. Just that you came all this way goes deep into my heart.

Life here gradually resumed its usual pattern, though how can it ever be "normal" again. It seems that everything has changed. I was a little quiet for a few days, trying to absorb many things. It wouldn't surprise me if you were feeling much the same—you were getting many new ideas thrown at you! But it was fun talking together. I loved your questions!

There's something I wanted to say to you when you were here but never found a good time. I don't know exactly how to say it. It's like a compliment, though it's not quite that either. I wanted to tell you how much I appreciated your open-mindedness to ideas that were new to you. Most people automatically reject or argue against ideas they are unfamiliar with—especially religious or political ideas. The doors of their minds are closed against new things. I don't know why people are that way. How are you going to learn if you don't expose yourself to new ideas?

But you were full of questions. You were eager to learn. I love that. Maybe you will decide in the end that you don't agree with some of the things I said about Christianity. And by the way I haven't forgotten what you asked me to do! But whether you agree or not hardly matters. You are thinking about things open-mindedly. That will lead you to truth in the end. I hope I can say the same of myself, that even though my beliefs are strong and I have held them for a long time, I want to continue growing all my life, growing into new understanding of ideas I haven't even thought of yet.

That's what I wanted to say! You are an open-minded man, hungry to know truth, and I admire that in you.

I'm trying to imagine where you are. How long did you spend in Seattle? How did your visit with Mrs. Hutchins go? Where are you NOW? I guess I will have to wait until I hear from you. But it's hard to be patient!

At last I am back to work on my regular schedule, and life is settling, like I say, back to normal—horses and old people, my two jobs and my two loves. I am so fortunate. I often wonder how it can be that I get paid for doing what I enjoy so much.

Let me tell you about my days. I don't want to bore you, but writing about it is a way to prolong your visit. Besides, I want you to know what I do, and I "think" you might be interested . . .

Okay, I've been adding to this letter for four days and it's getting way too long. I'm sure you will be bored with all the little details of my life! But I'm going to send it anyway.

Heather

August 4

Dear Todd,

I just got your letter after your visit with the Hutchins. It sounds like it was wonderful. It made me so happy to read it. When people come together in forgiveness and reconciliation, it is a wonderful thing. Do you mind if I share your letter with Mark and Grace? I know they will rejoice. But it may be too private and you would rather I didn't. I could feel your emotion as I read. I will say nothing about it until I hear from you.

Now more about my uneventful life . . .

Heather

August 11

Dear Todd,

Your "travelogue" letter from Seattle to Denver was so fun. It's a lot more interesting than mine. I hope you won't get tired of me writing almost every day!

I laughed so hard when you described your conversations with your friend. I know you still have a lot of questions, but if you keep that up you're going to get a reputation as a religious fanatic. Don't worry—I won't spread the news around Washington!

I'm glad you're enjoying the books. You're right about my mom and dad and grandfather. Talk about feeling like the low man on the intellectual totem pole! That's how I feel in this family. But I'm proud of them and am honored to be their daughter and granddaughter. As for me writing a book—forget it. I never could. So you might as well quit bringing it up!

Ginger has been pestering me with questions about you ever since you left. I think she has a crush on you. You'd better watch yourself!

Everyone sends their greetings and they're all interested in your travels. I tell them where you are but don't give any more details. I feel strongly about not sharing other people's business. Not that you're saying anything private, it's just something I take seriously. So even with mundane things, I try not to pass along other people's news. If you want me to share your letters, that's your call to make.

I had a really interesting exchange with an older woman at the care home yesterday . . .

Heather

August 16

Todd,

This is hardly a letter, but I'm going to be really busy the rest of the week—two of the other nurses at the care home are sick and I will be working twelve-hour days. I don't know when I'll have a chance to write again and I wanted you to know I received the letter you sent from Louisville. I enjoyed it so much!

Now I am off to work and may not have time to write again for a while. But I'm thinking of you as you resume your life in Washington.

Heather

44

New Victims of the Ally

SEPTEMBER 2050

FIRST EVANGELICAL Fellowship in Wichita, Kansas, suffered that common malady of self-proclaimed "enlightened" and "Bible-believing" churches in evangelicalism of thinking too highly of itself. It's head pastor, youth leader, and worship team had all been invisibly infected with the virus, which had spread to its elders and many of the assumed leaders of the church.

Gerald Stevens, longtime member of good standing who had contributed thousands to the church coffers over the years, had the singular misfortune to be too plain spoken for his own good. His wife Rebecca, former public school teacher, appalled by the gender and sexual atrocities being indoctrinated into children through the progressive public school system, had resigned and helped start what was now a thriving alternative in the form of Evangelical Fellowship's own private Christian school. It was unusual in being funded entirely by the church. Parents and students had to pay for nothing but books and materials, which amounted to less than two hundred dollars a year.

As a result of its financial policy and growing reputation for educational excellence, it was now the largest private school in the region, with more requests for new students than it could handle. The church, too, was prospering, adding buildings to its sprawling church and school campus. Talks were in the serious stage of building a college on the site.

All these factors combined to create the illusion—thoroughly endorsed by head pastor, youth leader, worship team, and school administration—that God was blessing and prospering First Evangelical because its head pastor, youth leader, worship team, and school administration were all perfectly in tune with God's leading and thus functioning in all ways in the center of his will. If a certain pride accompanied that assumption, it was only the humble pride of God's faithful and obedient servants to recognize the fruits of their obedience.

Gerald Stevens wasn't so sure. For several years he had detected unsavory whiffs of a very different spirit creeping into the church he loved. They were subtle and indistinct, and he did his best to ignore them. After returning from the weekend with the Marshalls at the Bar JG ranch in California in 2048, experiencing humility and unity with such a cross section of brothers and sisters, without a trace of puffed-up self-importance, the aroma prevalent during the worship hour every Sunday at First Evangelical Fellowship grew unmistakable—it was the stench of self-righteousness.

Within a month Gerald could no longer in good conscience continue. It broke his heart. But he knew he had no choice.

When he finally shared with her his grief over the direction of the church, he was almost shocked to discover that Rebecca felt exactly the same.

"I didn't want to say anything," she said. "But everyone at the school is the same. I take that back—not everyone. There are many truly good and sincere people, just as there are in the church. But if the leadership is setting the tone, it filters down and infects everything. You even hear the children parroting back a *We are the best* attitude that is in the air, even if no one actually says it. I wasn't sure how much longer I could remain. I love that school. I helped start it. But it's so changed now."

After more discussion and prayer, they reached the decision to leave the church. Rebecca finished out the final weeks of the school year, then handed in her resignation. They had been home-schooling their own four children for the two years since.

For such a high-profile family to leave the church caused "talk." Everyone wanted to know why. Gerald did not mind telling them he could no longer be part of it. And he was all too willing to tell them *exactly* why.

"It's become a country club," he said. "A wealthy country club so in love with itself that its leaders and members can't see the worldliness creeping in everywhere. The church is adapting to the world's methods and values. Spiritual pride blinds everyone's eyes from being able to perceive it."

All their friends knew that Gerald and Rebecca had spent a weekend in California not long before with a group of Christians they knew nothing about. They attributed the change to strange new views they must have picked up from them. When almost immediately Gerald became vocal in criticizing certain practices of First Evangelical, followed a month later by Rebecca's resignation from the school, then in the fall pulling their own children out to home-school them, word began to circulate that they had become involved in an anti-church separatist cult that had originated—where else!—in California's cauldron of socialist ideas, progressivism, and rampant ungodliness.

"But they *are* still Christians?" someone asked Rebecca's sister.

"In a way, sort of," she replied. "At least I *think* so," she added, her expression and tone clearly causing doubt in the mind of her listener. "I'm not really sure if they're going to church anywhere else or *at all*. How can they be Christians if they're not going to church?"

"I heard they had joined a cult."

"I think it is something like a Christian cult. I don't really know much about it. Rebecca says they still believe, even that they still believe *in* the church but that they don't believe in having to *go* to church every Sunday. And she's reading strange books she got from the people in California."

"Have you read any of them?"

"She gave me one and I tried to read it, so I would know how to talk to her and show her how wrong she is. I couldn't understand enough of it to know what it was talking about. I gave it back and told her I wanted nothing to do with it."

"What was it about?"

"Something about the things Jesus *didn't* say and how important they were or something like that. Like I said, I could make no sense of it."

"That *does* sound like a cult. What about the children?"

"That's what I'm most concerned about. Who knows what they're being taught. They need to be around normal children."

"Is there something you can do? You are their aunt."

"We try, when they visit us. Steve's been talking to the two older ones and keeping them involved in the junior high group."

"Rebecca lets them go?"

"Oh no, we have to take the children behind their backs. She would have a fit if she knew they were still involved in the youth group. But we have to do what we can to keep them from being lured into whatever false teachings Gerald may be filling their minds with."

"Good for you. *Something's* got to be done to protect them. You and Steve are the logical ones to step in."

Aware of the increasing talk and of the attempts of Rebecca's sister to divide the children from their parents, she and Gerald told not a soul about the letter that arrived in the fall of 2050, two years after the rumors about them had begun to spread.

Dear Gerald and Rebecca,

As many of you know, the readership of our dear Stirling's books, and the mail we receive as a result, continues to expand, often in the most unlikely ways and into the most unexpected places.

As a result, we have felt a growing sense that it is time to provide an opportunity for a wider cross section of this expanding fellowship to meet with others in whom God's Spirit is quickening similar truths. The living stones of God's eternal Church are being called out and up and are being knit together. We see many evidences of it, even worldwide.

In our little corner of this growth, we feel it important to foster and grow the connections of that knitting and bonding, strengthening and unifying work. To that end, we are planning to host what for lack of a better word we will call a "gathering" of some of those, like yourselves, whom God has led to Stirling's writings. The tentative date of the gathering, to be held at the Bar JG ranch in the California foothills, will be the second weekend in April of next year. More information will be sent out as the time draws closer. For now we want to personally extend our invitation to you in hopes that you may be able to join us.

In the fellowship of our common life in God the Father and in his Son,

Timothy and Jaylene Marshall

Below in Jaylene's hand was added:

Forgive the formality of this note. Since your time with us two years ago, we think of you often, always fondly, and hope you and your children are doing well. It would be wonderful to see you again. Both of us hope you will be able to come.

Jaylene

Immediately Gerald and Rebecca marked the days on their calendar and wrote back saying they would be there, asking if children would be welcome as well.

Leaving them with Rebecca's sister, as they had before, was out of the question.

45

Mark in Washington

October 2050

IF MARK Forster felt like a fish out of water on Bainbridge Island among the country's movers and shakers, at least Grace, Ginger, and Heather were with him. Landing at Obama International in Washington, DC, in October, he felt isolated and alone.

He'd asked himself through the entire flight why he was doing this. He knew why—because he and the others felt God saying he should.

But *why?*

The entire underlying message of Stirling Marshall's *Benedict Brief*, was that the kingdom of God and kingdom of man were intrinsically and fundamentally disconnected. The words *My kingdom is not of this world* were emblazoned on the minds of everyone involved in the FCL group and the rapidly expanding network of fellowship groups.

Yet here he was at the heart of the kingdom of man! He was about to become involved in a presidential commission, even act as its chairman, whose purpose was to bring the kingdom of God into the kingdom of man—to mingle the two things that Jesus said could not coexist.

How could he live that truth and also fulfill Jeff's commission? He had no interest in politics, yet here he was at the nerve center of the political world.

What was God's purpose for him here?

A limousine was waiting, courtesy of the president. After a forty-minute drive, the black Cadillac pulled into the Michelle Obama

Professional Housing Complex. A key was given him by the driver, who departed without fanfare.

A minute later he walked inside his rooms. A fully stocked kitchen and bar, a huge fruit and nut basket on the table complemented the completely furnished luxurious two-bedroom apartment. Jeff should have known he wouldn't use the bar, thought Mark, though the room was probably standard fare.

He set his suitcase on the bed in one of the rooms, looked briefly through the packet with his name on it next to the fruit basket, then telephoned Grace.

"Well, I'm here," he said when she answered.

"Good flight?"

"Routine, you know—five hours in an airplane. But flying first class was a new experience," he laughed. "Amazing how the other half lives. I must say, it was nice."

"Don't get used to it!"

"I'm sure you're right. As long as Jeff is picking up the tab, I'll enjoy it while I can."

"How are the accommodations?"

"First class—just like the plane. I think this is where visiting diplomats and lobbyists and assorted bigwigs stay—two bedrooms, sitting room, kitchen, office. I hope you can come with me next time."

"So now what? Are you going out on the town tonight?"

Mark laughed. "You know me better than that! I'll order something to be delivered—turkey with swiss and avocado on whole wheat—and rice pudding, of course."

"If you can find it!"

"I'll stay in and watch TV or read. You know I brought Stirling's *Brief*—I may read it over again. I want its principles deeply rooted before I set foot in the Presidential Manor. Wise as serpents, you know. I need to have my wits about me."

"Just guard the *Brief* with your life. You're in the belly of the beast, so to speak. You don't want it falling into the wrong hands. When will you see Jeff?"

"I'm not sure, or even if I will. There was a packet left for me. I'm to be picked up at ten tomorrow morning and taken to the Presidential Manor. There I'll be briefed by the president's chief of staff in preparation for an eleven o'clock meeting with those Jeff has apparently lined up to be working with me on this commission. I'm sure more will become clear then."

"It will be an adventure—personal guest of the president. Do you feel important?"

"Intimidated is more like it. I've changed since those days when I was comfortable standing in front of a crowd. I'm not the man I once was, Grace."

"You're *more* the man you were."

Mark laughed wryly. "If you say so. I guess I should take your word for it. You know me better than anyone."

"Then do take my word for it."

"I'll try. But now I think I will go out for a walk about the capital. It's 4:30 here. I want to see the monuments, though the new names and colors reflecting anti-white diversity is . . . I don't know what it is—certainly not representative of our country."

"Ugh—I hate it," said Grace. "They've turned them into monstrosities."

"I want to see the city anyway."

"Just watch yourself. I don't want all that progressivism rubbing off on you. I'm afraid Jeff's trying to corrupt you."

"Not a chance."

"I love you."

"And I love you. I'll talk to you tomorrow."

"Oh, that reminds me. David and Timothy and Jaylene and the Wests and as many as we could get together are meeting tomorrow afternoon to pray for you. I thought of it after you left."

Mark's two-hour walk through the streets of the capital and the National Mall, to Capitol Hill and back, past the Supreme Court building where he wondered if Linda was present, turned out less depressing than he had envisioned. The liveliness and energy of the city was invigorating. He was reminded again that people were still people, with the innate goodness of their Creator imbedded within them. Even in this hothouse of liberalism, most of those he saw were families showing their children the capital, businessmen and women, probably people of note whom he did not know, shoppers and storekeepers and all manner of men and women and children of every size and shape and color—mostly normal in appearance. Every one had been created in God's image. In spite of the lies with which most had been indoctrinated, they were yet *God's* men and women and children.

A great love for the universal brotherhood of humanity rose and filled his heart. It was all he could do not to stop each one on the street and say, "You dear child of God—you have a Father who loves you more than you can imagine. Let me tell you about him!"

He stopped at a deli on his way back to the apartment, ordered his turkey sandwich, though without the accompanying rice pudding, and returned to his temporary digs in an exuberant mood of optimism.

46

Surprise Visitor

AFTER HIS walk and stop at the delicatessen late the previous afternoon, the thought of breakfast the following morning never entered Mark's mind. The room was well supplied with coffee, sweets, fruits, and a few rolls. Nevertheless, he decided to go out, found a restaurant almost adjacent to the complex which no doubt catered to its clientele, and enjoyed a light fare of yogurt, fruit, coffee, and an English muffin.

As he walked back to the building where his unit was located, about 8:30, he saw a familiar figure milling about, apparently waiting for him. Seeing Mark approach, he walked toward him with outstretched hand.

"Hello, Mr. Forster," he said as they shook hands. "I'm Bradon Rhodes. I don't know if you remember me."

"Of course I do," smiled Mark. "I recognized you immediately. How nice to see you again. Did your father send you? Are you my ride?"

"No!" laughed Bradon. "I'm afraid my old rattletrap would hardly be fit to transport a presidential guest! But I knew you were coming and I wanted to come by and say hello and welcome you to the capital."

"That is kind of you. Would you like to come into my temporary home?"

"Oh, sure—if you don't mind. If you're not busy with something else."

"What would I be busy with!" laughed Mark, leading the way. "Someone is picking me up at ten. I have no plans. I think my week's agenda is being set by your father."

They went inside, sat, and chatted informally.

"My grandparents are in town too," said Bradon. "My grandmother says she knew you back when you and my dad were boys at some camp or another."

"Yes, we were quite the team back then!"

"You'll have to tell me about it. My dad never talks about his boyhood."

"I remember your grandmother fondly—please give her my warm regards."

"I will. She said she would like to see you, if you have time."

"I don't see why I wouldn't. I would love to see her again. Are your grandparents staying at the Manor?"

"No—they always stay at the Hilton. My grandfather would like nothing more than to be at the Manor, but my grandmother won't hear of it."

"And when your grandfather visits alone? Or does he?"

"He does. Then he roams the Manor like he owns it. He always dreamed of being president—at least that's my take on it. How's your wife, and . . . uh, Ginger?"

"Very well. Ginger's busy with her final year at Jessup."

"It's a Christian college, isn't it?"

"It is, yes."

"Tell her hello for me, and your wife."

"I certainly will."

When Mike Bardolf drove into the parking lot of the Michelle Obama complex, he saw the familiar old dilapidated green Mustang in the parking lot.

He swore under his breath.

What is that fool doing here! he muttered, then parked some distance away, and settled in to wait.

A few minutes before ten a knock came to the door. Bradon and Mark rose.

"That is probably my ride," said Mark.

He opened the door to see a Secret Service agent standing stoically in front of him. Observing Bradon behind Mark, the agent appeared to flinch briefly, as much as trained Secret Service agents ever displayed emotion. He nodded imperceptibly.

"Mr. Forster," said the agent, "I am here to transport you to the Presidential Manor."

"Yes, thank you. Just let me get my coat and briefcase."

He turned back into the room.

"Thank you for the visit, Bradon," he said, shaking the young man's hand. "Hopefully we will see one another again."

Bradon smiled and nodded, then left the apartment, nodding somewhat stiffly to the agent as he passed.

Five minutes later Mark was on his way through the streets of the busy capital. Minutes later they passed through the gates of the Presidential Manor, now painted in garish rainbow colors to reflect the diversity of the no longer "whiteness" of American society.

Even as Mark was going through the formality of showing his identification and credentials in his packet to the security guard at the gate, Mike Bardolf was letting himself into Mark's apartment at the Michelle Obama Complex with his pass key.

He glanced around briefly, then began a thorough search of the rooms, including bathroom, medicine cabinet, closet, and dressers, taking pictures of everything as he went. The tiniest detail might be useful later. Mike Bardolf was a thorough man and left no stone unturned, nor bedsheet, toothbrush, suitcase, book, or handwritten papers on the nightstand uninvestigated and photographed.

When he left thirty minutes later, the most minute investigation could not have detected a hair out of place. He was a man skilled in his work. Nothing betrayed a hint of his presence.

47
Presidential Commission

MARK WAS escorted to the West Wing and a small sitting room, complete with coffee and tea and assorted fruit and breakfast things. There he was left alone. Five minutes later the president's chief of staff walked in.

"Hello, Mr. Forster," he said, "I am Trent Randall, the president's chief of staff."

The two men shook hands. On behalf of the president and all of us here, welcome to Washington and to the Presidential Manor."

"Thank you, Mr. Randall."

"Are your accommodations acceptable? Is there anything you need?"

"Nothing. I am most comfortable."

"If there is anything that comes to your mind, please don't hesitate to get in touch with me personally. I will give you my private number."

"Thank you. I am sure everything will be fine."

"I have a packet here for you to review. It mainly contains a dossier on the other eleven men and women who will be at this morning's meeting and an agenda of the topics to be covered."

"Who will be moderating the meeting?" asked Mark.

"The president will meet with you all, give you some initial guidelines, then he will turn the meeting over to you."

Mark nodded, though he took Randall's final words with surprise.

"I'll leave you to familiarize yourself with the materials. Someone will call for you shortly before eleven. Help yourself to coffee and anything else."

Once again Mark was left alone, overwhelmed and more than a little bewildered but mostly intrigued with what would happen next. He had indeed entered a new world!

At five minutes before eleven, having reviewed the materials and recognizing only one name on the list, he was surprised when the door opened and the president walked in.

"Mark, my friend!" said Jeff exuberantly, approaching and shaking Mark's hand vigorously.

"Mr. President," said Mark.

"Please, Mark, I thought we dispensed with the formality last time."

"Just trying to observe protocol now that I am on your team, so to speak."

"That you are."

"I didn't expect you to see me personally."

"It's the least I could do. Come with me," Jeff added, turning back toward the door. "I'll escort you to the meeting and we'll get started."

"I'm still not entirely certain what you want me to do," said Mark as they started down the hallway of the West Wing. The place was alive with activity. Everyone they passed nodded respectfully at the president, casting Mark expressionless glances which he interpreted as silently meaning, "Who is *that* guy?"

Jeff turned at the corner of the corridor, opened a door, and Mark was shocked to find himself alone with the president of the United States in the Oval Office.

"Oh, my goodness!" he exclaimed softly, then caught himself.

Jeff laughed. "You are a special guest with an important new role to play in my administration," he said. "And in the country. Why shouldn't you and I meet here together. Sit down, Mark," he added as he sat behind the Obama desk that had replaced the historic Resolute desk that had been the centerpiece of the office for more than a century. "We'll just take a minute or two here before joining the others in the Roosevelt Room across the hall. I wanted to answer your question about what I expect you to do."

"Thank you. I still feel pretty much in the dark."

"That will change. I will explain my objectives to everyone in a few minutes. Much will come clear for you. Then I will leave you to chair the remainder of the meeting, fielding suggestions and moderating the discussion between the twelve of you preparatory for future meetings and an action plan which each of you will carry to the leaders of your respective constituencies. I presume the significance of the number of members I have chosen to sit on the Commission is not lost on you."

"Of course not."

"Notwithstanding its Jewish reference, I hope it will be an incentive for you all to bring groundbreaking change and unity to the religious world. The only other expectation I have is for you to appear with me in a press conference which I have scheduled in the press briefing room for the day after tomorrow. At that time I will announce the formation of the Commission, introduce you, and explain the high priority I place on the religious tradition and roots of our nation. I hope you will be up to fielding a few questions from the press."

"It would not be my first choice of pleasurable activities, but if it is what you want, I am willing."

Jeff laughed. "Good. After the press conference your responsibilities for this initial time getting the Commission set up will be concluded. You may stay on as long as you like or change your flight and return home whenever you want. Just talk to Trent. His people can make all the arrangements. The apartment is yours. Keep the key. It will be yours to use anytime throughout what I hope is a long partnership between us. Bring Grace next time. We will pick up all expenses for you both, of course. I would love to show her the Presidential Manor."

"Thank you, Jeff. That is very kind of you."

"Good," said Jeff. "I have individual packets for each of the individuals you will meet. I want you to distribute them. They will provide the basis for your discussions when I leave you alone."

He rose, came out from behind the desk, picking up the twelve packets, and handed them to Mark. "Let's go meet the others and get started."

Mark followed out the door where the two corridors met and to the Roosevelt Room, whose interior corner door sat directly opposite that of the Oval Office.

As they walked in, Mark's eleven co-designates rose from where they sat around the spacious and historic room.

"Hello everyone!" said Jeff expansively.

"Mr. President," said most of them in unison.

"Please, be seated," said Jeff amiably. "You have probably mostly met each other by now. Let me introduce the man who will act as chairman of this historic new Commission, my friend of, what is it, Mark, thirty-five years I think—Mark Forster from California."

Mark smiled and nodded, then proceeded to greet and shake hands with his new colleagues as Jeff walked around the table and introduced each one in turn. The full process, complete with Jeff's good-natured comments to each man and woman, took six or eight minutes, succeeding in breaking the ice before they all sat at the long rectangular table.

Mark immediately noticed the politically correct mix of individuals as approximating the percentage of diversity of the US population, as much as could be achieved in a small group of twelve. Around the table sat seven women, five men—three whites, two Hispanics, two Middle Eastern men, three blacks, one Middle Eastern woman, and one Asian.

"I know in my discussions with several of you," began Jeff, "there was some question about my choice of a white, evangelical man to head the Religion Commission, when, it must be admitted, Protestant evangelicalism in our country is on the decline. By many standards, it would be considered out of the mainstream of current cultural and political thought. Not only is Mark Forster a longtime friend whom I trust, it is precisely because of the challenges evangelicalism as a belief system presents to the march of our nation's progress that it is imperative that it be brought harmoniously into unity with its brother and sister faiths.

"You all obviously differ in major respects from one another on points of doctrine and creed and even on the nature of what constitutes faith and divinity or *God*, if you will. Those differences are not our concern here. I most strongly exhort you not to allow yourselves to become diverted into debates about what constitutes the truest form of religion. Such is not our purpose but rather to discover how all your faiths, your denominations, your belief systems can learn from the rest of our society to function and live together in diversity and harmony. For the purposes of the Commission, truth does not matter. Unity, mutual respect, and harmony will be our fundamental objectives. You will find Mark to be a man of goodwill, tolerance, kindness, and respect toward all men and women."

He turned toward Mark, and Mark nodded with a smile of acknowledgment.

"Whatever preconceptions you may have about evangelicals, you will find that Mark Forster does not have a judgmental or bigoted bone in his body. He will treat every one of you with kindness and courtesy. I know the rest of you will do the same toward him and toward one another."

Nods and smiles and comments of agreement went around the table.

"My plan," Jeff went on, "is for each of you to discuss strategies and protocols for implementing my agenda in each of your constituencies. They will obviously be unique for each of you but will share certain characteristics in common. Hopefully you will discuss and brainstorm and give one another ideas that will work across the spectrum of the diverse religious world. Remember, we are not seeking strategies based on what are very different *ideas* of truth and practice and organization but strategies to reduce strife and foster unity *in the midst of those* differences.

"You twelve must lead the way by working in unity and harmony yourselves, avoiding debate, disagreement, and argument over what constitutes truth, while emphasizing mutual kindness, respect, and cooperation toward a common goal. You men and women are my generals. You will come up with strategies and plans to pass down to your colonels, who will pass them to their captains and other officers and down to the leaders, whether called pastors or priests or imams or pujas, who will pass them thence to their congregations and followers. In time, it is my goal that what you achieve together, perhaps generations from now, will result in a religious world from which argument, bickering, squabbling, and debate will have been eliminated. Religion should lead the way throughout all society and culture toward the true brotherhood of humanity based on love, acceptance, harmony, and respect for all."

Hear, hear! and other comments of approbation spread around the table. Jefferson Rhodes had them in the palm of his hand. And he knew it.

"I have chosen each of you personally and carefully," he continued, "with as much care and thought as if I were appointing a new Supreme Court justice. Your role may be equally important. Perhaps more so. You are all highly respected. I have the utmost confidence that history will look on each one of you as pivotal in ushering in a new era in which the diverse religious tradition of America, so foundational to our roots, again leads the people of this great nation forward into a human brotherhood and sisterhood of which we can be proud. You have my deep gratitude for the historic cause you are about to embark upon.

"Yours is truly a historic and unprecedented enterprise. Think of it as a second Reformation. But not one of dissent, protest, or division, but a new Reformation where all breaches of the past are healed—a magnificent coming together of all belief systems in One Faith, the true faith of the unity of our common humanity."

As he concluded, the group broke into applause. Most stood, comments of admiration went around the room as the president, beaming and acknowledging many of the remarks personally, went around, warmly shaking hands with all twelve, then slowly left the room.

Feeling suddenly alone and on the hot seat, Mark drew a deep breath and walked around the table distributing the individual packets.

"Well that's the Jeff Rhodes I knew in college!" he said, laughing. "Never at a loss for an inspiring word, always the life and soul of the party!"

The others laughed with him. The enthusiastic and optimistic mood continued as they reviewed the information in their packets, and gradually the discussions began in earnest.

48

Prayer in the Foothills

When DAVID Gordon, Timothy, Jaylene, and Heather Marshall, Dewitt and Pearl West and their daughter Diane and her husband, Rod Statler, and their four children, DS and Ora Layne, Faith Silva, and several others arrived at the Circle F that same day about two o'clock Pacific time, the first question on their lips to Grace and Bob and Laura was,

"Have you heard from Mark?"

Grace waited until they were all seated.

"Yes," she said. "Mark called a few hours ago. I told him you were all coming. He said he'd call for a video chat at 5:30 his time. That's in fifteen or twenty minutes. His first meeting apparently went well. He said he felt skepticism on some of the faces at first at having an evangelical leading them. Probably some of the others—he especially sensed it from Cardinal Jordan from New York—thought they should have been selected. But he said Jeff gave him such a rousing introduction and explained why Mark would be the chairman or chair*person*—Mark said he had to be careful to watch his terms—that by the end of their time together, all twelve were talking easily with one another."

"Even the cardinal?" asked Dewitt.

"Mark did say that he had to work a little harder to win her over!"

"I'm not surprised—she's quite the feminist, and lesbian too, I think."

"So Mark saw the president personally?" asked Diane.

"Yes, Jeff and he met privately in the Oval Office."

"Our Mark has indeed hit the big time!" said DS.

"It was only for a few minutes," Grace went on. "But Mark was suitably awed. He said that Jeff's introductory remarks to the group were so grandiose and enthusiastic that he almost started believing all the wonderful benefits to the world of progressivism. It was a typical Jeff snow job, he called it. But that's Jeff—he could convince anyone of anything—sell sand to the Arabs and snow to the Eskimos, as they say."

"Does he actually think he'll be able to accomplish anything in such an environment?" asked Jaylene.

"He has no idea," replied Grace. "He's approaching it with the knowledge that he is supposed to be there, that, if we were hearing the signals correctly, God's leading is behind it. At this point he has no idea why."

A ring sounded from her computer on the table.

"And there he is! You can ask him your questions for yourselves."

She rose, answered Mark's call and transferred his image to the television screen. Greetings went around the room when his face appeared larger than life in front of them.

"You all look great," he said. "It is really true when I say, *I wish you were here*. Or I wish I was there!"

"You look great too, Mark," said Timothy. "You don't *look* like you've been tainted."

"Ah, but have you seen *Invasion of the Body Snatchers*?" rejoined Mark with a smile.

"That's not funny, Mark!" said Grace.

"Don't worry," he laughed. "I have not been invaded, though I could feel the presence and power of the lies Dreher and Solzhenitsyn speak of all around me."

He went on to tell them in detail about the meeting and his time with Jeff.

"Oh, and I forgot to mention it to you on the phone, Grace," he said, "and this may interest you too, Ginger—Bradon Rhodes paid me a visit. He says hello to you both."

"Daddy, please!" exclaimed Ginger.

“We actually had a nice visit. He was very respectful. He made a much better impression than in Seattle. I like him.”

Many more questions followed. As the call gradually wound down, Mark circled back to what he had said earlier.

“It’s been a somewhat surreal experience,” he said. “All around the city, so noticeable in the White House—oops, the Presidential Manor—the atmosphere was electric. People were walking about and talking and conducting their affairs with energy and optimism in the radiant glow of their belief that everything was wonderful—that the new world of progressivism represented the apex of humanity’s evolution to a glorious new genderless, colorless, godless world of ultimate freedom from past restraints. It was so different from the imagery in *Body Snatchers*—dreary, silent, ominous. Yet they were no less people who had lost their identity. They were zombies.

“That’s what’s so deceptive about this new Invasion of the Mind Snatchers. The masses are equally deceived—zombies of a new kind . . . spiritual, intellectual, moral zombies. But the exuberance of their so-called new life is all a lie. It is the energy of the chicken with its head cut off—the dying energy of death. They don’t know that their minds and hearts have been invaded and taken over by the great lie of atheistic progressivism. They exist in a living death, yet they think people like us are to be pitied.

“Walking through the halls of the Presidential Manor—life and exuberance all about me—yet I was aware that I was walking through a tomb in which the sequel to *Body Snatchers* could be filmed. Progressivism puts people to sleep, into a mindless stupor where they lose the power to think rationally and with common sense about truth. We are truly living in *1984* meets the *Body Snatchers*.”

The great room of the ranch house was silent.

“A chilling thought,” said Timothy.

“And with that!” laughed Mark, “I will leave you all.”

The room was thoughtful and quiet for some time after the video call ended.

“In spite of it all,” said Mark’s father, “he looked and sounded good.”

Bob's comment broke the ice, though the mood remained serious. It was David who spoke next.

"I met young Jeff Rhodes once," he said. "Briefly, when I was over here to see you, Bob, that Christmas vacation when you had him here for a week. How interesting now, all these years later, to picture the two boyhood friends together, as unbelievable as it sounds, in the Oval Office. Yet what a poignant reminder of the truth of the two roads diverging in a yellow wood, and of the Lord's parable of the four kinds of human soils. Or even more apt, MacDonald's image of two persons being at the same place on a mountain, seemingly at the same point in life and the development of character. But one is on the way up and the other is on the way down. They are not on the same life road at all. Their paths have merely intersected for a fleeting moment of time.

"Though perhaps we did not see it at the time, or maybe we did but didn't realize it, Mark's heart was pointed upward toward God's high mountains. He set his direction in life early and it was to follow the path of truth into God's high places. His friend Jeff was destined to follow a different path because he had *not* set his inner compass in quest of character, truth, and the Fatherhood of those high mountains."

He paused thoughtfully.

"How ironic for Mr. Rhodes to speak to Mark's group about a new Reformation, as I think he said to you, didn't he, Grace? In truth, unless I am misreading the signs of the times and misreading God's purposes for the days ahead, a very different kind of new Reformation is coming—indeed has already begun—which people like Jefferson Rhodes will be incapable of seeing. It may be in front of us even now in the form of Stirling's writings. *We* may be the ones to whom has been entrusted truths that will lead to that Reformation. But it will be an invisible Reformation, unseen, too, by organized Christendom, an invisible rapture, an unseen coming out, an unapprehended awakening. We are not called to nail a document to the door of a cathedral but to spread the principles of truth invisibly, like salt and leaven. Even now—Mark was in the Oval Office today!—what greater platform could God have placed within our grasp to nail the new *95 Theses* to a new Wittenberg door for the whole world to see and hear.

"But such is not God's way this time. I do not believe Mark has been put in this position to make a proclamation to the world. I don't know what God's purpose for him is. But I do not believe that this represents an indication of a sudden change in Stirling's admonition to caution and secrecy. Perhaps a time may come when some proclamation of truth *will* be nailed to a door, though probably a door such as we cannot envision. We have to be wise as serpents, innocent as doves. We are biding our time. We must walk warily.

"These are dangerous times. We don't know what the Lord's will is. What will be the catalyst for the invisible Reformation? The catalyst may already have come. The coming out has certainly begun. The remnant is being birthed in preparation. I believe Mark's role in this for however long it lasts, is part of the coming Reformation. However, it will be much different than that expected by Mr. Rhodes."

49

A Reflective Mother

WITH NOTHING to do for the next day, and unable to prepare for the press conference other than to be in prayer, Mark made several telephone calls to reschedule his fight home the day after the press briefing.

He read most of the morning, planning to go out for the afternoon. Having seen the highlights of the capital, however, he had no definite plans.

A little after noon came a knock on the door. He was expecting no one, though perhaps Jeff was sending for him again.

He opened the door to see a stately older lady, dressed in obviously expensive attire, every hair in place. He only vaguely recognized her yet knew her instantly.

"Mrs. Rhodes!" he exclaimed.

"Hello, Mr. Forster," said Jeff's mother, smiling a little nervously. "I am surprised you recognized me."

"I could say the same!" replied Mark.

"You are in the news these days. Today's *Post* has a photo of you and Jeff together with the caption 'The President's Mystery Guest.' I don't think I would have recognized you walking along the street. You and Jeff were just boys when I saw you last."

Mark laughed. "Well, I confess that I have seen your photo too. You and your husband were prominent during and after the election. I *think* I would have known you even if it was only from our brief meeting when you brought Jeff down to Pinecroft that second summer we were at camp together. You are looking well. It is truly wonderful to see you again. I am honored. Please—come in."

"It is I who should be honored," said the president's mother, as they sat opposite one another in the apartment's sitting room. "You have had a very distinguished career, Mr. Forster."

"Please, it's *Mark*. Just think of me as your son's Pinecroft friend."

"Then I must be *Sandra*."

"Fair enough—though I'm not sure it is exactly parallel. Mine has hardly been a distinguished career alongside your son's. You must be very proud."

Mrs. Rhodes smiled.

"I suppose it depends on what one values in life," she replied a little slowly. "I know this may sound strange, but in a way your mention of Pinecroft is why I wanted to see you again."

She paused and her expression became thoughtful.

"Do you know why I sent Jeff to that camp?" she asked. "Against my husband's objections, I might add."

"As I recall, you mentioned back then that you had attended camp there yourself when you were young."

"I had. I grew up in California in a Christian home and attended summer camp at Pinecroft three times. I loved it. I was serious about being a Christian, or thought I was," she added with a sad smile. "Then I met Harrison and was swept into his world and never looked back. I suppose sending Jeff was mostly an attempt to see if I could point him in a more spiritual direction than it turned out I had followed. Too little too late. Guilt maybe, for being such a lukewarm Christian myself, so lukewarm that a handsome face and charming smile could sweep me off my feet and make me abandon what I thought was a meaningful faith. Well, not abandon, really. I suppose I have always continued to *believe* in an abstract sort of way. As for any meaningful attempt to live as a dedicated Christian—that all evaporated with my wedding vows. Politics is not a world in which it is easy to hold strong spiritual convictions. Politics seeps in and disintegrates conviction."

Again she paused.

"I have thought of you many times through the years, Mark. I have followed your career as a minister. I probably know more about you than you realize," she added, laughing lightly. "And God forgive me, I have envied your mother to have such a son of virtue and conviction who has lived his faith publicly. Don't get me wrong, I love Jeff to death. But he is a politician above all else. He is not what I would call a man of sterling character. That may be a terrible thing for a mother to say."

Another quiet silence settled over the room. Mark did not intrude.

"I don't know," Mrs. Rhodes went on, her voice soft. "I am at an age where I find myself looking back over the years wishing I had been more courageous to hold onto my convictions. Maybe that's why I came, to ask you if it's too late, even at my age, too late to make amends, to begin doing what I should have done years ago, too late to say to God, 'I want to be yours again.' I didn't have anyone else to turn to, Mark. Somehow I knew that you—"

She looked away and began to weep softly.

Mark rose, sat down beside her on the couch, and placed a gentle hand on her arm.

Neither spoke for a minute or two.

"It's never too late, Sandra," said Mark at length. "There is no time with God. All our lives exist within his present. You are his precious daughter. You always have been. Today can be just as if you are still at Pinecroft sitting around the campfire whispering to him, *God, I want to be your daughter and live for you.*"

The image was powerfully present. Sandra Rhodes, mother of the president, burst into tears of remorse, healing, cleansing, and new hope.

50

Grilled by the Press

MARK FORSTER'S second day at the Presidential Manor was more intimidating than sitting alone with the president in the Oval Office.

Again, he was picked up at the apartment, driven to the Manor, escorted through all the security and other protocols, and to a small waiting room where he was briefed about what to expect, dabbed with makeup, and generally fussed over until Jeff appeared a minute or two before eleven.

"Hey, Mark, good to see you again!" he said jovially, sitting down beside him and allowing his own facial tones to be enhanced in preparation for the unforgiving scrutiny of the television cameras. The specter of Richard Nixon had been haunting presidents for ninety years. "Are you ready to be thrown to the wolves?" he asked.

"Probably not," replied Mark. "Is it really so bad? I thought the press loved you."

"Oh, they're generally pretty good to me. It's you I'm worried about."

"Me!"

Jeff laughed. "A Christian, and an evangelical to boot—that's red meat for the liberal media. I'm sure I'm not telling you anything you don't know."

"Thanks a lot!"

"It will be fine. But there are likely to be some pointed questions. Give straight answers. Don't go into detail. Don't get specific. Avoid your personal beliefs. Vagary is the key. If you get uncomfortable, just pass the buck to me."

"Will you want me to make any kind of statement?"

"No, I'll take care of that. I'll introduce you and what we're trying to achieve, then open it up for questions. Just keep calm, keep your sense of humor, smile and be friendly, and you'll be fine."

Five minutes later, Mark was following Jeff into the bright lights of the press room, looking out at forty or fifty expectant and, to him, inherently hostile faces. Every set of eyes seemed staring straight at him.

In California, Texas, Idaho, New York, Kansas, Louisville, and other homes throughout the country, dozens of Forster and Marshall friends sat in front of their televisions.

At the Circle F ranch, the five Forsters had been gathered with David Gordon since 7:30 anxiously awaiting the 8:00 a.m. telecast of the briefing.

"There he is!" exclaimed Craig, the first to spot his father walking in behind the president.

"That's my boy!" laughed Robert Forster.

Press Secretary Anson Roswell opened the press briefing with a few detail announcements, then turned the podium over to the president.

"Good morning, gentlepeople," began Jeff, smiling warmly in his charming manner that had turned the press into a docile cheering section throughout his presidency. Most present had got wind of something in the works involving an outspoken Christian. It sounded like something they could sink their fangs into. There were even rumors whoever it was had once been affiliated with Ward Hutchins. They were all sorry he had been shot. But he was such a kook that what else could have been expected? They had been chomping at the bit for some good old-fashioned, down-and-dirty journalistic sparring. This should be fun!

"Before I get to my opening remarks and give you a chance to ask a few questions," Jeff continued, "I want to briefly introduce my friend Mark Forster."

He turned to Mark. Both men smiled as the camera zoomed in on Mark's face.

"Mark and I have known one another for thirty-five years. We were teenage best friends, college roommates, and have kept in touch through the years in spite of following very different callings. As some of you know, for most of his life Mark has been a minister and has served in various churches in the West. I know Mark's whole family, his lovely wife, Grace, and his son, Craig, and daughter, Ginger, whom I am sure are watching. There is no man alive with more personal integrity of character than Mark Forster, which is precisely the reason he is here with me today."

Jeff paused. Before he could take a breath, a voice shouted out.

"Mr. Forster, is it true, as has been suggested, that you and Ward Hutchins—"

The importune reporter was interrupted by the president.

"Didn't you hear me, Ed?" he said loudly, smiling but with a commanding tone. "I will give you all a chance in a minute or two. But one more outburst like that and you won't get a chance to say anything."

The man sat and Jeff resumed.

"All right," he said, "let me continue. I have asked Mark here to Washington to chair a new commission I have established to promote religious unity. He met for preliminary discussions with the other members who have agreed to work with him. They are from diverse traditions of faith, encompassing most of the major religious groups of America. It is no secret that Mark is an evangelical from what might be considered a somewhat conservative religious tradition. I have tapped him to head the commission because of our long friendship and also in hopes of bringing conservative evangelicalism into the mainstream of America's future and into a brotherhood and sisterhood of unity with other faith traditions in a way that mitigates what has been an unfortunate skepticism toward evangelicalism in recent years. It is time for all criticism toward any and all faith traditions to end. I want America to know, and evangelicals to know, no less than Catholics and Jews and Orthodox and Muslims, that they have a friend in the Presidential

Manor who has been paying attention to the stirrings created by Dr. Reyburn's challenging book. Dr. Reyburn is right. America's roots extend deep into the soil of our religious tradition. I applaud his courage in challenging America toward a higher vision. We must reclaim that heritage together.

"But unlike so much of our religious history, we must reclaim that heritage in unity, not division. No more can religion be a source of debate, hostility, and judgment but a source of strength, healing, and unity in the midst of the great diversity of our many faith traditions. It is because I consider the role of religion imperative to our future, and the role of religion vital to the fabric of America's strength, that I am establishing the Commission on Religious Unity with my friend Mark Forster as its first chairperson."

Jeff continued for a few minutes, reiterating much of what he had said to the twelve members of the commission, emphasizing again his vision of a new Reformation based not on protest and schism but on unity.

When his remarks were concluded, had an evangelical minister not been standing at his side, it is likely that the questions to him might have become more vigorous, asking if he had had some kind of religious epiphany, a Jesus moment.

This was completely unlike the Jefferson Rhodes they knew. Praising Charles Reyburn's book, which every man and woman in the room, except for FNN's sole token representative, despised as a right-wing religious tract! What was the president thinking!

As it was, Mark took most of the heat.

The questions shouted from the floor were immediate and blunt.

"Will your evangelicalism prevent you working with Muslims, Jews, and Catholics?"

"Why are evangelicals so judgmental?"

"Do you oppose abortion?"

"Were you and Ward Hutchins lovers?"

"Do you approve of same-sex marriage?"

"How will you achieve unity with other faiths?"

Within seconds the onslaught threatened to become ugly. The press, it was clear, was not inclined to treat this conservative Christian minister with kid gloves.

Mark stood stoically at the podium and silently waited. Questions continued to be hurled loudly and rudely. Still he stood placidly saying nothing,

Gradually the flurry subsided. He waited until the room was silent, then another two or three seconds.

He opened his mouth and began to speak, but was instantly drowned out by another barrage of questions. He stopped again and waited.

This time he allowed the silence that finally descended to go on for ten or twelve seconds.

Again he began, his voice soft.

"I will engage in no shouting match," he said. "If all you want to do is listen to each other shouting among yourselves, that's fine. I will turn the podium back over to the president."

He paused and waited.

"If you have questions that you want to ask respectfully, one at a time, I will do my best to answer them. I will let Jeff—I'm sorry . . . I will let the president call on you. By way of responding to some of the cruder questions some of you threw out—which you ought to be ashamed of—not to dignify them but just to put all that behind us so we can engage in intelligent and respectful dialog, let me tell you a few things about myself."

He paused to see if the silence would hold. There was some shuffling, but after a few seconds he continued.

"My wife, Grace, and I have been married over twenty-six years. In fact, we celebrated our silver anniversary just last year. Neither of us have ever so much as touched another man or woman intimately. To use a phrase that used to be bandied about far too casually—such things should not even need to be spoken about, they should be taken for granted—the simple answer is that we saved ourselves for marriage, not because we're Christians wedded to an outmoded ethic. We were Christians and *are* committed to its ethic. But we did so because it was *right*. Sex before and outside marriage is wrong. It is always wrong. It is wrong for all people in all circumstances."

A great bustle of comments and objections spread through the room. Mark stopped and stood silently waiting until it subsided.

"Faithfulness to a single marriage partner used to be a badge of integrity and virtue in this country," he went on. "My wife and I have been completely faithful to each other. I do not believe I have ever intentionally told a lie in my life. Make of all that what you will. Call me what you will. You want to know who I am. I am a man who believes in right and wrong. We try to live by what is right, good, and honorable—in a nutshell, by truth. God's truth. We do not do so perfectly, of course. But we take our Christian faith seriously and try to regulate everything in life by it.

"There have been no affairs or scandals in our marriage or in any of our pastorates. We are a simple, traditional man and woman. Neither of us smoke, drink, or have touched a marijuana cigarette. We believe in virtue. Call us old-fashioned and Victorian if you like. We will hold our hands up proudly to that charge in this day when virtue and morality are crumbling. Our son and daughter, both in college, are, like ourselves, Christians—not because we indoctrinated or forced our beliefs on them but because they have chosen the road of truth they believe Christianity represents.

"About myself, I will say that I believe in right and wrong. I believe in American exceptionalism. I do not believe that many of the trends in our culture today promote truth or virtue or are based on right and wrong. But those matters lie outside questions of religious unity. Beyond that, please do not question me on matters of religious doctrine, biblical interpretation, or divisive cultural issues. I will answer no such questions. That is not why we are here. The president has honored me to participate in an attempt to bring religious unity into the national and political discussion. If you have questions about that, I will do my best to respond."

He turned to Jeff.

"Perhaps the president, who knows you better than I do, can call on you."

Hands immediately shot into the air, to the accompaniment of another volley of shouted questions.

"I believe Mr. Forster has made the format of this morning's briefing clear," said Jeff with a smile. "He has set his ground rules and I will abide by them. Shall we try again."

He waited a moment.

"Yes, Blythe."

"Mr. Forster," said the well-known WNN reporter, "I mean no disrespect but in general evangelicals are known for very definite and mostly conservative viewpoints. You said yourself that you believe strongly in what you consider right and wrong. Would you see these perspectives as an impediment to your ability to work with leaders of other faiths?"

"That is a very good question," replied Mark, "and one I'm sure that has occurred to my fellow commission members! You are right, we tend to have definite viewpoints. But evangelicalism cannot be characterized quite as one-dimensionally as the media often assumes. It is a broad tradition. There are evangelical liberals as well as conservatives. Evangelicalism is part of an extremely diverse Christian spectrum. The president has not called us to haggle over our differences but to lay them aside for the greater good of discovering ways to foster unity. Of course I have personal views, as will the others who are involved. I am also a believer in the universal brotherhood of humanity. That brotherhood not only links me with those of other faiths but with all men and women, including those of you in this room."

"What about those claiming no gender and transgenders?" came a shout from the floor.

Mark stood silently.

"Do you refuse to answer?"

Still Mark said nothing.

Jeff stepped again to the podium. "One thing you will soon discover!" he laughed, "is that my friend is a man of his word. If he says he will not answer such questions, you can ask them all day and be met only with silence.—Yes, Diego."

"Thank you, Mr. President.—Mr. Forster, do you have any comment on the death of Rev. Ward Hutchins?"

"Though not exactly apropos to the unity commission, I will answer that by saying that I miss my friend. I have no other information. Ward was a good and honorable man of virtue and integrity who did not deserve the treatment many of you gave him."

"Do you hold to his view that the end times are imminent?"

Mark stood silently and did not answer. Beside him, again Jeff laughed, clearly enjoying Mark's deft handling of the press corps. He then acknowledged another hand in the air.

"Doreen—"

"Will you step down from your current pastorate to chair the president's commission?"

"I resigned from my last church two years ago," replied Mark. "I am no longer in the pastorate."

"Are you retired then?"

"My family and I operate the horse ranch where I grew up. It keeps us busy."

"Will you and your family move to Washington?"

"No."

"Do you have political ambitions?"

"No."

"Are you a Progressive or a Republican?"

The room was silent.

"Have you read Dr. Reyburn's book?"

"Yes."

"What is your opinion of it in light of the commission?"

"It is prophetic—a blueprint for getting America back on track."

"Back on track from what? Do you consider America off track?"

"I should not have said that. Let me amend my reply to say simply that I consider Dr. Reyburn's book prophetic and leave it at that."

"Yes . . . uh, Mason, isn't it?" said the president.

"Yes, sir—Mason Templeton, NBC."

"Go ahead, Mason."

"Thank you.—Mr. Forster, could you shed light on how you perceive what you call unity actually working out practically among what are admittedly not merely diverse religious faiths and views but those which involve diametrically conflicting, even hostile ethnic and cultural, divisions as well. How will you and your colleagues practically implement policies that Jew, Hindu, Muslim, Catholic, Protestant, to name just a few, will all be able to follow and practice when the historical, ethnic, and doctrinal divisions are deep, visceral, and of such long duration? It would seem that the president has set you an impossible task."

Mark stood silent and reflected for several long seconds.

"That is perhaps the question of the hour, Mr. Templeton," he said at length. "A probing and perceptive question. And as I do not like to speak unless I have something to say I have thought about, I will have to decline to attempt an answer—not because your question does not deserve one, but because it *does* deserve one. I will need to give the matter more thought and prayer. I *have* been thinking about it, actually, but am not ready with a response. If you are in earnest and will get your contact information to me, I will be in touch with you when I feel I have a response worthy of the importance of your question."

Todd Stewart had been back in Washington, DC, nearly a month.

He watched the new young rising star who had replaced him at NBC ask what was doubtless the most probing question of the day, he could not help smiling. After today's performance by Templeton, he was unlikely ever to get his job back!

He could tell the president was also impressed. Once a young journalist caught the president's eye, as he once had himself, there was no direction to go but up.

Thus far he had not renewed his former acquaintances at NBC. The more people who knew he was back in town, the more pressure would mount to resume life in the fast lane. Knowing he had to do *something*, however, he had visited several of the local television stations to explore the possibility of working out of the national spotlight.

He and Heather continued to write, talked occasionally on the phone or by computer. Their visits—whether by letter or voice or face-to-face on screen—were the highlight of his days.

He hadn't known Mark Forster was in Washington. As soon as the press briefing was over, he made a few calls to track down where he was staying.

Where she sat watching the replay of the press briefing in her chambers during an early afternoon recess, Linda Trent smiled to herself. In some ways Mark was a babe in Washington's cutthroat woods. Yet he was so quietly self-assured that nothing the roomful of journalists threw out fazed him.

It was delightful watching him refuse to take their bait and be lured into a polemic debate. He had been just the same in college—quietly watching Jeff and Ward go at each other's throats over Trump. He was actually a perfect choice to lead a commission on unity.

But how long could he possibly last in DC?

51

Another Visitor

THE RESULT of Todd Stewart's inquiries was a knock on the door of Mark's apartment at the Michelle Obama Professional Housing Complex about four o'clock that same afternoon.

When Mark answered the door, Todd could see at a glance that he had probably woken him.

"Todd . . ." said Mark through somewhat blurry eyes. "Is that you—Todd Stewart!"

"Yes," said Todd, laughing lightly. "I'm afraid I disturbed you."

"No, please—come in!" said Mark, regaining control of his wits. "I must have dozed off. I just laid down for a minute to rest my eyes—what time is it anyway?"

"A few minutes after four."

"Gosh—I really conked out! Last I knew it was three!"

"I really don't want to bother you."

"Don't be ridiculous—I could not have asked for a more welcome intrusion. A friendly face is just what I need. It is wonderful to see you again. I've been through a rather trying ordeal. I need a diversion."

They sat in Mark's small sitting room.

"If you're referring to the press briefing at the Manor . . ."

"Ah, you know about that. Yes, that's it. I was exhausted when I got back here, totally drained. You saw the result!"

"I watched the whole thing. You handled yourself like a pro."

Mark laughed. "It did not feel like it from where I was standing!"

"Believe me, take it from one who has been in that room many times shouting out the questions, you presented them with such a calm demeanor, such quiet confidence to speak your mind and not be ruffled—most of them have never encountered someone like you in the political arena. They won't know where to pigeon-hole you—a nice, thoughtful, respectful, gracious, dedicated conservative Christian man. I broke out laughing when you told them they should be ashamed of themselves. Old Paul McCormack deserved it. You'll probably take a beating in his column tomorrow. But *everybody* takes a beating in his column. He's an old Washington curmudgeon. The point is—you were a star! Believe me, people around town will be talking about you."

Mark broke into a roar of laughter. "If you say so! I hope I don't have to go through it again. What about you? Why weren't you there?"

"I haven't returned to work yet. After the show-stopper by Mason Templeton, I'm not sure I'll have a job to go back to! The young upstart!" laughed Todd. "Your reply to him was brilliant. Those guys never hear anyone say, 'I don't know . . . I don't have an answer . . . I'll get back to you.' Actually, I take that back—the president's press secretary Anson Roswell says that all the time, but it's just a way to sidestep a question and not answer it. He never gets back to anyone. I have the feeling you *will* contact Mason."

"Of course. I said I would."

"That's the difference."

"So you're still undecided about your plans?"

"I am. But you—my goodness. At the president's side!"

"I'm still not sure how Jeff . . . how the *president* is going to sidestep the church and state argument about all this. Some group is bound to challenge the Commission. Who knows, it might go all the way to the Supreme Court."

"That would take years. Until then, you're a member of the administration."

"Quite overwhelming, I'll admit. I'm still not sure why I'm here."

"Didn't you say when I was in California that you felt God leading you to say yes?"

Mark nodded. "I did. But I'm at a loss to understand why he would want me to do this. It's so opposite to how God's been leading us about politics and the world and everything that's going on."

"Us?"

"I mean Grace and our family and the Marshalls and some others in the unofficial fellowship we're part of."

"How does God's leading work exactly? Heather used the same words."

"Your journalistic instincts are coming through."

"I am genuinely interested. I've never heard people talk about spiritual things the way you do. Heather was my first exposure to a completely different perspective. She said what sounded like the strangest things. Yet to her they were part of everyday life. We've been writing quite a bit. The ideas she talks about are so enormous. Some of it is really hard to get my head around."

"Such as?"

"I don't know—like God's leading for important decisions. Like feeling God's presence. And laying things on the altar—that was another thing. Relinquishing self, I remember that particularly. She talks a lot about God's Fatherhood and the commands of Jesus. She's been explaining it to me as best she can, but it's like learning a foreign language."

Mark could not help laughing.

"Walking daily as a Christian, in an ongoing moment-by-moment relationship with God the Father and the Spirit of Jesus—it involves all those things. Boiled down there's little more to it than recognizing God as a good Father, acknowledging ourselves as his children, then finding out what Jesus said to do and trying to obey those instructions because that's what good children do. Jesus came to teach and show us how to be sons and daughters of his Father and our Father. He prayed to God for leading, so in saying I pray to God for leading, I am merely following his example."

Todd shook his head. "It's a different world. But hey," he said rising, "I don't mean to take up your whole day—"

"Nonsense," rejoined Mark. "I've got nothing else to do. My obligations are done. I'm flying back to California tomorrow. What about you—do you have plans for the rest of the day? How about my taking you to dinner?"

"I would like that. Would you like me to show you the city a little between now and then?"

"Absolutely. I've had my nap. I'm feeling revitalized. I haven't had a car so all I've seen has been within walking distance."

"Then let's go!" said Todd.

"Being the native, you pick where we eat. And my treat! I'm the president's religion man now, and you're a starving unemployed reporter."

52

High-Profile Voting Member

January–February 2051

When the call came two weeks before Christmas, though it was probably inevitable, the news was nevertheless as surprising as it was welcome.

"Mike, it's your father," said the familiar voice on Mike Bardolf's private phone. "How goes it at the center of world affairs?"

"The usual," he replied. "Trying to keep the president in line."

From anyone else the comment would have been humorous. Spoken between the two men who each bore the most important name in Palladium, it was not far from the truth.

"I've a bit of news," Loring went on. "Old Jason McNab died yesterday."

"I heard."

"Then you'll know he'll have to be replaced."

"Of course."

"I'm putting your name before the membership. You will be unopposed and approved immediately."

"I see. Thank you."

"It is long overdue. I should not have waited so long. I am sorry—though it has not seemed to inhibit your rise. You may one day rise higher than us all."

"I doubt that," replied Mike, though that was precisely his intent.

"The seventy-two are scheduled for the first of the year annual meeting next month. Your approval will be a mere formality. You will be inducted and cast your first votes at that time. You will need to arrange a clandestine trip, more difficult now with your high-profile responsibilities in Washington."

"I will be able to arrange it."

"We're scheduled for the seventeenth. If you want to come see me first as your cover, we can fly into Mira Monte together."

Mike ended the call with a sigh of relief. It was about time, he thought. This would smooth his way in setting up the PDA. Since the entire voting membership would be present, he might hold some private meetings at the same time.

When Mike Bardolf arrived at the Roswell estate in Mira Monte, California a month later, he walked into the secret Palladium headquarters with head held higher than on previous occasions. He carried himself with the sense of confidence not only that he belonged but that he was poised to take his rightful place at the highest level of Palladium's leadership.

This would be the first time he and Anson, grandsons and scions of Palladium's legendary founders, would serve together on the seventy-two. Both would in time replace their fathers as Grand Masters of the League of Seven, and they were thus treated with respect, even deference. Along with Hamad Bahram, they would be the two youngest of the seventy-two. But all the others knew it behooved them to keep on their good side. Storm Roswell was noticeably slowing down. And Mike's reputation as Viktor Domokos's biographer and his present stature as a man who had the president's ear—notwithstanding that Anson's role in the administration was a more public one—made him even more the center of attention at the compound than his father.

It had taken a little fancy logistical footwork to arrange his and Anson's simultaneous departure from Washington. He told the president that his father's health had taken a turn for the worse and that he needed to pay him a visit for a few days or a week. It was arranged for

Anson to receive an invitation to speak at an event in Phoenix. Thus, when they greeted one another at the secret compound where Anson's great-grandfather had built his fortune, no one in the capital even knew they were in the same state.

Mike's induction ceremony took place on the second night of the august assembly following the unanimous vote. The darkened room and candles and incense and chants and vows and rituals and signatures with pens dipped in blood would have sent chills down the spine even of a 33rd-Degree Mason, Bohemian, or Eulogian.

Mike Bardolf was a practical man and put little stock in the superstitious hocus-pocus begun by his grandfather. Once the black robes and swords and crosses and vials and concoctions and goblets were all put away, not to be brought out until the next induction, and the Latin anti-Christian slogans forgotten, he was anxious to get down to business, make his new quarters at the compound his own, and then proceed with the meetings and interviews he had planned.

He envisioned each of the new presidential commissions proposing a series of initiatives—innocuous at first as cover for their ultimate goals which would be instituted over the coming years and decades.

He had nearly completed the initial draft of the document which would outline those objectives both in general and specific terms. It was far more detailed than the broad outline he had put together several months before. He had been adding specificity ever since. The Domokos Final Declaration provided a foundational perspective. To it he had added his own far-reaching ideas which would take the country through to the end of the twenty-first century.

He called the written articulation of his life-vision "The Freedom Manifesto."

53

The Interviews

LORING BARDOLF left the Palladium compound the day following Mike's induction. The rest of the membership gradually made their own plans to depart. Anson Roswell would be back at his duties in the Presidential Manor well before the head of the president's Secret Service detail returned to the capital.

Mike delivered private memos to eighteen men and women requesting them to remain for an extra two or three days. He had matters of national import to discuss with them and would be grateful for an hour of their time. Their discussions and his requests were matters of utmost secrecy, he added, and must remain absolutely confidential, even from their Palladium colleagues.

His first meeting late that morning was with Hamad Bahram, president of the Consolidated Alliance of Muslims, Jews, and Christians for the Unification of Jerusalem. He had been a member of Palladium for eighteen years. Like Mike and Anson, he was a third-generation member who had served simultaneously with his father, Sonrab, until the elder Bahram's death a dozen years before. Mike had tentatively earmarked Hamad Bahram to replace the president's friend Forster, at some propitious future time, as head of the Religion Commission.

"I am conducting preliminary inquiries on behalf of President Rhodes," began Mike when he and the highly placed Harvard professor were seated in the private apartment that was now his. "The president of course knows nothing about Palladium. He has asked me to gather names from various fields for consideration to head his series of presidential commissions. The purpose of each commission will be to carry out the more sweeping and it may be controversial, aspects of his long-term agenda on diverse fronts. Most of those whom I have designated to speak with such as yourself, for obvious reasons, I have selected from Palladium's membership, though that fact will never be known. Like Palladium, much of the work of the commissions will operate below the public radar. The recent highly publicized Religion Commission is an anomaly. If I may speak frankly, it is but a smoke screen to initiate the idea of the commissions in a non-threatening manner. Those aspects of our social, cultural, political, financial, and religious agendas which will follow are more far reaching and will be implemented slowly, invisibly, inoculating the public by such slow steps that they never perceive where those steps are leading. This will eventually be the case with the Religion Commission."

"Of course. I understand," nodded Bahram. "Such has been my strategy for fifteen years with the Jerusalem project. Christians and Jews must be lulled to sleep with promises and bland proposals, never seeing the body of the camel following the nose into the tent. Before I am done I will have the Jews themselves dismantling the Wailing Wall."

Bardolf laughed. "Very shrewd, Hamad. I knew I had not misjudged my man. We think alike."

"It is the only way to accomplish large objectives. The masses must be herded like cattle."

"A somewhat hackneyed image, yet still true as ever. As I was about to say, the president's commissions, which I have dubbed PDA—with its obvious double entendre, whose deeper meaning will be known only to us—will be led by twelve chairpersons or czars, if you will. Some will have more public faces than others, as is the case with the president's first appointment as the chairperson for Religious Unity. In order to mitigate the recent resurgence of interest in conservative Christianity, the president has made a public show of the establishment of the religion commission and his first appointment—"

"The man he chose is an imbecile," interrupted Bahram.

Mike smiled. "Of course. I know it. You know it. The president knows it. You could almost hear the snickering through the press room with all that nonsense about right and wrong and saving himself for marriage. The fool is an anachronism from another century. It's all part of the master plan to ensure that the 10 percent of the country still clinging to some vestige of Christianity doesn't become 20 percent. Forster is a temporary figurehead. His only purpose is to lull evangelicals back into the slumber where we have kept them politically toothless for thirty years."

Mike paused briefly.

"Once we had most of the Christian denominations accepting gays and lesbians and transgenders into their pulpits," he went on, "and performing marriages between them all, even endorsing President Samara's Three-Party Marriage Act, Christianity as a cultural force was dead. Then without warning this Reyburn menace woke up the sleeping bear. President Rhodes is simply trying to gently settle the bear back down so that his next hibernation will be permanent. Mark Forster is a tool toward that end. He will be replaced in time by one whose objectives are more in line with the president's, and ours."

"Someone such as?" said Bahram, arching an eyebrow.

"I am conducting interviews," rejoined Mike with hint of a smile. "All I will say is that you are my first appointment of the day."

Bahram took in the statement thoughtfully.

"One of the important features of the PDA Commissions," Mike went on, "will be that its twelve chairpersons act in concert, speak with a single voice, present a united front. Each will be responsible to implement the agenda in his or her chosen field of leadership and expertise—religion, as we have been speaking of, finance, education, legal, international affairs, the media, and so on. As a group, all will be committed to the objectives of what we might call the master plan. Many of these goals go back decades and have been intrinsic to Palladium's strategy and the originating vision of Viktor Domokos. Others are more recent and stretch far into the future.

"Toward that end, I have prepared an overview memorandum outlining the major points the Commissions will be charged to implement.

This includes questions and talking points I will be discussing with select individuals from Palladium's membership. What I share with you remains fluid. I have been working on it for some time. The president has not yet seen it. You and others I have earmarked for these discussions will help me refine my final document prior to its presentation to the president.

"I want you to see the document as it presently exists, with its proposed objectives. I want you to write down your ideas, reflecting on what you would add or expand upon. I want to canvas your thoughts, especially were you in a position to join the president and myself in their implementation. I am looking for specific proposals, timetables, and standards and guidelines where appropriate, if, as I say, the time should come when you should be tasked with heading the Religion Commission. However, you should not consider your responses limited to the religious sphere. I want you to be free to address the entirety of those areas encompassed by the memorandum."

54

The Bardolf Memorandum

As HAMAD Bahram sat in his own quarters to a light lunch of fattoush, dates, and yogurt, he pulled out the document Mike Bardolf had given him. As he quickly perused it, many of the points raised caused even *his* eyes to open wide, and he was probably the most radical member of Palladium of all. Though his radicalism, like his father's and grandfather's, was of an altogether different kind than any of his colleagues knew.

He had only met the first-term American president once, on Bainbridge Island. His impression of Jefferson Rhodes was not as quite such a revolutionary thinker as would be indicated by what he held in his hand. He strongly doubted Rhodes had had much of a hand in this document. It was the kind of thing that might have originated with Karl Marx if he were alive today!

Or Viktor Domokos, thought Bahram.

Neither had he ever spoken personally with the legendary old Romanian, gone now for fifteen years. He had not yet been brought into Palladium back in 2032 at the time of Domokos's now famous Final Declaration speech at Mira Monte. His father told him about it.

It was well known that Mike Bardolf had been closer to Domokos than anyone during the aging icon's final days. Was this so-called memorandum in reality Mike Bardolf's amplification of the Domokos Declaration, the old man's dying utopian dream for the world? If that

Declaration was anything like what he suspected, this document had probably come straight from it.

After a glance through the eclectic and thought-provoking entries, Bahram settled into a more careful reading, continuing to bounce from topic to topic, taking liberal notes and running many things through his mind.

Legal and Judicial Priorities and Protocols:

The present progressive outlook required of Supreme Court justices must be greatly expanded to include all levels of the judicial system, ensuring that the nation's legal systems continue to reflect cultural progress, eliminating the possibility of a future reversion to the white, conservative values of the nation's unfortunate . . .

Nothing so controversial there, Bahram thought to himself. The judicial system had been moving in these directions for decades. He skipped ahead.

Medical, Vaccination, Health, and Wellness Objectives, Talking Points, Priorities, and Protocols:

The Harris-Cortez Freedom Affirmation Bill of 2031 and Youth Rights Act of 2032 shall be expanded. Parental permission for gender reassignment surgery shall no longer be required for children eleven and older. Parental permission for children ten and under shall still be required. Parental objection shall be countermanded if teacher recommends gender reassignment surgery, and if deemed in best interest of mental and psychological well-being of child. Operations in both cases to be paid for from funds allocated by the Youth Rights Act of 2032.

Transgender surgery shall continue to be publicly funded according to the terms of the 2034 Gender Neutrality Act. To that act shall be added 50 percent public funding for biological birth-males to be implanted with uterus and other necessary organs enabling them to bear children and carry them to term, and for biological birth females to be implanted with organs and provided hormone treatment enabling them to produce sperm and impregnate an identified female of either biological birth-gender. Fifty percent of such operations and hormone treatments and follow-up to be paid for by parents. Gender reassignment surgeons shall be immune from lawsuits or prosecution for any cause. Pre- and post-surgery gender affirmation therapy shall be provided at public expense.

Cut-off period for post-birth abortions in cases of mental or physical handicap remains controversial. This to be discussed. Additional query: What should be the government mandated method of termination and disposal?

Research accelerated into isolating various "proclivity genes," especially the religion gene and conservative gene. Funding for the research expanded, with the goal of increasing predictability of culturally destructive influences, and responding accordingly. Parallel research expanded to determine most appropriate means to turn off such genes within the human response system, using worldwide vaccination dissemination through insect RNA and DNA modification technologies, with the goal of bringing all races, cultures, and societal groups into uniformity of outlook according to the Global Progressive Mandate.

It will become increasingly necessary to mandate societally beneficial abortion on the basis of genetic predispositions as determined by mandated DNA testing of all couples applying for marriage licenses, and all fetuses. Genetic predisposition to be determined: criminality, conservatism, religiosity, illness, drug use, and others. Query: Which potentially negative cultural and societal influences should be included, which should be excluded on the basis of preferred racial or other genetic markers?

Many of the world's nations are far ahead of us in dealing with the problem of the aged and their drain on the financial health of the nation. We must work aggressively to transfer the vast resources used to prolong life to the needy in our society.

Pursuant to the Pérez/Samara Right to Die Initiative and the Dignified Freedom of Death Act of 2035, which legalized a range of death drugs and a patient's right to euthanize themselves . . . the next step must be a bill authorizing, and in time mandating, euthanasia on the terminally ill, those with irreversible dementia, and those unable to care for themselves. Medical professionals will be brought in to begin discussions about forced euthanasia, possibly setting certain age limits to life, and a list of terminal conditions which should not be prolonged after confirmed diagnosis. Query: What should be the parameters which should regulate those decisions, and how should potential religious objections be met?

Bahram set down the pages in his hand and leaned back, exhaling slowly. He hardly knew whether to be outraged and withdraw his name from consideration—or laugh at the boldness of it.

Mike Bardolf was stirring up a hornet's nest! Would President Rhodes actually endorse these proposals?

He looked over what he had just read, made a few notes, then turned back to the protocols for the Education Commission.

Educational Objectives, Talking Points, Priorities, and Protocols:

The heavy taxation and regulation of private, charter, and home schools has not produced the desired effect of eliminating their steady drain on the public educational system, or their persistent Christian influence. The options to rid America of this destructive menace seem to be two: To abolish home and charter schools altogether, forbid them by law and enforce the prohibition with the stiffest fines, seizures of property, and jail sentences for non-compliance. Or to establish stringent curriculum requirements with mandatory testing and oversight. These would mandate the teaching of government-approved diversity, social justice, and gender-neutrality curriculum in all subjects. Non-compliance to be severely punished. Ongoing non-compliance would result in closure, and/or removal of children from homes deemed unfit educational environments and placed in government housing where their proper education would be assured.

The Department of Education to be expanded to include the new Education Enforcement Agency, with a related regulatory commission for home and charter schools. If home and charter schools are allowed to continue, unscheduled and random inspection visits must be instituted ensuring that government-mandated curriculum is being taught. Test results must be open to inspection. Inspectors to have authorization to enter any home or charter school without prior notice. These visits to interview any and all children and students, in private, to ensure they are being taught according to established guidelines.

A more stringent LGBTQ curriculum will be developed for use between kindergarten and third grade, mandated for use in all home schools and charter schools. The presentation of gender choice will be mandated in all home and charter schools. Prior to entry into second grade, all children will be required to identify their chosen gender and give themselves a chosen name. Affidavits to be registered with the Department of Education, ensuring home and charter school compliance. Failure to complete affidavits for every student in a timely manner to result in school closure.

All curriculum at all levels, both public and private, completely bi-lingual. All natural-born English-speaking children required to be taught and demonstrate fluency in Spanish by Grade 8. One year of Chinese language and one year of Russian mandatory for all public and private high schools.

African and Latin American history mandatory for all high school juniors. US history shall continue to be considered optional.

No high school, college, or university diploma shall be issued, including those from private, charter, and online institutions, until a signed affidavit of compliance from each student is registered with the Department of Education, certifying under penalty of perjury that they have received mandated diversity, social justice, and gender-neutrality curricula at all levels, and acknowledging their obligation to adhere to governmental mandates set by those curricula in their future professional and business vocations. Proven failure to do so would result in revocation of diploma and potential indictment on charges of perjury.

Bahram shook his head and smiled.

If anything could cause a revolution among Christians, this could be the catalyst. On the other hand, these proposals might successfully end the Christian home-school movement for good. Obviously Mike Bardolf was banking on the latter result.

He continued reading.

Social Engineering Objectives, Talking Points, Priorities, and Protocols to be Incorporated into the Action Point Objectives of all Commissions:

It has become clear that we cannot achieve full ideological conformity until there is linguistic conformity. Language is a powerful tool that shapes thoughts and beliefs. We began our experiments to control language in the culture back in the 2010s with pronouns. The goal was to move beyond mere pronouns eventually to encompass all forms of expression so that it became impossible to speak with terminologies contrary to the progressive worldview. We were successful by employing a two-fold process: the elimination of all terms incompatible with the agenda, and introducing new mandatory terms bolstering and infiltrating the culture with our chosen nomenclature. With the open-ended mandate of the Linguistic Reform Bill of 2031, all the Commissions will continue to monitor and penalize the use of words or phrases in their specific fields deemed offensive or exclusive, adding their own outlawed terms as needed. Through linguistic control, we will continue to mold the collective mindset to reflect the values of the agenda.

As but one example, though an important one, Christianity must be rendered powerless with a carefully controlled program which will redefine its terms. The definition of sin, for instance will be stripped of its Christian presuppositions in order to promote the secular religion of progressivism. Racism, sexism, bigotry, hate speech, homophobia, and patriarchy will constitute a new composite definition of sin. Repentance for such social sins will be encouraged. Former Christian terms like sin and repentance will be co-opted to serve our ends. Counseling for white guilt will be offered at governmental expense. This new perspective of religion, which exalts racial groups of color, sexual minorities, and encourages the subtle subjugation of men, will become the new religious morality.

Though great strides have been made, systemic bias, personal preference, and individual choice lying outside the framework of the agenda must continue to be eliminated, criminalized as necessary for eliminating racism and inequality. Through social engineering, we will continue reshaping personal preferences to align with our vision of a more equitable inclusivity throughout every level of culture.

To ensure a society free of oppressive ideologies, we will implement mandatory reeducation programs for those found expressing dissenting views. These programs will be carried out through the workplace and enforced, if necessary, by removal to reeducation centers whose priority will be the elimination of all remnants of non-conforming thought. Full collective consciousness aligned with the ideals of the agenda will be instilled through whatever means are necessary, including incarcerative, electric, aquatic, hypnotic, and drug and deprivation therapies.

In our pursuit of diversity and inclusion, mandatory quotas of equitability in all aspects of life will continue to be implemented based on the Universal Income, Opportunity, and Communal Ownership Executive Order of 2033, with the ultimate goal of removing every trace of former white privilege and societal hierarchies.

He set the pages aside for several minutes. What he had just read sent his brain off in many directions. Mike Bardolf had no idea what he was setting in motion. The *true* agenda, *his* own agenda, thought Bahram, would indeed employ all these measures and more. But not in the way Bardolf imagined!

After several minutes, he settled back in his chair to read Bardolf's talking points on religion, which he himself might be charged to implement.

Religion Objectives, Talking Points, Priorities, and Protocols:

All Christian churches to be regularly monitored for compliance in teaching materials and content, including content in small groups, literature distributed, and sermon and homily content, according to governmental FCP Presidential Alliance standards and guidelines. All licensed clergy shall be required to sign a contract of compliance under penalty of perjury. Churches and clergy not complying shall be closed and church assets forfeited and sold at auction, proceeds set aside for funding of abortions and transgender operations.

Under terms of Ocasio-Cortez Truth and Freedom Act of 2031, Christian churches will continue to be taxed at corporation rates based on gross receipts. Quarterly audits to be conducted by Department of Finance, with heavy financial penalties for non-compliance.

Tax-exempt status for Muslim mosques shall continue.

Bahram smiled. Had Bardolf included this last to win him over? How little the man knew what a fool's game he was playing!

He continued scanning the pages. The mere list of topics was enough to send his brain spinning. What would Mike Bardolf think if he knew what the future of the country *really* held? Progressive visionary as Bardolf considered himself, he still had no idea what was coming.

Expanded statehood . . . unification . . . world constitution . . . police . . . intelligence . . . standards and guidelines . . . technology—he would go over those recommendations later, thought Bahram. Mere window dressing. But he would continue to agree with everything. Every rung higher he could climb moved *his* agenda closer.

He rose and fixed himself a cup of tea. When he resumed ten minutes later, he turned to Bardolf's literacy and publishing objectives.

> *Literacy and Publishing Objectives, Talking Points, Priorities, and Protocols:*
>
> *Provisions of the Literacy Management Initiative of 2032 shall be expanded. Publications presenting one-sided, white, Christian, and Western perspectives of history, culture, and religion will continue to be eliminated from public libraries and educational institutions and destroyed. Standards established to ensure that gender and racial diversity are represented in all publications. More stringent controls established on publishing houses and printeries, with rigorous inspections and controls of all self-publishing and Print on Demand services. AI technologies more aggressively used to isolate and ban Christian books not in compliance with Commission guidelines. The works of authors promoting pure Christian content without equal attention to alternate points of view shall be banned. Underground publications by authors known to be non-compliant shall be considered a felony and punishable by fines, confiscation of assets, and imprisonment.*
>
> *All publishing companies, including Christian publishers shall be required to publish a certain percentage of their line focusing on topics in keeping with the government's FCP Presidential Alliance guidelines. Publishers not complying shall be closed.*
>
> *Current guidelines for publication of Bibles to be expanded. The Love Bible shall be edited and brought up to current terminology of usage, presenting parallel teachings throughout from the Koran. All other Bibles will be required to contain equal content from the Koran by percentage. Bibles published prior to 2020 shall be confiscated and destroyed. Possession of a*

Bible without equal percentage of the Koran will be criminalized and punishable by fine.

All new publications, including self-published and privately published literature shall be required to include a bar code indicating compliance with governmental FCP Presidential Alliance guidelines. The duties of the Literacy Compliance Agency shall be coordinated with the Technology Commission to scan all new publications for compliance or imbedded non-compliant content before filing barcode applications. Publications without a compliance barcode—including private newsletters and online mailings—shall not be distributed or sold by retail or online outlets or given away for private use. Publication of such material shall be considered in violation of law and those responsible subject to fine or arrest.

All publishing facilities, public or private, including private homes where literature originates for distribution, shall be required to register with the Literacy Compliance Agency and shall be subject to unannounced inspection. Facilities not complying or found in violation shall be shut down and will be subject to forfeiture of assets.

All libraries—educational, regional, college, university, and private—shall be required to conduct an assessment of their holdings under supervision of the Literacy Compliance Agency with the ultimate objective of removing books and other materials in conflict with governmental FCP Presidential Alliance guidelines. Some historical works, though anachronistic and not in keeping with current racial and cultural trends, may be allowed if deemed generally unlikely to offend. Books promoting overt Christian bias and message published prior to 2020 to be removed and destroyed by statute. Libraries not complying to be shut down and their holdings transferred to nearby libraries.

55

Reflections

HAMAD BAHRAM remained in his Palladium quarters for three hours, reading through the entire Bardolf memorandum. His reactions were mixed. He had to read through two opposite lenses—that of the public façade in which he must continue walking as a third-generation Palladium member but also through the eyes of the secret persona represented by his legacy as Husain Bahram's great-grandson.

Holding the two personas in a single consciousness might have turned most men into confused schizophrenics. But the progeny of Husain Bahram had been balancing their two selves now for three generations.

Successfully navigating that tightrope was intrinsic to the Bahram family legacy and the ultimate objective to which they had committed themselves.

Reading Bardolf's memorandum, with its obvious anti-Christian bias, sent Hamad's thoughts back to his twenty-fifth birthday. His father, Sonrab, perhaps beginning to feel his own mortality, though he would live another thirteen years, had celebrated the day with the symbolic passing on to Hamad of the ornately fashioned ring of pure gold that had been his great-grandfather's, grandfather's, and father's before him. It had come with old Husain from Iran and belonged to more past generations than his father even knew.

With it, Sonrab solemnly told his son, the Bahram legacy now passed to him, a legacy that would lead to Islam's ultimate triumph over the West.

Hamad had heard it all before—many times. The narrative of Islam's jihad was inbred into every Muslim youth. The more specific hidden jihad that Husain Bahram and his posterity made their special life's vision had been inculcated into him from before he could remember.

On that day of his birthday, when yet again his father laid out the oft-told vision of infiltration, Hamad articulated the question that had long perplexed him about the entire plan. Reading Bardolf's memorandum brought that conversation almost twenty-six years ago vividly back into his mind. He had turned twenty-five that day. Now he was fifty—at the midpoint of his life thus far. At last he understood clearly what on that day had been nebulous and indistinct.

"Father, I still cannot entirely understand," he had asked, "why America's liberals and progressives despise Christianity and Judaism and call them backward and bigoted but tolerate our Muslim faith. We are more rigid and intolerant of Christianity's ideals and Judaism's cultural norms. I understand the strategy of pretending to go along with progressivism. Yet I do not understand its tolerance of *us*. Why do they not hate Islam with equal or even greater venom? Why do they welcome and encourage our religion to flourish in America, while trying to eradicate Christianity? It seems backwards."

His father merely nodded, betraying the hint of a smile.

"We despise homosexuality, feminism, abortion, rap music, divorce," Hamad went on. "We hate *all* those cultural evils. Our belief system is rigidly patriarchal. Women's rights are anathema to us. Yet American progressivism tolerates and encourages us. Let's be honest, Father, the history of Christianity is *more* tolerant than ours. Yet they hate Christians and Jews."

The smile on the elder Bahram's face widened. "You have put your finger on a great irony—one of progressivism's countless blindnesses.

It is bewildering but true. Yet this mystifying hypocrisy is one we will use to overthrow the West when our time comes."

"But why? Do they not see their folly?"

"I have no answer to your *why*, my son. It is entirely inconsistent—they do *not* see it. Why a Christian nation welcomes Islam with open arms knowing our avowed objective of *destroying* the very fabric of its foundations is a great dichotomy. America is engaged in a slow self-inflicted suicide. But as long as this illogic exists, we will exploit it.

"Two significant dates may go down in history as pivotally foreshadowing the ultimate success of our jihad. The first took place, as you well know, the year you were born. I take it as an omen from Allah that you were born almost coincident with the New York attack. Allah's hand is on you. I believe that the triumph of 9-11 bestowed Allah's favor on you to take the jihad into future generations."

"What is the second date?" Hamad asked.

"It occurred three years ago," his father replied. "Surely you see the significance of the attack of Hamas against Israel in Gaza. In both instances, defying all reason, rather than inciting public outrage against Islam, in a curious perversion of logic, the attack on New York's Twin Towers and the Hamas attack turned the world *more* favorably toward us, and led to a great outpouring of sympathy for our cause.

"The upshot is that within a few years, Muslims were not viewed as terrorists or aggressors, but as *victims* of Islamophobia and Christian judgmentalism. It became progressivism's mantra to call Islam a religion of peace, and Christianity a religion of hatred and bigotry. There is no logical explanation for it. If ever a religion taught peace, it is Christianity. If ever a religion taught hatred toward one's enemies, it is Islam. Yet such was the result of 9-11. Much effort was made to differentiate between terrorists and the great majority of so-called *peace-loving Muslims*. They chose to ignore the historical reality that the avowed objective of *all* Muslims, even those pretending to be peace loving, is to destroy Christianity and Judaism, and to replace Western culture with Sharia Law."

Sonrab chuckled. "I still laugh when I think of it. *We* became victims in the public eye. The US became almost militantly pro-Islam in a way never seen before. The few isolated incidents of violence toward Muslims became a rallying cry for a nationwide embracing of Islam as a religion of peace. Islam may be many things," he added chuckling again. "But it is certainly *not* a religion of peace. Jihad is at the core of Islam's lifeblood.

"Similarly, after the Hamas attack in 2023 there was an outpouring of antisemitism and hatred of Israel—and *sympathy* for Hamas and the Palestinian cause. Within a year it was the Palestinian terrorists who were the *victims* of Israel's aggression."

"I can think of no plausible reason for it, Father. But obviously this explains why Muslims get a free pass for our stand against homosexuality, divorce, feminism, and abortion."

"Exactly. Progressives *always* give victims and minorities a free pass. It is a compulsion with them. Ignoring facts and misinterpreting history, they turn most minorities into victims for no reason other than that they are minorities. Illegal immigrants get a free pass for breaking the law because they are a minority. Inner-city blacks are considered victims of systemic white racism, so the black community is not held accountable for its crime rate and the disintegration of its family structure. Victims of hard times, the homeless get a pass. Victims of high rent prices, squatters get a pass. Unwed mothers get a pass and their loose morals never enter into it. Women getting abortions get a pass and murdering human life never enters into it. Gays get a pass. Shoplifters get a pass. Almost everything in progressivism's lexicon of right and wrong, good and evil, truth and falsehood, is upside-down.

"We are the benefactors of that inconsistency. Muslims, too, are perceived as a minority—which obviously we are not—and our views on homosexuality and feminism are overlooked. We get the same free pass because we make common cause with progressivism against Christianity and Judaism. Though Islam is the West's mortal enemy, in a bizarre twist we are perceived as allies. Since Islam is against Christianity and Judaism, progressives have unknowingly made a pact with the devil, so to speak, exactly as the allies did in embracing Russia in WWII."

"What this recent second Trump victory?"

"Like his first administration, it will prove to be an aberration. It will serve our long-term goals."

"How?"

"By lulling conservatives to sleep. They won't realize that the gravest danger to Western civilization is not progressivism, except as the means we will use to destroy America from within. Their true enemy is our jihad against progressive and conservative alike to destroy their culture.

"By the same inverted logic, in spite of the fact that Sharia Law is directly opposed to every principle the United States was founded on, Islam, as you say, continues to get a free pass. Unless conservatives *and* progressives wake up to their collective blindness, you may lead the jihad to its final victory."

He paused and his voice grew solemn.

"Every time you look at this ring I give you today," Sonrab went on, "remember that it is imbued with the spirit of the jihad of the ages, the spirit of the Great Prophet himself. That spirit is upon you and within you, my son. Its destiny has marked you for its own. *Allahu Akbar . . . Insha Allah Jihad.*"

"Allahu Akbar," repeated Hamad. *"Alhamdulillah."*

Hamad glanced down at the ring on his finger, smiling as he thought back to that day. His father's prophetic vision was at last coming to fruition. The ultimate progressive president now occupying the Oval Office and his lackey Bardolf could well be the ones setting the stage for the revelation of Islam's glory.

56

Return to the Manor

MIKE BARDOLF continued to conduct similar interviews throughout the day, vaguely but shrewdly assessing each candidate, despite his or her Palladium *bona fides*, for potential cracks in the armor of unswerving allegiance to the cause as he defined it. If he was to be successful in taking all the elements of his master vision to their fulfillment, even surpassing his mentor Viktor Domokos, loyalty must be unquestioned.

During his stay at the compound he managed to sneak the copy of the Domokos Final Declaration back into the office safe now that he had his own copy. He was moving beyond it now anyway.

He should have made his own copy years ago—it was a foolish oversight. But Viktor hadn't told him *everything*—whether intentionally or because by then his mind was slipping, he would never know. If old Storm had even noticed it missing, its reappearance would leave him wondering if he had imagined the whole thing—the doddering old fool.

As much as the aura of the Domokos legend hung over Palladium like a shroud, even that document hadn't gone far enough. His present proposals—outlined only in brief in the memorandum he had shared with potential Commission chairpersons—took his agenda much further. Even they would not yet be privy to the final Manifesto—not yet.

The men and women interviewed treated him with deference and respect. It was more than having been initiated into the voting membership. Storm Roswell sat with the other Seven in front, slumped in his chair and looking half dead. He did not speak. It was clear he was fading. His own father, emcee for the induction ceremony and moderator for the annual business meeting the next day, was still fully in command of his wits. Yet climbing the three stairs to the raised dais, he'd stumbled momentarily. Quickly recovering himself with a remark about his knees, it was a minor incident. Yet its significance was not lost on the membership.

It might not be long before Mike Bardolf was effectively the man in charge of Palladium.

Given Storm's condition it was obvious that Anson would probably be elevated to the League ahead of him. With his seniority, he could probably make an issue of it—the equivalent of a constitutional crisis in Palladium's leadership. The organization had never encountered such a situation before.

But whereas Anson's elevation would have grated on him several years earlier, the fact that he occupied an office but a ten-second walk from the Oval Office raised his stature in Palladium sufficient to keep him focused on the larger picture. Of course, the same could be said for Anson. But he had the president's ear in a way Anson never would. When those he was interviewing walked into his new apartment-office at the compound, most of them carried themselves as if entering the presence of the president himself.

The perception was not inaccurate.

He returned to Washington three days later, the interviews complete.

When Mike met with the president the next day, his report was necessarily vague. In spite of Rhodes's occasional enigmatic references to *Four-Six*, Mike remained convinced he knew nothing. Where he had picked up the number reference was still of some concern. But not serious. Few in the organization used the secret code anymore. They had moved beyond cloak-and-dagger methods. Rhodes had probably heard the numbers years ago with no idea of their meaning within the Palladium group.

"How was your trip—you're looking bronzed and fit—you must have spent time at the beach," said Rhodes. "Where is it your folks live?"

"Denver—no beach, I'm afraid."

"How is your father?"

"Doing better."

"You must bring him to the Manor. I would like to meet him."

"He would be honored. I'll mention it to him. I did manage to use the time to jot down a few more specifics about the commissions. I am working on the preliminary list of names you requested."

"Very good. I am eager to see it, as well as your ideas for the various departments."

"I will organize my thoughts and recommendations. Have you spoken with your man Forster again?"

"Not since he was here for his first meeting of the Religion Commission."

"Do you really think he could accomplish anything?"

"I don't know. It doesn't matter. Once the religious fervor settles down, we can disband the thing next term."

"I should tell you that the recommendations I am putting together are far reaching. Your friend will definitely not be happy about them."

"There's no reason for Mark to see them. If he gets wind of anything, I'll smooth it over."

"I hope your assessment is right. It's a risky strategy having an outspoken Christian so high up. There have been rumblings of discontent from the gay sector."

"I know what I'm doing. Friends close, enemies closer, you know. Besides, he'll be ready to resign before the next election. Then we can install one of those on your list. Who do you have lined up to take his place?"

"Tentatively Dr. Hamad Bahram."

"Muslim—head of the Jerusalem Alliance, isn't he?"

"That's right."

"Didn't I meet him at Bainbridge?"

"You did, Mr. President?"

"What's his background?"

"Third-generation, American-born Iranian, father and grandfather before him loyal Progressive Party members. He is following in their footsteps. We can depend on him to further our agenda."

When Jefferson Rhodes sat with the document Mike Bardolf presented him a week later, titled, "A Presidential Prospectus for Change—The President's Eyes Only," he had only begun reading before his eyes were wide in disbelief. Mike Bardolf was more visionary than he had any idea.

This was a revolutionary document!

57

The Essence

January–February 2051

HEATHER'S HUNDRED-WORDS-OR-LESS letter to Todd arrived just after the first of the year. She had obviously labored long and hard over it. Todd read it three times in succession and had done so more methodically half a dozen times in the month since. At a cursory glance, it seemed simple enough. Yet it probed depths that helped put much from the previous months into perspective.

Dear Todd,

This is about the sixth draft of this I have tried to write. I told you I was no writer! I hope it will make sense to you. My mother could do a better job. Eventually you should ask her to do the same thing! For now, you asked me. All I can say is that I've done my best. This is the essence of Christianity as this one young woman sees it. I realize I am young. I will continue to grow in my understanding. My answer to the same request twenty years from now would probably include ideas that are beyond the scope of my present sight.

That said, here I go:

Genesis 1:1 is one of the most powerful verses in the Bible. It lays the foundation for everything. God created the universe and everything in it. How he did it, and over what span of time, and what processes he used (micro-evolution, for example—billions or thousands of years—whether Adam and Eve were real people, etc.) are, in my opinion, side issues. They are interesting, but not fundamental to the essence of God's being. God exists and is creator of the world and mankind. That is the foundational FACT. Everything hinges on that.

He is a *personal* creator. He created man in his image. Though we can't know exactly what that means, we know that in some way we are like God.

Having birthed and given mankind life, he is mankind's *Father.* We are his children, in something like the same way that physical children are created in the image of their parents. Therefore, we are inextricably bound in relationship to him. We can never sever that Father-child relationship. We thus owe God our honor, allegiance, love, and obedience *because* we are his children.

Modernity would scoff, but I believe this Father-child relationship is intrinsic to understanding the nature of our humanity and our place in the world. We *owe* God our obedience because we owe him our life. He created the universe and humanity to function in certain ways. We are *supposed* to obey and live by the laws he established.

He is also a *good and loving* Father and creator. Because he is good and loving, his laws are also good and loving. They are designed for our best, our happiness, our fulfillment.

For reasons that are both a mystery and wonderful, God not only gave mankind life, he gave him free will. Though we cannot cut ourselves off from his Father-role in our lives, he gave us the power to try to do that very thing—to live apart from and independent from him. He gave man freedom to *not* obey, to *not* live by his laws if we choose to do so.

God set that choice before Adam and Eve in Genesis. Moses emphasized the same thing. He said over and over: "I set before you a blessing *and* a curse—life *and* prosperity or death *and* destruction." The choice is always in man's own hand how he decides he wants to live.

The word *curse* is greatly misunderstood. It wasn't a curse that God imposed. God simply said, "Live by my principles. Be my good and obedient children and it will go well with you. Life will be a good thing. I will bless you because I love you. However, if you do *not* obey, if you do not fall in with the created order as I established it, you will be at odds with life and the world. It will not go well for you, because you will be out of harmony with the world, with those around you, and with yourself. You will be out of sync with the created order."

People think that God punishes those who disobey. It's not that at all. It's a matter of natural consequences. When we fall in with the created order, we are in harmony with life and the world, with our Father and the rest of humanity, and with ourselves. The punishment, the curse so to speak, of disobedience is a punishment we bring on ourselves by choosing to resist, choosing not to live by the principles by which the universe functions, to go against the grain, to oppose the created order of things.

God wants us to *choose* to live in harmony with the created order of the world, and with him. That's why he gave mankind free will.

Some people choose to fall in with God's ways and live as his obedient children. But most men and women throughout history have been too in love with their independence. They don't want anyone telling them how to live. So they choose to go their *own* way and ignore God's laws—what I called the created order of things.

As a result, God has been greatly misunderstood. He has been perceived as an almighty tyrant of legalistic laws intent on punishing every violation. That's why the Old Testament is so misunderstood. Disobedient ancient people developed wrong ideas about who God was. They forgot that he was their Father, that he was a good Father, and that his instructions were for their good, their happiness, and their fulfillment in life.

The word *law* is as greatly misunderstood as the word *curse*. What are the "laws" by which God intended humanity to live? They're nothing so complicated—*Be good, kind, righteous, unselfish, respectful, giving, generous, forgiving.* The Ten Commandments and all the rest of the commands of the Old Testament can be summarized simply as *Live as God's good children—live in harmony with the created order of life, with who you were intended to be.* God wants us to use our free will to *choose* to live in harmony with him as our Father.

But because people have misunderstood all that and deeply resent anyone—especially God—telling them they have to obey, even telling them something as simple as, *Be good,* the image of God as a vengeful tyrant persists to this day. But it's all wrong. That's not who he is at all.

When Jesus is called "God's Son," no one really knows exactly what that means. It's very mysterious. There have been thousands of explanations through the centuries—from Jesus being a good man who taught about God, to Jesus being *God himself* who came into his own creation as a man. It's easy to get lost in all the theories and doctrines and miss the essence. The bottom line is that Jesus came from God to teach and show mankind how to get back to a right understanding of who God is and get back into a right relationship with him as our Father.

Jesus came to teach men what they should have known all along—that God is a good Father, that we are his sons and daughters, that the way to live an abundant life is to fall in with life as he established it. Not only did he teach it, Jesus *lived* it. He is life's ultimate example and mentor. We are supposed to follow his example.

Then Jesus told his followers exactly what God's instructions were. They were the same as they had always been: *Be good, kind, righteous, unselfish, respectful, giving, generous, forgiving.* But he simplified God's laws and explained how to live in sync with God's life in such practical ways that no one would ever misunderstand them again: *Turn the other cheek, do unto others as you would have them do unto you, give more than is expected, pray for your enemies, do good to those who persecute you, speak with grace, don't talk too much, love truth, don't follow the ways of the world, serve others, apply yourself to understand God's ways, honor your father and mother, don't speak carelessly, don't be a hypocrite.*

Christianity's thousands of doctrines, in my opinion don't matter alongside that. You and I have talked about it many times—doing what Jesus said by daily *choice*. That's how to live in harmony with God, with the world, with each other, and with ourselves.

This isn't to say that Christianity is all peace and love. Jesus also makes clear, as God did in the Old Testament, what we're *not* to do. Obedience is a two-sided coin. We are told what to do, and what not to do. *Sin* is a very real and important component of life with God.

Jesus is as clear about right and wrong and sin and what God *doesn't* want us to do—unforgiveness, gossip, sexual sin, lying, speaking against others, immorality, crude talk, wanting what other people have, cruelty, hypocrisy, unkindness. Those things are *wrong*. They are sins.

We are commanded not to sin just as we are commanded to be good. Right and wrong isn't relative. Sin is sin and is sin for everyone. Modernity's loss of absolutes cannot change that. Truth is not relative. Right is right, wrong is wrong, sin is sin, and truth is truth—for everyone.

One final thing I will say, and I probably got this from my grandfather and father and mother. Being a Christian is not just getting a ticket into heaven. In one way, Christianity has nothing to do with heaven either. It has to do with learning to live as sons and daughters of Jesus's Father and our Father. We learn that by doing what Jesus told us.

That's the essence of Christianity, in my humble opinion—learning to live as God's sons and daughters by making yourself a disciple of Jesus, living by his commands, trying to model your life after his, and thus living in sonship and daughterhood to God's Fatherhood.

In a way, nothing has changed since Genesis. Free will is the method of discipleship. Free will is still the engine of Christianity. We still have to choose every day, a hundred times a day, to live by what Jesus told us to do. We will always have the freedom to choose or not choose to fall in with God's created order.

The words of Moses and Joshua from over three thousand years ago still explain everything in life, and everything about the essence of Christianity: *Choose this day whom you will serve.*

I'm sorry, Todd, that's three times more than the five hundred words you gave me! I hope it will help you understand my walk with God a little better.

Let's see if I can summarize it in twenty-five words or less. This will be hard!

God is the Father of mankind. He gave us free will so we could choose to live as his children. Jesus came to give his life to pay the price for the sin that separates us from God and to show us in practical and daily ways how to live God's instructions. Christianity describes the surrendered life and learning to live as God's children by obeying Jesus's commands. There's obviously a lot more to a complete understanding of the Gospel than this brief overview, but this at least tells you in an introductory way how I see it.

Hmm . . . I still couldn't do it—it's almost a hundred words! I just counted them.

I wish we could talk about this in person! I know you will have questions. I love your questions. It's hard being so far away.

I am praying that you will hear and understand my heart in what I have written here.

With much affection,
Heather

In his next letter, Todd thanked her for what she had written but added that he wasn't ready to talk about it further or ask any of the hundred questions he had. He needed time to digest it, he said.

Heather heard no more about the letter for three months.

58

Distilling a Great Man's Thought

Early March 2051

MARK FORSTER returned to Washington, DC, twice more during the winter months for meetings of the Religion Commission. Grace accompanied him in late January. During his meetings, she was taken under the wing of First Lady Marcia Rhodes and given a royal tour of the capital—by limousine not Cessna—followed everywhere by photographers, who, by the end of the day were revisiting the exploits of the same two women in the skies over Seattle the previous May.

Mark used one of those visits to invite Mason Templeton to coffee, with the stipulation that their discussion would be off the record. The meeting was friendly. After much thought, Mark gave the best explanation he could of his view of unity among those of widely differing perspectives of faith and belief.

Templeton listened attentively, then asked, "Don't you think it would be beneficial and instructive to say what you've told me publicly? You've made some good points. It seems that it would help the cause of your commission."

"I think it would be more likely to precipitate debate, even argument, about what comprises unity," replied Mark. "That would be to trample on the very thing we're talking about. No, I'm sorry. I told you I would try to answer the perceptive question you asked, but I must insist that it remain between the two of us."

When Mark returned in early March an unseasonably warm spell succeeded in bringing out the first of the cherry blossoms a few weeks early. He regretted that Grace hadn't come with him on this occasion too.

Though perhaps it was for the best. Serious things were on his mind. He needed time alone, to think and pray, even perhaps to walk the streets of the city again like he had on his first visit, asking himself, as he had then, what he was doing here and what God wanted him to do now.

He had been asking that ever since Jeff's offer, the question rising into prominence more forcefully with every meeting of the commission. His present reservations were more serious. It was not merely the sense that he was accomplishing nothing. That almost went without saying. The whole thing was an obvious exercise in futility.

Two factors had changed. The first was his conviction that Jeff's offer might have been a ploy from the beginning. Whatever were his motivations in setting up the commission and asking him to act as its chairman, Mark had grown suspicious of Jeff's motives. He was convinced Jeff wasn't being straight with him.

Not to put too fine a point on it, he was being played by his onetime best friend. To what purpose, he had no idea.

His most important reservations stemmed from the gnawing sense that the time was coming when God might want him to step away. What had been the purpose for him to accept Jeff's offer, he might never know. But whatever it was, he sensed it coming to an end.

One thing he *was* sure of—that the time was approaching for a more widespread dissemination of Stirling Marshall's *Benedict Brief.* Any final decision about the *Brief* would rest with Timothy. But until there was a change, an urgency had grown upon him in recent weeks that he needed to prayerfully pore over Stirling's words again, asking God to disclose its greater depths more than he had apprehended earlier.

He'd brought his copy to Washington, determined to uncover whatever new secrets it had to reveal. As was his custom after unpacking in his familiar condo, he went out for a walk, taking what had become his usual route through several parks and the National Mall, then stopping by what had become his favorite deli before returning for the evening.

On this occasion, by the time he settled in, it was after 7:00 and well past dark. He pulled out Stirling Marshall's *Brief*, and began to read from the beginning—sandwich, sweet potato chips, vegetable smoothie, and a package of fig newtons on the table beside him, looking forward to a feast for body, mind, and spirit.

Even as his eyes fell on Stirling's first words, however, his uplifted mood of hopefulness changed. He sensed the heaviness of heart Stirling must have felt as he wrote the words twenty years before, concerned for a world and a church disintegrating into darkness.

Mark paused after only reading two pages, then went to his briefcase and took out his pen and several blank sheets of paper.

From Timothy, a far more experienced writer than himself, he had learned the technique of rewriting an author's thoughts and ideas, trying to cast them into one's own words, sometimes summarizing, occasionally simplifying the language or syntax, at other times amplifying. The intent was to communicate the author's essential message and ideas and purpose in one's own way, as if writing it oneself. Or, equally important, to recast it in order for someone else to absorb the author's essential message which might be obscure as originally written.

It was a supremely helpful process, Timothy always said, to penetrate the heart and mind of an author. Trying to recast the flow of ideas, he said, forced him to probe below the surface of those ideas, digging deep to understand them intimately and personally, to know the ideas as they had originally coalesced in the mind and heart of the author.

The process took him *inside* the author's mind and heart in a way no intellectual analysis ever could. Timothy had done so with his own father's writings many times. As a result, he now knew his father's heart far better than he had before.

He would do the same thing, Mark thought. He would summarize, in a sense, *rewrite* Stirling's *Brief* for himself. He wanted to probe Stirling Marshall's heart and mind just as Timothy was doing. Twenty years had passed since the writing of the *Brief*. Incapable as he felt to do so, he wanted to interpret Stirling's vision afresh for a new time, probing his intent from new angles, through a new lens. He wanted to *know* the man truly, deeply, accurately, personally, intimately.

He drew in a deep breath and turned back to the beginning, trying to place himself inside the heart of Stirling Marshall during his final days almost twenty years before.

He waited for several long seconds, then set his pen to paper and began to write on a fresh sheet of paper.

> *The Benedict Brief—a prophetic word to the sons and daughters of God's true Church to combat the Ally in their personal lives, and to triumph over the insidious progressivism of the age by standing resolute in the invisible unity of the saints. In God's time, a remnant will be raised up and is now being birthed and prepared for just this time of tribulation in the world's history when Christ's army will again defeat his enemy. The visible and practical face of that enemy is the world and kingdom of man and all it stands for. In these days, that enemy is assiduously at work seducing the minds and hearts of superficially believing men and women through the cancer of progressive perspectives that have entered the bloodstream of man's church as a result of its alliance with the world. In this invisible war, God's remnant is being birthed and called out from both the world and man's church, that it might be molded and strengthened for the coming revelation of God's eternal kingdom into the hearts of mankind.*

He read over the words he had written. A little cumbersome, perhaps, he thought with a smile. He did not have the gift of concise communication Stirling had.

It would do for now. No one but himself, and maybe Grace, would probably read it anyway. This was his interpretation, thought Mark, to help *him* probe the depths of the *Brief.*

Mark continued, reading, jotting down notes, adding a sentence, now a paragraph, to what he had begun. He was reminded of the significant week he had spent years before responding to David's challenge, at the end of which he had compiled a list of the New Testament's commands. It was a week that had changed his life. He had done the same thing then—tried to summarize the commands of the Lord and his apostles in the most succinct way possible, to capture the essence, the heart of the Lord's intent and purpose. He was doing the same thing now—trying to succinctly set down the *essence* of Stirling Marshall's heart.

When he finally stopped a little before eleven, he was tired yet exhilarated from the effort. He had written only two and a half pages and was only a third of the way through the *Brief*. But he would be here a week. For the first time, he was excited about his time in the nation's capital.

He set his pen and his papers and the *Brief* aside on the desk where he had been seated and prepared for bed. It had been a long day and he needed to be rested for tomorrow.

59

JACKPOT!

MIKE BARDOLF had been trying to get something on Mark Forster for years, all the way back to his association with Ward Hutchins. To call Mark Forster a nemesis would be overstating it. But he didn't like an evangelical Christian being in a position to influence the president. It grated on him that the man was so calm, so infuriatingly sure of himself, so confident in his idiotic religion.

He wasn't really worried about anything Forster could do to derail his plans. The man was a fool. He was determined to bring him down off his holier-than-thou pedestal. Yet he had to be careful not to run afoul of the president.

He had been sneaking into Forster's DC apartment every time he was in the capital, thus far without success. He even thought of enlisting the services of a hooker to entrap him but had decided against it. The president would never believe it, and the thing could backfire.

He had to find something else. But the man never left for his meetings without all his personal papers and briefcase with him. For anything he had been able to turn up, the small apartment might as well have been sanitized and emptied of all personal items.

He was waiting at the far end of the parking lot of the complex as usual when the Secret Service driver came to take Forster to the Presidential Manor a little after nine.

Mark had awoken early. After dressing and turning on the coffee maker, he spent the morning so absorbed again in the *Brief* he had not even paused to eat.

When the doorbell rang, he started, then glanced at his watch. The time had completely gotten away from him!

He quickly grabbed the *Brief*, tossed it into his briefcase and shut it, then rose, still distracted and preoccupied from being jarred so suddenly back to the present, strode to the door, and answered it.

There stood the familiar stoic face of the agent usually assigned as his chauffeur when he was in DC.

"Good morning!" said Mark. "I'm afraid I didn't realize what time it was. Just give me a minute."

He turned back into the room, grabbed his coat from the closet, looked around hurriedly, picked up his briefcase, then returned to the corridor, closed the door behind him, and followed the agent to the parking lot.

It was not until they were well on their way through the morning traffic as he sat in the back seat of the limo and Mark gradually calmed and tried to ready himself for the day, that he suddenly realized he'd left his notes on the desk where he'd been at work on them all morning.

A pang shot through him. Grace's words to watch himself flashed through his brain. They were followed immediately by Stirling's own warnings.

He opened his briefcase where it lay on his lap. There sat Stirling's document on top where he had put it. He exhaled a sigh of relief. At least he'd left nothing on the desk in the condo but his handwritten notes and thoughts. Not that anyone would see them anyway. But he had to be more careful. The *Benedict Brief* must *never* leave his sight.

He stuffed it at the bottom of his briefcase beneath his other papers. He could take no chances that anyone at the meeting might see even so much as its title. That alone could raise red flags.

A few minutes later he was on his way through the now familiar gates of the Presidential Manor.

As Mark made his way into the historic residence, across town at the Michelle Obama Housing Complex, after a suitable wait and making sure he wasn't seen, Mike Bardolf let himself into Mark's apartment.

He glanced about briefly, expecting to find nothing more than he had on every previous occasion.

Suddenly his gaze fell on the desk across the room strewn with papers. His eyes shot open. Like a homing pigeon he hurried across the floor, then bent for a closer look.

Caramba! he breathed silently. He'd hit the jackpot! Forster's personal writings!

Taking care to note the exact position of everything on the desk, then taking out his phone to photograph it, he then set each of the five or six pages carefully in place and photographed each, checking to make sure every word was clearly legible.

When he was finished, he replaced them exactly as he had found them, swept through the two rooms hoping perhaps that his good fortune might extend to more discoveries. But there was nothing more.

Leaving the apartment as he had found it, he raced back to his car, eager to print copies of the pages he had discovered and read them thoroughly.

Might he at last have stumbled on a smoking gun that would bring down Mark Forster for good!

60

Code of Treason

MIKE BARDOLF'S high hopes for what his discovery might divulge quickly proved disappointing. That he was reading highly personal thoughts in Forster's own hand was clear enough.

But he couldn't make heads or tails of it. He might as well have been writing in a foreign language.

Tribulation . . . ally . . . saints . . . remnant . . . prophetic word . . . enemy . . . it was all nonsense!

There were, however, a few phrases that leapt out at him.

What could he mean by Christ's army that would be strengthened to defeat his enemy? *What* enemy?

There were other sinister hints . . . *cells . . . private gatherings . . . prayer warriors*, whatever that meant . . . avoiding electronic and other media communications between cell groups . . . keeping below the radar. It was clear there were cell groups throughout the country.

And these quotes, he presumed from the Bible. He glanced down at the words again.

> *Then Zerub'babel the son of She-al'ti-el, and Joshua the son of Jehoz'adak, the high priest, with all the remnant of the people, obeyed the voice of the Lord their God, and the words of Haggai the prophet, as the Lord their God had sent him; and the people feared before the Lord.*

What gobbledygook!

Little wonder no one took the Bible seriously anymore.

And yet . . . it had all the earmarks of a cleverly devised code!

Could it be a secret communication preparatory for an uprising of some kind? It wouldn't be the first time right-wing wackos and militia groups used religious manifestos to conceal their sinister plans.

What did the underlined words and phrases mean?

Putting them together, they gave a clear message: *All the remnant of the people obeyed the voice of the prophet, and the people feared.*

If ever there was a coded message hidden in a passage, he had just found it! That would be just like them—use the Bible to send their secret messages.

It was a call to arms!

When the Prophet spoke—obviously the leader of an underground movement—his *secret army* would obey and rise up and strike *fear* into the country!

It could mean nothing else!

This *Prophet* was obviously at the heart of the conspiracy. Might it be Forster himself?

But would Forster speak of himself using such terms? More likely their leader was someone—

What was that other name mentioned in the notes?

He sifted through the pages again, scanning up and down quickly—there it was—*Stirling Marshall.*

He'd never heard of him, but it must be him!

This Marshall had to be the so-called "Prophet."

And what could be the document he'd supposedly written—the *Benedict Brief*? What was it—*where* was it!

It must contain the group's full plan and agenda—unvarnished, uncoded. That was obviously the reason it was kept secret and why Forster was translating its key elements into some kind of weird biblical code.

He had to get his hands on that brief!

With the document in his hand, he'd be able to take down the whole organization—this Marshall prophet and Forster and all of them. It was a good thing Ward Hutchins was no longer around. With a nationally known figure like him, there was no telling how dangerous this thing might have become. There was talk back then of a secret group. With Hutchins out of the way, he assumed nothing more had come of it.

His pal Forster must have picked up the threads and taken up where Hutchins left off.

As things stood, nobody had heard of the fellow Marshall. Though Forster's name was somewhat known, he had no national reputation. Not yet! At this point the thing probably wasn't dangerous, as long as it could be snuffed out before it got out of control.

One thing was certain—he needed to get rid of Forster.

He was too close to the president. His coming and going in the Presidential Manor put him at the very center of power—the perfect place to launch an underground movement.

He had discovered treason!

61
Eager Enlistee

MIKE LEANED back and let out a long slow thoughtful breath.

He needed to go over every word of the Forster notes in detail. Better yet, find a Christian somewhere in the administration—though that might prove difficult, there weren't many of them around—who knew the Bible and all the Christian lingo who could help him decipher and make sense—

Mike snapped straight up in his chair.

Wait a minute! he thought. There were those people out west that Anson was involved with in the Ward Hutchins affair.

Thirty seconds later he had Anson Roswell on the phone. Three minutes after that he was entering the number Anson had given him.

"Mr. Holt?" he said when a voice answered.

"Yes—I'm Lionel Holt."

"It's Mike Bardolf calling—from the Presidential Manor in Washington, DC."

His throat suddenly dry, Lionel swallowed hard. Trying to keep his composure, he was glad the man on the other end couldn't see him. His face went white hearing his name. He knew well enough who Mike Bardolf was.

"Hello . . ." he said, trying not to sound nervous. "I, uh—I've heard your name."

"Yes, we have a mutual friend, Anson Roswell. You and he used to work together in Sacramento. He's told me you were a big help in our

Ward Hutchins investigation. He gave me your number. I'm calling to ask if you'd like to get into the game at a yet higher level."

"Uh, yeah . . . sure. That'd be great."

"What are your present commitments? Are you still with the governor's office?"

"Yeah. But after Anson left I was moved to the governor's environmental initiative—adding to protected lands, shutting down the oil companies in southern Cal, working to ban timber harvesting and the few remaining lumber mills in the state, cracking down on the underground combustion engine black market—"

Bardolf laughed. "In other words, all the usual suspects."

"That's about it. But I'm going nowhere. It's not exactly the kind of job that keeps you up nights."

"Well, I'd like you to work directly for me. It's a top-secret matter. I can't say how long the assignment will last. But if you agree to come on board, I can promise that I'll take care of you. For now, I'll clear it with the governor for you to go on a leave of absence. I'll make sure you still have a job to return to, although I may want you permanently. You won't be able to tell a soul what you're doing. You okay with that?"

"Absolutely," replied Lionel, still trying to sound calm but perspiring freely.

"Are you still involved in that church where the Hutchins event was held?"

"More or less. I'm not all that active anymore."

"You still have connections?"

"My parents are on staff as assistant pastors and chairpersons of several committees."

"Is Ward Hutchins's friend Forster still there?"

"Not in the church. He resigned a few years ago. He's still around."

"I assume you know him?"

"Yes. My folks don't like him much."

"What about you—are you on good terms with him?"

"I would say so."

The phone was silent a few seconds.

"All right," said Bardolf after the pause, "are you with me?"

"Uh, yes, sure—what do you want me to do?"

"First, I want you to come to DC so we can meet in person," answered Mike, giving his voice a tone of urgency and import which he knew would not be lost on his future lackey. "You cannot breathe a word of it to anyone. Again—this is absolutely top-secret. Not even your parents can know you are connected with me or the president. In working for me, you will be working for the president on a matter of utmost importance for the future of the country. Do you understand?"

Trembling with eagerness, Lionel desperately tried to remain calm.

"I understand, Mr. Bardolf. You can count on me."

"I will talk to the governor. In the meantime, you make the necessary arrangements to get here as soon as you can—don't worry about the cost. We'll pay all your expenses and make it worth your while. I'll make arrangements on this end for your hotel and everything you'll need. When you have your plans set, let me know the specifics and I'll make sure everything is paid."

Four days later Lionel Holt was on a plane bound for the nation's capital.

62

Marching Orders

MIKE BARDOLF knew exactly which buttons to push.

When Lionel Holt checked in for his flight from Sacramento, he was informed that his reservation had been ungraded to first class. Arriving in Washington, he was met by a uniformed chauffeur and driven by limousine to the Marriott. There he found himself already checked in to a three-room suite. He was told that the hotel's room service, bar, coffee shop, and restaurant were at his service. Anything he wanted would go on his room tab, compliments of the Presidential Manor.

Mike Bardolf called on him the following morning, drove him to the Manor, and led him upstairs to his private office. By the time they got down to business, Lionel was putty in his hands. Preliminaries taken care of during the drive in, Mike wasted no time.

"What I am about to share with you, Lionel," he began, "is strictly top-secret. Though I am now the president's top advisor, I have been with the Secret Service for years. I am still technically with the FBI. That should tell you what you need to know about the importance of secrecy. Everything we do must remain just between the two of us. Do you understand?"

"Absolutely. I can keep a secret."

"Good. You recall my asking you about Rev. Forster, the former pastor of your church?"

Lionel nodded.

"You were involved some years ago with our friend Anson Roswell. You informed him of a secret group in your church with connections to both Forster and Rev. Hutchins prior to his untimely death. I had assumed it to have died down. I have reason to believe I may have been mistaken. Do you have information on whether the group is still active?"

"Not much," replied Lionel. "My mom would know. She knows everything that goes on in every church for fifty miles."

"That may be useful. She can know nothing about me, you understand?"

"Of course. I can get it out of her. She'll never suspect a thing. Get my mom talking and she won't come up for air for fifteen minutes."

Mike laughed. "It sounds like you have her pegged! Tell me, what's your sense of the thing? The group I mean?"

"As far as I know it's still active. I don't think they're making such a big deal of secrecy. I think anyone can go to their meetings."

"They have meetings?"

"As far as I know."

"How often?"

"I don't know. Not that often—a few times a year, I think."

"I'm sure you'll be able to find out more details. Is there anyone you're close to who's involved, anyone you could pump for information without arousing suspicion?"

"Not really. There's a girl I grew up with in the church, a couple years younger than me. She's had a crush on me ever since high school. She's a loser, unmarried, still lives with her folks. I think they're all involved."

"What's her name?"

"Heather Marshall."

"*Marshall*! What's her father's name?"

"Timothy."

Mike thought a moment. "The whole family's involved, you say?"

"Used to be. They may be, I don't really know. The girl's dad used to be high up in the church too, with Mr. Forster. But they both mostly dropped out of sight a few years ago. What's it all about, Mr. Bardolf?"

Mike glanced around the room, then lowered his voice for maximum effect.

"We suspect this group, and Rev. Forster in particular, of what may be treasonous activities," he said in what was barely above a whisper. "We think the group in your area is the nucleus for a national network of cells which may be plotting against the government."

Before he was finished, Lionel's eyes were as wide as golf balls with conspiratorial intrigue.

"Their dropping out of church and this secret group of theirs confirms my own information."

"I knew they were up to something!" exclaimed Lionel. "My folks have suspected it all along. But why is Mr. Forster on the president's commission?"

"I'm working on that. I suspect he views his proximity to the Oval Office as a power base to use once they make their move. I am hoping to get him away from Washington before the threat materializes. Obviously, the ideal scenario is to get him behind bars. But I have to have proof. That's where you come in."

"What can I possibly do? I'm no one of importance."

"You may be more important to the future security of the country than you realize. You are in a unique position to infiltrate this group, go underground as it were, find out what you can and report back to me. If we can uncover their plot, we'll be able to bring the whole organization down. You're a clever young man. I'm sure you'll be able to use your wiles to get information out of this young woman you say is infatuated with you—what's her name?"

"Heather—Heather Marshall."

"See what you can learn from her, especially about her father."

"I can do that," nodded Lionel eagerly. "She'll be a pushover."

"I knew I had the right man for the job!" laughed Mike. "Then, too, we'll need to find out about their meetings, when they meet, who's part of it. If we can get a line on the cells around the country, so much the better. Have you ever heard of someone associated with the group called the Prophet?"

"I don't think so."

"Could it be the girl's father?"

"I've never heard that. He's just an average kind of guy—college professor. Though I think he's sort of the leader of the group, he and Mr. Forster."

"Well, keep your ears to the ground. If you hear anything about a Prophet, that could be the key. Let me know whatever you find out—who's involved, upcoming meetings, what they believe, any plans they have—anything at all."

"I will, Mr. Bardolf. You can count on me."

"Good. I'll have my driver take you back to your hotel. You'll be in DC two more days before your flight home. See the sights, have some fun. Do up the city! Here's some spending money," he said, handing Lionel an envelope. "If you need more, call me. Anything you need, Lionel. Though you won't officially be on the FBI books—we can't risk that for the sake of your cover—you can consider yourself an undercover agent for the bureau as my personal operative."

He paused, then handed him a brand new expensive mobile phone.

"This is programmed with my personal number," he said. "It is to be used for nothing else but to call me. If it rings, answer it. It will be me. If you call and I don't answer, leave a detailed message."

Lionel did not open the envelope until he was inside the limousine.

He could hardly keep from whistling softly as he pulled out forty crisp hundred-dollar bills.

63

Sleuthing

LIONEL WAS so eager to get back to Sacramento to begin his top-secret assignment for the president that he was scarcely able to enjoy his two days in the nation's capital. He did, however, manage to spend half of the $4,000 and run up a healthy tab at the Marriott.

Mike Bardolf smiled when he saw the bill. Money in the bank, he thought. Lionel Holt was his for life. Though once he managed to topple Mark Forster and whoever the Prophet was and dismantle their underground group, he would have no more use for a bottom feeder like young Holt. It would be interesting to meet the mother, he thought. Even without seeing her, he knew the type. Who could tell, she might come in useful before this was done.

Lionel wasted no time.

His first call to Mike Bardolf came four days later. Mike did not pick up but opted to let Lionel leave a message. He couldn't let him think he was sitting around waiting for him to call.

> *Mr. Bardolf, it's Lionel Holt. Just to keep you up on what I'm doing—I asked Heather Marshall out for a date but the little vixen turned me down. I don't know what she's thinking, it's not as if she has any options. I doubt if she's ever been on a date in her life. But I'll find out what's going on without her. It so happens that my mother's birthday is in two days. It'll be a perfect cover. I'll invite her and my dad out to dinner at a swanky restaurant in Sacramento. It will be easy to get them*

talking. I'll tell them about what happened with Heather. They'll wonder what possessed me to ask her out but it will be sure to get them talking. They can't stand the Forsters. I should have more for you after that.

True to his word, Lionel called again the day following the evening with his parents. This time Mike answered in person.

"Lionel—how'd it go with your folks?"

"All I had to do was tell them Heather had turned me down and my mom went off. I didn't know this, but Heather's working at the ranch."

"What ranch?"

"The Forster ranch. Circle something, I think. It's where Mr. Forster grew up—his parents' ranch. When he quit the church, he went back to running the ranch with his father."

"Preacher turned cowboy, eh?" laughed Bardolf. "An interesting twist."

"My mom said that's why Heather's so uppity all of a sudden, from being around the Forsters. They're all the same, she says, the Marshalls too and everyone else in their group—think they're better than everyone else, my mom says."

"So the group is still active?"

"It seems so."

"What's it called?"

"I don't know. I don't know if it has a name."

"Who are its members?"

"People from various churches, I think. My mom let slip some names of people she knows who go to the meetings. I'll see what more I can find out. I'll go to church this Sunday. I'll find some of the people she mentioned and chat them up."

"Find out when the next meeting is. Maybe you can figure out some way to be there."

"I think you have to be invited. But what are they going to do—throw me out? I did find out one more thing—Heather's not living with her parents anymore. She bought her grandparents' old house."

"Her grandparents—are they still living?"

"No. Old Stirling and his wife have been dead for years."

"*Stirling*?"

"Stirling Marshall—Heather's grandfather."

Bardolf did not reply immediately. So the man from Forster's notes who wrote the mysterious *Benedict Brief* was the girl's grandfather! *The plot thickens!* he thought to himself.

"Have you ever been there?"

"To the grandparents' house, no. I never had much to do with the Marshalls."

"Does the girl live alone?"

"Not sure."

"And the house—would it still have any of old Stirling's possessions—books, files, papers?"

"I don't know. Sorry."

"Not a problem, Lionel. Okay listen—see if you can find out the girl's schedule, when nobody will be at the house—her grandparents' place. I'll have an agent from the FBI field office in Sacramento contact you. He can get you in. See what you can find out about the group or the old man's writings. You up for a little B and E?"

"Absolutely!"

"She can *not* know you were there. The agent will help make sure of that. Don't make a mess or move anything. He'll have the equipment to photograph anything you find. We've got to find out what their group is up to."

Lionel ended the call tingling with excitement. This was the real thing, he thought—breaking and entering as a secret operative for the FBI!

64

Give All and Follow

AT HEATHER'S recommendation to avoid the Old Testament, Todd had bought a copy of the New Testament the previous autumn. He'd dabbled through it, turning pages, glancing here and there, reading randomly. But also following Heather's advice, he'd mostly concentrated his reading in the first four books.

Though he'd never held a Bible in his hand before, he was surprised how much of it was familiar. There were a million questions it raised in his mind. But over the next few months, without either of them putting it in exactly those terms, Heather guided his reading, referring often to the books she'd given him, making sure he did not become distracted by the myriad side issues of those million questions.

"Watch mostly for four things as you read the Gospels," she told him. "The most important is what Jesus tells his listeners to *do*. Whether he's talking to his disciples or crowds of people, he's really talking to us. The practical *doing* is everything. How does he distinguish between right and wrong, righteousness and hypocrisy, faith and doubt, obedience and sin, goodness and badness."

"Then second, watch for how people respond. Some obey what he says to do, others don't. It's a constant undercurrent through the gospel story. People have to *choose* what they're going to do about what Jesus says. Some are hungry to be good and are eager to obey. Others are angered by being told what to do and reject what he says. Compare how the disciples respond, how the Pharisees respond, and how the people in the crowds respond.

"Also watch how people *grow and change*, especially the disciples. The Christian life is one of growth. Obedience leads to growth. It is fascinating to watch that process taking place in the gospels. The more the disciples grow, the more Jesus expects of them. He is constantly challenging his followers higher, both in their understanding and in their obedience. He never lets his followers coast along. There's no spiritual laziness allowed. One of my grandfather's favorite authors, and mine too, said that God is easy to please but hard to satisfy. In other words, you have to *keep* growing.

"And finally, the fourth might be the most important—pay attention to what Jesus says about *God his Father*. Nothing in Christianity makes sense until you get rid of the notion that God is an ogre whose main purpose is to punish sin and recognize that he is a good and loving and forgiving Father who wants the best for his children. That truth is the foundation of everything."

It wasn't hard for Todd to recognize the first of the four. The Sermon on the Mount at the very beginning of Matthew's gospel was almost entirely comprised of *do*-commands. It was more difficult to see the practical *do* in the first chapters of John's gospel. But the repetition he noticed between the accounts of the other three reinforced the *do* all the more.

Every time he read a passage, he noticed things he hadn't seen before. As he read the story of Jesus's encounter with the wealthy young man in Mark 10 in early February, though he had read it several times, especially as it was repeated almost verbatim in both Matthew and Luke, suddenly the words leapt off the page and hit him between the eyes: "Sell everything—then come, follow me."

Those were words the gospel writers had written, but they entered his brain as: *Give up all and follow.*

In that moment, Todd knew the words were being spoken directly to *him*. Not to some unnamed wealthy young man in the first century, but to Todd Stewart in the year 2051. It was exactly what Heather had said—*he's really talking to us.*

Todd knew that meant *him.*

He wasn't wealthy by any means, but he had done pretty well for himself. As Jesus's words slammed into his brain, however, they did not speak to him about emptying his bank account and selling his few investments and giving all the money to the homeless. The words meant something very different—to give up all he had known until that moment in his life, to give up his past, to give up his security, to give up his reputation—to give *himself*, to give *all* of himself—and follow Jesus.

He could not see into the future. He could not see what might be the consequences of such a radical change in his life. But he knew that Jesus was saying to him, *Follow me anyway. Trust me. Give all and follow.*

The thought sent chills through him.

Was this man who had lived and died more than two thousand years ago speaking to him? Now, *today*? Was such a thing actually possible?

Was Jesus really *alive*!

Like the young man in the story, Todd knew that Jesus was looking straight into his eyes with life's ultimate challenge. A moment of truth had come. It was time for a *yes* or *no*. It was time to follow or turn away. If, like the young man, he chose to turn away, it was time to face the consequences.

Everything reduced to choice, just like Heather said. If he turned away, he had to do so in the full knowledge of what he did. He had to know if the man people called the Son of God had invited *him* to follow. And he had to know how *he* intended to respond.

It wasn't so easy. To follow required giving all.

With Heather's long letter still fresh in his mind from repeated readings, he did not write her again. He could not rely on anyone else now.

What came next in his life was on him.

65

Oblivious to a Legend

TWO WEEKS after his mother's birthday, Lionel Holt was on his way out of the valley on Highway 50 toward Dorado Hills, seated beside FBI agent Rich Sneed, whom Mike Bardolf had enlisted to supervise the break-in at the Marshall home. Lionel had to struggle to stifle his excitement. Agent Sneed, suitably stoic and untalkative, obviously did not share his eagerness. "All in a day's work" about summed up Sneed's demeanor.

They pulled into the driveway. Despite his information, Lionel was nervous that Heather might be at home after all. He followed Sneed to the front door. Breaking in was child's play. They were inside in less than sixty seconds without so much as a scratch on the brass exterior of the door lock or dead bolt.

"I'll leave you to it, then," said Sneed. "You know what Bardolf is looking for. I'll nose around too. Let me know if you need me."

The house was eerily quiet. Though Lionel had only seen Stirling Marshall a few times at church from afar when he was young, the man's reputation was enough to create a preternatural aura deepened by the silence, the bookshelves, even the mystique of Heather's presence, all affecting him with unexpected ghostliness. He shook it off as best he could, oblivious to the reminders of the legendary lives surrounding him.

He wandered about, found Heather's office, then settled in looking about her desk and the papers and files on it, then the folders in the two file drawers beneath it.

When he was ready, he summoned Agent Sneed who photographed everything Lionel thought might be useful. When they left an hour later, not a hair was out of place.

It was somber as they drove out of the foothills. Lionel felt queasy. He had crossed a line of honesty and ethics, and he knew it. He had betrayed one he had known most of his life. As much as he had always looked down on Heather, both literally and figuratively, the moment he walked into the house, he knew that she was on one side of truth, and that he had chosen the other.

When the inner compass of motive has not decided which direction to point, however, qualms of conscience are fleeting, easy to ignore, and quickly die down. Lionel was in too deep to turn back. His moment of truth had come when they walked into the house. Like most crossroads of truth, it came and went in a few seconds. The life-choices of seemingly insignificant men and women produce influences that ripple outward and echo into innumerable individual histories. Lionel never knew that he had passed a life-changing Rubicon that would bring grief and heartache to hundreds.

"I'll make two copies of the photographs," said Sneed when he left Lionel at his apartment in the city. "I'll overnight a set by courier to Bardolf in DC and bring the other set to you. You'll need to go over them in case he needs help interpreting what it means."

Two days later Sneed appeared at his door and handed Lionel a thick packet.

He spent the next two days going over all the documents. By then Bardolf would have his own copies. It was time to call him.

The call went to voice mail.

Mr. Bardolf—it's Lionel. I've been over all the photographs we took at the Marshall home. I think I can give you a pretty clear picture of what's going on. I'll be home the rest of the day. Give me a call when you want to talk.

Bardolf returned his call two hours later.

"There's a lot here to go through," he said. "But nothing from the girl's grandfather."

"No, I couldn't find anything either," said Lionel.

"No hint of anything called the *Benedict Brief*?"

"No. I went through every file cabinet. There was nothing of the old man's. Well, except for hundreds of books. The grandparents have been dead twenty years. They probably got rid of their files or put them into storage when Heather moved into the house. All I could find in the office were Heather's files—mostly copies of letters to people."

"I saw the few you included. Were there more?"

"Hundreds—whole file drawers of letters and copies of her replies. I gather that Heather is sort of the secretary who keeps track of the family correspondence."

"What family?"

"Hers, the Marshalls. Her father and mother write books too. Letters come to them, and even to her grandfather from people who don't know he's dead, from all over the world. Heather writes back. Some of the letters are pretty interesting. I had him photograph those that talked about the group—there doesn't seem to be any name other than calling it a gathering when they get together, though they use the phrase *the common life* a lot."

"What does it mean?"

"I don't know. I tried to get you as many names and addresses of other groups in other places as I could."

"I saw that. They should be helpful. I'll get some of my people investigating. If these are cell groups scattered around the country, we'll plan a coordinated move to take them out. From everything I've seen, I think the Forster and Marshall group is the command center of the thing."

"They've been meeting for a long time. I've heard my mom talking about it for years."

"It's clearly expanding now, with all these other cells involved."

"You found nothing about any prophet?"

"No, only that the word *prophetic* is used a lot in the letters."

"I saw that."

"They're probably talking about Heather's grandfather. I don't know who else it could be."

"It sounds to me like someone still alive—that coded message about the people obeying when the prophet speaks worries me. They're getting ready for some kind of move, I'm certain of it. The gist of the correspondence points to an underground grassroots movement. That's the most dangerous kind. They seem particularly intent on not being allied with churches. That's my chief concern. We can manage the churches. We've had them under control for decades. But whatever this is, it won't be so easy to manipulate as the organized church."

The line went quiet.

"All right then," said Bardolf after a few seconds. "We'll continue perusing what you sent and running down the names on these lists. That's the most useful thing you uncovered. Well done, Holt. This is a good start. You keep digging, talking to people, nosing about. Don't give up on the girl. She's at the heart of this thing, along with Forster and her parents. You might be able to worm your way closer to her yet."

"I don't think she likes me much. I wasn't very nice to her when we were young."

"Use your wiles. Turn on the charm. You're a good-looking guy. Wine her and dine her—take her someplace expensive. Sweep her off her feet. I'm picking up the tab, remember. I have confidence in you. In the meantime, let me know if you learn anything further."

66

Manifesto for Revolution

MIKE BARDOLF put the phone aside, leaned back and again perused the sheaf of documents photographed from the Marshall home.

The biggest surprise was the extent of the movement. By all accounts it was an international conspiracy—with cells in England, Germany, Poland, Scotland, Australia! They clearly had wider designs than merely the US.

But *what* designs?

He glanced through some of the letters again. He could hardly make sense of them.

A letter addressed to Alexandria caught his eye. That was close by. It could be important.

Dear Mr. and Mrs. Nason,

Thank you so much for your letter and for your interest in my mother's and father's and grandfather's writings. I am Heather Marshall, Stirling Marshall's granddaughter. I help my father and mother—Timothy and Jaylene Marshall—with the correspondence. It is amazing how much mail still comes to my grandfather twenty years after his death. His books continue to strike a chord in many hearts.

It is not too much to say that there is a growing movement building that regards my grandfather as nothing less than a prophet for his wisdom in having seen much that would transpire in our country and in the church in the years after his death. You said as much in your letter. All around the country, small cell groups are springing up, reading and studying and discussing his books and seeking to put into practice the principles he articulated so profoundly. It is nothing less than a quiet revolution as hearts are knit together in common cause around the country and around the world—dedicated to making a difference, to rebuilding the Church from the ground up, to changing our failing nation and changing the world. I'm sure you, Mr. Nason, being a member of Congress, are acutely aware of that need. You mentioned seeing every day new and more scandalous policies becoming law, and you are powerless to stop it. It must be heartbreaking to be so close to it!

Caramba!

Of course—how could he have missed it on the letterhead. This letter was from Pennsylvania congressman Nason, chairman of the House Armed Services Committee! He was a man thought to be a loyal member of the Progressive Party!

The conspiracy had infiltrated that far!

He continued reading the Marshall girl's reply.

A remnant of God's people is being called out from the influences of the world and its systems, called out from its politics, from its depraved culture, called to arise and stand for truth, even to fight for truth against the lies of our times. You are surely of that remnant!

It sounds like the small group you are meeting with is already doing that, like so many others. We are all joined together, underground, invisible cells committed to a common purpose. We will be praying for you and covet your prayers for those who gather here and elsewhere.

How wonderful it would be if you could join us for a gathering we have planned where people from around the country, even from around the world, will be coming to pray and strategize how to live the life my grandfather wrote about—a truly revolutionary life in these perilous times.

I am enclosing a brochure of books we have for sale and information about next month's gathering.

I will pass your letter on to my parents. They may want to reply also.

I hope to hear from you again, and maybe, God willing, meet you one day.

Many blessings,
Heather Marshall

Mike sat shaking his head. This thing had tentacles reaching into the government. A cell in the heart of Congress!

He sifted through the rest of the papers but did not find the brochure the girl had mentioned. That would have been helpful to see. He'd have to ask Lionel about it.

This was an obvious solicitation both for money and an invitation to affiliate Nason's cause to their own. It was so thinly veiled as to be laughable. It was a recruitment letter for the movement!

The conspiracy was wider than he had imagined!

He rose and returned to his desk. He opened the file containing the copy of Mark Forster's notes. Reading through them again, the coded language and innuendos were unmistakably similar to what he had just read.

As individuals and small groups spontaneously come together, Forster had written, an underground, silent, hidden movement will organically act as leaven in a church that has become complicit in the worldliness of the times. This invisible army, unknown to the world and its system, its methods of warfare incomprehensible to the carnal mind of progressivism, will grow and expand into a revolution of world separation unto Christlikeness.

Whatever Christlikeness meant, he hadn't a clue. Everything he had seen and heard and read about these people showed clearly enough that they were intoxicated with preposterous notions.

That's what made them dangerous. Their leader of the first century had been a revolutionary too, equally full of idiotic ideas. It had cost him his life on a cross, though the revolution ignited by his followers had turned the Roman Empire upside down.

He didn't intend to let it get that far in this millennium!

If it took equally stringent measures to quash it before the danger became too widespread, Bardolf would see to it.

Who else could the prophet be than the girl's grandfather, the author of the elusive *Benedict Brief*?

He had to get his hands on that document! It was clearly a call to arms with the power to revolutionize Christianity and make it a force again.

All doubts were swept from his mind—the *Benedict Brief* was a manifesto for Christian revolution!

I will gather the remnant of Israel; I will set them together
like sheep in a fold, like a flock in its pasture. . . .
He who opens the breach will go up before them;
they will break through and pass the gate,
going out by it. Their king will pass on before them.

— **Micah 2:12–13**

PART 3
A GATHERING
SPRING 2051

67

ARRIVALS

APRIL 2051

MARK FORSTER'S trips to Washington, DC, through the winter and spring coincided with the planning and preparation for the gathering Timothy and Jaylene had set in motion. The invitations and notifications sent out through the final months of the previous year resulted in an unexpected outpouring of enthusiastic response.

No sooner had the holiday season turned the corner and given way to the new year than plans for the weekend got underway in earnest. The four women—Jaylene and Heather Marshall and Grace and Laura Forster—got busy planning meals and lodging possibilities, also trying to anticipate expenses. Once it became obvious that both ranches would be needed, Mark, Timothy, and David planned out the weekend's schedule, logistics of parking, tables, chairs, and how to coordinate activities and transportation between the Circle F and Bar JG.

Grace had only been able to accompany Mark during his January trip to the capital. The highlight of those few days for Grace were her visits with First Lady Marcia Rhodes, including a very personal time of sharing between the two wives at the living quarters of the Presidential Manor. Their embrace at the conclusion of the visit gave clear evidence that a lifetime friendship had begun. After Mark's trip to the capital alone in March, it was obvious to Grace that reservations had set in about how much longer he could participate in what seemed may have been a charade all along.

When the first week of April arrived, with spring bursting out in the California foothills from an unseasonably warm March, over a hundred had signed up for the "Marshall Gathering" from out of the area. The organizing and arranging for food and lodging became a planning nightmare.

Those signed up included six overseas couples: Leon and Alita Morales from Ecuador, Moira and Alexander Campbell from Scotland, Richard and Jessica Constable from London, Fynn and Monika Sievers from Germany, Grigor and Anya Popov from Russia by way of Poland, and Paddy and Charlene Ayscough from New Zealand.

Also scheduled to come for the weekend were Gerald and Rebecca Stevens from Kansas, Matthew and Sarah Gardner from Idaho, Geoffrey and Martha Powell from Texas, and Violet and Trevor Langdon from New York, along with dozens of individuals, couples, and families, from Maine to Washington, from Florida to Hawaii. At the very last minute, they were surprised and delighted to receive a letter from the Nasons in Alexandria, Virginia, whom Heather had only written a week earlier, asking if it was too late for them to participate. Excitement rose all the more to hear that a high-ranking congressman was scheduled to attend.

Fortunately, there was plenty of help from all the members of the FCL group—all the ladies baking for two weeks in advance. Both large Gordon and Forster ranch houses and the few former bunkhouses that were in condition to be cleaned up and made suitable, with cots and rented beds brought in, were sufficient for twenty or twenty-five each. The rest would stay with local couples, some in motels in Grass Valley, along with others who were bringing tents to pitch at the two ranches, several also pulling trailers for which there was ample room. David's ranch would be used for the large group meetings, lunches, and suppers, with breakfast handled individually at the two ranch houses.

With now fifteen or twenty men and women from Foothills participating regularly in FCL's periodic get-togethers, it could not be helped that talk circulated. Their most diligent efforts to downplay the meetings over the last eight or ten years had not been completely successful. Curiosity mounted in the Foothills congregation.

It was well-known that the leaders of the group—David Gordon and Timothy and Jaylene Marshall—were long-time members of Foothills, though not active in recent years. Word of a large event to be held at the Gordon ranch where tents would be set up, especially with people coming from all over the world, created the impression of a Christian rock festival. That set tongues wagging even more. All they could do was keep the plans as low-key as possible. As the time approached, however, the whole church knew about the upcoming "Marshall Gathering."

A loose schedule was planned from Friday through Sunday—with those arriving Thursday evening getting together for an informal buffet supper in the Gordon ranch house.

As the guests made their way out of the Sacramento valley into the foothills and began arriving at the Bar JG Ranch—the organizational headquarters for the weekend—Timothy, Jaylene, and Heather felt like they knew everyone already. They had been corresponding with most of the newcomers for years. For the three Marshalls, the greetings were reunions more than first-time meetings.

The Langdons from New York were the first to arrive Thursday afternoon. Jaylene knew them immediately from photographs. She ran to the car as the passenger door opened.

"Oh, Violet, I can't believe it!" she exclaimed. "To see you at last!"

The two women embraced with tears flowing. Timothy followed and shook hands with Trevor as he also climbed out.

"It's warm!" said their first guest, gazing about. "We left forty-five degrees in New York!"

"What can I say—it's California," laughed Timothy. "This is actually a little warm for April.—Oh, and here's our daughter Heather."

Heather and Violet embraced with equal warmth, and the three Marshall hosts led them toward the house.

The Gardners from Idaho, with whom there had been several visits through the years, were only thirty minutes behind. As they pulled in, they found themselves greeted by a committee of five.

"Sarah," said Jaylene excitedly, "meet my new friend Violet Langdon. She and her husband just arrived from New York.—Violet, Sarah and Matthew live in Idaho."

"New York!" said Sarah as she and Violet shook hands. "That's a long trip."

"From what I understand we haven't come nearly so far as some of the others."

"When did you leave?" asked Sarah.

"Early this morning. And you?"

"We drove down. It's eight hundred miles. We stayed over in a little town in the middle of Oregon called Crescent."

Court and Stella Masters drove up in the midst of the greetings. Whenever they were introduced, their names were familiar to everyone from the *Master's Helps Newsletter*, which had become a written network connecting most of the unofficial but expanding fellowship.

Mark had driven to the airport with their van. He arrived about forty minutes later with the Stevens from Kansas and Powells from Texas, whose flights had arrived near the same time.

Richard and Jessica Constable drove in about 5:00. They had arranged flights from London to San Francisco with Moira and Alexander Campbell. The new friends spent two days together before driving northeast into the Sacramento valley and foothills.

"Richard!" exclaimed Timothy, shaking his hand warmly, "I cannot tell you how much I have looked forward to meeting you."

"And I you.—Meet my countryman from the north, Alexander Campbell."

"Alexander," said Timothy, "—welcome to California's gold country."

"My wife, Moira," said Alexander.

"The Bible study leader! Hello, Moira—welcome. I am Timothy Marshall.—Oh, and here comes my wife and daughter.—Jaylene, Heather, meet the Campbells and Constables."

"Moira—Jessica—we are so happy to have you," said Jaylene. "Come and meet some of the others who have also just arrived."

Grace, Ginger, and Craig Forster and several more local families arrived by the time Mark drove up with the Stevens and Powells. Though only a third or quarter of the full contingent would arrive on Thursday, so many cars were parked in front of David's barn that Mark could hardly find room for the van. With much of the local group on hand and another twenty from across the country, the ranch house was by now full of lively conversation, all the women bustling about with supper preparations.

To all appearances everyone had known the others for years. Walking in with Gerald and Rebecca and Geoffrey and Martha, Mark had to squeeze his way through the kitchen and introduce them before Jaylene and Grace put the two women to work while Mark continued into the great room to introduce Matthew and Gerald to the others.

The evening was full of a deeply shared camaraderie of spirit. No one was anxious to leave, yet the weekend was only beginning. They would all meet another four or five dozen new brothers and sisters the next day!

An hour or two after supper, the exuberance of many new friendships and the fatigue of travel was taking its toll. Everyone was exhausted from pure joy.

The guests departed to the homes of their local hosts, some crammed into the van or followed in their cars to the Forster ranch. Those remaining at the Bar JG adjourned to David's bedrooms and bunkhouse, and several families to the tents they had pitched about the ranch earlier—with much help from a multitude of advisors.

Only her parents and closest friends noticed Heather's subdued spirits as the day advanced into evening. She left shortly after supper and drove alone to the Circle F where she would spend the weekend.

68

What Does It Mean to Be a Man?

TODD STEWART'S flight into Sacramento was four hours late. He had hoped to arrive before evening supper to give him time to find a motel. Now here he was heading out of the city into the foothills in his rental car with the afterglow of the sunset fading into darkness at the horizon in his rear-view mirror. He still had an hour's drive ahead of him.

Though no one was expecting him, he had pored over the weekend's schedule. By now he knew it by heart. He'd received the invitation three months ago, enclosed in one of Heather's letters. He'd asked her a few initial questions, but they had not discussed it since. Nor had he RSVP'd.

He wasn't sure such a gathering was for him—or that he *should* attend. It was obviously designed for serious Christians. He had never considered himself a Christian. Would it be right to attend under false pretenses? He had been completely open and honest with Heather about his uncertainties. He knew his mere presence would lead to assumptions, especially, though he hated to think in such terms, given his former notoriety.

It wouldn't be fair to the others attending, *or* to Heather and her parents, for him to show up, crash the party, as it were, knowing full well, to put it bluntly, that he wasn't one of them.

His perplexity mounted as the weeks passed. He remained silent, avoiding Heather's persistent questions.

Now he hadn't written or called in three weeks. He could only imagine what she must be wondering, especially with all her calls going to voice mail, and his returning none of them. But he couldn't talk to her again until he had some answers.

Far more was on his mind than Heather or the April gathering. Ever since that day he'd read the gospel of Mark, he knew that his own appointment with destiny was approaching.

Finally, a week ago he told the station manager of the local station where he was working that he needed a few days. They had been so delighted to add *the* Todd Stewart to their staff—though he refused to appear on camera and only agreed to write copy and help with their online news blog—that he could pretty much do as he pleased, especially in that he had only requested an entry-level salary.

He'd left the city and driven west into the Virginia hills. There he spent two days at the Big Meadows Lodge walking the trails and drinking in the solitude in and around Shenandoah National Park.

On his second full day in the Blue Ridge Mountains, while walking deep in the forest along the Dark Hollow Falls trail, not another soul in sight, he gradually sensed a Great Silence descending upon him. It was eerily like a physical presence.

His steps slowed and came to a stop. Words from Heather's letter came back to him, pouring over him out of the silence like a warm, gentle, comforting rain.

God simply says, "Live by my principles. Obey me as your Father. Be my good and obedient children, and it will go well with you. Life will be a good thing. I will bless you because I love you."

He knew the Presence he felt wasn't Heather. A chill swept through him in spite of a hint of coming warmth in the fragrant spring air.

He was not alone. Again came words out of the silence into his brain—personal words meant only for him.

Be a man. Become my son.

Long seconds passed. "God," he whispered almost inaudibly, "is it really *you* whose presence I sense?"

He did not encounter another human being for more than an hour. Yet he was almost embarrassed to have spoken aloud.

Had he just *prayed* for the first time in his life!

He felt no different. It wasn't spooky or weird as he might have thought. It actually felt natural, somehow calming, soothing—like feeling his hand in his father's before his father's death, like drifting to sleep in the back seat as his father drove home through the darkness, like a gentle rain on the roof of his bedroom. The memories of his father were faint but evoked a deep sense of contentment.

Heather said that God was just the best Father who ever was, a Father whose only desire was to grow and nurture sons and daughters to be like Jesus.

What an astonishing thing for someone to say in this modern progressive technological age—that obeying Jesus and growing her soul to become like him was the only thing she wanted—her supreme goal of life. Heather *had* said it. In the time he had known her, she had continued to be exactly what he had sensed on the day he first laid eyes on her—the most real, grounded, and *at peace* individual he had ever met.

By now he realized, too, that he just might love her. That was one of the reasons he hadn't written or called. He was afraid he might say too much. She had never been involved with a man. He had to be very careful of her feelings. He could say nothing until he was sure.

At this moment his thoughts about Heather were so intermingled with his thoughts about God and life and what it all meant that he could hardly disentangle them. Were they just two people who chanced to meet at a moment of time but whose lives would continue moving in different directions? Or had something more lasting begun? Only time could answer that question.

In the meantime, if what Heather said was true, and God was a good, loving, nurturing, forgiving, kind, and compassionate Father, why shouldn't he talk to him, pour out his thoughts to him as he used to do with his own father before his untimely death? He no longer had an earthly father. That was all the more reason he should get to know his heavenly Father. Why shouldn't he confide in him, ask him all the questions he could think to ask? Heather said he would speak back, but that he spoke in the silence . . . *out* of the silence . . . *within* the silence . . . that his Voice was hard to hear . . . that you had to learn to hear it in the midst of your own thoughts and feelings.

God, if you are my Father, I want to know it, said Todd, though he said the words silently in his mind. *I want to hear your voice, though I hardly know how I would recognize it if you did speak.*

He was praying again, yet was no longer thinking of it as prayer. He was simply talking to God, to the Father he could not see but who was around him in the silence. The Father who *was* the Presence.

He drew in a deep breath of the clean forest air.

I want to know you, he continued, whether whispering or silently thinking the words he could not even tell. All he knew is that they were bubbling up from hidden wellsprings within him. *I want to know the truth—If you are real, if you are mankind's Father, if I am truly your son, then I want to be your son. I don't even know what that means. I don't know how you speak, but I ask you to speak to me.*

He found a fallen log nearby and sat. He remained a long while in the deep, resonating silence of the forest trying to absorb what these last few minutes meant. Whispered prayer again rose up.

God, show me what to do now, show me what it means to be your son, to be a follower of Jesus. Do with me what you will. Make me the man you want me to be.

His thoughts and prayers fell silent. He had just uttered the most profound prayer in the universe, the prayer of yielding the will of sonship into the heart of eternal Fatherhood.

69

Face in the Crowd of Decision

TODD'S THOUGHTS drifted back to the reading he had done in recent months, the people he had met in the pages of the gospel—Peter with his tumultuous outbursts and eager enthusiasm, the Pharisees with their hard hearts, those who believed instantly and those who doubted, those who followed and those who turned away. At the heart of it was Jesus himself.

As he sat, the reality of everything he had read swept back over him with such power it seemed he was there with them, watching and listening with the disciples, with the crowd. He was part of the gospel story.

The incidents he'd read filled his memory one upon another. The forest around him gave way to the hot dusty roads and countryside of ancient Galilee. The sights and sounds and commotion of that remarkable intersection of history filled him with such reality that he was *there*, being pulled along with the rest. He could feel and hear the crowd pressing to get as close to Jesus as they could.

Suddenly in his mind's eyes he saw the wealthy young man surrounded by the hubbub and noise. The expression on his face was anxious, eager, uncertain. Would he have courage to step forward and ask the question that had prompted him to join the crowd on this day? All around men and women, proud scribes and priests, beggars and tax collectors and soldiers, mothers with children, the sick and lame, young men and old, clamored to get close to the man in their midst.

The wealthy young man squeezed through. Sensing his presence, Jesus turned, scanning the multitude. His eyes come to rest upon him.

Seeing him gazing intently at the young man, slowly the crowd stilled and quietly moved away, leaving the young man isolated and alone in its midst. The eyes of the two met. The young man suddenly felt exposed, vulnerable, naked amid the silent stares around him.

As the reality of the moment became overpowering, Todd stared straight at the young man. He was as clear in his mind as if he was standing in front of him. The face before him came into focus. Chills and goosebumps swept through him and he began to tremble. Standing in front of him was no first-century rich young ruler. He was staring at his own face!

It was *him*! Todd Stewart was at the center of the crowd!

Jesus's eyes bored straight into his. A hush descended. All his friends, his family, everyone he had ever known—the whole world was watching to see what would come next.

Todd *was* the young man!

Jesus's expression was warm, friendly, inviting. Todd sensed that he had known him for years, from long before he met Heather. He had known him his whole life. He had been waiting all this time for the right moment to gaze deeply into Todd's eyes.

At last he nodded imperceptibly.

"I want you to come with me," he said.

A moment more he waited, then Jesus turned and began walking away.

Todd stared after him. He was no longer a mere spectator. Jesus had found him in the midst of the multitude. He had issued the timeless invitation and challenge, "Come."

Then Jesus turned and spoke again.

"Are you ready, Todd Stewart?" he said. "This is the moment. Will you give all and follow, or will you turn away?"

As unexpectedly as the startling image had filled his consciousness, suddenly it was gone. Todd was again alone in the forest seated on a fallen log. The quiet of the solitude around him deepened.

Give all to follow echoed out of the silence.

He rose, drew in a deep breath, stood, and gazed up into the canopy of the trees above him.

Jesus, he whispered, *I am ready to follow. I don't know all it means, but if you show me I will try to do what you want me to do. I want you to live with me and inside me. I am ready to give myself to you for whatever you want to do with me.*

He began walking back the way he had come. He felt a strange emptiness. Yet it was also a clean fullness of something—he knew not what—he had never felt before.

A longing rose within him to tell Heather what he had done. Yet he knew that he had to wait for the Presence, the Voice, the Silence to speak. It was not Heather's voice he needed to hear from next.

It was God's.

70

Souls in the Foothills Moonlight

ALONE IN her room at the Circle F in the evening, Heather heard the Forster van return, followed by the several cars and trailers of those who would be staying at the ranch for the weekend. The new arrivals poured into the house in a boisterous mood laughing and talking as Mark and Grace organized sleeping arrangements. Her door was closed. She did not go out all evening. She knew she would find it difficult to enter the spirit of the weekend.

An hour passed, then two as the evening slowly crawled by. Eventually the house quieted. By eleven, the house, outbuildings, and grounds of the Circle F were mostly asleep. She had been trying to read but couldn't concentrate.

Another thirty minutes went by. It was no use. She might as well go to bed.

Ten minutes later at last she lay down, the lamp at her bedside still on. She opened her *Pocket Thomas Kempis*. She had been in the bathroom moments before and hadn't heard the crunching of tires of a late arrival on the gravel outside.

As she tried to concentrate on the familiar words—

Make me a dutiful and humble disciple. O that with your presence you would wholly inflame me, consume, and transform me . . .

—an indistinct sound startled her. Was that a faint knocking on her window! A sudden fright of girlish boogieman fancies sent goosebumps up and down her spine.

Quickly she reached over and turned off her light, then lay deathly still.

There it was again!

What could it be? A raccoon on the window sill?

Then, in no more than a whisper, she heard her name.

Heather . . . Heather!

Terror seized her, yet at the same moment an awful trembling hope. The next instant she was out of bed dashing for the window. Remembering the light, she spun around and turned on her lamp. In seconds her quivering fingers were fumbling with the window latch.

The light from across the room shone on a face in the darkness.

"Todd!" she gasped as she lifted the sash. "What are you . . . oh, my goodness . . . wait a second . . . I'll just—!"

Seconds later, wrapped in her robe but still in bare feet, Heather crept through the door of her bedroom into the chilly night, wondering if she'd been dreaming.

There he stood waiting, all six foot three of him!

Neither said a word. He stooped and swallowed her in his arms. Heather was glad for the darkness as she returned his embrace. She was crying and knew she could not stop the tears.

"I'm sorry I didn't let you know I was coming," said Todd as they stepped apart. "I didn't know myself until yesterday. I know it's late. I need to go find a motel somewhere, but I had to see you before I did anything."

"Don't be . . . I mean . . . I can't believe you're . . . it's . . ."

Heather was trembling and could hardly get the words out.

"We'll find a place," she went on. "Go get your things—I'll be . . . come here to my room—I'll be right back."

She turned back inside, wiping frantically at her eyes. She opened her door into the house, tiptoed down the hall to Ginger's room, and crept inside. She turned on the bedside lamp. As gently as she could, she placed a hand on her shoulder.

"Ginger . . . Ginger . . ."

Groggily Ginger turned toward her.

"Heather," she said sleepily.

"I'm sorry," said Heather, "but I need to bring in a blanket and pillow and sleep on your floor tonight. I thought it best to wake you so you don't stumble over me in the night."

"What's going on?"

"An unexpected guest just turned up. He will be using my room tonight."

"That's nice," said Ginger, rolling over again. "Just turn my light out when you're done. I'm going back to sleep."

Ten minutes later, Heather dressed warmly and arrangements made for them in both bedrooms, Heather and Todd left the ranch house. A three-quarter moon gave ample light to walk by, though Heather carried a flashlight. It was still early enough in the year that at this elevation the nights turned cold. Neither said a word until they were well away from the house, and the three pitched tents and trailer parked near the barn. Heather led the way along one of the well-worn trails through the pasture. Gradually they began to talk softly.

"I'm sorry I stopped writing and calling," said Todd. "There were some important things I needed to think about."

"I knew you had a good reason," replied Heather. "Well, I *mostly* knew," she laughed lightly. "I admit I sometimes couldn't help worrying. I thought you might be getting sick of me."

"Not a chance!"

"Or that I was saying too much in my letters."

"It wasn't that at all. That one you wrote, you know explaining what being a Christian means to you—or I guess more how you see the Christian faith as a whole—I've been thinking about it ever since. I'm so glad you didn't keep it to five hundred words. It was such a help putting things into perspective for me. I've probably read it ten or twelve times. But it's hard to absorb it all. I needed alone time, I guess you'd say."

He went on to tell her about his time in the Shenandoah hills. By the time they returned to the ranch house, it was well after midnight. Both were shivering. But their hearts were warm, quiet, and at peace.

They walked into Heather's room.

"I hope you can get some sleep," said Heather. "The house will probably be bustling early getting breakfast going for the guests. Then we'll be heading over to David's by noon."

"I'll manage," said Todd. "I'm still on Eastern time, so I'm sure I'll be awake. If not, come and roust me out of bed!"

They looked at one another a moment.

"I'm really glad you came," said Heather.

"Me too," said Todd.

They smiled, then Heather turned and left for her accommodations on Ginger's floor.

71

Friends and Brothers, Sisters and Notables

THE FIRST inkling Timothy and Jaylene had of a change in their daughter's destiny came as they drove into the precincts of the Circle F ranch the following morning about ten. They had stopped on the way to David's to see if rides were needed. In the distance they saw a very tall young man and a very short young woman with a slight limp walking toward the house hand in hand.

"Oh . . . my . . . goodness!" said Jaylene slowly. "Is that—"

"The one at barely over five feet, the other several inches over six, I don't think there is much doubt about it."

"But are they—"

"They are!" replied Timothy, starting to laugh. "Is something happening with our little girl!"

They parked and got out, then stood by the car and waited. As the two drew closer, the glow on Heather's face said all there was to say. She let go of Todd's hand and bounded somewhat jerkily toward them with the happy exuberance of a child.

"Look who came!" she said.

"We can see!" laughed Jaylene.

Todd walked up behind Heather. "Hello, Mr. Marshall," he said, shaking Timothy's hand. "And Mrs. Marshall," he added, turning to Jaylene. "It is wonderful to see you both."

"When did you arrive?" asked Timothy.

"Not until late. My flight was delayed. I sort of snuck in."

"He knocked on my window!" said Heather, giggling. "I was still awake and was so shocked to see him standing outside. Everyone else was asleep. I gave Todd my room and I slept on the floor in Ginger's. She woke up and said, 'What are you doing here!' She didn't even remember that I'd woken her the night before."

"I wanted to see Heather first," said Todd. "I had planned to find a motel, but she wouldn't hear of. I didn't want her to sleep on the floor. I could have slept in my car, but she was insistent."

Timothy and Jaylene laughed. "You're telling us!" rejoined Timothy.

"Daddy! He was three hours ahead of us and with his flight delays he needed a good night's sleep."

"Well, let's go in and see how we can be useful," said Jaylene. "I'm sure Grace could use some extra hands."

"If there's anything I can do," said Todd.

"We'll be loading up some tables and chairs to take over to David's," said Timothy. "We will definitely put you to work."

While Timothy, Jaylene, Heather, and Todd drove over to David's in three cars, car-pooling with as many of the early arrivals as would fit to keep the congestion to a minimum, Mark departed again in the van for the airport. There he awaited the Popovs and Moraleses, both arriving Friday morning, the Popovs coming in on a connection from an overnight flight via Amsterdam.

The drive into the foothills in the van, English being spoken with three distinct accents, was lively. By the time Mark pulled the van under the Bar JG sign, the South American and Eastern European couples were talking excitedly amongst themselves. Weary as they were from long multiple flights, once they arrived at the ranch, Grigor and Anya refused to lie down even for a brief nap. They didn't want to miss a minute! By then, the Ayscoughs had arrived from New Zealand. The newcomers walked inside to laughter, Paddy keeping the group entertained with a description of his first experience driving on the right side of the road as he navigated their rental car from the airport to the ranch.

As the great room in David's house would accommodate thirty-five or forty at most, once RSVPs began pouring in, David and Timothy came up with a plan. They would meet in David's largest barn. Once used for cattle and large equipment storage, the huge building normally sat unused and half empty except for the two hundred or so hay bales needed for David's five horses, now in early spring the number of bales depleted to fewer than fifty.

Three weeks before the event, they invited the local members of their FCL group to the ranch for a Saturday workday to put the barn in order. Most of the rusting old equipment, two tractors and miscellaneous implements and paraphernalia of a hundred years of ranching life was moved outside behind the barn. David declared he should have gotten rid of half of it long before now.

What cleaning was possible followed, though it amounted mostly to raking away loose straw and hay from the floor and sweeping the hard-packed dirt, and as much as possible raking or brooming away what overhead cobwebs they could reach. When they were finished, a large center area was cleared that would have been suitable for an old-fashioned hoedown or, more for their purposes, that would hold a hundred or more chairs.

David closed all the doors and other openings as best he could and set off a dozen pest bombs. But it was an old barn. They could not hope to eliminate all the spiders and bugs and insects that might consider it home and that had been roused out of their hiding places by the clean-up activity. If they reduced the native population even by a third, he hoped it would make for a more comfortable time of it for everyone.

A few days before the first arrivals, early one morning, Mark and Timothy, still members though of somewhat dubious standing, drove David's forty-year-old flatbed to the church and loaded a 120 folding chairs from one of the storage rooms, along with several long folding tables. By the time the guests arrived, the chairs were set up in the barn. Some of the men and many of the young people, however, chose instead to sit on the hay bales scattered about the perimeter, a few with legs dangling over the ledge of the hayloft at the far end. The tables sat outside the house for outdoor buffet meals. Happily, the weather remained cooperative.

As more guests arrived throughout Friday, most of the time was spent in informal visiting and walks about the ranch, with David conducting trail rides for the intrepid horsemen and horsewomen among them.

Word had spread, especially among the local group, that a number of individuals of note had responded to the personal invitations they had received.

Between 1:00 and 2:00 Mark left for the airport. When he returned several hours later, he had with him Eloise and Deidra Hutchins and Sandra Rhodes, who had flown in on the same flight from Seattle. Meanwhile, Charles and Regina Reyburn drove in from the south about the same time that Harvey and Harriet Jansen drove down out of the Sierras on Interstate 80 from the east, then made their way from the highway into the foothills ranch land.

By supper that evening, most of those who would be attending had arrived. Tents and trailers were spread about the grounds and the outdoor buffet meal was festive, introductions and greetings flowing everywhere throughout the diverse mix of by then 120, with a few more arrivals scheduled the following morning. Timothy and Jaylene, official hosts of the gathering did their best to make personal contact with everyone, meeting most for the first time. They were eager to personally introduce their international guests to as many as possible.

The arrival late in the afternoon of such high-profile guests as the president's mother, the former Republican presidential candidate, the recognizable face of NBC's former Presidential Manor reporter, and the author of *Roots: America Reclaims its Heritage*, which the country was still talking about, heightened excitement and kept the atmosphere electric with anticipation. There were so many "guests of honor" everyone wanted to meet that the informal supper and milling around afterward could have gone on for hours.

With the aid of a large resonant bell which David's grandmother once used to call their ranch hands to meals a century before, and with the help of Mark and Todd and Jaylene and Heather and Court Master's authoritative presence, Timothy managed to herd the boisterous assembly toward the barn. Settling the subdued roar of dozens of individual conversations even then proved a daunting task. It was approaching eight before they were all seated and Timothy, standing in front, could make himself heard.

"It seems entirely unnecessary to open with words of welcome," he began. "We've barely begun, yet it seems you have all been friends for years. Seeing you here, meeting many of you for the first time, is more special than we can express for Jaylene and me. We feel we know most of you from the rich correspondence of many years. Yet our hearts are full to share our common life in the Spirit face-to-face.

"You are all special guests and dear to our hearts. As you know by now, we are honored to have a number of singular men and women among us. I only call attention to them to tell you that they are ordinary men and women like the rest of us. They do not want to be treated with deference but as brothers and sisters in the common life we share. So introduce yourselves and meet them and share God's life with them in our mutual brotherhood. I am speaking especially of the man I am now privileged to call my friend, Professor Charles Reyburn and his wife, Regina, Congressman Alfred Nason and his wife, Catherine, and our family's new friend—I am speaking on behalf of my wife *and* daughter," he added, smiling as he glanced to Heather and Todd where they were seated together, "Todd Stewart. Also our new friends whom it is such a privilege to welcome to California under what are happier circumstances than his visit to our state three years ago, Harvey Jansen and his wife, Harriet."

Timothy paused to allow the glances and the buzz of comment and some light laughter and nods of acknowledgment from those he had mentioned to die down.

"Is it true, Dr. Reyburn?" asked one of the new arrivals, "that you are going to run for president?"

The room went suddenly silent. The expression on Dr. Reyburn's face said clearly that the question took him by surprise.

"I have no idea where you would have gotten such an idea," he answered slowly. "No—of course not. I would never run for public office."

"I've heard rumors."

"About *me*?"

"Yes."

Reyburn shook his head. "Honestly, this is the first I've heard about it. I can tell you categorically that there isn't an atom of truth to whatever you've heard."

"What about you, Senator?" the man asked, turning to Harvey Jansen. "Might you run again?"

"My answer would be identical," answered the former candidate. "I will never run for office again. But I will say it is nice to be back in California, as Timothy said, under *much* happier circumstances than my previous visit! Stay away from police departments in Los Angeles, is my advice—am I right, Todd?"

Todd sighed at the reminder. "Don't remind me!" he said.

"For those of you who may not have seen his interview with Harriet and me," Jansen stood and went on, "I should tell you that Todd and I have become quite good friends since the unfortunate events prior to the election. He's embarrassed, so don't ask him about all that. But I don't mind. Harriet and I laugh about it now, and I wish the president the very best."

He glanced toward Sandra Rhodes with a nod and a smile.

"Sorry to interrupt, Timothy," Harvey added, and sat down.

"Not at all," said Timothy. "You have many fans and admirers here. I know they will enjoy anything you have to share. I also want to introduce our special guests who have come from great distances—Grigor and Anya Popov from Russia by way of Poland, Leon and Alita Morales from Ecuador, Paddy and Charlene Ayscough from New Zealand, Monika and Fynn Sievers from Germany, Moira and Alexander Campbell from Scotland, and Richard and Jessica Constable from London. I know you will make them feel at home.

"I'd like to bring my fellow host for the weekend, Mark Forster, up now to introduce three more special guests we have with us, all from Seattle where Mark and Grace pastored for several years."

Mark rose and went forward.

"I know they would all rather remain anonymous," he began, "but I feel I need to acknowledge these three Seattle women whom I have known for many years." He smiled and glanced toward the three where they were seated together. "Believe it or not, I have actually known the president's mother, Sandra Rhodes, longer than anyone here, since I was fourteen and she brought her son, Jeff, to a Christian summer camp not far from here. That's where Jeff and I met and became boyhood friends. I am happy to say that Sandra and I have had a very warm resumption of what I now consider a deep friendship in the Lord. We have shed some tears together, prayed together, and I know you will want to talk with her and become better acquainted with her as your sister in Christ."

He paused and smiled toward Mrs. Rhodes again. Fighting tears, all she could do was mouth the words back to Mark, *Thank you.*

"As most of you know, Ward Hutchins and I met in college, were roommates with the president, and served as pastors together for many years. His death a little over two years ago was shocking to us all and left a huge hole in the lives of those who were close to him—most of all to his mother, Eloise, and his wife, Deidra, who are with us here. I have known Eloise since those college days, and of course Deidra and Grace and I were close during our time in Seattle serving in the pastorate with Ward. We are so glad you both are with us," he said, smiling at the mother and daughter-in-law. "Nothing can make up for the loss of a man like Ward who was bigger than life. But we hope you can receive the love all of us here have for you, and let it enfold you as the love of our Father binds our hearts and enfolds us in his arms as one."

Mark returned to his seat beside Grace. Jaylene stood. After her personal introductory remarks of welcome, David rose and recounted his lifelong association with Stirling and Larke Marshall, and the import of their spiritual vision on his own.

Questions and discussion followed, lively and animated, with laughter punctuated by moments of poignant sobriety as many others reflected on the life of the man and woman who had now been gone twenty years and whose writings were the basis of the fellowship that had sprung up between them.

As the group broke up and began making its way to the many rooms, tents, trailers, bunkhouses, homes, and motels where they would spend the night—though no one was anxious to leave—Mark walked toward Eloise Hutchins.

"Still no word from Linda," he said. "I've been checking my phone for a text."

"I've heard nothing either," said Mrs. Hutchins. "I know she was moved by your invitation. I think she still feels awkward. She's trying to figure out after all this time how serious she is about wanting to be a Christian, or even if she considers herself a Christian at all."

Mark nodded. "It's an important time in her life. I know she's thinking hard. Her spiritual self is awake after many years of dormancy. I have no doubt she'll get where the Lord wants her."

72

The Gathering

ON SATURDAY morning, Timothy told his personal story as the Marshall's son and that he was privileged to be doing a small part to further his father's vision of a centered life based on obedience to the commands. Jaylene also shared her perspectives.

Timothy's downplaying of his role was interrupted numerous times by those who had written to express what a help he and Jaylene had been to them, many adding that Stirling could not have given more perfect counsel and encouragement than had Timothy and Jaylene.

Many personal stories also confirmed that to many of those in attendance, Timothy's and Jaylene's own writings of the past two decades—with now twelve books between them—had in some ways taken up where Stirling's left off. In addition to investigating topics of their own interest, they had sought to expand Stirling's vision of life with God into regions he had not thoroughly explored. Praise for Jaylene's clear articulation of the scientific and historic factuality of Christianity and the Bible was shared by nearly everyone.

Both were overjoyed when all four of Timothy's brothers and sisters called through the early months of the year expressing their desire to attend. Timothy therefore planned his talk when he knew all four would be present. Cateline arrived Thursday evening and remained for the entire weekend. Woody and his wife drove up from San Luis Obispo on Friday and had only planned to be at the ranch a few hours on Saturday. Woody was so taken with the proceedings, however, that he and Cheryl remained through Sunday, spending Friday and Saturday nights with Timothy and Jaylene. Graham and Jane came without their spouses and spent a night each in the extra beds at the ranch house. All four listened with wide eyes as Timothy shared, and then to what was said about their younger brother afterward, having no idea to what stature he had risen in the eyes of many of those present.

Though none of the four were avowed Christians, they had decided to stretch the invitation parameters and had also invited Jaylene's two brothers and their wives. Both older Gray men were professional geologists like their father. They too listened with amazement to hear their younger sister spoken of with such honor as having changed the lives of many through her writings. When the weekend was over, they had much to think about.

Timothy introduced his two brothers and two sisters and gave them the opportunity to share their thoughts and memories about growing up in the Marshall home. He was surprised when they did so. All four seemed genuinely appreciative of the opportunity. Graham told several stories about Timothy that had everyone in the barn in stitches.

Discussion and personal sharing about the impact of the diverse Marshall corpus of writings, and about Timothy's and Jaylene's ongoing correspondence with many, might have continued all day. Timothy's siblings drank it in with wonder, seeing not only their brother and his wife, but also their parents, in a new light. They had known about their father's writing all their lives. Yet it began to dawn on them in a new way what an ongoing impact his life's work had had around the world.

Gathered in David's large barn, few even noticed as a car drove slowly into the precincts of the Bar JG, nor heard its lone occupant walk toward the meeting in progress, then take a place outside its side wall. There he was able to hear every word through the ample cracks in the weathered siding.

Though urged to do so, Mark did not speak to the group, preferring, he said, for the sake of his former position at Foothills and his current role with the president, to remain an observer.

Each of the international guests was invited to share, as well as those whose correspondence with Timothy and Jaylene over the years had led them to start their own groups with like-minded Christians.

Moira Campbell told of her experience leading her first Bible study, recounting her initial fears and her correspondence with Timothy that helped her overcome them. She and Alexander had been leading a Bible study in their home ever since. The sound of Moira's Scottish accent quickly made her a favorite. After listening to her story, it was obvious why their Bible study had proven a success. She was an engaging speaker with a gift for drawing others into the discussion in personal ways.

Leon and Alita Morales shared about their ministry with students in Ecuador using their Spanish translations of Stirling Marshall's book.

Matthew and Sarah Gardner shared the story of their church's reaction to Stirling's New Testament commentaries, which led to the beginning of a home group involving other couples. Their ongoing study now boasted twenty-five men and women from different churches throughout northern Idaho and eastern Washington.

Richard Constable shared about the reaction to his refusal to perform same-sex marriages. Discussion became extremely animated after Timothy posed the question: "What should be our response to unscriptural practices in the congregations we are part of? Do we speak up, do we leave, or do we silently go along?"

The experiences of the Gardners and Constables opened the floodgates for the sharing of a multitude of diverse church experiences and quandaries.

One of the most lively discussions followed Trevor and Violet Langdon's personal story from their Albany church and their choosing to walk different roads in response to their frustrations and concerns.

Stirling's *Benedict Brief* was never mentioned. Yet the conversations and discussions about withdrawing from the world, living the centered life in churches where the emphasis was far removed from that quiet center, silently reminded the few who had read it of exactly what Stirling had so forcefully written in the months prior to his death.

Grigor and Anya Popov made the greatest impact of the weekend. That they had come so far, and that their story of escaping out of Russia and getting safely to Poland was so moving, made them the courageous rock stars of the gathering.

Midway through lunch, with people of all ages seated at tables or walking and talking in small groups about the grounds, everyone sharing excitedly as dozens of new friendships quickly deepened, a car drove up the drive. A few heads turned, but not until the new arrival stepped tentatively out did Mark and Grace have any idea who it was.

They leapt up from where they were sitting and ran to meet her.

"Linda!" exclaimed Grace, embracing her warmly.

Linda burst into tears even before Mark had a chance to greet her.

"I wasn't sure I should come," said Linda softly after a moment.

"We are so glad you did!" said Grace.

"Your mother and sister-in-law are here," added Mark.

"I see them!" said Linda, wiping at her eyes and laughing lightly.

"The next moment Linda was surrounded by an impromptu welcoming committee of four as the two other Hutchins women hurried to join them.

"We've got quite the Seattle contingent!" said Mark.

"Who else?" asked Linda.

"We flew down with Sandra Rhodes," replied Eloise.

"Jeff's mother!"

"She's become quite the celebrity here!" laughed Mark. "Though she's not the only one. Now they'll have to compete with you."

"I just want to sit in the back and be anonymous."

"I doubt that will be possible. Come and join the others, have some lunch, and let me introduce you around."

Even as they stood talking beside Linda's rented car, word began to circulate who it was that had just arrived—none other than Supreme Court Justice Linda Trent. One of the first approaching to greet her was Congressman Nason.

At two o'clock, Jaylene and Timothy led a lively interactive Bible study based on Stirling's book *Unspoken Commandments*, which nearly all those in attendance had read. For many it was the book most instrumental in beginning the personal journeys that had led them to this place at this particular time.

As the study broke up an hour later, though animated conversations continued and spread out on his ranch, David Gordon, now just months shy of eighty and in many ways the patriarch of a spiritual family burgeoning before his eyes, was unusually quiet. His face wore an imperceptible smile. He stood back watching as dozens of men, women, and children of all ages moved about the grounds and lawns, some walking in the pastures, talking, laughing, sometimes praying together.

How amazing it was for the man who had written to Stirling Marshall as a young twenty-two-year-old, now as a shepherd to be watching his flock—*Stirling's* flock, he would say—feeding on the spiritual sustenance of true body-life. He had known such rich fellowship existed yet had only been capable of imagining it flowing out of the heart of God.

Now he was overwhelmed to witness a faith-vision he had been nurturing in his heart for years coming to life.

73

The Holt Report

"MR. BARDOLF, it's Lionel Holt. I'm glad you answered. I have some big news I think you'll want to hear."

"You said you were going to the Forster ranch, that there was some kind of event going on."

"I had the dickens of a time finding out about it. My mom's right—they keep their activities close to the vest. But I overheard two ladies who are involved talking last Sunday at church. So I drove up this morning. Turns out it was at a neighboring ranch, though people are staying at the Forster's too. There's some connection between the owner and old man Forster, Mark Forster's father. I'm there now and they've seen me. I'm just milling around, keeping my ears open. I'm not trying to hide but am staying in the background. Heather hasn't said a word to me. She's not pleased to see me crashing their party, but they're not going to kick me out."

"So, what's your news?"

"It's bigger than I imagined. There must be a hundred or more people here—tents and trailers spread about the ranch. It's a big deal. But get this—you'll never guess who's here—Linda Trent."

"*Justice* Trent!" exclaimed Bardolf.

"None other. I wouldn't have recognized her from Adam, but I wasn't far away when Mr. Forster greeted her. Everyone's talking about her coming. And she's not the only one. There's an older lady I had noticed and didn't recognize either until Mrs. Trent went up and started talking to her. It's Sandra Rhodes."

"The president's mother—*Caramba!*"

The phone went silent. It didn't usually take much to disturb Mike Bardolf's equilibrium. But this news jolted him.

"That *is* surprising," he said after a moment. "Good work, Lionel. Call me again if there are more surprises. See if you can get your hands on a guest list. And pictures. I'll need proof to take to the president. When I move against these people, I need to have ironclad evidence of what they're up to."

74

Saturday Afternoon

OBSERVING DAVID later that afternoon gazing out over the pasture between his house and barn and the woods in the distance, its grasses now lush and green from the spring warmth and rains, Timothy walked in his direction. David was leaning against the wood fence he and college student Mark Forster had built some thirty years earlier

"Amazing, isn't it," said Timothy as he walked up behind him. "It's more than I could have hoped for."

David turned. "It's your father's vision come to life," he said in a soft voice. "Why should we be surprised?" he added. "*He* saw it all those years ago. He knew it would happen. His vision of a community of what he called the *common life*, the life of the Center, is being birthed, just as he foresaw. These are the people he was writing about—these and many more. The remnant is being called out of the church that the Church may be birthed in power."

"Are we watching it with our own eyes?" said Timothy.

"I believe we are, my friend," rejoined David. "I have no doubt there are hundreds, perhaps thousands of birthings just like this taking place simultaneously all over the world. Today, next week, next month, next year, three or four, ten or twelve, or a man and his wife who feel a rousing toward something more as they sit together in the evening. It isn't the numbers; it is the nature of what is stirring to life. Many of them do not yet recognize what is happening, that they are part of something much larger than themselves."

He stopped, gazing toward Grigor Popov, Paddy Ayscough, Alita Morales, and Rebecca Stevens talking together—four nationalities blended as one. A great laugh burst out of Grigor's mouth from something Paddy—regarded by now as the witty comedian of the gathering—had just said.

"But they *will* recognize it," said David at length, "as I think everyone here is sensing a uniqueness to what they are part of. Many around the world will be drawn into unity just as these are. As in the physical world, cells grow and divide and join and expand, so too will the cells of God's remnant grow into an unnumbered invisible Church. We are privileged to be witnessing something mighty in God's plan, Timothy."

Their conversation stilled briefly as Lionel Holt, whom they had not noticed listening from a short distance away, now sauntered toward them.

"Hello, Lionel," said Timothy. "I hadn't known you were coming. Nice to see you again."

"And you, Mr. Marshall. Hello, Mr. Gordon," he added, turning toward David with a curious expression.

David smiled but said nothing.

Lionel walked on somewhat aimlessly toward nowhere in particular. The two men watched him go.

"His presence here surprises me," said David at length. "I didn't think he was on the list."

"He wasn't," rejoined Timothy. "Heather was livid when she saw him making the rounds among the Foothills people at lunch. I have no idea when he arrived. She feels responsible. He's been phoning her—even asked her out on a date—asking questions. She thinks he's up to something. Spying for his mother, she thinks," Timothy added laughing. "But there's nothing to do but make the best of it."

The eyes of both were drawn in the distance where Todd and Heather were walking alone together.

"Your daughter would seem to have a new friend who appears more than a mere friend," said David with a smile.

"So it appears indeed!" laughed Timothy. "Jaylene and I are surprised, delighted, apprehensive, feeling protective—all the normal parental emotions, I suppose. But at this stage of her life, it is an unexpected position for us to be in. Jaylene is concerned, their being from such different worlds, that she's liable to get her heart broken."

"Young Stewart seems like a fine young man," said David. "Heather has a good head on her shoulders. She will keep her wits about her. If I know Heather, she will prove to be a match for anything young Stewart can throw at her."

"Agreed!" laughed Timothy again. "My only concern is that he has been steeped in the liberal deception for so long. Those lies can be hard to break."

"God can bring light even in the midst of progressivism's darkness. We must be diligent in praying for him. His coming among us can be no accident. God may have mighty things in store. Good will come of it, I have no doubt. I believe the hand of the Lord is on the young man."

Mark and Court Masters walked toward them. A minute or two later, Harvey Jansen and Charles Reyburn, the two deep in conversation for the past hour, also joined them. Soon the six men were talking and laughing freely, while from some distance away Lionel Holt, who had been listening as intently as he was able to the conversation between Jansen and Reyburn, was busy taking photographs with his phone.

Walking arm in arm as they left the ranch house, Grace Forster and Jaylene Marshall, full sisters now in every way, paused as they saw the men in the distance.

"Our men," said Jaylene. "Doesn't it warm your heart to see them together?"

"Oh, it does!" replied Grace. "You cannot imagine what it means to Mark to have older friends and mentors like Timothy and David. The pastor's life can be a lonely one. Now he has a growing support team of strong like-minded men.—Oh, excuse me a minute."

She hurried off to where she had seen Linda and her sister-in-law. Harriet Jansen and Stella Masters also left the house together. Jaylene walked over to meet them. Grace, Linda, and Deidra Hutchins soon joined them. The six continued to the paddock next to the barn where Sandra Rhodes and Eloise Hutchins were standing at the rail watching three of David's horses nibbling at the grass while a young colt scampered between them.

75

Bombshell

MR. BARDOLF—LIONEL Holt again. I'm back home. It's a little after seven. I didn't think I should press my luck and stay longer. The people from our church were keeping their eyes on me. I knew what they were all thinking—the hypocrites, thinking I didn't belong. My mother's right about them. But that's not why I called. I have more big news—bigger than Justice Trent. You won't believe it. I have pictures! Call me when you get this, no matter how late. I'll be up.

The return call to Lionel's phone didn't come till 9:30.

"Lionel," said Mike, "you sounded keyed up. What's your news?"

"Are you sitting down?"

"Just spring it, Lionel. I'm a big boy. I can take it. Did you find out who the Prophet is?"

"No, not that. Well, I don't know—maybe. There were quite a few blacks there—maybe fifteen or twenty—so he just blended in and I didn't notice. I wasn't paying close attention until this afternoon when there were no meetings or anything. Everybody was spread out around the ranch—"

"The Forster ranch?"

"The Gordon ranch down the road. They were in small groups talking informally. I was just wandering about, watching, listening, taking pictures. I wanted to try to get photos of everyone who was there for you."

"Good boy. Just what I need."

"I couldn't be too obvious. Anyway, in the distance I saw three men talking seriously between themselves. A tall black man in his fifties, a white guy maybe a few years older, and a younger man whom by then I knew as the congressman because people were talking about him. The three were talking seriously. Then the congressman wandered off. I think he connected with Forster, but I was watching the other two. Then I realized that I recognized the older white man, though I couldn't place him at first. I wandered a little closer, trying not to be obvious. Then suddenly it hit me where I'd seen him—it was Harvey Jansen!"

"Senator Jansen!"

"In the flesh. Then I heard him call the other man by name, the black man. It was Dr. Reyburn—Charles Reyburn!"

"My God—it's a convention of right-wing nut jobs!" exclaimed Bardolf. "Though what is Justice Trent doing mixed up with them? And the president's mother, for God's sake!"

"And Congressman Nason. There's another guy too, a Secret Service agent by the name of Masters."

"Court Masters! Yes, I know him, though he's now retired. There were rumors about him getting religion a while back."

Mike Bardolf's brain was spinning. This explained much! Religion or not, Court Masters wasn't someone to take lightly. He'd been around. He knew things. He'd been tight with Director Parva for a while and was one of the lead investigators on the assassination of President Hunt—not a man he'd want to tangle with.

"What were Jansen and Reyburn talking about? You said you were listening."

"I couldn't get it all. But once I realized who they were I turned on my phone's video recorder. I've been listening to it all evening. I re-recorded it into my Audacity program and have cleaned and scrubbed it. You can't make out everything, but it helped some. I think you'll get the gist of it. Here—let me play it for you. The first voice you'll hear is Jansen's."

". . . what you said last night . . . asked you . . . run for president . . ."

"Absolutely . . . no plans."

Muffled laughed.

"... wise decision ... been there done that, as they say!"

"... difficult time," came Reyburn's voice again, speaking seriously, "... felt for you ... in my prayers, believe me ... what they did ... your poor wife ... unconscionable ..."

"... not a pleasant time ... sitting in jail ... no one enjoys ... laughingstock. Harriet ... furious ... but one learns ... roll with the punches ..."

He laughed again.

"You were a brave man," said Reyburn as Lionel managed to inch closer.

"Don't know ... not an experience ... soon forget. But ... even in just two years ... country might be ready ... think you might have ... legitimate chance ... country needs grassroots revolution ... traditional values ... dying around us ... think there might be ... enormous groundswell ... untapped support ... a Reyburn candidacy."

It was silent between the two men for several long seconds.

"Don't get me wrong Senator," said Reyburn, "love our country ... do anything that lay in my power ... yet I am not convinced ... not of this world ... need an awakening, a revolution ... absolutely certain ... standard-bearer ... if what you say ... that now is the time ... you would be more likely ... try again ... need to band together ... people are ... widespread hunger to take the country back ... time for courage ..."

"... never convince my wife!" laughed Jansen. "Though perhaps if you would ... consider ... with me in the ... slot."

"I'm a professor, Senator ... never make a politician ... might convince ... Secretary of Education ..."

"Rather we were ... roles reversed ... my educational qualifications ... as yours ..."

"... academic not politician ..."

"Promise me ... pray about the possibilities ..."

"Pray about everything ... definitely a commitment I am prepared to make."

Then two men turned away. Though Lionel continued to video them, no more of their conversation was audible.

The phone went silent again as Mike Bardolf let out a long sigh.

"That is an explosive exchange," he said at length. "Any *more* big news?"

"That's my only bombshell."

"Well you did good. Send me over all the photos and that video. We'll have to work on identifying as many as we can who were in attendance. Facial recognition should get most of them."

76

Listening to the Silence

ONE OF the most extraordinary group sessions of the weekend took place on Sunday morning. It was not intended as a "church" service, though the coincidence of timing with thousands of services throughout the land taking place during the same few hours could not be helped.

Between seven and ten that morning, groups of two or three, couples, here and there a solitary individual, or five or six together as husbands and wives found themselves bonding with other couples, could be seen leaving the two ranch houses where buffet-style breakfasts were set out.

The Sunday mood was subdued. Some quietly visited, some read, others walked about, a number found a place in the cool quiet barn to be alone. Some wandered toward the woods, not to be seen for an hour, others sat on one of many outdoor benches or chairs or were seen leaning against a fence, some carrying Bibles, others with books.

Gradually cars and vans drove in, bringing those staying at the Circle F to David's. Even as the stream of arrivals continued, little was said. The newcomers joined and spread out in the reverent solitude of the morning.

The grounds surrounding David's house and barn and outbuildings were of such extent that the group numbering over a hundred could wander indefinitely and encounter no one, though there might be a dozen others doing the same. The peaceful warm morning air did not invite boisterous dialogue.

Groups and individuals came and went from the house and tables set in front of the porch for a refill of coffee or tea.

Brief laughter from Paddy, Grigor, and Leon, by now fast friends, broke out in the distance.

The sound did not disturb the mood between Richard Constable and Matthew Gardner, the two pastors, sitting on a bench deep in thoughtful conversation.

Charles Reyburn and Harvey Jansen, with their wives, were sitting at one of the tables near the house with coffee and breakfast rolls. The four had forged what would be a lifelong friendship. The Reyburns, who had taken the opportunity for a road trip and had driven out to California, were already planning to return to Kentucky through Wyoming where they would spend a day or two at the Jansen ranch.

David, with Fynn Sievers and Alexander Campbell, disappeared behind the barn chatting comfortably. When they appeared again, they had been joined by Gerald Stevens and Violet Langdon.

Todd Stewart, Court Masters, and Alfred Nason were talking politics, the journalist and former DC detective sharing similar experiences and their convictions that the world of Washington, DC, was no longer for them, though fourth-term Texas congressman Nason, younger even by a year or two than Todd, had not quite yet given up on the system.

Linda and Mark and Grace walked arm-in-arm in the distance.

Heather, Ginger, Grace, Stella Masters, and Catherine Nason wandered away from the house together. The question on Ginger's mind was what was going on between Heather and Todd!

"She'll tell you when she's ready," said Stella. "Give the poor girl time to figure it out herself."

Heather laughed. "It's nothing so mysterious," she said. "I invited him. He came. I like him. If there's more to it than that, you will be the first to know. I take that back—maybe second or third after me, probably Todd, and my parents. After this weekend, I may never see him again. For now, I'm just enjoying the moment. And I am really glad Lionel didn't show up again today."

"I can't imagine what he was doing here," said Ginger. "He's the last person who would be interested. I don't think he even talked to anyone."

"Probably spying for his mother," said Grace. "Though that's not very nice of me. But honestly, that woman is the living personification of what James said about the tongue. Mark and I invited her to one of the FCL meetings. We thought that would satisfy her curiosity. But she's not interested in coming, only gossiping about everyone who does. Although shame on me—I guess I just did the same by talking about her. Forgive me!"

"Everything you said is true, Mom," said Ginger. "It's not wrong to speak the truth."

"Maybe not, but truth has to be tempered with kindness. I'm not sure my heart is always full of love toward poor Edith—and that's on me, not her."

"I'm afraid Lionel's being here is my fault," said Heather. "He somehow heard about it and pestered me with questions. I don't remember saying anything definite."

"You didn't invite him?"

"Heaven's no."

"I'm sure Edith knows all about it," said Grace. "It's not as if we're trying to keep the group secret anymore. That would be impossible. Lionel could have found out anything he wanted to know from Edith."

As they continued to talk, from the house to the pine wood beyond the pasture, other small groups moved about, coming together, separating, then coming together again in delightfully spontaneous intermingling.

The two Seattle women—Eloise Hutchins and Sandra Rhodes, both with secret sorrows—walked arm in arm across the lawn. They had shared tears together in the past two days and would probably share more. They had been tears of healing. Each had found a new friend, which was worth any number of tears.

By the end of the weekend, Sandra Rhodes reached a personal decision that cost her some of those tears she had shared with Ward's mother. It might be too late to influence her son spiritually. She would have to live with that. She had not been forceful enough either to sustain her own faith—if she even had one back in the early days of her marriage—or pass on meaningful spiritual values to her son beyond hoping he might absorb something from the Pinecroft experience.

But there was another generation to consider. She hoped she hadn't waited too long to build meaningfully into the lives of her grandchildren. One of the truths she had absorbed this weekend, exactly as Mark had said during their visit the previous fall in Washington, DC, was that with God it was *never* too late.

Maybe she *could* have some influence. She could at least try. She would pray that the next generation would discover a spiritual grounding that had, to all appearances, bypassed her son. She would look for an opportunity for God to use her in answering her own prayer.

Even before she left the gathering, she was turning over in her mind the idea of another trip to the nation's capital. She didn't really *need* an excuse to see her grandson and granddaughter. But she would use his upcoming birthday to keep her deeper motives from being *too* obvious.

As they beheld what was happening around them, and the deepening of many relationships on so many levels, Mark and Grace said to one another more than once that in all their years in the pastorate they had never known such bonds of unity and spiritual connection.

"This is what I have been longing for in Christian fellowship all my life," said Grace. "All that time in the church I never knew what it would be like. Now we are surrounded by it!"

The morning advanced. Gradually the intersecting circles of wanderings drifted toward the barn where the next session was scheduled for 10:30.

After the leisurely breakfast and many impromptu conversations, and because of the hundreds of eternal bonds forming, the mood as they entered the darkened barn was reverent. Knowing it was their final day together, everyone realized that something extraordinary had taken place among them this weekend.

As the barn grew silent Timothy stood. Shafts from the morning sun slanted through the wooden planks of the walls, piercing the darkness with arrows of light.

"It is Sunday morning," Timothy said with a smile. "I suppose it cannot be helped that there is an aura of a church service as we sit here together. I hope we can put that aside except to remember our brother and sister Christians throughout the country sitting in a thousand churches, including the home churches of those of you who have them. I hope we can all be mindful of the expansive body of Christ, as God's Spirit slowly wakens the remnant to come out of man's worldly church and out of the world itself to be part of God's eternal Church. We need to pray that God gives his people wisdom—his leaders, pastors, priests, men, women, Bible study leaders, deacons, elders, young and old, rich and poor alike—as he spreads his silent invisible leavening throughout his body, wisdom how to practicalize that coming out in their lives and churches, exactly as we pray for that same wisdom for ourselves."

He paused briefly.

"I have nothing to say, no planned talk this morning, no *sermon*, as it were," he went on as light laughter circulated among them. "Having participated in many 'prayer meetings,' as I know you all have," Timothy went on. "I would like to ask, instead of praying aloud, in a sense, for the benefit of each other, that we allow a spirit of *listening* to descend among us. We do not need a sermon. We need only to hear what God would say to us. Neither do we need to pray so that others will hear our prayers. If we pray, it is to the Lord we pray, not one another. Therefore let us talk to *him,* and *listen* to him, in the quietness of our hearts."

He paused a moment.

"I think we all recognize that we have experienced the life of God's Church this weekend. Soon we will separate and go our own ways. This is not an end but a beginning. Something has come to life among us. I believe we are intended to take that life literally unto the corners of the world to share it—in New Zealand, Russia, Germany, England, Scotland, Ecuador, yes, and in Texas and Kansas and New York and Indiana and Georgia and Idaho. Even in California and Washington, DC.

"This is bigger than any of us—bigger even than all of us. Therefore, as we pray, let us pray for guidance, for wisdom, that God would guide our steps and show us what he wants each of us to do to grow his eternal Church in the corners of the world where he has planted us."

Where they sat, Woody, Cateline, Graham, and Jane almost felt that they were listening to their father.

Timothy took his seat beside Jaylene. Stillness deeper than merely the absence of words settled upon those gathered in that humble

Church. A potent and enlivening presence inhabited the hundred-year-old barn. The Spirit of the Lord hovered over them, then descended and came among them, informing and infusing the very air, moving in and through it, playing a silent aeolian melody on every heart.

Those hearts were joined as in a silent symphony of a hundred unique spirit-instruments fashioned by God, each to make a timbre of music unlike any other, tuned in perfect intervals to create an uplifting of prayer none could make on their own.

Not an audible word was uttered. Yet prayers were swirling among the vibrations of the many individual heart strings. Whether the Spirit of the Lord was making the prayer music or whether the prayer-thoughts of those gathered were intertwining in harmonics that resonated with his leading, such mysteries lay outside human ken. It was what Thomas Kelly called a "gathered meeting," when, from out of the silence, a "hush and solemnity" steals over a room and "the worshippers are gathered into a unity and synthesis of life."

As much as each was able, they let their petitions, thanksgivings, yieldings, and inarticulate sighs pour into the Lord's heart. All the prayers flowed into each of the others. The entire human orchestra, receptive to the divine breathings, was swept up into a single heart-cry: *Lord, reveal your will, show us what you want us to do, and help us to faithfully obey.*

They had entered into the great Silence that was at root in the historic foundations of Quaker prayer. Perhaps no Christian people had ever so practically obeyed the Lord's command—*And in praying do not heap up empty phrases as unbelievers do, thinking that they will be heard for their many words.*

As a result the Lord's promise was operating among them: *For your Father knows what you need before you ask him.*

What an extraordinary thing for more than a hundred people to become one, no one anxious to be heard, intent only to listen.

It was the prayer of listening silence.

Eventually David stood and left the barn. Others gradually followed over the next hour, coming and going, praying outside alone, some returning to the barn. Silence continued to hang suspended over the ranch.

77

Sinister Schemes

"MR. BARDOLF, it's Lionel," came the voice on Mike Bardolf's private cell midway through Sunday morning.

"Yes, hello, Lionel. You have something more for me."

"Nothing yet. That's what I was calling about—do you want me to go up there again today?"

"What time is it there?"

"Just after seven. I'm a little hesitant to make another appearance. I'm sure you don't want them getting suspicious."

"No, we don't want that. Today's the last day, isn't that what you said?"

"I think so. They'll probably have a church service and that will be it."

Mike thought a minute.

"I think your instincts are right. Let's leave it as it is. What you sent me last evening is a gold mine. I have to sift through all of that and it will take me a while. Have you had more thoughts about who the Prophet is?"

"Other than either of the Marshalls, Forster, or Reyburn—no. It seems that it must be Heather's grandfather, the man named Stirling."

"You're probably right. However, I have the sense it's someone living. Best you lay low for now. If I need more I'll get in touch."

Mike set his phone aside and fell to musing. It had been an eventful two days. How much of what he had learned should he tell the president?

He needed to wait until he had more specifics and had some idea how he wanted to proceed. Rhodes was an emotional guy. He would go ballistic hearing that Justice Trent and a former Secret Service agent, not to mention a congressman and Professor Reyburn and Senator Jansen—and his own mother!—were all present.

Just the hint of a Reyburn presidential run would send him over the top. There was no telling how he might react.

He had to pick the moment with care. One thing was certain, he must accelerate his plans against this group before its cells gained a stronger foothold.

The first step was to take down its California nucleus. He must walk with care. Mark Forster, in some peculiar way, was still the president's friend. He couldn't just order a hit on the man. He had to bring this movement down with more finesse than before. It hadn't worked with Hutchins anyway. Reyburn, too, would have to be neutralized with cunning, not a frontal attack.

Court Masters's involvement was one of the troubling pieces of new information the Holt kid had uncovered. It smelled of militia involvement. That made the thing doubly dangerous. If he could prove it, taking out their cells militarily would be quick and effective. With the media building up the conspiracy angle, the FBI would be lauded for protecting the nation. But he needed to consider the wider ramifications.

One thing was certain—the plot was more widespread and had infiltrated deeper than he realized.

He *had* to learn the identity of the Prophet! Whatever plans he made hinged on that.

78

A Prophetic Word

ABOUT NOON, as of one accord, most were again seated inside David's barn. David had also returned. He rose and turned to face them.

"I have observed this weekend what I think you would all agree is a profound knitting together of the living stones of God's Church. What do we do with that fact now that we will soon separate? What do Fynn and Monika do when they return to their farm and none of you—their fellow living stones—are with them? What do Grigor and Anya do when they return to Poland and are separated from the living stones they have been joined with here? What do all of us do?

"What do Court and Stella and Todd and Alfred and Catherine do when they return to the eye of the progressive storm in Washington, DC? What do Charles and Regina do when they return to one of the few campuses left in the country that stands as a bastion of truth against the onslaught of the spirit of antichrist ruling the modern age? How does Charles build virtue into his students when untruth, evil, and immorality are in the very air they breathe when they leave his class or lecture hall?

"We must pray to be led and be joined with other living stones. God's living Church is growing throughout the world. It will grow as living stones join with other living stones. Not with the purpose of starting Bible studies or prayer meetings. That may happen, it may not happen. The Church is not a collection of groups, it is an eternal collection of hearts.

"I sense that to each of us the Spirit has shown, or will show, some portion of how we are to proceed. I have felt profound movings, as I am sure each of you have, confirming that momentous times are ahead. God has much for us to do, much for *all* his people to do amid the perils that lie before us. I sense that he has been preparing us for times when strength, courage, and wisdom will be required.

"We have heard stories of courage from our brothers and sisters. Richard, Matthew, Violet, Geoffrey and Martha, Grigor and Anya—their stories have moved me. Who could not be moved by Harvey and Harriet's courage two years ago to give bold testimony to their convictions in the face of the persecution hurled against them. We will face that, and more, as the spirit of the Tribulation rises ever more viciously against God's people.

"I question whether I have ever had to exert the kind of courage they demonstrated. Mine has been a peaceful life. But times are coming when such may be required of *all* of us. Such persecutions may come upon every one of us here in this barn today—they *will* come! May we share the courage of these, our brothers and sisters who have suffered and have stood strong. May we all stand as God's people against the lies of the age. May we have courage in Aleksandr Solzhenitsyn's words to live not by lies.

"Our world is sinking into what the old Calvinists called depravity. I used to dislike that term. I wanted to believe in the goodness of man. More and more around us in the world, however, I see what I can call nothing but depravity. As we face it, persecution is sure to come to the living stones of God's temple. The depravity of the world today is an angry, self-righteous, hostile depravity intent to stamp out the Christian faith. May God give us courage to be his faithful sons and daughters against it."

He paused, clearly drained from the emotion of what had poured out of him.

"As I was lifting my thoughts to the Lord earlier," he went on, "there were moments when a great heaviness came over me. With it came a vision of our nation as a once flourishing garden lying abandoned, unkempt, windblown, and overgrown like the desolation of Israel being overrun and taken into exile. Others of you may have felt the same for your countries. The sight, even if only in my imagination, nearly broke my heart. Yet behind the desolation, stretching into the distance beyond, I saw a long line of men, women, and children, exiles and refugees from a time of suffering and great trial, seemingly waiting to enter that garden, desolate as it appeared. But it is not the garden of the United States or England or any other nation they seek. They are seeking a new kingdom, God's kingdom—the Church where his people live.

"That Church will soon also be a Church in exile from the nations of the world plunging into darkness. To be part of its remnant will mean joining an exiled community of people even as God's people Israel have lived for two thousand years. True Christianity will soon, in the lifetimes of many of you, be a faith of *exile*, persecuted and ostracized for refusing to embrace the manifold lies of the age. I do not know what it all means or what will characterize that exile. I cannot see what is coming. But we must continue to pray for wisdom, clarity, and courage. An exile *is* coming to God's true Church. But he who endures to the end will be saved."

After lunch came a time of many tearful partings. One after another family and couple departed, several traveling together for airports, others to begin their drives home.

79

SECRET COMMITTEE

MIKE BARDOLF slept little Sunday night. He was not a man given to superstitions or premonitions. But this organization he had uncovered was growing into an obsession. It represented everything his grandfather and father, Viktor Domokos, and the entire Palladium organization had been trying to stamp out for three quarters of a century.

Now here it was springing back to life!

He assumed getting rid of Ward Hutchins would stop the thing. Without a dynamic public leader, how could any movement succeed? Personality drove visionary movements. Grassroots were fine but *somebody* had to be at the vanguard galvanizing the imagination and energy of the masses. Except for a few high-profile personalities around the edges, as far as he could tell, this was a collection of nobodies, ordinary men and women. How had it gained such momentum? There had to be a leader!

The Prophet!

Reyburn was a possible candidate. But he was just a college professor who happened to have written a book. He was no Obama. He was not capable of galvanizing a movement. It seemed unlikely that he was the illusive prophet.

Unless . . . he was thinking about being a *literal* candidate!

Why was the thing gaining momentum *now*—just when he was on the cusp of rising to the pinnacle of Palladium's leadership and the apex of power in the government?! He had worked for years to get where he was. His entire legacy as Viktor's visionary heir was at stake. Now a handful of religious zealots were conspiring to undermine everything!

He was not about to let that happen!

Not on his watch. He would destroy them—destroy them all. Whatever it took!

He was up by five on Monday morning, at the FBI field office by six. Over the years he had developed a small cadre of agents so loyal they would kill for him. He called them his "Enforcement Committee," though never said so openly. He would probably require their services for more delicate assignments in the future. They would form the nucleus of the PDA Intelligence Commission when it was formed.

Today, however, all he wanted was a list of names and dossiers on every man, woman, child, dog, and horse who had been at that gathering in California. He had delivered the file of Lionel's photographs to the technical expert of his committee. With state-of-the-art AI facial recognition software and the vast FBI database of files on every individual in the country, he expected to have what he needed in four or five days.

"I want the names, addresses, employment, tax and military records, educational histories, marital status, extended family relationships, and obviously any legal issues for every individual in attendance. I need whatever might be used against these people—business activities, memberships, affairs, divorces, legal problems, complaints, police records even if just a parking ticket. Obviously political affiliations, public statements, writings, websites—home schoolers, protest activities—no doubt there will be many Trump supporters among the older ones. We'll hang that on them, even get them arrested under the Trump Treason Act—anything at all. I want to know *everything* about these people."

With a thorough investigation underway, he began to breathe more easily. In early afternoon again he took out the copies of the papers he had photographed from Mark Forster's DC apartment desk.

Surely there was something more here, something he had overlooked that could bring Forster to his knees. And bring Reyburn and Jansen and Nason and everyone else down along with him.

80

The Brief Goes Quietly International

BEFORE THE Gathering had culminated, Timothy and Jaylene realized they might never again see many of those coming from long distances. As had been the case three years earlier at the smaller gathering, they again prayed about the possibility of sharing the *Brief* with a few, especially their foreign visitors. This might be their only chance with some of them.

They had therefore privately asked the foreign visitors in making plans earlier, to stay over an extra day, though to keep their plans to themselves, only saying, if asked, that they would be leaving the area on Monday or Tuesday.

On Sunday afternoon Heather told Todd about the meeting of the smaller group but, somewhat sheepishly after all that had taken place, said that she felt it best he not be present.

"I understand completely," said Todd. "I'm flying out later tonight anyway."

"What—no!" exclaimed Heather. "You can't go so soon!"

Todd smiled. "I made plans before I came. The way it was, showing up unannounced, I didn't know how it would be, you know, with us. There was a lot going on. The rest of you had so many people to think of, I didn't want to add to that. I thought it best to make my exit with everyone else and assume we would talk later."

A select group gathered at Heather's home in Dorado Wood for breakfast on Monday. The Masters, Jansen, and Reyburn couples were among those present. After the weekend just past, the fellowship between so many new friends was stimulated all the more by finding themselves in Stirling's and Larke's home surrounded by reminders of their lives. In a smaller group the exchanges were even richer. It could have continued for hours. It was all Timothy and Jaylene could do to settle everyone down and proceed with the business at hand.

Timothy gave a brief history of the document written by his father, mostly kept secret since his death, that he and Jaylene now felt led to share with those present. Finally, he read aloud Stirling's injunction to discretion.

"Before I hand out the *Brief*, I've asked Mark to share his thoughts."

Mark rose and the room quieted,

"A month ago, during my last trip to DC," he began, "and which may truly be one of my last," he added, "I read through the *Brief* again in great detail and wrote down some thoughts, trying, I guess you would say, to summarize it, to isolate its essence, its key points, its overarching significance. I was doing it for my own benefit, but I think it might help you put it into perspective for me to share a few of the thoughts that came to me during that time."

He paused briefly.

"Boiled down," he went on, "I suppose I would say that in his *Brief* Stirling was calling God's people to discipleship obedience by separating themselves from the world's value system and outlook. In one sense, that doesn't seem so earth-shattering. At the same time, Stirling's stark indictment of the church of man as the world's Ally, unknowingly doing much that actually *prevents* the kingdom of God being lived within worldwide Christendom—it is a bold word. If it were widely read in man's churches, his *Brief* would be denounced and Stirling Marshall condemned as a false prophet rather than the *true* prophet I believe he was. Thus his injunction to great care is vital. We must treat this as a hidden cache of gold, the treasure buried in a field."

He paused again.

"Let me just read a bit from Stirling's preface," said Mark. He glanced down at the first page of the document that by now he knew so well.

> *"This will not appear revolutionary or controversial beyond what others have said at various times in history," he read. "If given closer and prayerful attention, however, the far-reaching consequences of these ideas, if followed to their imperative conclusions, and put into practice by dedicated disciple-Christians, contain the power both to shake and remake the body of Christ—to shake the church of man, and to remake Christ's true Church into a bride capable of fulfilling his final commission. Therefore, I exhort all to whom these words chance to come through the years after I am gone, to read prayerfully, expansively, and implicationally—probing beyond formularistic interpretations of man, and to hear and discern what the Spirit may be saying to Christ's Church."*

He paused to allow Stirling's words to sink in.

"I think Timothy and Jaylene and Heather—all three who wear the mantle of Stirling's legacy—would agree that this day represents a major turning point when Stirling's *Brief* expands from this very house where it was written nineteen years ago. We in this room share both a great privilege and a solemn responsibility to be faithful to his legacy and to this message God gave him.

"Everything we do and say may be misunderstood, our words twisted and turned upside down. If we say light, the world will interpret it as darkness. Expect to be maligned for trying to do good and bring light. We will be accused of falsehoods. We will be maligned and persecuted. We cannot even anticipate what is coming. I have no doubt that true Christians will one day be accused of trying to destroy this country we love, not save it. Some of us in this room may one day be jailed for our convictions. Our government has been on a collision course with Christianity for four decades, since the Obama years. That collision may be explosive, and I believe we will see it in our lifetimes. The Trump presidencies only slowed it but did not stop it. He was a man with his finger in the dike, but the tidal wave could not be stopped.

"Stirling felt that the Tribulation was underway as he wrote the *Brief.* If he was right, that Tribulation is still underway, and gathering momentum as the antichrist tries not merely to discredit the true Church but kill it.

"Count the cost, my friends. Stirling's *Brief* is a revolutionary document. Those who attempt to live by it will be attacked and persecuted by the minions of the antichrist. Our local group here is already being called a cult. It may be that we who attempt to live by the Lord's commands will be a cult of the Tribulation. We may be called many things. Light will be called darkness by those who love the darkness.

"Therefore, I would emphasize Stirling's own words—we must count the cost of the life we are attempting to live together. I believe that those who read Stirling's *Brief* will find themselves in the crosshairs of the enemy. If you have second thoughts, no one in this room will think less of anyone who feels this step is not right for them."

He returned to his chair beside Grace. No one moved. Timothy rose again and began handing out individual copies of his father's *Brief,* which, he added, must remain with him when they were done.

The group disbanded into the neighborhood and yard. They gathered again ninety minutes later.

"Now you must all prayerfully decide how God would use this word he gave my father," said Timothy. "I would only emphasize again my father's cautions to privacy."

As the final meeting of the weekend's Gathering broke up, the tears and embraces continued for over another hour.

Then the momentous weekend was over.

81

Activation of the Network

THE RESULTS of the facial recognition search were adequate, though not complete. Mike Bardolf's DC agent identified eighty-five faces beyond those high-profile names he already knew and had supplied dossiers on most. He still hoped Lionel Holt might manage to get his hands on a copy of the guest list. Except for the handful he knew, the rest were insignificant people with no police records and nothing noteworthy in their biographies. Beyond half a dozen divorces—an unbelievably low number—and three bankruptcies, there was little he could use, except perhaps some dozen families who homeschooled their children.

Not that homeschooling was unusual these days. But with the required curriculum regulations and standards for sex education, American history, and Myths of Religion all enforceable by law, it was assumed there were more Christian private schools in violation than in compliance with the new mandates. That could be a perfect door into some of the families. He would have to find other avenues of infiltration with the rest.

Now he had names and addresses, thought Mike. He could begin moving against the individual cells around the country. The big names would have to be handled separately. The president's mother was one of the most problematic. Implication of *her* in a right-wing group could damage Rhodes. Especially if she endorsed Reyburn next year.

Mike opened his computer and began formulating instructions for his enforcement committee. The first order of business was to uncover the identity of everyone involved in the individual cells who *hadn't* been in California.

He needed men he could trust in the cities where it appeared the cells were most active and had been in place the longest: Albany, Wichita, Chicago, Eureka, Haymarket, Austin, Indianapolis, Coeur d'Alene, Miami, Phoenix, Minneapolis, Louisville, Houston, and several in Sacramento, ground zero of the movement's leadership. He needed to expand his network, with an eye to the final makeup of the Intelligence Commission.

He also needed men specifically watching the Forsters, Reyburns, Masters, Nasons, and Jansens.

He still wasn't sure what to think about Justice Trent. Along with Sandra Rhodes, she was a wild card in this.

An hour later he was typing rapidly on a new document. It bore the title: *A private dispatch outlining strategies to uncover and neutralize right-wing collaborators associated with the Marshall-Forster conspiracy.*

82

Grandmother and Grandson

Second Week of May 2051

SANDRA RHODES told her daughter-in-law no details about her trip to Washington other than that she hadn't seen Melissa or Bradon for some time and decided to use Bradon's twenty-fourth birthday as an opportunity to make a trip to the East Coast. Though the president would be gone, Marcia assured Sandra that she would be welcome to stay at the Manor. Thanking her, Sandra declined. She would make her own arrangements, she said.

After lunch with Melissa on an afternoon she had no classes at Georgetown, Sandra arranged to take Bradon out the following day for a birthday dinner. Nothing else had been planned by the family. Marcia had a speaking engagement that evening anyway. Bradon tried to make light of the fact that his parents were too busy for more than a bland birthday card. But he was still young enough that birthdays mattered. He hadn't relished the idea of spending his birthday evening alone or giving himself a party with casual acquaintances who would be less interested in him than free drinks.

His grandmother's invitation therefore, had touched him more than he let on. In spite of living on opposite sides of the country, the two had always had a special relationship. Sandra told him to make reservations at his favorite restaurant and pick her up at her hotel at 6:30. He went so far as to wash and vacuum out his Mustang that afternoon.

"Oh, my goodness!" exclaimed Sandra when Bradon appeared at her door. "A tie and sport coat! I feel honored."

"It's the least I could do, Grandma," he replied. "You were nice enough to want to spend the evening with me and invite me to dinner."

"Well it is your birthday, after all. And by the way, *Happy birthday!*"

"Thank you," laughed Bradon. "And with the president's son and mother together," he added, "we'll no doubt be spotted. I thought I should look the part. You look very nice too."

"Thank you."

He offered his arm. She took it, beaming with pleasure, and they left the hotel together.

"I'm afraid my old car won't be a very classy ride," said Bradon as they walked toward the parking lot.

"I've been in worse!" laughed Sandra. "As I recall you gave me a spin around the city soon after you bought it at that vintage car show."

"That's right—I'd forgotten."

They walked into Barribault's twenty minutes later. They had been seated for several minutes before a few heads began to turn, accompanied by whispered asides to one or another of the waiters, "Is that . . .?"

A few phones came out to photograph the two. Both the mother and son of the president were well-enough used to it from years in the spotlight and took it in stride.

"I hope you won't mind if I speak to you personally," said Sandra midway through their meal.

"Of course not, Grandma," replied Bradon.

Sandra grew thoughtful. Bradon waited, wondering what could account for the change in his grandmother's tone.

"I'd like tell you a little story," Sandra began after a minute. "Well, not a story exactly . . . something about when I was younger and your dad was about your age."

She paused briefly. "Have you heard your dad mention Pinecroft?" she asked.

"I don't think so," replied Bradon. "Doesn't ring a bell."

"It was a summer camp in California . . . a Christian camp. Your dad went to the camp twice when he was in high school."

"A *Christian* camp . . . my dad?" said Bradon in surprise.

"I pushed him to go. Your grandfather thought it was ridiculous but went along. That's where your dad met Mark Forster."

"Oh yeah—that sounds familiar. I didn't remember the name of the place."

"Mr. Forster and your dad went to the same camp for two summers in a row, heard the same talks, shared the same experiences. Yet their lives turned out much differently. They've followed different life paths. Do you see what I'm trying to say?"

"I'm not sure, Grandma."

"Mr. Forster has remained a dedicated Christian all his life. As much as I love your father, I wouldn't call him a dedicated Christian. What I'm trying to say is that everyone makes choices in life about what road they're going to follow. It's like the old poem about two roads diverging in a yellow wood. I always think of your father and Mark—*Mr. Forster*—when I hear those words. They were bosom pals, best friends, inseparable—but eventually the two roads diverged and they chose different directions."

She stopped and drew in a thoughtful breath. "What I want to say to you, Bradon, is to think carefully about those two roads *now*, when you're young, with your life ahead of you, and choose wisely. I'm sorry to say, I didn't do that. You probably don't know this, but I was raised as a Christian. I went to Pinecroft when I was in high school too. That's why I wanted your father to go. But I slipped away from my Christian roots. I didn't think of what life-road I was on. When the fork in the road came, I didn't maintain my Christian convictions."

She paused and a poignant expression came over her face.

"I love your grandfather," she went on. "I have no regrets on that score. We've had a good marriage as marriages go. But God hasn't been part of our life together, as he should be in all marriages. I allowed the life of a politician's wife to relegate my faith to the back seat. Eventually I quit thinking about spiritual things. Everyone develops their own roots of belief. My spiritual roots weren't strong enough, and that's my own fault. So I had no faith to pass on to your father to help him develop spiritual roots. Sending him to Pinecroft wasn't enough. I blame myself that he did not follow a spiritual path, that he did not seek spiritual truth. How could he? I wasn't an example of faith to him."

Again she paused and glanced away briefly.

"When Mr. Forster was in the capital last year, he and I had a serious talk about all this."

"You know him?" said Bradon in surprise.

Sandra nodded. "I hadn't seen him in all those years since he and Jeff were at Pinecroft together. But yes, we knew each other. Since our talk last year, I've been thinking about my life and have been trying to be more attentive to spiritual things. Last week I saw Mr. Forster again, and some other people . . . serious Christians."

"How did you happen to be with them?"

"There was a gathering of some people—in California. Being with them helped me turn a corner. For however long I have left, I intend to pay closer attention to the road of life I'm following. I'm getting a late start, but I'm going to do my best to live by God's truths and principles as much as I know how. Please, don't mention this to your father or mother about my being in California, I mean. I don't think your father would understand. I don't like secrets, and I will tell him everything. But I want him to find out from me, not third hand."

"Sure, no problem," said Bradon. "He's so busy, we don't really talk much anyway, and never about anything serious."

"It was an extraordinary time in California," Sandra went on. "It helped me regain my spiritual footing. When I was there I decided that I wanted to talk to you and encourage you—I don't know how to say this, it sounds terrible . . . but encourage you to follow Mr. Forster's example rather than your father's. You and I both love your father, but like I said before, he's not a deeply spiritual man."

Bradon nodded. He understood what his grandmother was delicately saying.

"When the roads in your life diverge, Bradon," Sandra added, "follow God's road. That's what I want to say to you. When you find the two roads diverging in a yellow wood, follow the road of God's truth."

Bradon took in her words more thoughtfully than Sandra had expected. The expression on his face made it clear that these were not foreign thoughts, that similar things may have been passing through his mind.

"Did you, uh, see Mr. Forster's daughter, Ginger?" asked Bradon. "Was she there?"

"Why yes, she was," replied Sandra. "Do you know her?"

"We met briefly at Dad's bash at your place last year. She said some similar things to me. I guess it got me thinking too."

"Maybe if the group ever gets together again, you could go with me."

Bradon nodded, then slowly began to chuckle. "I can't even imagine what Dad would say to *that*!"

It was quiet a minute. Bradon again grew serious.

"Thank you, Grandma," he said at length. "Probably a lot of young people would be put off by what you've said to me. But I appreciate it. I know you love me and care about me. I am grateful. I will take your words to heart. I mean that. Thank you."

Tears flooded Sandra's eyes. When grandmother and grandson embraced two days later at the airport, where Bradon had driven Sandra for her flight back to the West Coast, a yet deeper bond had been established between them. Their love and mutual respect for one another would grow over the coming years and become an anchoring strength in Bradon's developing maturity as a young man of deepening character.

83

Conspiracy!

May 2051

PRESIDENT RHODES'S overseas trip to Taiwan for a meeting of the Superpower Alliance with the twelve-nation Chinese Federation of States, Germany, and the Russian Union gave Mike Bardolf the time he needed to formulate his plan of attack against the California group.

It was thus toward the end of May, immediately after the president's return, that the two met in the Oval Office. The hour was late. But Bardolf considered the matter urgent. He was not a man who was accustomed to waiting, even for the president of the United States. He had privately texted the president on Air Force One to plan to meet with him for half an hour after his arrival.

"I hope you have some good news for me, Mike," said the president. "It was a long trip. I'm tired. And I've been taking a beating in the press. They're saying it's only a matter of time before China, Germany, and Russia squeeze us out of the Big Four altogether. They're calling me the weak member of the summit. They say I was manipulated by Golubev, Jiang, and Mueller. Someone even compared me to Biden and Chamberlain!"

"I'm not sure you're going to like what I bring you much better," said Mike. "I'm sorry for the late hour, but what I have to tell you is too important to wait. And I know your schedule will be packed tomorrow."

"Get on with it, then. I want to get to bed. You said there were developments on the home front during my absence. You're telling me it's bad news too."

"Nothing we can't handle. I'm confident we can nip it in the bud."

"Nip what in the bud, Mike?"

"A conspiracy, Mr. President."

"A *conspiracy*! You've got to be kidding. Coups are the purview of the Progressives, not our enemies."

"That may be about to change."

"We're not some banana republic. What kind of conspiracy?"

"An underground right-wing organization—"

He paused. Rhodes waited.

"The most worrisome aspect of it for you personally," Mike went on, "is that your friend Mark Forster is involved. He's one of the ringleaders."

"What! Mark's no politico. It was all I could do to get him on my Commission."

"A ruse, Mr. President. I'm convinced he intends to use his position to infiltrate the government at the highest level."

"Mike, you're imagining this. Mark didn't even want the assignment."

"A clever ploy, I'll admit," rejoined Mike. "He had me fooled too. When you hear what I have to tell you, I think you'll see that he's been using you. The whole thing is an outgrowth of what I believe was begun years ago by Forster and Ward Hutchins. I'm sure you recall the secret group we heard about in Forster's church?"

"Come to think of it, I do remember," the president replied, growing serious. "It was just some Bible study in Mark's church, wasn't it? Nothing so sinister."

"It's grown since. There are similar groups around the country, all linked to the Sacramento group."

By now Jeff was listening intently.

"But Mark retired from his church," he said slowly.

"That's true. Nevertheless, the group has continued to expand. It doesn't seem to be connected to the church. It may have begun there. Now it's a national movement with cells throughout the country, even in other countries."

"Other countries! Surely it's just a religious thing. That's how churches proliferate—people break off from one and start a new one."

"It's more than that, Mr. President. There was a gathering three weeks ago, with over a hundred people in attendance."

"What kind of gathering? Sounds like a church thing to me."

"It was more political than religious. I have a contact in the area who was able to infiltrate the group. When you learn who was in attendance, and some of the things that were discussed, I think you will see what I mean."

84

Voices in the Manor

Bradon had been working on his final paper for his World War II history course on the development of the atomic bomb, the pros and cons of its use, and whether or not it prevented the war in the Pacific from lasting another three or four years, even perhaps saving Japan from annihilation at its own hand. He had grown up schooled in the modernist perspective that the United States had been the aggressor in the war and Japan the victim of a new American president's thirst for revenge. But ever since stumbling on the obscure seventy-five-year-old book by William Manchester, *The Glory and the Dream*, he had been intrigued by what he now considered a more historically accurate perspective. Manchester's description of Japan's obsession with honor, to the point of refusal to surrender under *any* circumstances, even to the point of what amounted to national suicide, was so compelling he had to research it further. His professor had been censored by the university for his controversial view of Islam's connections to 1940s German fascism and its potential danger to the West. Fascinated by both unconventional interpretations, and whether they might be linked, Bradon tried to weave the two disparate narratives together into a *weltanschauung*, or worldview, that was perhaps more contemporarily relevant than many would imagine. His final paper was the result.

After working for several hours trying to set down his notes and references coherently, his brain was fried. He needed a break.

He still couldn't entirely get his head around the idea that the entire civilian population of 1945 Japan would be so stubborn as to take its nation down in flames to the last man, woman, and child, if in the process they could take a million young American soldiers with them.

His dad had minored in history. He wondered if he had ever studied the Oriental mentality toward honor, surrender, and suicide in connection with the events of 1943–1945. It would be interesting to get his point of view. Maybe he'd heard something from his own father or grandfather that would shed light on it.

He rose from his desk, stretched arms and back, and glanced at his clock on the wall—11:15. The Presidential Manor never completely slept. There were Secret Service men and women, guards and secretaries and filing clerks working round the clock. But mostly the place was quiet.

He wandered out of his room and along the corridor. He had nothing in mind other than to see if there was an off chance his father was still in his office. He needed to bounce the thesis of his paper around with someone.

The night staff of the Manor was used to his random wanderings. No one gave him more than a nod or brief greeting. The president's ne'er-do-well son was not exactly considered the black sheep of the Presidential Manor, though the appellations of unpredictable, flighty, and impulsive would not have been far wrong. They paid little attention to his movements. That he had the run of the Manor caused no more concern than if First Lady Marcia Rhodes was seen anywhere in its labyrinth of passages and stairways.

He descended to the first floor and into the West Wing. The security here was heightened for obvious reasons. He continued to make his way casually, still without raising more than an eyebrow or two. He passed the Roosevelt Room, entered the small private dining room, through a short corridor, and tried the door of the private presidential study, hoping his father might still be up. The light was on, but the room was empty.

He walked into the small room. In the quiet of the night he heard voices coming through the wall from the Oval Office. It was late for his father to be entertaining visitors. But he definitely heard his father's voice.

He sounded angry.

85

Familiar Faces

BARDOLF OPENED his briefcase and handed six or seven color 8 x 10's across the presidential desk. The president began to scan them casually.

"There's Mark, of course," said Jeff, "and Grace . . . and—*what!*" he exclaimed. "Is that Linda with them? And . . . my God—that's my mother! What in the world . . . what connection could she possibly have to any of this!"

"She seems to be acquainted with Mrs. Hutchins, who's also from Seattle. I've been looking into everyone's movements. They flew down together. Ward Hutchins's widow was also with them."

"That might explain Linda's presence—visiting her mother," said Jeff slowly. "She's no right-winger."

"People change, Mr. President."

"Not Linda. She's been a card-carrying liberal . . ."

His voice trailed off as he fell to perusing more of the photographs.

"Is that . . . it looks like Jansen," he said after a few seconds.

"Do you recognize the tall black man with him?"

"Should I?"

"It's Charles Reyburn."

"Reyburn—I can't believe it!" exclaimed Jeff. "—With Jansen! That's as unlikely an alliance as—"

"And the other man with them," added Mike, "—that's Texas congressman Nason."

Jeff sat back and let out a low whistle.

"Now do you see what I mean—more political than religious."

Jeff nodded. "You know what this looks like, don't you," he said, "—an exploratory gathering for some political purpose, if you know what I mean."

"I think you may be getting the idea," said Mike.

"But it's preposterous! Jansen would never run again. I killed him last time. He was humiliated. His wife hates my guts. Jansen makes no move without her."

"True, which is why I am convinced there's more to it. The election may be only one part of their plan. And look at this photo here."

He stood, walked around to the president's side of the desk, then set another photograph on the desk in front of him. He pointed to a tall, muscular man.

"That's Court Masters," he said, "former DC cop who has a long association with the FBI, though unofficial. He's now retired. I knew him a few years back. He's nobody's fool."

"Okay, what's your point?"

"I've been tracking his movements. It is my belief that he's in charge of the military component of what I believe is nothing less than a conspiracy against your administration, Mr. President."

Jeff exhaled slowly and leaned back in his chair. A somber quiet descended over the room.

"I cannot believe a word of this, Mike," he said at length. "Yet if you're right, I may be looking at the evidence right in front of me."

"When you see all the groups growing around the country, combined with Masters's movements to at least a dozen locations where we've identified cells, it looks serious."

"Masters has visited the cells?"

Mike nodded.

"Where was this thing held—this meeting?" asked Jeff.

"Jointly between Forster's ranch and an adjoining ranch, owned by a fellow named Gordon. His place hosted the meetings, though guests were staying at both ranches, as I understand it."

Jeff nodded thoughtfully.

“There is something else,” Mike went on. “There is a secret document, a manifesto of sorts. As yet I have been unable to get my hands on a copy. Your friend Forster is involved in that too. I managed to obtain his notes about it, handwritten, a précis of the document.”

“I don’t even want to ask you *how* you got your hands on it,” said Jeff wryly. “It’s good I don’t look too closely into your methods!”

“Leave the dirty work to me,” rejoined Mike. “In any event, Forster’s summary is several pages long—I will leave you a copy of my typed transcription. You will have no trouble seeing the implications. There is reference in Forster’s notes to a man called the Prophet. I assume him to be the head of the organization. The unknown document is called *The Benedict Brief.*”

“Who’s Benedict?”

“No idea.”

“And the Prophet?”

“I don’t know.”

“What’s it all about, then—this manifesto, or whatever it is?”

“You will see the inflammatory language for yourself. Forster uses terms like *underground grassroots movement* and *revolutionary.* His abridgement, I believe, is but the tip of the iceberg. The original *Brief* as it’s called, I believe, sets out a blueprint, using Forster’s own words, for an underground grassroots revolution being planned to coincide with the election of 2052.”

“In other words, a conspiracy against me, as you said before.”

“I believe so, Mr. President.”

Where he stood listening, Bradon could hardly believe what he was hearing. When his father was angry, his voice was unmistakable. He would also know Mike Bardolf’s voice anywhere. Both were talking so loud that he was able to make out most of the conversation.

They were talking about a conspiracy involving the Forsters—and the gathering his grandmother had told him about. She had been there!

He leaned his ear against the wall separating himself from the Oval Office as carefully as he dared and continued to listen intently.

86

The Elusive Prophet

FOR ONE of the first times in his life, Jefferson Fitzsimmons Rhodes felt like he'd taken a blow to the gut. He sat speechless, then slowly shook his head in disbelief.

"Do you realize what you're saying, Mike?" he said softly. "It's treason."

"I believe that is exactly what it is."

"And who is this so-called *Prophet*?"

"That is the $64,000 question. There's an old author, dead now twenty years. They all read his books. His son, along with Forster, is spearheading the group."

"His name's not Benedict?"

"I'm afraid not."

"Maybe it's the son. Or could it be Mark?"

"Possibly. But I doubt Forster would speak of himself as he does in his notes if it were him."

"It must be the old author."

"My sense is that it's someone living."

"Reyburn?"

"He's a relative newcomer to the scene, as is Jansen."

"What's the dead author's name?"

"Marshall . . . Stirling Marshall."

"I know that name. Mark used to talk about him. He tried to get me to read his stuff when we were young."

"Forster was interested that long ago?"

"From before college."

"Then this thing has deeper roots than I realized. That would place its origin in the Trump era. I knew Trump had long tentacles—this could be a resurfacing of the treason and other stuff the Democrats used against him."

"It makes perfect sense!" said Jeff leaning forward in his chair. Anger now replaced the feeling of being sucker-punched. "Mark and Ward were Trump lunatics when we lived together. They must have hatched this thing then!"

"I think it likely, Mr. President."

"Have you picked up any links to Trump—his kids or one of the outgrowths of Trumpism that keep popping up?"

"Nothing specific."

"There was another man too," said Jeff, continuing to think back to former times "older than either of us, a disciple of old Marshall's. Mark took me to meet him once. Now that it comes back . . . he had a ranch nearby. He talked a lot of religious claptrap, much of it about the fellow Marshall and his books. Let me look at those pictures again."

He picked up the glossies and scanned through them more intently than before.

"Yes . . . there he is—there's Gordon. Thinner than I remember him, white hair. Gosh that was thirty-five years ago. The old coot must be a hundred by now! You say this gathering was held at his ranch?"

Mike nodded.

Jeff continued thoughtful. "They called him a mystic. I remember Mark saying that before I met the old duffer. He was right—the man was a religious nut job. That's got to be it! He fits the profile. He's obviously the elder statesman of the group, a disciple of old Marshall. Just look at this little group around him—they're hanging on his every word, spouting his nonsense. He's probably been planning this for years."

He sat back, nodded as if in decision.

"There's your prophet, Mike!" he said. "No doubt about it."

"I see what you mean," nodded Mike. "If this Gordon was tight with old Marshall, he's probably been spreading the man's views all this time. What *are* his views anyway?"

"Who knows? I could never make sense of it. I didn't take old Gordon for a politico any more than Mark. Apparently I was wrong about both of them."

He turned away and let out a barrage of expletives. "I can't believe Mark betraying me like this!" he said heatedly. "And to infiltrate my family—my own mother, for God's sake. I'll have Mark's head on a platter!"

Bradon's eyes shot open. Was he actually talking about killing Grace's father! It couldn't be possible. It was obvious that his grandmother's concerns meant little now. His father knew his grandmother had been with the Forsters in California even before she told him.

He seemed to know everything!

87

Take Them Down!

"WE MAY have more problems than your mother and your pal Forster," said Mike, as he continued to scan the photographs over the president's shoulder. "I'd forgotten to mention someone else who was there—look . . . there," he said, pointing down to a tall young man in his thirties walking between two older men, one in his fifties, the other in his sixties.

"Is that . . . it looks like the reporter from NBC," said Jeff. "He was at my election bash. What was his name?"

"Todd Stewart."

"Right. I haven't seen him around for a while. As a matter of fact, I haven't seen him since Bainbridge a year ago. You said he'd been gone and you had trouble tracking him down."

"He was in Scotland, of all places."

"He seemed to be on my side."

"So I thought too. Then he went off the deep end, quit NBC, and left the country. When he accepted your invitation last year, I thought we had him back in our corner. Suddenly he did that idiotic apology tour with the Jansens."

"I'd forgotten about that. Off the deep end is right. When did he become a right-winger?"

"No idea. Now here he is with these people. That's Forster and the Marshall son he's walking with."

"So young Stewart is in the middle of it too. And Linda! God, I can't believe it! Ward's death must have unhinged her. Though she was always sweet on Mark—maybe that's what's going on. And here's Stewart again off by himself with a little girl."

"I will have to confirm this with my source, but that may be Dr. Marshall's daughter—the granddaughter of the old author.—Oh, I'd almost forgotten," he said.

He strode back to where he'd left his briefcase and pulled out a single sheet of paper.

"I have a copy here of a letter from the granddaughter—it may be the girl in the photo with Stewart. Apparently she handles the correspondence for the group."

"How did you obtain it?"

"Like I said before—don't ask! I'll leave this with you too. It's addressed to Congressman Nason. It's full of the same coded language as the Forster notes—*revolution . . . underground . . . cell groups*."

"But Nason's a Progressive."

"Probably just a ploy. Who knows how many moles like him are in the Progressive Party secretly working with the Forster-Marshall group."

"I can hardly believe it!"

"Some of the letters refer to a newsletter of some kind that circulates among the cells. I haven't been able to get my hands on a copy yet. It's what they will use, in code of course, to activate their plans."

"You need to get a copy!"

"I'm hoping to find one or two among the names we're accumulating that we can turn. If I can get on the mailing list myself, using an alias, I'll know what they have planned."

"As long as you can break their code."

"That's why I have to turn one of their followers. I've got something else to show you," Mike went on, opening his portable monitor. "My contact who was at the gathering managed to get this brief video of Reyburn and Jansen. The audio isn't the best. But I've typed up a transcript of what can be made out. You can follow along as you watch."

He handed the president the paper, then set the monitor down in front of him.

"You'll see clearly that they're talking about a presidential run, and probably more.—Press *Play*, Mr. President."

When the recording was finished, Jeff sat back in his chair and exhaled slowly.

"We definitely need to know what those two are up to," he said.

"I have already taken steps," rejoined Mike. "You know how reverse 911 calls were established to alert at-risk regions of earthquakes and fires? I am arranging to have those systems expanded so that all calls can be monitored with AI algorithms programmed with an extensive list of problematic words that will alert us to subversive activities, especially of Christian groups—sort of a national alert in reverse," he added. "My system will be impervious to passcodes and firewalls or any security measures."

"You can do this?"

"Easily. The NSA, FBI, and CIA have been doing it for decades. All I have to do is expand the algorithms. I've already taken steps to target every name on the cell lists my people are gathering. There will be no secrets left. Along with getting copies of the newsletter, within months I will be able to monitor all communications between every one of these people."

Jeff thought a second or two.

"What's the bottom line, Mike?" he said. "What do you make of all this? What's their master plan?"

Bardolf did not answer immediately. When he did, he chose his words carefully.

"Even without a copy of the Benedict Manifesto, with Forster's summary and these photographs and the Nason letter, I think we have a pretty clear idea what's going on. They are putting together the pieces in every venue of government and society to pull off something big. It's obvious they're targeting the next election—probably with Reyburn as their public face to run against you. However, I believe their plan is more far reaching. They've got Forster now in the Executive Branch—"

"Not for long!" interrupted Jeff angrily.

"Even without him, they've got Justice Trent in the Judiciary, and Congressman Nason in Congress. I have it on good authority that he is being considered for Speaker. That would put him third in line to the presidency. Add academia with Reyburn and both Marshalls, a former presidential candidate in Jansen, and the media with young Stewart. They are poised to mobilize every segment of the country."

"Except high tech," put in the president. "I haven't heard of their involvement."

"It wouldn't surprise me if we uncover individuals involved who are high up in tech and banking," rejoined Bardolf, "possibly in one of the cells. They will need major financial backing. I'm convinced that's shaping up too. Surely there's wealth in the Marshall organization."

"Add Masters to the mix, who's perfectly situated to raise an underground militia, and you've got the military. Who knows how many former or disgruntled servicemen and agents in the bureau he's recruited. And with everyone taking orders from this Gordon and Reyburn as their candidate for next year through the network of cells—the grassroots may be more extensive than we imagine. If not Speaker, they may have Alfred Nason slated for the VP slot. They may even be grooming your man Forster to run on the ticket. Then Masters becomes head of the FBI or Attorney General. It all fits together."

"I can hardly believe it," said Jeff, shaking his head. "There simply *cannot* be enough conservatives and Christians and Republicans left in the country to mount a serious threat. We've had a lock on the presidency for years."

"Fringe movements like this have a way of galvanizing the uneducated classes," said Mike. "Stupid people get one vote just the same as those who know what's best for the country. That's one of the flaws of our system I wish we could correct. Conservatives who want to take the country backward should not have the same power as everyone else. But there are still millions of ignorant people clinging to their religious myths. Reyburn's book was a wakeup call. The response was completely unexpected. And the best-seller *Endangered Virtues* tapped into the same backward-thinking mentality. People will believe any lie if they think the majority believes it."

Jeff let out a sigh of mingled fury and more concern than he wanted to admit.

"But, Mike . . . realistically—there is no way Reyburn could beat me in the election. There just aren't that many conservatives left! Once I'm reelected, all this will die down."

"You haven't been hearing me, Mr. President," said Mike. "The election is only to legitimatize Reyburn or whomever they run. Their plan is not dependent on victory. Even if their candidate is defeated, they will have the pieces in place in every sphere of government to pull off the kind of coup they accused Trump of after the 2020 election, false as it actually was. This time the coup might be for real and could be successful.

"This is exactly how conspiracies become dangerous. When they talk about taking the country back, there can be no doubt about what they mean. They are planning a takeover, Mr. President, no less than the Russia collusion fiction attempted by the Democrats to take down a sitting president. But this will be a right-wing coup by people who want to return us to slavery and bigotry and *In God We Trust.* All the pieces are on the chessboard right in front of us."

Again Jeff sat shaking his head.

"Then we've got to snuff it out," he said, "before they can get a viable candidate on the ballot. I presume you have some ideas?"

"I'm formulating a plan, Mr. President."

"Just do what you have to do. Get on it, Mike. We've got to stop this thing in its tracks. Take them down, whatever it takes!"

☆ ☆ ☆

Bradon had heard enough. He had to warn his grandmother and Mr. Forster and whoever else Mike Bardolf and his father were talking about. He didn't know Mike Bardolf except in passing. But the look in his eyes was enough to know that he was a dangerous man. When his father told a man like Bardolf to use whatever it took to destroy people, that *whatever* in a brain like Bardolf's made him shudder.

He doubted there were any limits to how he would interpret the orders his father had just given him.

With great care, Bradon backed away from the wall and tiptoed slowly and softly out of the private study. He had to get out of here and find some way to get word to his grandmother and the Forsters!

88

WARNINGS

WHEN MIKE Bardolf exited the main door of the Oval Office a minute or two later, expecting to be greeted by a silent empty corridor and one of his stoic S.S. underlings standing like a statue at the end of the hall, he was surprised to see Bradon Rhodes creeping furtively through the door of the private dining room twenty feet away from him.

Bradon glanced toward him as he carefully shut the door behind him. Their eyes met. To a man like Mike Bardolf, the expression on the face of the president's son betrayed all. It was the unmistakable look of guilt.

Quickly Bradon turned and hurried away. Bardolf watched him go. He was a man who suspected everyone. His naturally suspicious nature knew instantly that Bradon had been listening. Somehow he must have found his way into the private presidential study. How much might he have overheard?

Bradon's retreating form was now rounding the corner adjacent to the vice president's office. Bardolf followed. Thinking it best to say nothing to the agent on guard, he passed with an expressionless nod. Keeping his eye on Bradon, expecting to see him return upstairs up to the residence, instead the young fool appeared making for the outside door.

Bardolf pulled out his phone and called the main gate.

"This is Mike Bardolf," he said when a guard answered. "Call me immediately if you see the president's son or if he leaves the premises."

"Do you want me to stop him, sir?"

"No, just notify me immediately."

Mike paused in thought. He'd scarcely given Bradon Rhodes more than a passing thought in all his years working closely with his father. But that look on his face spelled trouble.

The call came three minutes later.

"He just left, Mr. Bardolf," said the guard. "In his old Mustang."

"Can you tell where he's headed?"

"Hold on . . . I'm watching—he's turning right on Pennsylvania."

Mike made for the door and ran for the private parking lot. Three minutes later he sped onto Pennsylvania, though without a clue where Bradon might be bound. As he drove he was on his phone to the on-duty precinct chief of the DC Metropolitan Police.

"This is Mike Bardolf, Deputy Director of the FBI and assistant to the president," he said. "I need an immediate all points on the president's son's car—1965 Mustang, highland green . . ."

"No, don't apprehend. Should be easy to spot, you've got his license on file. No lights or sirens—just get me his location."

With no idea a stealthy citywide manhunt was on the lookout for his car, Bradon took no precautions about being seen. He parked in front of one of DC's all-night hangouts and AI cafés. He ordered a coffee and sat down at an available computer as far away from anyone else as possible. No one seemed to recognize him, but he did not want to be overheard.

He connected the headphones, logged into AI Connect, and entered a number. Seconds later he heard the phone ringing on the opposite side of the country.

"Hello," the familiar voice answered.

"Grandma, hi—it's Bradon," said Bradon, speaking softly.

"Hello, Bradon—it's good to hear your voice. And so soon again. It must be late there."

"A little after midnight. Grandma, something's come up here . . . a dangerous situation."

"What is it, are you . . .is everyone—"

"No, nothing like that—we're fine. But I just found out that my dad knows about that thing you went to in California. He knows you were there."

"Oh, goodness—I was hoping to tell him myself. What did he say?"

"Nothing . . . not to me, I mean, I overheard a conversation he was having with one of his henchmen, a really bad guy. Dad went ballistic. He told this guy to take the California group down."

"Oh, my!"

"Obviously you're in no danger. But I'm afraid Mr. Forster may be. I need to warn him. Do you have his number or know how I can get in touch with him?"

"Yes, I think I do . . . wait just a minute—I've got addresses and phone numbers of everyone who was there. Hang on."

☆ ☆ ☆

The car phone rang as the president's powerful right-hand man drove slowly through the streets of the capital glancing down every street he passed for a sign of Bradon's car.

"Mike Bardolf speaking," barked Mike the instant his car phone rang.

"Mr. Bardolf, Bert Dexter, Metro Police. The Mustang's been spotted—it's parked outside an AI café at Del Norte and Williams. I've got men standing by if you need them."

"Tell them to keep surveillance until I get there. Make sure the kid stays put. Once I'm on the scene I'll handle it personally."

☆ ☆ ☆

Sandra Rhodes came back on the line.

"Here's the number, Bradon."

"Got it . . . good—thank you. I'll call him immediately. And, Grandma," Bradon added in a serious tone, "be careful. Obviously nothing's going to happen to you, but this guy Bardolf is a nasty piece of work. We've all got to be careful. Dad is on the rampage about Mr. Forster's group. There's no telling what Bardolf might do. I think you need to get out in front of it and call Dad tomorrow and tell him you were there. He'll probably be mad. But better you tell him so he doesn't think you're keeping it from him. Don't let him know you heard anything from me. If you're straight with him, hopefully he'll see there's nothing sinister going on, and maybe this will blow over."

"I will, Bradon. I'll call tomorrow. And, Bradon . . . you be careful too."

Bradon disconnected the call. Immediately he entered the number his grandmother had given him and sent the call through.

"Mrs. Forster," he said when Grace answered. "It's Bradon Rhodes . . . no," he added to Grace's surprised exclamation, "I'm calling from Washington. I need to speak to your husband. It's urgent."

His tone making clear it was no social call, Grace walked across the room and handed the phone to Mark.

"It's Bradon Rhodes," she said. "He's calling from DC. He sounds serious."

Mark took the phone.

"Bradon, hello—it's Mark Forster," he said. "How are you?"

"I've been better, Mr. Forster. I've just learned that my father knows about the gathering you folks held last month that my grandmother attended."

"We made no secret of it. No harm in his knowing."

"Except that people around him are putting a much different construction on those events. They are reading conspiracy into it, Mr. Forster."

"What! I hope you're kidding, though I can tell from your tone you're not."

"I am deadly serious, Mr. Forster," replied Bradon. "I only learned of this in the last hour. I overheard some things. I left the Presidential Manor immediately and called to warn you. I believe you are in danger, you and possibly others—serious danger, Mr. Forster. The man behind this who is very close to my father, I believe he may—"

The sound of squealing tires outside interrupted him. Bradon glanced toward the street in time to see Mike Bardolf come crashing through the door.

Bradon leaped to his feet, bolted through the large open space filled with tables, desks, and computers toward the back, sprinted down the corridor, and raced out the rear security door.

"I'm FBI!" Bardolf shouted over the blaring alarms that suddenly erupted from the security breach at the back of the building. He flashed his badge toward the two terrified attendants at the counter. "I'm confiscating anything that boy was using!"

He ran to the corner where Bradon had been sitting. He looked down at the number on the screen. The call was still active. He drew in a breath and tried to calm his voice.

"Who am I speaking with?" he said.

"Bradon?" said a man's voice on the computer's speaker.

"Who am I speaking with?" Bardolf repeated.

In California, Mark disconnected the call, then turned to Grace.

"That was very strange," he said. "Bradon stopped speaking in mid-sentence. I heard what sounded like running feet. An alarm sounded a few seconds later, then someone else came on demanding that I identify myself. I did not like the sound of the man's voice."

89

The Streets of DC

BRADON RACED around the building, slowing long enough as he came out front to make sure the coast was clear, then sprinted for his car. By the time Mike Bardolf ran outside with the computer under one arm, the Mustang's distinctive taillights were speeding away, the roar of its vintage engine echoing through the darkness.

Bardolf flew to his car and threw the computer onto the passenger seat. As his high-powered electric engine whined into life, he was on the phone to the FBI's twenty-four-hour line reserved only for top-tier agents.

"I need you to run a phone number immediately," he yelled toward the mic and speaker on his dashboard.

Racing after the Mustang, he managed to keep it just in sight three hundred yards ahead. The reply to his request came back less than a minute later.

"The number belongs to a Mark Forster, Grass Valley, California."

A string of expletives exploded from Bardolf's mouth.

"Will that be all, sir?" came the woman's voice from his phone.

"Yes, thank you."

"Do you need the address?"

"That will not be necessary."

Mike disconnected the call in a white fury and jammed his foot down on the accelerator.

There was more traffic about than one would expect at midnight. Keeping one eye on his rear-view mirror, however, it was easy enough for Bradon to see that he was being followed. The distinctive headlights weaving in and out of traffic behind him, were as easy to recognize as his own tail-lights. He knew Mike Bardolf was bearing down on him.

He loved his Mustang, but it was no match for Bardolf's Tesla-BMW. It would take some fancy wheelwork to elude him. He had one advantage—he had grown up in this city. He knew places a man like Bardolf, in spite of his few years here, couldn't possibly know.

In a brief dangerous move, he flipped off his headlights, took the next right much too fast, skidding slightly on tires he knew he should have replaced before now. Regaining control, he glanced again in his rearview mirror. A few seconds later he saw the Tesla speed past behind him.

He turned his lights back on, slowed to a stop, jumped out, and was at the point of smashing in his taillights to keep Bardolf from recognizing his car. Suddenly he stopped. What was he thinking! He would get pulled over by the Metro police within five minutes.

He had to risk it. He jumped back in, threw the car into gear, and with tires squealing sped away. He would make for Rock Creek Park. He knew every inch of the place. He could get lost there.

He glanced up at his mirror as he entered the park—Bardolf had backtracked, found him, and was again on his tail.

"Dang!" Bradon muttered. He had hoped to make the park before being spotted again! It was not going to be easy to shake him!

The main cycle path winding through the park was eight to ten feet wide. Bradon knew several places where it crossed the main road. There would be no cyclists out in the middle of the night. One of the crossings was just ahead. If he could manage to reach it and get off the road before Bardolf caught up, he could lose himself in the trees. Bardolf would never suspect a thing.

He flew into a sweeping bend of the pavement curving around to the left. Momentarily he was lost to Bardolf's sight.

Reaching the cycle path, again he flipped off his lights. Braking slightly, though not as much as he should have, he ground the steering wheel hard left, careened off the road onto the wide dirt path. But without his headlights he misjudged the angle of the crossing.

As he hit the loose dirt of the cycle path, his two left tires raised off the ground. His rear right tire skidded dangerously away beneath him. Losing control the Mustang flipped twice and came to rest on its side in total darkness, lights still off, in the ravine of the small creek below the cycle path.

Seconds later Mike Bardolf sped by on the road, unaware that his quarry was lying unconscious only a hundred feet from him.

Gradually realizing he'd lost sight of Bradon's tail-lights, he slowed, cursed silently, then drove about through the park aimlessly for half an hour. At last, confessing himself stymied, he returned to his condo revolving many stratagems in his mind.

90

THE PLAN

THE SWEEPING strategy devised by Nasim Bahram during the 1970s was cunningly brilliant. Whether by coincidence or some cosmic design, the liberal and progressive movement spawned during that and the previous decade ordered itself precisely according to Bahram's ultimate and prophetic objectives. He and his protégés had to do little but sit back and wait for progressivism's agenda to ripen.

They could not have had more perfect accomplices during the formative years when that agenda turned American culture on its head than the 42nd, 44th, and 46th US presidents. Neither the first nor the last of the three ever knew themselves as pawns in Islam's great design. Debate continued about 44, and what might have been his deeper thoughts.

To succeed in the West, Islam had long eyed three primary objectives:

Western *religion*.

Western *history*.

Western *culture*.

All three needed to be undercut and eventually destroyed so that Islamic religion, history, and culture could replace them.

For centuries these targets had been the chief roadblocks barring Islam from making significant incursions into the Western world.

Yet within a mere three generations, the West's demise was now being orchestrated from within! The hidden jihad was being furthered by the West's own death wish. The threefold spheres whose changed paradigms they would seize upon would have been unthinkable to Americans of the 1950s. The revolutionary new perspectives in all three areas were now taken for granted in the 2050s.

Since the 1960s, liberal progressives had been systematically destroying US religion, history, and culture. Western Europe and its allies had followed the US on its downward suicidal spiral. All they had to do was wait patiently, then step in and pick up the pieces. Events were now moving so quickly under America's succession of recent radical presidents that the culmination of the hidden jihad was suddenly at hand.

In *religion*, Christianity and Judaism had been all but eradicated as significant forces in American life. The progressivist agenda had turned them into scourges in the public mind. The majority of Americans now so despised both Christianity and Judaism that their few remaining zealots were treated as societal outcasts, deprived of the rights, privileges, and freedoms enjoyed by the rest of society.

This would permanently mitigate Christianity's resurgence as a united world force. Christianity was effectively dead. The Christian antidote both to the progressive poison, and to the ideas of Islam, had been eliminated.

In *history*, that of America as well as the history of Western civilization had been so thoroughly reinterpreted and rewritten by revisionist liberal scholars that an entire generation of Americans now looked upon the United States as one of the world's foremost evil empires of history. The pro-minority, pro-Islamic, anti-white, and anti-Christian perspective of the histories written and taught for the last thirty years could not have suited the jihad better had they originated in Baghdad or Tehran. The majority of Americans now despised the country's white, racist, and capitalist roots.

It would be an easy matter to shift this antipathy to its history into receptivity for Islam's promise to deliver America from its years of bondage to an inherently evil system. Here too, America's liberal academic community had helped carry out the jihad on its own. When Hamas attacked Israel in 2023, the world turned against Jews and Israel, not against Islam's jihadist foundations. The gullible American public would be indoctrinated into accepting Sharia law as effortlessly as it had been brainwashed into its new wave of antisemitism and thinking Christianity racist and accepting the LGBTQ depravity. For all its wealth and power, the American populace was a vast society of lemmings that had lost the ability to think.

And *culturally*, America's ethics, morals, and family values had been so thoroughly undercut by liberal policymakers, educators, think tanks, judges, filmmakers, and politicians, that the moral fabric of the country was in tatters. Thus, the third of Islam's roadblocks to success had been removed as effectively as the other two.

The three generations of Bahrams knew that they would have to carefully monitor events. Timing was everything in war, even a hidden war. They would especially watch as their progressivist pawns continued to use four of liberalism's most bellicose combative groups to finalize the erosion of America's spiritual, historical, and cultural character.

Hateful to Islam as they were, their cunning use must continue a while longer. They would be swept away once Sharia became the law of the land. For the present, however, they remained useful to complete the final annihilation of what had once been America's intrinsic strength.

Militant *feminism* would continue to emasculate the male-dominated order.

Militant *anti-white minorities* would continue to replace the white majority in cultural influence.

Militant *homosexuality* would continue its destruction of marriage and the traditional nuclear family.

Militant *a-genderism* would continue to unravel cultural mores at their foundations.

As the feminist, anti-white, homosexual, and genderless coalitions infiltrated more and more segments of American society, the internal moral and ethical fabric of America would eventually crumble and bring down the entire US house of cards.

91

The Bardolf Gambit

JUNE 2051

IN EARLY June, having convinced the execs of NBC that he had a major scoop worthy of leading the nightly news broadcast—though only divulging enough to persuade them—Todd Stewart's replacement, now making a name for himself in his own right, took his place in front of the cameras and lights, the Presidential Manor behind him, awaiting the cue to begin his bombshell report.

"This is Mason Templeton reporting for NBC News," he began in the resonant baritone eerily reminiscent of Bing Crosby. Templeton was the new young star of the journalistic world, with good looks to match his silky voice. "As you can see," he continued, "I am standing in front of the Presidential Manor with breaking news that could have major implications for its future occupancy. I have learned—"

"What can you tell us about Bradon Rhodes?" shouted a voice from the small crowd of onlookers. "Is he back in the Presidential Manor?"

Impromptu questions were not part of the evening's script, but Templeton took it in stride. Knowing the high level of interest in the president's son, he judged it best to answer the question.

"Yes," he replied, "he is back home in the Manor behind me. He was released from the hospital two days ago. He is resting comfortably and doing well. His injuries, though somewhat severe, were not serious or life-threatening. He will make a full recovery."

"Are the reports true he had been drinking?"

"That has not been ascertained. I have no information about that."

"Why was he in the park so late? What caused the accident?"

"That, too, remains uncertain. I simply have nothing to give you. Now if I may, let me return to the breaking news I mentioned a moment ago."

He paused as his cameraman zoomed in for a head shot.

"I have earlier today been informed by high-placed confidential sources," he resumed, "that a nationwide grassroots campaign is underway with the objective of unseating President Jefferson Rhodes in next year's presidential election behind a Republican duo of Dr. Charles Reyburn and former candidate and senator Harvey Jansen."

Again he waited for his words to sink in. Within seconds the revelation had millions of viewers changing channels as word of his announcement overloaded telephone services and social media.

"It is unclear at this time which of the two men would occupy the top slot on the ticket," Templeton went on. "Speculation favors Professor Reyburn as the most likely candidate for the presidency. His bestselling book has placed him in the national spotlight. Nor are my sources convinced that Senator Jansen would be capable of mounting a serious campaign after his defeat three years ago.

"The film clip we have obtained of a recent meeting in California between the two men, where many influential supporters were present, is inconclusive, though the purpose of the clandestine meeting at an undisclosed West Coast location was reportedly to discuss the election with supporters and potential donors."

As he spoke, the thirty-second low-resolution video recorded on Lionel Holt's phone played on millions of television screens across the country.

"A week later," Templeton went on, "as will be seen from the next clip, Dr. and Mrs. Reyburn were seen at the Jansen ranch in Laramie, Wyoming. There they spent two days, presumably outlining the preliminary strategy for a campaign which will obviously be an uphill battle against a popular incumbent."

As Templeton continued with brief biographies of the two men and footage from the previous campaign and what was available of the somewhat reclusive Reyburn, including clips from his interview several years earlier with Phil Simons, Mike Bardolf leaned back and took a slow sip from the glass in his hand.

It was a risky gambit. He had known that when he set up this morning's meeting with Templeton.

"You're a bright kid, Mason," he said. "Play your cards right and you'll have a friend in high places. But if so much as a hint leaks out where you got this video and how you learned what it means, I'll ruin you. You've heard of Todd Stewart, I presume."

"Of course."

"Three years ago he was where you are today, on his way to becoming NBC's anchor. Where is he now? I'm sure I make myself clear what can be the consequences of crossing me."

"Don't worry, Mr. Bardolf," said Templeton. "I can keep my mouth shut."

"Okay then, go out and make some news."

It was a calculated risk, but he needed to get the president fired up. He wanted to get out in front of it. By leaking the announcement himself, he could control the narrative. Just as he had with Stewart, he would set up young Templeton as his mouthpiece. After two or three stories which he would leak, the public would look to Mason Templeton as the authority on anything connected with the election. Over the next year he would continue to feed him exactly what he wanted the public to hear.

Getting the news out early and Jansen and Reyburn in the public eye would also ensure that whatever early enthusiasm their candidacy generated would burst long before the primaries.

He would follow Templeton's early reports at the right moment with news of the conspiracy. By then he should have all the evidence he needed.

As for the president's son, whatever had happened in Rock Creek Park had hopefully knocked some sense into the young fool's thick skull. Whatever he may have told Forster wouldn't matter now anyway.

92

The Device

HOW LONG it would take for the spirit of America's strength to die, Hamad Bahram's grandfather could not have foreseen. Their predecessors had waited centuries. What was time to Islam so long as the Great Satan was eventually cast into the lake of fire?

Whether the objectives of Islam's hidden jihad would come through the electoral process, or be precipitated by a new civil war, an attempted military coup, or events impossible to predict, old Nasim always said that circumstances would dictate the strategy. They must be ready, he said, whether that culmination came in years, decades, or after still more centuries of patient waiting.

At some future confluence of favorable circumstances, Nasim was convinced, in the confusion and hedonism to which its failed Christian ethic and historic capitalist system would lead them, America's people would be ripe to turn to Islam to provide hope and spiritual strength in the vacuum thus created.

Nasim's son Sohrab had warned that feminism would be difficult to bring under the umbrella of Sharia law, as would the gay and lesbian communities. But after a century endorsing abortion, US feminism would be so dead of conscience that it could be convinced of anything. As for the homosexuals, they would ultimately have to be eliminated. But that need not be made public before the fact.

The Achilles heel of the plan, of course—tacit acceptance for a time of the progressivism which was abhorrent to Islam—prevented its widespread acceptance among most leaders in the Islamic world. But those few who embraced the elder Bahram's vision to use the liberalism they hated as a Trojan horse to take down the West, recognized that the prize was the Caliphate, even if it took controversial means to bring it to fruition.

Hamad Bahram's Iranian cousin had shared his commitment to the hidden jihad as long as either could remember. On those occasions when the aging patriarch visited Iran, Ada Bahram had listened to his grandfather Nasim's vision as eagerly as did young Hamad.

The two boys did not see one another often. But the bonds of their friendship and shared commitment to their grandfather's strategy deepened as they grew into youths and were unbreakable by the time the two were in their twenties.

As young men they continued to plot and scheme in anticipation of the day it would rest on *their* shoulders to carry their grandfather's and two fathers' shared Islamic vision forward into the age of its fulfillment.

☆ ☆ ☆

Trained in Iran's nuclear program, Ada's brainchild was to develop a device, technically "nuclear" but with limited or of little long-lasting global radiation, and of generally predictable explosive radius. He envisioned a tactical weapon that could judiciously be used without triggering the long-feared nuclear holocaust. The idea was to cause maximum panic without crippling a nation—the perfect tool to render opponents incapacitated but with systems still intact, which they would be in a position to bring under their own control.

His chief difficulty had been how to conduct tests in secret. Seismic sensors around the world were so sophisticated that any land explosion would be detected. Testing would remove the element of surprise and raise undesirable questions within the international community.

Without testing, however, Ada could not predict with 100 percent certainty just what would be the impact or how large would be the kill zone.

He had every reason to trust his computer models. But atoms were tricky things to control. With surprise so vital, the element of uncertainty must be reduced to a minimum.

By the time he reached his twenties, Hamad Bahram saw just what a strategic genius his grandfather was. All he had to do was ask himself which he hated more, homosexuality or the Great Satan. To temporarily blind himself to the depravity of America's sexual perversions, even pretending to be its advocate in the insular fellowship of Palladium, was a sacrifice he was willing to make.

And now, much sooner than his grandfather could have predicted, the stage seemed set to strike the decisive blow that would place him at the very center of power. The stars were aligning in their favor!

The progressive poison had nearly completed its work on their behalf. The foundations of America were so weak that when they struck, America's economy, government, and national identity would cry out for radical new directions that would change the course of world history forever.

☆ ☆ ☆

Hamad's thoughts were interrupted by the sound of his phone. Almost as if his thoughts had prompted the call, he heard a familiar voice in Arabic. Quickly he turned on his electronic scrambler to keep prying ears being able to translate their conversation.

"Hamad, it's Ada—I have devised a test for the device."

"What about detection?" asked Hamad.

"There will be a risk. But I will test only a quarter or third of the fissionable material we will need."

"Will that prevent notice?"

"I cannot say with complete certainty. But I must know that the signal will activate the timing device reliably from a distance. Also the exact technology I am refining has never been used. I must track the radiation to see if my computer algorithms are correct. A small test will be enough to gauge size and fallout and tell me what I need to know. If we conduct the test under cloud cover and away from shipping lanes—"

"Shipping lanes . . . you mean, at sea?"

"It's the only way to avoid seismic detection."

"Surely it will be seen by satellites."

"Perhaps. But where I have in mind, I don't think it will be investigated by the major powers. We'll float something in the news about fire or explosion on a private vessel. The plume will be too small to be seen from a distance and will dissipate quickly. With no conclusive or incriminating evidence found in the wreckage, I consider the risk a reasonable one. It will be so far away no country will risk a diving operation to investigate. It is the only way for me to know for certain exactly how to configure the final device."

"*Far away* . . . where are you thinking?" asked Hamad.

"Off the coast of Antarctica," replied Ada.

93

Faux Campaign

MIKE BARDOLF continued to reflect on his Templeton strategy, as he called it. The eager young journalist's report and its aftermath would be enough to smear the Republican Party and whatever pockets of conservatism remained. He would publicly destroy Mark Forster and his group, in full view of the nation.

If his gambit succeeded as he was sure it would, it might place him even closer to his ultimate objective as Jefferson's Rhodes right hand man, and even his potential succ—

His thoughts were cut short by the ringtone of his phone.

It was the president.

"Mike!" Rhodes's voice barked into his ear. "What do you know about this—how did they find out!"

"I don't know, Mr. President. But the gathering in California wasn't secret. Anyone could have learned of it. Obviously Reyburn's visit to Laramie wasn't kept under wraps. The two men were in full view."

"What are we going to do!"

"Nothing. This is good, Mr. President. Let the enthusiasm for the two fools die down before it can hurt you. You take the high road—act the statesman."

"What about their conspiracy? I don't like this, Mike. What if it grows? Reyburn's still riding a wave of popularity."

"Exactly what we want. We *want* it to grow. The more conservatives and Christians get swept up into it the better. Then we will divulge that it's part of a paramilitary conspiracy. The disillusionment will be so great that Christianity will never recover as a political force. This couldn't be better."

"How can you be so sure?"

"Have you forgotten the last election? When Jansen rose in the polls, you were worried. I told you I had everything covered. When he fell, he fell so hard that your majority was record breaking. I had it in the bag, just like I promised. I have it in the bag now. Don't worry, Mr. President. The more momentum they build will ensure that their fall is all the more catastrophic. Trust me. I've got this. Leave everything to me, Mr. President. I haven't failed you yet. I won't fail you now."

In California phones were going off throughout the Sacramento valley and foothills.

Almost simultaneous to the president's call to Mike Bardolf, Mark and Grace Forster heard the news from Timothy Marshall, who had been notified by Dewitt West who had been called by their daughter Diane Statler.

As for the Jansens and Reyburns, whose phones also began ringing and beeping in their respective homes, Harvey could not keep from laughing. When Charles called within three minutes, however, he was noticeably upset.

"It will blow over, Charles," said Harvey. "There's obviously nothing to it. Unless you've changed your mind."

"Don't joke about it, Harvey!" said Charles.

"The best thing we can do is ignore it. I've been through it before. The news hounds will be all over us tomorrow. We'll have to ride it out. Let's talk and pray with our wives tonight, then talk again in the morning and decide on a uniform response. I'll also try to schedule a conference call with Timothy and Mark and the two of us. We need to be careful to divulge nothing about the group or what we were doing in California so that no one else gets mixed up in it. We'll let Mark and Timothy tell us what they want us to say. But hold onto your hat, brother—it's liable to be a bumpy couple of days."

The next day, exactly according to Mike Bardolf's plan, letters were delivered throughout the country to every address he had been able to obtain of the gathering attendees, along with those in their cell groups who hadn't been there. The letter announced the Reyburn-Jansen presidential candidacy and included a request for donations. Mark Forster was named as campaign manager, with his address listed for correspondence and donations.

He still hadn't got hold of a copy of the group's newsletter. But he added to the mass mailing that a campaign website would be made public shortly.

He'd anonymously secured the domain name REYBURNJANSENCAMPAIGN.NET and was already having the site designed. It was a website he would control personally.

94
The Yacht

ARRANGING FOR the secret purchase of a luxury yacht was easy for one with Hamad Bahram's connections, as was circulating the cover story of its fictitious drug-lord owner and his excursion with a party of dubious clients to the bottom of the globe during the Christmas season when daylight in those regions would be twenty-four hours long. A story would follow in due course that threats on the owner's life had been made by a rival drug kingpin.

Sailing under the Venezuelan flag and departing from Caracas with a hand-picked crew, the yacht made its way around Brazil's Cape Branco, then south along the South American coast, with stops at Salvador, Rio, and Buenos Aires, ostensibly to take on board the owner's wealthy clients and enough young women to keep them all happy. In reality, the three-man crew was met by the two Bahram cousins in Rio Gallegos at the southern tip of Argentina, paid well for their services, and dismissed. Under cloak of secrecy, Ada Bahram outfitted the vessel both with the device that had come with him by private plane from Tehran as well as the complex electronics which effectively turned the yacht into a floating drone-ship.

Launching the yacht into the world's southernmost ocean without a human being aboard, the two scions of the long-fermenting Bahram vision followed on a rusting non-descript trawler they hired for the purpose manned only by the owner and his son. Ada and Hamad shadowed the unmanned yacht slowly south of perilous Cape Horn, then west through the dangerous Drake Passage, awaiting a propitious cloud cover.

Arrived a hundred miles off the western ice floes of Graham land on the Antarctic Peninsula, which Ada judged sufficient distance to prevent the blast arousing unwanted attention from the international scientific stations along the peninsula, he put the yacht into a circular holding pattern.

Aboard the trawler at a distance of ten miles, with binoculars and photographic and sensor equipment in place, Hamad and Ada waited.

On the third morning, though night and morning were virtually identical at this season, Hamad was awakened early in his small quarters.

"Come, Hamad," said Ada eagerly. "Today is the day. Allah has given us a perfect cover of clouds. Nothing will be seen from above."

Hamad dressed quickly and followed Ada up to the stern deck where their equipment stood in readiness.

"Where are the men?" asked Hamad.

"Only the father was on the bridge," replied Ada. "I sent him below. They'll see nothing. They think we are filming icebergs and penguins."

Ada hurriedly made his final preparations, checking his equipment, then activating the sensors, camera, and recording devices. Both men picked up their powerful binoculars and stared across the expanse of water.

"You shall do the honors, Hamad," said Ada, flipping the activation switch attached to the sensor platform. The timer on the yacht is set for twenty seconds but is inactive until receiving our signal."

"It is your device," said Hamad. "You should—"

"It is you who will soon be at the center of the world stage," interrupted his cousin.

Hamad smiled. "If all goes according to plan."

"It will," nodded Ada. "Our grandfather Nasim is with us. He will be proud."

Both donned their masks, then turned again toward the white yacht in the distance. Hamad reached forward, then pressed the red button.

Eyes glued through their binoculars, they waited as twenty seconds passed.

In the distance a silent, blinding red and orange fireball erupted hundreds of feet into the air. Splintered flaming fragments of the yacht blew nearly as high, then fell burning back into the ocean as a familiar circular cloud of white rose above the blast.

They watched in deathly silence as the plume billowed up into the clouds.

The eerie silence continued about fifty seconds. Suddenly a warm wind blew against them with surprising force. It was followed seconds later by the great *boom* of the explosion as the sound reached them. The thunderous echo of the blast quickly died down, but the warm breeze continued for several minutes then gradually subsided.

The four-foot swells that hit the trawler twenty minutes later sent the vessel rocking, though not dangerously. By then Ada's readings were complete. No perceptible radiation had been detected, and they removed their masks. He would continue to monitor the aftermath of the explosion from Stanley in the Falkland Islands for a week.

It was time to return to Rio Gallegos. By the time they left them, the father and son were convinced of the story they had been told about the sound they had heard and the sudden turbulence of the sea.

THIS ENDS BOOK 3

Tribulation Cult Book 4: *Freedom Manifesto*
Coming Soon

Character List

THE MARSHALLS—THREE GENERATIONS

Stirling and Larke (Stevens)	1941–2032, 1942–2031
Woodrow (m. Cheryl Burns)	1973
Cateline (m. Clancy Watson)	1974
Graham (m. Lynn Davies)	1976
Jane (m. Wade Durant)	1978
Timothy (m. Jaylene Gray)	1980, 1983
Heather	2014

THE FORSTERS—THREE GENERATIONS

Robert and Laura (Clay)	1973, 1976
Janet (m. Collis Nason)	1998
Mark (m. Grace Thornton)	2000, 2001
Ginger	2028
Craig	2030
Gayle (m. David Dowling)	2005

THE GORDONS—TWO GENERATIONS

Pelham and Isobel (Hamilton)	1939–2014, 1945–2041
David	1971

THE RHODES—THREE GENERATIONS

Harrison and Sandra (Nelson)	1975, 1977
Jefferson (m. Marcia Bergen)	2000
Bradon	2027
Melissa	2029

THE HUTCHINSES—TWO GENERATIONS

Truman and Eloise (Warton)	1972, 1973
Sawyer (m. Inga Daven)	1995
Ward (m. Deidra Lindberg)	1999–2048
Linda (m. Cameron Trent)	2000

THE REYBURNS—TWO GENERATIONS

Hank and Valerie (Hart)	1974, 1977
Charles (m. Regina Stone)	2001
Summer	2003
Loni	2005

THE BAHRAMS—FOUR GENERATIONS

Hussain	1905–1977
Nasim	1932–2009
Sonrab	1967–2039
Hamad	2001–

POLITICAL INDIVIDUALS

Viktor Domokos	1939–2035
Akilah Samara	1993
Slayton Bardolf	1949–2014
Loring	1976
Mike	2001
Amy	2004
Talon Roswell	1950–2043
Storm	1983
Anson	2010
Adriana Carmella Hunt	1989–2033
Harvey and Harriet Jansen	1991, 1992
Elizabeth Wickes Hardy	1996
Todd Stewart	2013

ABOUT THE AUTHOR

MICHAEL PHILLIPS was born (1946) and raised in the small northern California university town of Arcata. After a year at Lincoln University in Pennsylvania, Michael completed his higher education at Humboldt State University (now California State Polytechnic University), where he was a standout miler and half-miler, graduating in 1969 in physics, mathematics, and history. During his final year at Humboldt, he began a small bookstore in his college apartment. He and his wife, Judy, music major and harpist in the university symphony, were married in 1971, the same year they discovered the life-changing influences of C. S. Lewis and George MacDonald. Moving to nearby Eureka, their One Way Book Shop grew rapidly. For the next thirty-five years, while carrying on their writing and harping pursuits, Michael and Judy's bookstore ministry was a fixture in the life of Humboldt County's Christian community.

MacDonald's profound influence in their lives, coupled with the realization that none of his books were in print and the Victorian author was in danger of being lost to posterity, prompted Michael, amid the busy life of a rapidly expanding business and homeschooling their three sons, to begin the ambitious task of editing and republishing MacDonald's works. At the same time he began writing seriously in his own right, publishing several books in the 1970s.

Michael's efforts inaugurated a worldwide renaissance of interest in the forgotten nineteenth-century Scotsman. In the years since, Michael has been known as one whose skillful diligence helped rescue George MacDonald from obscurity. Throughout the following forty years, he has published more than eighty studies and new editions of MacDonald's writings in diverse formats and is recognized as a man possessing rare insight into MacDonald's heart and spiritual vision.

Paralleling his work with MacDonald, Michael's own author's reputation in Christian circles expanded quickly. He became one of the premier novelists of the Christian fiction boom of the 1980s and 1990s, his books appearing on numerous CBA bestseller lists with an enthusiastic worldwide following.

In 2021 Michael and Judy celebrated their fiftieth anniversary. Michael continues to write as prolifically as ever. Judy continues the ministry of her harp music, teaching and as a therapeutic musician in several hospitals and medical facilities.

Recognized as one of the most versatile and prolific Christian writers of our time, Michael's wide-reaching corpus and the multiple genres of his work now encompass well over a hundred titles. For many years his books have demonstrated keen insight and uncommon wisdom to probe deeply into issues, relationships, and cultural trends. His writings are personal and challenging. He encourages readers to think in fresh ways about the world and themselves.

Michael Phillips's corpus of more than a hundred titles is praised across a wide spectrum of readership. The impact of his writing is perhaps best summed up by Paul Young, who wrote, "When I read Lewis and MacDonald, and now Phillips, I walk away wanting to be more than I already am, more consistent and true, a more authentic human being."

OTHER NOTABLE TITLES BY MICHAEL PHILLIPS

FICTION

Rift in Time
Hidden in Time
The Secret of the Rose (4 volumes)
Secrets of the Shetlands (3 volumes)
American Dreams (3 volumes)
Angel Harp
Legend of the Celtic Stone

NON-FICTION

Endangered Virtues and the Coming Ideological War
George MacDonald, Scotland's Beloved Storyteller
George MacDonald, A Writer's Life
The Commands of the Prophets
The Commands of Jesus
The Commands of the Apostles
Make Me Like Jesus
The Eyewitness Bible (5 volumes)

INFORMATION AND BOOK AVAILABILITY CAN BE FOUND AT:

https://michaelphillipsbooks.com
https://fatheroftheinklings.com